A LADY
DIVIDED

Books by Sandra Ardoin

Contemporary

Hidden Veil Hometown
A Musician's Heart
A Horseman's Mission
A Hero's Nature
A Father's Promise
(Next in Series)

Love at Christmas Inn
Love in Second Bloom
Leaving the Past Behind
Lost in Winter's Wonderland
Longing for Second Chances
Box Set

Stand Alone Books
A Love Most Worthy
Renee

Historical

House of Fire
A Lady Divided
A Lady Unveiled
(Next in Series)

Widow's Might
Unwrapping Hope
Enduring Dreams
Rekindling Trust

Barnes Brothers
The Yuletide Angel
A Reluctant Melody

Short Stories
Daphne's Day Out

A LADY DIVIDED

HOUSE OF FIRE

Book One

SANDRA ARDOIN

Corner Room Books

Scripture quotations are taken from the King James Version of the Bible.

Print ISBN: 979-8-9905848-2-2

"Dearly beloved, avenge not yourselves, but rather give place unto wrath: for it is written,
Vengeance is mine; I will repay, saith the Lord."

Romans 12:19 KJV

CHAPTER ONE

Texas Hill Country, 1877

Quinn Spencer stopped humming. Back rigid in the McClellan saddle, he gathered facts from the surrounding sounds. The rattle of tumbling leaves. Water flowing in the nearby river. His horse's shoes kicking small rocks. Still, a chill rolled over his skin—an evil finger that tickled his spine. He'd experienced such feelings a few times during his cavalry years. They never bode well.

The chill intensified when his mare's ears pricked forward as far as they would go. Snorting, her nostrils puffed in and out like a blacksmith's bellows. Did she react to his unease, or was something out there? He patted her neck. "Easy, Ruthie."

Quinn tightened his grip on the reins and searched the rolling landscape that ran from the trail to the trees along the south bank of the Pedernales River. He saw no threat in the tall grasses or on the hills or within the clumps of cedars and oaks. Yet his stomach muscles clenched.

A wisp of breeze plastered the linen shirt to his damp chest. He scanned the late August sky—no ominous clouds that might suggest a sudden storm.

His stalwart military horse danced a step to the left. He readjusted in the saddle and spoke in a whisper. "Easy now. Everything's fi—"

The cat rose from a rocky bluff at the riverbank like a fawn-colored monster from the sea. A handful of yards to his right, the creature stared at him, eyes spitting fire. It crept forward one step at a time. Quinn fought to keep his mount steady while he eased his hand toward his hip, never taking his eyes from the mountain lion.

The skin along his arms and neck prickled. The mare pawed the ground, adding a squeal to the eeriness.

The tips of his fingers reached the holster of his Army Colt revolver. As if sensing his intent, the mountain lion pounced. The mare whipped around. She kicked out with both back legs, jarring his hand away from the weapon.

Pain seared Quinn's right leg as fangs tore through his new trousers, the leather of his boot, and into his calf. The skin tore, and he drew a quick breath and released it with a loud, anguished groan. It was all he could do to remain in the saddle.

Ruthie screamed again. She bucked and kicked, jerking Quinn free of the predator's grip but missing her target. She paid the price when the mountain lion raked her with its claws, its weight knocking her sideways. The mare went down with a thud. Her body pinned Quinn's left leg under her side. Bone snapped.

Through shock and throbbing agony, he called out, "God, help us."

The cat released its hold on Ruthie, eyed the tree line, and ran off as dirt kicked up in the spot where it had stood a mere breath before a sharp report sliced the air.

Quinn turned his head toward the sound. A puff of smoke drifted upward at the edge of the tree line across the river. Branches shuddered, and a horse broke from the wooded area. The rider spurred the buckskin forward to splash across the shallow water covering the limestone bed, and his wide-brimmed hat flew up in the breeze. He caught it with one hand, but not before a honey-colored braid escaped.

The buckskin skidded to a stop. Quinn studied his rescuer's face and blinked, sure the pain played tricks with his mind. No man possessed skin that smooth.

Laurel Tillman stifled the curse on her lips. Not in deference to the man on the ground or because her mother would wash her mouth out with soap. She smothered it because the word came from her old life, and she wanted that life to stay in the past.

She had tracked the cat for over three hours after being alerted to trouble by her dog, finally finding the carcass of one of her ewes hidden in scrub and partially covered with dead leaves. The survival of La Casa del Fuego depended on every sheep she raised, yet killing any living thing, including a predator, left Laurel nauseous. Unfortunately, she felt fine right now.

Not fine, exactly. Boiling mad. She'd missed. She couldn't remember the last time she'd missed a target.

It was that blasted man's fault. He must have moved, drawing the cat to move at the last second. And she would stick to that story. In a way, she was relieved after seeing a cub follow its mother into the scrub. It would have torn her apart to shoot it, too.

Her gaze drifted to the saber in the scabbard hanging from the stranger's saddle—a military man. She turned away, fighting to swallow the bitter gall rising in her throat at the sight of the weapon of war.

The injured bay struggled to her feet, and her rider sucked in a breath. Wounds slashed the horse's neck near the shoulder—ugly, but not life-threatening. While the mare stood strangely calm, Laurel's gelding pranced and snorted at the stench of blood. Or, more likely, he reacted to the bucking of her nerves.

A grunt brought her attention back to the man pinned beneath the mare. His muffled cry of pain pierced the shell of indifference she tried to maintain. She winced at the condition of his right leg, torn and bright with his life's blood flowing in a rivulet a few inches below the knee. His left foot turned out unnaturally.

Laurel dismounted with care, her own right leg stiff from hours without full movement. She took a step before turning to search the landscape, and waited, her carbine at the ready. Instinct told her the cat had fled, leaving nothing but carnage and the mark on the ground where her bullet had pierced the dirt.

The man struggled to stand. He fell back to the ground with a moan. "I think my leg is broken."

She lowered the weapon. Swiping the back of her leather glove across her damp forehead, she straightened her back and readied herself to face the stranger—if she'd heard right, a Yankee stranger.

A wavy lock of dark hair sprawled across his forehead. His was an impressive build—a thick neck, wide shoulders, and broad chest. Muscles bulged under the shirt sleeves. Her husband would have called them a field hand's muscles. An intimidating man, even with the pain contorting his bearded face.

Laurel turned her head at the sound of hoofbeats. Her daughter, Becky, and friend, Camille Arneau, slid their horses to a stop a few feet away.

Bounding to the ground with all the femininity of a rambunctious nine-year-old boy, Becky's eyes widened, the apple green irises so like Laurel's. "Jumpin' Jehoshaphat!"

"Rebecca Irene Tillman, I will not abide such language. Do you hear you me, child?"

Becky scowled and hung her head, her blonde braids falling forward. "Yes, ma'am."

Even wearing trousers, Camille dismounted in ladylike fashion with a grace Laurel hoped her child would adopt one day. "*Merci, mi Dios.* I began praying once I heard the shot, Laurel." Camille gripped her arm. "Are you all right?"

Laurel suppressed a half-hearted chuckle. When Camille became flustered, her French and Spanish ancestry burst forth in a combination of languages. Leave it to her friend to pray at the tiniest inkling of trouble. She sobered at the thought. Between the two of them, God would not hesitate to answer Camille, whose darkest sin—whatever it was—could never match Laurel's.

"I'm perfectly well." She jabbed a thumb over her shoulder. "See what you can do for him."

Camille checked on the wounded man while Laurel shuffled over to examine his horse. Both the mare and her master would need stitching. She would leave that task to her mother, a woman who had trouble deciding which of her two best dresses to wear to worship or what flowers would look right near the porch. Unlike her daughter, though, Ellen Chamberlain possessed flawless expertise with a needle and excellent nursing skills.

Laurel ran her fingers down the trembling mare's blazed face and whispered in her ear. "There, there now. Those nasty wounds will heal. We'll take good care of you." The horse blew out a noisy breath and nuzzled her hand.

"What about him, Momma? Are we gonna take care of him?" Becky pointed to the man.

Too many lives depended upon Laurel's common sense, protection, and determination to see her husband's ranch outlive her. Too many lives to risk on a stranger.

The "him" grimaced. "How is Ruthie?"

Laurel huffed. Her earlier guess had been correct. A Yankee born and bred. Most likely, a mule-headed Yankee to boot. "The cat missed the windpipe. She'll be fine."

She turned to her friend without answering her daughter. "Well, Camille?"

"I believe he broke the small outer bone, but the larger looks to be intact. The right leg needs to be stitched."

Laurel raised a hand over her brows and searched the landscape. "Where's Charlie?"

"I left him to guard the flock."

"Momma, I don't see the cat." Becky scanned the ground. "Where is he?"

"He ran off."

Her daughter's eyes widened. "You telling me you missed?" She raised on tiptoe and stretched her hand to feel Laurel's forehead. "Are you sure you're not sick? Did you shoot *him* instead?" She pointed to the man.

Laurel brushed the pale-yellow bangs from her daughter's eyes. "No. I did not shoot him."

Becky slowly nodded. "Then I reckon you saved him."

Laurel shut her eyes and drew a deep breath. *Yes, I did.*

There had been a day when she would have taken that man's life without a shred of remorse.

Through the burning and throbbing pain, Quinn thanked his heavenly Savior for his life and Ruthie's. As an afterthought, he added a reluctant appreciation for his earthly savior, the gun-wielding southerner with a foul temperament.

The woman named Camille Arneau smiled down at him, her odd accent faint enough to be deemed imagination. Warmth swept through him while staring into her deep brown eyes, as welcoming as a hot cup of chocolate on an Ohio winter's eve. There was nothing brazen or flirtatious in her conduct, but her femininity, hidden under masculine attire, raised too many memories. He turned his face away.

He considered himself blessed not to have his wounds tended by the one with the icy manner and a mouth that seemed set in a perpetual frown. Miss Arneau called her Laurel. If she were a battlefield surgeon, she would have amputated his leg by now.

Tall and slender, her slim face tapered to a pointed chin. If the woman ever removed that dour expression and smiled . . .

She limped over to her daughter. Despite her hostile attitude toward him, she lovingly stroked the girl's cheek. Quinn's opinion of her rose half a notch.

"Laurel, we must have the wagon."

The woman's eyes narrowed and lips parted, ready to argue with Miss Arneau. After eyeing Ruthie, her face relaxed. "Becky, ride back to the house. Have Issy prepare the buckboard and bring it here. Tell Granmomma about the man's legs."

"Yes, ma'am." The little girl mounted and sent her horse running toward the trees.

"What is your name?"

Quinn turned his attention back to the angel-faced woman at his side. He clenched a handful of grass and held his breath when she carefully removed the boot from his broken leg. "Qu-Quinn Spencer, Miss Arneau."

"And your rank?" The question came from the surly one with the distinct drawl, one he'd heard too often during the war.

"Mister. I resigned my commission as a major and left Fort McKavett a week ago."

He followed her glance to the saber hanging from the scabbard, a gift from his former superior and another obvious mark against him. He had grown used to seeing that same bitterness in other southerners during Reconstruction. Even after twelve years, some Rebs couldn't stop licking their wounds long enough to allow them to heal.

"My name is Camille Arneau." The brown-haired angel spread her arms, indicating the vastness of their surroundings. "I work for Mrs. Tillman on her ranch, La Casa del Fuego." She tipped her head toward the woman who stared at him with almond-shaped eyes.

Quinn refused to wither under that sharp emerald gaze. "Thank you for saving my life, Mrs. Tillman, and Ruthie's." If that cat hadn't flinched at the last second, it would be dead. He'd never seen a woman shoot with such accuracy from such a distance. In fact, the best shot in his company couldn't have done better.

She rubbed the mare's neck. "A fine horse is a treasure and one not to be wasted . . . *Mister* Spencer."

He coughed, disguising the laughter that tickled his throat. She'd made her priorities clear.

Whenever Quinn moved, pain shot through his broken leg and

sent his head spinning. He had never broken a bone before now, but had such an occurrence caused Mrs. Tillman's limp? Though not extreme, perhaps it added to her dour attitude.

He had been fortunate during the war to have received only a jagged scar from a stray ball. It ran along his left jaw line and remained hidden when his beard was long enough, like now. Had he—like the cat—not moved at the last moment, Quinn would be buried a few feet under the Virginia soil at Spotsylvania.

"May I ask what you were doing on my property, Mr. Spencer?"

"Traveling to the town of Bold Creek, Mrs. Tillman." The removal of the right boot produced an inward grimace from Quinn. He held his breath until it was over.

"And will you be settling there?" Miss Camille pulled a lace-edged handkerchief from her trouser pocket and doused it with water from a canteen. She cleaned away the blood caused by the cat's bite. After offering him what remained inside the canteen, she picked up his black slouch hat from the ground and set it on his head.

Quinn gulped the water and brushed the back of his hand across his wet lips. He snatched at the conversational lifeline that took his mind off his legs. "I'm to work for Arthur Bruner in his law office— a temporary position until I open my own. His son, Henry, was a boyhood friend of mine back in Ohio and a corporal in my regiment during the war."

"You are a trained attorney?"

"Yes, Miss Arneau. I completed my studies and a good portion of my apprenticeship before the war. Recently, a Texas judge pronounced me competent to practice the law."

"Perhaps, with that practice, you will one day acquire the competence to be successful."

Camille's eyes widened at her employer's rudeness. "Laurel! What is wrong with you today?"

Quinn pitied the husband of the woman. Under other circumstances, he might consider her smooth face and intelligent eyes attractive. Instead, she looked as though she had drained a pickle

14

barrel.

"It's all right, Miss Arneau. She's correct. I intend to take advantage of Mr. Bruner's years of experience and knowledge. In a sense, I will be practicing. My goal is to work hard to become a well-respected attorney . . . perhaps engage in politics in the future."

"Well respected? Then I suggest you keep your distance from us, Mr. Spencer." Mrs. Tillman stood as erect as a private at attention, looking in the opposite direction.

From that moment on, they waited in predominant silence for the expected help to arrive.

It seemed forever before the wagon rolled into the clearing. A well-endowed young woman in men's trousers and a plaid shirt set the brake. She leaped to the ground. Becky jumped off the back of the bed. Her mother closed her eyes and shook her head.

A stately woman, who appeared to be in her mid-fifties, remained on the wagon bench—the only female present wearing a dress. She glanced around and wrung her hands as if uncertain about whether to leave her post on the seat.

Mrs. Tillman moved to the buckboard and held out her hand. "I'm glad you're here, Momma."

"Becky said someone was hurt. I brought your father's bag." Her gaze fell to the hands twisting in uncertainty on her lap.

"Good. Here, let me help you down."

The older woman smiled like a schoolgirl receiving approval from the teacher. She clasped her daughter's hand. "I am sure I can help."

"I'm sure you can."

"Mr. Spencer, this is Mrs. Tillman's mother, Mrs. Ellen Chamberlain." Miss Arneau then pointed to the wagon team's driver. "The young lady is Miss Isabel Krueger."

What an odd lot—females wearing trousers, shirts, and chaps. Surely, they took no pleasure in being seen this way. He tried not to stare—nor see his beloved Amy in their faces.

Where were the male ranch hands and Mrs. Tillman's husband? Where was this Charlie she had mentioned?

"It's a pleasure to meet you, Mr. Spencer." Mrs. Chamberlain's voice held a hint of home.

"New York?"

"Eastern Pennsylvania. And you?"

He smiled, glad to hear a friendly accent. "Ohio. Do you still have family there, ma'am?"

"No." She examined the bite first and then ran her fingers along his left leg, a few inches above his ankle. He tried not to wince. "You're very fortunate, Mr. Spencer. Only the fibula, the small outer bone, fractured. However, we must set it before we move you. Laurel, I need—"

"Yes, ma'am. Issy, bring the bag."

"And the quilt, Issy dear."

Ellen Chamberlain opened the medical case and dug through the contents, removing a large roll of bandages. She stared into Quinn's eyes. Her brown gaze was stronger and more resolute than he had seen from her thus far. "I am sorry, but this will hurt."

Quinn nodded. Miss Arneau and Miss Krueger held his shoulders. He thought he had prepared himself. Then the pain shot through him when the older woman straightened the two broken pieces of bone by pulling his foot into its normal position.

Though he vowed to show no weakness in front of a group of women, even ones who seemed to defy proper society, a loud groan betrayed him.

Laurel had worked to harden her heart against feeling sorry for this blue belly in his suffering. Now, she wrestled with an urge to reach down and smooth the wrinkles that creased his damp forehead. His teeth clenched so hard against the pain, it was a wonder they didn't crumble like crushed rock.

Her mother rolled each end of a baby's quilt and eased his leg between the rolls. She wrapped the blanket with the bandages. "This will hold the bone in place until we reach the house. We need to keep that foot raised so it doesn't fall outward again."

At least Spencer hadn't passed out, which would have made settling him into the wagon bed harder. Afterward, Laurel left him to the ministrations of her mother and Camille while she led his horse over to her own.

Ruthie. What brawny military man named his mount something so namby-pamby? She shook her head and chuckled under her breath. At least his mare had a name, something she couldn't say about her gelding.

"Issy, take Camille's horse and check the sheep in the north pasture. I'm taking the mare to the house."

"Don't you want me to ride for the doctor?"

She met the quizzical gaze of her young ranch hand. "That's twelve miles one way. He's in no danger of expiring."

Laurel mounted and pressed her gelding's sides until he broke into a trot, followed by Ruthie. Five pairs of eyes bore into her back, willing her to change her mind. Momma would see to his injuries well enough.

She slowed the buckskin to a walk and kept the pace for nearly a rolling mile back to the ranch house. What would she do with the man? Neither he nor his horse were in any condition to be fed and sent on their way. Yet, hers was a homestead with four women, one child, and no man. Where would he stay?

Wherever she housed him, it would not be for long. She'd held her home and business together for the past six years without the presence of a single male—a single *human* male. And she would continue to do so, no matter how much she longed to live the traditional life of a lady.

Laurel frowned and her stomach tumbled with the peculiar feeling that this man's presence would throw into turmoil those rare moments of calm she had found in Texas.

CHAPTER TWO

Laurel raised the braided loop made from the material of one of Becky's old dresses and opened the gate to the small enclosure next to the barn. One day soon, she needed to fix the gate properly. She had allowed places around the ranch to fall into disrepair, but nothing was as bad as the burned condition of the house when John purchased it. Upon first seeing the place, her husband had insisted they name the ranch *La Casa del Fuego*—The House of Fire.

Slapping the hindquarter of the unsaddled buckskin sent him across the sod, kicking up his heels. She would groom him after settling her *guest.*

Laurel stalled Ruthie for Momma to tend to her injuries. What provoked her to shoot Spencer with words as sharp as porcupine quills? She had met other Yankees over the past twelve years. Many of the residents of the county had supported the Union in the war. So what riled her about Mr. Spencer? The saber?

A shiver rolled down her spine. The sooner he left, the better.

The wagon rolled into the yard, and Becky hopped out of the bed before the wheels stopped spinning. "Granmomma wants to know where they should put Mr. Spencer."

18

Oh, to share her daughter's enthusiasm about life. "She could have shouted that out for herself, Peanut."

Once Laurel made the hard decision, she refused to change her mind, a stubborn trait that had caused her no end of trouble in her life. With Issy gone, she must help Camille get Spencer into the house. Cursing her southern upbringing and the code that required hospitality, Laurel lowered the end gate of the wagon. "We'll take him to my room."

"I don't want to put you out, ma'am."

"Don't argue, Mr. Spencer, or you'll keep company with your horse."

His low chuckle vibrated her shoulder. "It wouldn't be the first time, ma'am."

An image of him using Ruthie's belly as a pillow almost made her smile. "I am not above temptation, sir."

It took all three women to help him to the house while Becky kept his foot in place. He was a solid man, and with the weakness in her right knee, Laurel strained to keep her balance. Together, they must be quite a sight—the lame carrying the lame. All were huffing and puffing by the time the women eased him onto Laurel's bed.

Camille smiled down at him. "I hope you feel better soon, Mr. Spencer." She frowned at Laurel and left the room.

When the others followed, abandoning her, Laurel wished to join them, but someone must see to the man's comfort. Besides, she loathed leaving this stranger alone with her possessions. The war taught her how Yankees treated a southerner's property.

She sighed. The man couldn't walk. How would he steal anything?

A chorus of bleats from the ewes and lambs recently separated during the weaning period penetrated the walls of the room. Stepping to the window, she drew aside the flimsy yellowed curtain. During the past six years, her flocks had multiplied many times over. They grazed the small hills and pastureland of her acreage. Sheep were such skittish things, bolting at the least little intimidation.

Laurel moved to the corner. She would not bolt. Neither would she carry on a conversation with the man lying in her bed.

Momma entered the room carrying an enameled pan. Steam rolled upward in the air and in front of her face. With clean rags tucked under her arm, she tiptoed so as not to slosh the water over the edge. "Would you bring Daddy's bag, dear? And some whiskey?"

"Right away, Momma." Laurel dashed from the room as if that mountain lion licked her heels. So much for not bolting.

Quinn took a deep breath and leaned back against the bed's headboard while Mrs. Chamberlain cleansed his wound with hot water. Mrs. Tillman could have sent for a doctor, but he assumed she had faith in her mother's ability. Clearly, the older woman's confidence benefited from the task given her.

To quell the physical sting, he concentrated on the faint scent of lilacs on the pillow and sank into the straw mattress under his body. For years, he'd slept on the ground or—when not on patrol—on a straw-filled tick in his quarters. The first thing he would look for in Bold Creek would be a boarding house with goose down bedding.

His gaze strayed to the frame sitting on the bureau a few feet away. The mustachioed, one-eyed man in the wedding photo wore his butternut uniform with authority. Despite the groom's lack of a smile, the eye without the black patch flashed with humor, as if the photographer had made an amusing comment. He sat in a plush, fringed chair while his younger bride stood partially behind him, her hand resting on his shoulder.

Laurel Tillman appeared to have been in her late teens when wed. Her loveliness would have pumped pride through any man. She still retained the same regal bearing, the slung-back shoulders and raised chin, the slim frame and soft tresses—and the same melancholy stare. An unhappy match?

The eyes of his men held that same look after a wearying Union defeat. In his spirit, Quinn sensed this woman had experienced things

20

in her life that had damaged her character. Beyond repair? He shivered at the voice inside that assured him no vessel was beyond repair when placed in the hands of the Master Potter."

The mattress shuddered, sending a sharp spasm through Quinn's broken leg. He bit back a groan as Becky bounced on the edge of the ticking. "How you feelin', Mr. Spencer?"

Better until you jumped on the bed. Quinn mustered a half-smile. "Good."

"This is Prudence." The multi-colored collie whined in pleasure at Becky's loving pats on her head. "Her husband, Charlie, is guarding the flock."

Charlie was a dog, not a male ranch hand? So where were the men? He found it ludicrous to suppose Mr. Tillman only employed females.

"They're going to have babies soon. Did you know dogs can have lots of babies at one time, Mr. Spencer? Why do people have only one or two? Two are called twins. I didn't have a twin. I had a big brother, but Momma was a twin, wasn't she, Granmomma?"

Mrs. Chamberlain turned a sharp gaze to her granddaughter. "Rebecca, you have no business in here. Now scoot. And take that hairy mutt with you." Becky's expression said she considered spouting a rebellious reply. "You heard me. Go."

"Yes, ma'am." The girl slid off the bed and sulked out the door. Prudence trotted behind her.

Quinn bit his bottom lip to hold in laughter mixed with physical misery.

"I am sorry, Mr. Spencer. I love my granddaughter, but she can send a teetotaler on a regular trip to the sherry decanter. She's just like her mother at that age—more boy than young lady."

Quinn released the laughter, his mood improving with the woman's unexpected admission. "I am sure she'll grow out of it and into a woman as handsome as her mother." He cringed at having freely shared such a private assessment.

Mrs. Chamberlain provided him with an old quilt and took the scissors to his new trousers. "Oh, I hope it won't take as long with Becky as it did with Laurel. Of course, the war didn't help."

"Didn't help what, Momma?"

Ellen Chamberlain examined the gash as her daughter came into the room carrying the medical bag and a large clear bottle holding a golden liquid. "I think we can agree that the war helped nothing, dear."

Quinn settled the quilt over his body, leaving his lower legs exposed.

"I depleted my store of carbolic acid." Mrs. Chamberlain raised her head and smiled at Quinn as she dabbed a small amount of whiskey onto his wound. "This will have to do."

He gripped the sheet on either side of his body to keep from shooting off the bed. So this was what being on fire felt like. He clamped his teeth together and pressed his eyes shut until he figured they'd fused together. Quinn inhaled a series of quick, shallow breaths during her ministrations with the alcohol.

"Would you like me to blow on it, Mr. Spencer?"

He glared at the woman standing in the corner. "N-no, Mrs. Tillman. I would not."

She shrugged and turned toward the window as she had earlier.

Ellen Chamberlain dug through the bag. "I'm afraid I'm out of catgut as well. Dr. Cameron was to provide me with more, but his shipment of supplies has been delayed. Laurel, we must resupply your father's bag soon. In the meantime, well, I guess . . ."

"Thread, Momma?"

"Yes, thread will do."

"I'll get your sewing kit." Mrs. Tillman returned a minute later with a box.

Mrs. Chamberlain dug through it and held up two spools of thread. "Now, Mr. Spencer, which color would you like?"

She may as well have asked a man facing a firing squad which color blindfold he wanted. "I'll leave it up to you, ma'am, as long as it isn't red."

"The red is not silk, Mr. Spencer. Only the black and brown are suitable for sewing wounds." She spent several moments in decision.

"I believe the black would be proper, Momma."

"Black it is, then. Unless you have an objection, sir?"

For Pete's sake, woman, get on with it. "No, ma'am. Black will do."

She disinfected the thread with the alcohol and held out the bottle of whiskey. "You might need this."

"I don't imbibe."

Mrs. Tillman returned to her corner of the room. "You will shortly."

Her smirk made him even more determined to refuse the liquor. "Go ahead, Mrs. Chamberlain." It took all his willpower, but Quinn survived the next few minutes with his pride intact.

After dressing the wound and wrapping the leg with bandages, the older woman patted him on the shoulder. "I fear that's all I can do for you. However, you cannot remain in these torn and dirty clothes. Laurel, will you get one of John's nightshirts from the trunk?"

The young woman's jaw resembled a rock. "Momma—"

"Please, dear."

Laurel threw her hands up and sifted through the large, humpbacked trunk at the end of the bed. She dropped a bundle of brown-striped muslin onto the mattress and stomped back to her corner.

Ellen Chamberlain handed him the nightshirt. "I imagine you can manage this yourself?"

"Yes, ma'am." Quinn would do so if the process killed him.

"Should you need anything, Mr. Spencer, let me know."

"Thank you for all you've done, Mrs. Chamberlain." As the women prepared to leave the room, Quinn called out, "Mrs. Tillman, I have no desire to drive you from your room. I saw a bunkhouse. I'll stay with the other ranch hands."

"I don't believe so, Mr. Spencer. Besides, you won't be here long enough to cause me much additional inconvenience."

He nodded once. "When will I meet Mr. Tillman?"

Her hand wrapped around the doorknob in a claw-like grip. She stared at—or was it through—him?

"It depends."

"Depends? On what?"

"On how soon you want to meet your Maker."

"I do not understand you, Laurel." Camille stabbed a beet with uncharacteristic violence. "You only treat our friends the MacMahons with such contempt."

Issy choked on her coffee. "Friends? How can you say that? They're arrogant—"

"Issy." No matter how often Laurel had tried to shift the subject at the supper table to business, it eventually strayed back to Quinn Spencer.

Issy frowned. "You know it as well as I do, Laurel. How can you tolerate either of the MacMahons? All they want is La Casa del Fuego land. And, Camille, don't you ever see the bad in anyone?"

Laurel peeked at her friend while slathering peach jam on a biscuit. Although her past contained a deep hurt she had never revealed, Camille looked for the good in people. Her benevolence both intrigued and irritated Laurel.

Issy didn't wait for Camille's answer. "So far, all I've found wrong with Mr. Spencer is his typical male attitude toward women."

"What male attitude?" Becky crammed a large piece of biscuit into her mouth.

Laurel tapped her daughter's arm. "Never mind. And don't put so much in your mouth at one time. It isn't ladylike." She nearly laughed at Becky's rolled eyes. The girl had inherited too many of her traits.

"Did you see his big eyes when he found himself surrounded by a group of women wearing trousers?" Issy exaggerated Spencer's expression, drawing laughter from everyone seated around the table. "Men. It's as if they didn't think God gave women legs under all these

24

petticoats."

"Limbs, Issy. And men should see us differently. Frankly, I am thankful we dress like this in the evening." Camille fingered the hand-tatted lace at the collar of her blouse and glanced at Laurel. "I have no desire to look like a male twenty-four hours a day. As much as I appreciate the necessities of my employment, I am female, and I do not desire anyone to forget that."

Issy picked up her fork and grumbled at the potato on her plate. "As if any *man* could."

Pity welled inside Laurel at the sour note. The physical difference between Camille and Issy stood out like the only sheared lamb in a flock. The younger woman failed to see that her sense of humor and outgoing spirit reflected an inner loveliness. And how could any man look past those striking eyes, the blue-green of the Atlantic Ocean at midday?

Of course, too many louts lacked the strength to raise their eyes higher than Issy's ample bosom.

Laurel intervened before the discussion deteriorated into another argument over the role of women in society. "I'll stay in the bunkhouse tonight."

Her mother stared at her. "Becky and I will make room for you with us."

"Momma, that room is hardly large enough for the two of you. Since sleeping on the sofa in the sitting room does not appeal to me, I'll sleep in one of the extra beds in the bunkhouse. It'll only be for one night." Had it not been that Mr. Spencer's injuries left him unable to walk properly, Laurel would never consider leaving her mother and daughter in the house alone with him. "I want you to place a chair under the bedroom doorknob."

"Where do you plan to go tomorrow night, dear?"

"Back to my own room, of course."

Camille set her coffee cup on the saucer. "What about Mr. Spencer?"

"Mr. Spencer will not take up a prolonged residence in this house. I'll go to Bold Creek tomorrow for supplies. He'll go with me."

"I'm siding with Camille on this." Issy narrowed her eyes. "What is wrong with you, Laurel? You wouldn't allow me to fetch Dr. Cameron and now you want to throw an injured man out on his ear? He can hardly walk. How can he take care of himself?"

"I'm sure the man will—"

"No." Silence ruled the room as everyone focused on Laurel's mother. Her eyes were downcast, and she played with her napkin, but her voice had been strong and decisive. "You will not cause that man further agony, Laurel. I realize this is your home, but what you want to do is wrong. Allowing him a few days of recovery will hurt none of us."

Laurel gazed around the table. Each face expressed agreement, even Becky's. She rubbed her temples, tired of the fight and willing to surrender—under certain terms. "Fine. He'll stay until he can walk with a crutch. Not one day longer. Is that clear?" She slid her chair away from the table and stood.

"I just thought it might be best . . ." The strength and determination on Momma's face faltered, replaced by the typical uncertainty.

Laurel wished to bite her offending tongue in two. "No, Momma. You're right." She dropped her napkin on the table and limped from the room, no longer hungry.

I deserve to feel no peace.

CHAPTER THREE

Laurel bent her stiff right knee and stepped on the hub of the wagon's wheel, groaning at the annoyance that seemed especially bothersome this morning.

"Wait, dear." Momma trotted toward the wagon, waving something white in her hand.

Once seated on the bench of the buckboard, Laurel straightened her indigo cotton skirt and glanced at the sky, its bright shade the opposite hue of the cloth.

"Mr. Spencer asked that you deliver this letter to Mr. Bruner."

Laurel stared at the folded paper. "Now I am to be his messenger?" She took the missive from her mother's hand and stuffed it inside the embroidered reticule hanging from her wrist, not caring if the paper wrinkled. The sooner he left La Casa del Fuego, the better.

She ran her fingers across her eyes, the grit of a restless night stinging their lids. Almost two years had passed since the last dream. Laurel thought she had finally outgrown waking in the wee hours with her damp gown clinging to her skin after ill-defined faces raced through her mind. She blamed her night terror on the presence of the former cavalry officer.

She slapped the reins across the backs of the mules, harder than she'd meant to do. "Get up."

The eastern sun peaked above the hills without a cloud to disturb its ascent. She had hoped for a grayer sky to cool the seven miles to town. At least her bonnet's brim would shield her eyes from the sunshine.

Once in town, Laurel stopped the mules in the alley beside Schuler's General Merchandise. She set the wagon's brake, eased onto the ground, and limped around to the front of the building. She preferred to come into Bold Creek during the week rather than on Saturday when the stores and streets teemed with people.

Her supply order given to Mrs. Schuler, she walked toward Arthur Bruner's office above the bakery. At the door to May Simpson's dress shop, she collided with a stout body backing outside while a stream of last-minute orders to the dressmaker flowed from the customer's mouth. Laurel reached out to steady the woman.

Florence Cade took a step backward and eyed Laurel's simple apparel. Before walking away, the woman glanced toward May's shop as though wordlessly suggesting Laurel might want to frequent the establishment.

The snubs from the town's biddies had long since failed to rile Laurel. Admittedly, to her shame, she sometimes gained a wicked sense of righteousness from their rebuffs. At other times, they made her feel as though she had ridden into town on the back of a cockroach.

"Decent women shouldn't wear trousers and do the jobs of men willing to work."

But the women of La Casa del Fuego had no choice thanks to Royce MacMahon and his bootlickers. And they could hardly ride through the hills and brush in their Sunday finest now, could they?

"You shame your husband."

Of all people, John would understand.

"God will punish you for raising your daughter in a den of iniquity."

That one always made Laurel laugh. What den of iniquity? Until

Quinn Spencer, only her husband slept under her roof. And she had news for them. God had been punishing her long before she rejected Royce MacMahon's proposals, long before she hired Camille and Issy, and long before her husband and son died, leaving her to run a sheep ranch with only female help.

"*Guten morgen, Frau* Tillman." The rotund owner of Oberlin's Bakery cleaned the front window of his shop, his reflection smiling at her. Laurel was never sure whether his ever-present reddened cheeks were natural or the result of heat from the brick ovens inside the bakery.

"Good morning, Mr. Oberlin." She sniffed the air, and her mouth watered at the smell of yeast, cinnamon, and sugar. "How is Mrs. Oberlin?"

"Ach, my Frieda she is much improved. *Danke*." He turned and waved a wet sponge through the air. Happiness glowed in the man's face. "The fever is over, but the cough lingers. *Gott* bless the dear one who provided the doctor's fee."

Anton and Frieda had accepted Laurel and the others, treating Becky as if she were their own grandchild. Their loyalty had prompted her to scrape together enough cash to pay Dr. Cameron anonymously for Frieda's care.

"That is fortunate." Laurel smiled for the first time that morning. "Please tell her I hope she's well real soon. Do you know if Mr. Bruner is in?"

"*Ja*. I see him earlier."

"Would you mind wrapping one of your delicious *Butterküchen* for me? I'll get it once I finish my business upstairs."

"You will have the freshest in *mein* shop." He bobbed his head and scurried inside the bakery.

She grinned again and started up the steps to the attorney's office above the bakery. Laurel opened the door to the office and stepped inside. "Mr. Bruner?"

A man, tall and straight as a telegraph pole, walked out of the room to her right. He removed his spectacles and rubbed the glass with a handkerchief. With his gray-streaked, brown hair running past the collar of his coat, she supposed he sought to prove to himself that the large bald spot on top of his head wouldn't keep him from growing hair in other areas.

His smile was strained. "Mrs. Tillman, what a pleasure to speak with you somewhere other than the cemetery." Arthur Bruner's accent matched that of Laurel's house guest. However, he did not spark the irrational animosity she felt toward the former officer.

"We do often pay respects to our loved ones at the same time."

She pulled the wrinkled notepaper from her reticule and handed it to him. "This is from Major Spencer. He said you were expecting him this week."

"Quinn? Yes, I am." He pointed to a small chair by the wall. "Please sit down and tell me why you're here and not him."

Laurel smoothed the back of her skirt and sat on the edge of the straight-backed chair he'd pointed out. Like Camille, she preferred wearing women's clothing when not working around the ranch. Issy, though, took pleasure in scandalizing society and her family by wearing bloomers to town whenever she could get away with it.

"Unfortunately, a mountain lion attacked Mr. Spencer. He's recuperating at my ranch." She pointed to the note in his hand. "I'm sure the message explains everything."

While the attorney unfolded the paper and read the letter silently, Laurel looked around the austere reception room. Two doors opened into offices. A small portion of the one straight ahead was visible from where she sat. It, too, contained a simple décor and plain, dark furnishings.

"He says it will be some time before he's able to travel." Mr. Bruner paused with his graying eyebrows drawn together. "Would you mind if I stop at your place on Saturday? Quinn and I go way back. He was my son's friend and his lieutenant during the war. I am eager to see him again."

Laurel perked up. Surely, Mr. Bruner would insist upon returning to Bold Creek, accompanied by her unwanted guest. "That will be fine."

Laurel hesitated for fear of sounding too inquisitive, but her curiosity overcame the concern. "Until he mentioned it, I never realized you had a son, Mr. Bruner."

"Henry is dead, Mrs. Tillman."

At the sharpness in the reply, she wanted to ask if his death came during the war, but it wasn't her business. "You have my condolences, sir."

He shrugged and refolded the letter. "How badly is Quinn hurt?"

"A broken leg bone. Momma is taking good care of him."

"Good. I look forward to the visit."

Laurel smiled as she left the office. Spencer's absence would bring her better sleep.

Mr. Schuler's clerk heaved a sack of rice on top of the bags of flour and sugar in the bed of Laurel's wagon. He dusted off his hands. "That should do you for a while, Mrs. Tillman."

"Thank you, Peter."

The young man steadied her with a hand to her elbow as she climbed onto the wagon bench. "How's Miss Issy?"

"Outspoken as always."

He laughed. "She's a wonder, ain't she?"

"Yes."

Laurel gazed at the rail thin young man with the rosy cheeks and contagious grin. Issy needed someone like Peter Belton to show an interest and temper her zeal for women's suffrage—not that Laurel didn't agree with women being treated in a more equal manner. Her life proved it. Still, she sensed the nineteen-year-old woman desired to shock more than to reform. Besides, Peter was one of the few men willing to accept her behavior. Not even Issy's family did so.

Laurel took up the reins and urged the mules back onto the street. As she left the buildings of Bold Creek behind, she glanced at the empty wooden bench beside her. She scanned the floor by her feet.

Nothing. She turned her head and shoulders to peer into the bed of the wagon. Not there. Her lips twisted into a scowl. "Where is that Butterküchen?"

Laurel well remembered laying the paper-wrapped cake on the seat before her visit to the cemetery. Either it had fallen off unnoticed when she turned the wagon, or a stray dog had found a tasty meal. She shook her head in disgust. "I'd set my mouth for that treat."

The hoofs of the mules kicked up small puffs of road dust. She relaxed the reins, allowing the animals to travel at their own pace. Even with the load in the wagon bed, they stepped lively toward home.

A movement at the top of the hill caught her attention, and she squinted as a small figure dodged into the trees next to the road. She reached under the seat for her carbine and set it beside her. A lone woman couldn't be too careful.

The mules plodded closer to the trees and Laurel kept watch on the foliage. Scrub rustled, and she tugged on the lines. "Whoa, there." Picking up the weapon from the seat, she rested the butt on her upper leg. Whoever hid at the side of the road would not waylay her. "Come out this instant."

Stillness and silence.

"I mean it. Come out now."

Leafy branches parted. "Don't shoot, ma'am."

Laurel eyed the young stranger in the loose, dusty trousers and dirty, rumpled shirt. Tendrils of red hair poked out in all directions from a wide-brimmed hat with sweat stains around the beehive crown. "Who are you?"

"Name's Ernie Goodman, ma'am."

"Your full name?"

"Ernaline Marie Goodman." She kicked the dirt. "Nobody calls me by my rightful name."

Laurel lowered the weapon. From a distance, Ernie could pass for a boy. She took a deep breath, fighting back the desire to flee the young girl's presence and the memories flashing in front of her.

"Just passin' through, ma'am."

"On your way to where?"

"Can't rightly say. I reckon I'll know the place when I see it."

Appearing to be only a few years older than Becky, the girl was too young to travel the roads on her own. Laurel stiffened, subduing a familiar urge with the excuse that she could not afford to take in any more strays. She scanned the child from her booted feet to her covered head and snorted wry amusement. *Ernie* fit in perfectly with the rest of the ranch family.

"Where are you from?"

"Arkansas."

Such a far distance. "Why are you traveling alone?"

Ernie stared at Laurel. She opened her mouth and shut it again. The girl straightened her shoulders and raised her chin. "Ain't nobody gonna make me marry Virgil Hicks. He's old enough to be my grampap."

Words failed Laurel, but an ache of silent pity burned in her heart.

Ernie swiped her dirty sleeve under her nose and looked away. "If'n you don't mind, ma'am, I best move on." She turned and started down the road. Her back pocket bulged with a piece of brown paper—the butterküchen.

Before she could stop herself, Laurel called out, "How do you feel about sheep, Miss Goodman?"

CHAPTER FOUR

Quinn grimaced as he shifted on the bed until his back was vertical. Although each day brought less discomfort, he had been abed seventy-two hours and fourteen minutes and was ready to climb the cabin's walls, sore legs or no.

Resting with his back against the headboard, he celebrated the expectation of deeply missed male company. The women had been gracious, but work took them away from the house during the day. Only Mrs. Chamberlain remained to cook and clean or teach Becky her lessons.

The women spent the evenings in the sitting room discussing female topics, sheep, and ranch tasks he knew little about. He couldn't wait to partake in a good political argument.

At a rap on the bedroom door, he covered his full body with the sheet. "Enter." Quinn wished to take back the command. After all, this wasn't his room.

Mrs. Tillman strode inside. She extended an open hand and stopped, a look of indecision on her face. The expression turned to galled resolution when she reached out and pressed cool fingers to his forehead. "Momma asked me to check that you had no fever. She's still concerned about infection."

"Please tell her I'm fine. She's a skillful nurse."

Laurel lifted her hand and slid it down her denims. Quinn almost laughed. She couldn't abide the feel of his skin on her own?

She walked over to the bureau and removed another set of clothing, hiding the women's undergarments inside men's work clothes and out of sight. Almost. A slight bit of lace peeked from between a pair of trousers and a plaid shirt.

Why did Mrs. Tillman employ only women? The ones he had met were a varied lot—the lovely Miss Arneau, the rebellious Miss Krueger, the ambivalent Mrs. Chamberlain. Were there more on the ranch?

His gaze drifted to the woman in the photograph on the dresser. What was her story? "Your husband was a Confederate officer, ma'am? May I ask where he received the injury to his eye?"

"You may ask." She walked toward the opened door as though to leave without answering his question. Before completely passing through to the hall, she stopped and turned around. "Bentonville, Mr. Spencer."

"March of '65. Less than a month before Lee surrendered."

"A long month." She left, softly shutting the door behind her.

The conversation might have been short and strained, but he had conversed with the woman who, heretofore, had done her best to ignore him. Perhaps by the time he left the ranch, they could discuss something neutral, like the weather, in an amiable manner.

Quinn yawned. At another knock on the door, he bid his visitor to enter. Arthur Bruner stepped into the bedroom with a smile on his face. "It's good to see you in one piece, Quinn."

"Thank you, sir. It's good to be in one piece." Quinn studied his friend, whose hair was thinner than he remembered. He wore spectacles, and the skin sagged around his jawline. Years of life and loss had dimmed the sparkle in the man's brown eyes.

"Please sit down, Mr. Bruner." Mrs. Chamberlain followed him into the bedroom, carrying a kitchen chair. She positioned it to allow the two men to face one another and talk with ease.

"Thank you, madam." The lawyer presented her with a slight bow.

"I'll leave you gentlemen alone. I'm sure you have a great deal to discuss. I'll bring supper in half an hour, if that's all right? Unless you would prefer to wait a while, then—"

"No, ma'am. That would be fine, Mrs. Chamberlain." Quinn smiled to put her at ease.

Once Ellen Chamberlain left them alone in the bedroom, Arthur sat in the chair and squinted at Quinn's bandaged legs. "How are you, son?"

"Sore. Though, as Mrs. Tillman likes to say, I'll live."

"Good, good." Arthur's mouth spread into a smile that never parted his lips. "I would recommend you join me at my home for your convalescence, but I'm afraid business calls me away for at least two weeks. As much as I hate to say it, you are better off here with the women to care for you."

"Don't worry about me, sir."

"I can't help but worry. I'm counting on your hasty recovery. I need a partner like you."

Quinn stopped in the process of plumping the pillow behind his back. "A partner? When you invited me to work with you, sir, you said nothing about becoming a partner."

Quinn had planned to study for a couple of years under the experienced lawyer, then open his own office, maybe nearer Austin. Before the war and before life changed so drastically, politics had held his interest. What better place to learn how Texas lawmakers worked than in the capital itself?

"I am honored to be considered for the position, Mr. Bruner, but—"

"Now, we'll have none of that. My name is Arthur."

"Arthur." Though in his mind he had referred to the man as such, the name sounded strange on Quinn's tongue, like calling Colonel Peck by his Christian name of Bill. "I deeply appreciate the offer, and I look forward to working with you, but I haven't decided where I'll settle. As I stated in my letters to you, I can't promise to make a permanent home in Bold Creek."

The man's brown eyes lowered. His lips curved into a self-conscious grin. "I am sorry to hear that. I had planned . . . well, I had hoped Henry would one day follow in my footsteps, but the war ended that dream."

It ended the dreams of many a man. Henry had only himself to blame. However, Quinn decided long ago to never burden this man with his son's failing.

"Sir, I am very sorry if something in one of my letters gave you the wrong impression."

"Nonsense." Arthur leaned forward and laid his long fingers on Quinn's forearm. He gave it a fatherly squeeze. "I apologize for making an improper assumption."

Doubt dried Quinn's throat. Was he being foolish? He might risk losing the man's respect by not accepting his generous offer at once. At thirty-seven, he had little experience to warrant such an excellent opportunity. And it wasn't as if he had recently met Arthur. Their friendship spanned many years and too much hurt. Still, more thought and prayer was required before assuming the position offered him.

"Shall we wait and see whether you think me worthy of a partnership?"

The older man eased back in his chair, his face relaxed. "That is acceptable."

"I never heard of a girl named Ernie." Becky tugged a small cucumber from the vine and tossed it into the basket at her mother's feet.

"Don't be rude, Peanut."

"I was just saying—"

"We don't need to say everything on our minds." Laurel straightened and rubbed her lower back, ready to turn the pickings over to Momma and go on to the countless other chores awaiting her.

Ernie laughed. "It don't bother me none. B'sides, I ain't never heard of nobody called Peanut."

Laurel raised the basket. "This is nearly it for the season. Granmomma's going to put up more tasty pickles."

Becky turned to Ernie. "Nobody makes better sweet pickles than my granmomma."

"She's a right fine cook, all right. I ain't had meals so good since my ma . . ." Ernie traced a line in the dirt with the toe of her worn boot. "She used to whip up vittles that'd melt faster'n sugar in your mouth."

Laurel smiled. Did Ernie's mother make butter cakes, too? If so, were they as tasty as Mr. Oberlin's? She hadn't the heart to scold the hungry girl and had let her keep the rest of the sweet treat. Eventually, Ernie broached the subject, admitting to having taken it. The confession eased Laurel's mind over the concern of having invited a thief into her home.

"How old are you, Ernaline?"

Ernie hesitated, seeming to carry on an inner argument as to the necessity of a lie. Like two days ago, her grimace said the truth won out. She might lack formal schooling, but her momma had raised her to be an honest girl.

"Fifteen, ma'am."

A mere girl of fifteen, traveling alone for weeks on end. Laurel shut her eyes, recalling her own fears when leaving home at nearly seventeen, not knowing where she would go, how she would accomplish her goal, or if she would see her mother again. An immature, selfish need for vengeance had overshadowed her trepidation. She blinked away the unpleasant memories. "Where are your folks, Ernie?"

A flush rose to tint the girl's already ruddy skin. "My pa lit out a ways back. Ma said he had a bigger hankerin' for John Barleycorn than his kin. Last spring, she plain saddened herself into a hole in the ground."

"Who's John Barleycorn?"

"Never mind, Peanut."

"Aw, nobody tells me nothin'." Becky stomped off toward the barn with Ernie following at a plodding gait.

Tempted to call her daughter back to reprimand her for her poor word choice—something exacerbated in the past two days—Laurel kept her mouth shut. She tired of chiding Becky. No doubt the child found the correction equally maddening.

Her lips puckered. It might prove more practical for Ernie to sit in on her daughter's schooling sessions. Could the girl read and write?

"Becky reminds me so much of you and Lance at her age."

Laurel turned. Her mother stood at the edge of the garden. "We gave you ample trouble back then. I suppose I am reaping what I sowed."

"No, dear. You are raising a precious child. She'll grow up to become a woman we'll be proud to know . . . like you."

How could she say that after all Laurel had confessed of those seven months she'd been away? She hugged her mother. "Thank you, Momma. I don't know what I'd do without you."

"Not a person on this ranch would say any different about you." Momma squeezed Laurel's hand. "Dear, I pray every day that the Lord will open your eyes and allow you to see your worth to Him."

"Oh, Momma, He'll never—"

"Hush now, girl. That's John speaking, not God."

Laurel recoiled. For the second time this week, her mother spoke to her with authority. This was the first time she had ever spoken a word against John. What had gotten into Momma?

Arthur dabbed at the corners of his mouth with a napkin and then patted his flat stomach. "It's been some time since I've enjoyed a woman's cooking. You're a civilian like me now." He winked. "A bachelor civilian, I might add. You no longer have army cooks to satisfy your hunger."

Quinn winced at the reminder. Amy's cooking should fill his stomach morning, noon, and evening. On good days, he acknowledged that his deceased fiancée had been no different from him—fighting for what she believed was right. Other days, he railed at her memory, struggling to understand why she chose a dangerous and unorthodox way to fulfill the task she'd believed God had assigned her. Why her?

He swallowed his last bite of carrot cake. The first portion of the dinner was delicious, but he tasted little of the dessert once both legs began to throb and ache. After insisting he could sit on the side of the bed to eat, all he wanted now was to ease back onto the down-filled ticking and prop his legs on a pillow.

"You look pale, son."

"I believe I'll scoot back and put my legs up again."

Arthur rose from his seat and reached out to help Quinn raise his right foot. During the process, the older man bumped the tray on Quinn's lap, which held his plate and a cup filled with coffee. The cup tipped, sloshing hot liquid that splashed onto John Tillman's nightshirt and coated Quinn's skin underneath. He sucked in a breath when heat seared his abdomen.

"I am sorry, son. Here, let me help." Arthur blotted the material with his napkin, leaving a light brown circle on the muslin nightshirt.

"No. It's all right, sir. I'll be fine." The burn subsided, but the saturated cloth clung to his skin. "I should change. Will you ask Mrs. Chamberlain if she might supply me with another nightshirt?"

"Of course." Arthur returned a short time later. "There's not a single woman inside the house and the yard is empty."

Quinn frowned, uncomfortable in the wet clothing he had hoped to change. "The ladies confiscated my clothes to wash. I haven't seen them since." Once he reached Bold Creek, he would shop for the type of attire he hadn't needed while in the military.

He pointed to the end of the bed. Though he hated going through the woman's things, he couldn't stay in the wet clothing. "Mrs. Tillman pulled this nightshirt from that trunk. Maybe you can find another one in there."

Arthur opened the lid and shuffled through the belongings. The rustling of the items inside abated. He looked toward the dresser, then peered into the trunk again.

"Did you find one?" At his lack of answer, Quinn called out, "Arthur?"

"Hmm? Oh, yes." He closed the lid and held up a nightshirt that matched the one Quinn was wearing.

His faraway expression disconcerted Quinn. "Is something wrong?"

Arthur scowled at the dresser. At the photo of John and Laurel Tillman? "It's difficult to go through the possessions of one no longer with us."

"And why would you go through those possessions?" Laurel stood in the doorway with her hands on her hips, a foot tapping with impatience, and the scowl on her face trumping that of Arthur's.

Quinn opened his mouth to explain as Arthur dropped the lid on the trunk and said, "I beg your pardon, Mrs. Tillman. You see, my clumsy movements caused Quinn's coffee to spill over his nightshirt. It seemed all the women were occupied elsewhere, so in seeking his comfort, I opened the trunk. My apologies."

Laurel's narrowed gaze slid to Quinn and the wet brown spot on the material of the nightshirt. Seeking evidence that Arthur told the truth?

She hobbled inside the room, opened the trunk, and rummaged through the contents. Did she think they had stolen something? Finally, she pulled out another nightshirt and shoved it at Arthur. "We certainly wouldn't want the poor man uncomfortable."

After her uneven gait carried her from the room, Arthur whistled. "I suppose the rumors are true."

"What rumors?"

"Mrs. Tillman is anything but a well-mannered lady."

Though Quinn couldn't deny the statement, he wouldn't disparage his hostess by vocalizing an agreement.

CHAPTER FIVE

"What do you think of Checkers, Mr. Spencer?" Becky sat on the porch steps near Quinn's chair, chattering nonstop.

His gaze shifted from watching Camille gather eggs at the henhouse to the cute little girl who so resembled her mother—minus the glowering looks. He recalled his desire to melt into the goose down over two weeks ago. Quinn hadn't blamed Laurel for feeling as though they had violated her privacy. They had. Had he caught a man under his command—even one he liked—going through his belongings without permission, he would have thrown him in the guardhouse quicker than the soldier could catch his breath.

"What do you think, Mr. Spencer?"

He focused on the young girl. "Checkers? It's an amusing game."

"Checkers is not a game." Becky ran her hand along the fur of the large and sleepy calico cat sprawled across her lap, then held the animal in the air. It let out a loud, extended meow. "This is Checkers."

He chastised himself for letting his attention wander during a good portion of the chiefly one-sided discussion. "I beg your pardon, Becky." He reached over and carefully shook the front paw of the offended cat. "And I beg your pardon, Checkers."

The little girl laughed. "You're a funny man. Isn't he, Checkers?"

Quinn considered his daily visits with Becky to be like a rich dessert—enjoyed in small servings. To his surprise, he was becoming rather fond of the treat. Through fourteen years of military life, his contact with children had been sparse. Officers sometimes brought their families to live on the post, but he spent as little time as possible in their presence. Any desire for children died years ago with Amy.

"Where are the other ladies?"

She cuddled the cat against her cheek. "Momma was walking up the hill."

Off and on in the evenings, he had watched from the bedroom window as Laurel walked the knoll nearly fifty yards behind the house. "What's up the hill?"

Becky lowered the cat to the porch floor behind her. "The top of the world, I guess."

The top of the world? He should have known not to ask.

Time spent with the sheep lady continued to tax him, yet Quinn sensed a soft spot toward him expanding somewhere within Laurel's hardwood shell. He had noticed the rare grins she tried to hide when he said something the others found amusing. He just didn't know how to grow that soft spot, or if he should make the effort. Planing her splinters really wasn't to his advantage.

"Good morning, Quinn." Camille joined him on the porch. She eyed the sky. "It is a nice day. I am glad you can take in the fresh air each morning."

"Yes, ma'am. It's good to feel the sunshine."

With the aid of the crutches Arthur had given him and the continued healing of the broken bone in his left leg, Quinn could dress in trousers and hobble along for short distances. That discovery brought no end to Mrs. Tillman's joy.

A gunshot echoed, and Quinn jolted. He would have jumped to his feet to make ready to defend the ladies . . . if he could.

"Do not worry about the shooting. It is only Laurel practicing behind the barn."

"Practicing?"

"Yes. She is an amazing shot." Camille laughed. "I believe missing the mountain lion hurt her pride."

He looked at Becky. "You said she was at the top of the world."

The girl shrugged as more shots sounded. With no need to worry over danger, he ignored them to focus on Miss Camille.

"I've asked Mr. Bruner to drive me into Bold Creek on Wednesday."

Camille turned to Becky. "It is time to milk Princess. Please take Checkers with you to the barn. And put the stool back in its place when you finish. You do not want your *mamá* to see that you left it out again."

"Yes, ma'am. If I hurry, I can watch Momma." A loose board wobbled under Becky's foot when she jumped to her feet. The little girl ran across the yard, carrying the cat.

Miss Arneau called out, "Be sure to let your *mamá* know you are present."

Quinn watched as Becky disappeared inside the barn. "Is it safe to let her near Mrs. Tillman while she shoots?"

"Becky has watched Laurel practice since she was a small child and knows to be careful."

Quinn chuckled. "That little girl is full of life."

"Becky is a good girl. Forgetful sometimes, but she will learn as she grows. It must be difficult for her to have four women mother her."

"I would imagine Mrs. Tillman appreciates the help. Running this place can't be easy. Then adding motherhood . . ."

"People do what they must."

Camille transferred the egg basket from her left hand to her right, careful not to scramble the contents inside. The biting of her bottom lip said she considered how to address a problem, so he waited to hear what she had to say. "When you have settled in Bold Creek, I hope you will hold only good thoughts of Laurel. She feels a great responsibility for those in her care."

Was that responsibility the reason for the continued shooting? Did she feel threatened?

Quinn nodded. "I have no personal argument with Mrs. Tillman. In fact, I'm grateful for her generosity. However, I can say she has an argument with me. I raised her hackles the moment she got a good look at me and the evidence of my military life."

"I do not know Laurel's entire story, Quinn. What I do know, I will not share. Except for the small circle of family and friends on this ranch, there are few she believes would provide her the time of day. Because of our way of doing things," she tugged on the leg of the trousers she wore, "the way we dress, Issy's vocal beliefs about the rights of women, and Laurel's refusal to attend worship services, we all have experienced the disapproval of many of the townspeople."

"What about when her husband was alive? They must have had friends."

"I was not here then. But not long after John Tillman died, Gavin MacMahon and his older son pressured her to sell to them, eager to expand their holdings. Royce even proposed marriage—something he considered of equal advantage to both of them. The man acted offended when she refused such a romantic offer." A breath of disbelief escaped her lips. "Two of the three sheep herders who worked for her husband found they could not stomach working for a woman who refused to relinquish the control of her business to a man."

"And the third?"

"The MacMahons' threats drove him away, as well as anyone else who sought jobs on the ranch."

"What about the law?"

"Bold Creek only recently hired a town marshal, and Royce knows how far to push." She sighed. "Laurel hung on and expects a small profit this year. But Royce is a powerful man. Some of the townspeople and Laurel's neighbors have suggested she was a fool not to accept at least one of his proposals, either marriage or the purchase of the ranch. They believe a woman with options should not run a place like this." Camille's laugh tinkled like a fragile bell, light and pleasing to Quinn's ears. "Their censure was enough to make her determined to keep La Casa del Fuego . . . and hire women."

So that was how it started. His mouth ticked up. "Are you suggesting she's obstinate?"

Camille laughed with greater enthusiasm. "As a mule."

He smiled at the woman's honest assessment of a friend. "Who are these MacMahons?"

"Neighboring ranchers. The father is gone. Royce and his younger brother Murphy raise cattle and horses."

"So she thumbed her nose at them and the people of Bold Creek." Quinn could well imagine Laurel Tillman thumbing her nose at all of society if it suited her.

"You might judge it so, Quinn, but Laurel considered it self-preservation." Her dark eyes drilled into him. "She is a determined, good-hearted woman, who has made . . . decisions some deem inappropriate. But then, we all have sins and regrets we wish to hide from prying eyes. My prayer is that Laurel will see that those choices are not beyond God's willingness to forgive. Will you not make that one of your prayers?" With a sad smile, Camille stepped off the porch and walked toward the bunkhouse.

As she walked away, he mumbled a quick, half-hearted entreaty for wisdom on Mrs. Tillman's part. Then he eased back in the chair while his mind worked to conceive the circumstances that brought Camille Arneau to the ranch. What sins did she hide away from prying eyes?

Compared to the women of La Casa del Fuego, Quinn's life was an open book, neither interesting nor scandalous. And he thanked God for it.

Curious, he hobbled to the barn and peered out a small rear window. Laurel stood with her back to him, Becky a few feet behind her. Raising the carbine to her shoulder, Laurel took aim and fired at a row of six tin cans on a fence post around two-hundred-fifty feet away. One by one, they sprang into the air to land in the grass.

Quinn blew out a breath. Her shots equaled some of the best made by men under his command.

Laurel fingered the long braid that rested over one shoulder. She promised herself years ago that, never again, would she cut her hair above her collar. When freed of braid and pins, it touched the lower portion of her waist and would remain that way until she died.

Exhausted from a day spent herding and culling the flock, but unable to sleep, she stepped from the bunkhouse doorway and breathed in the mixed scents of prairie grass and livestock.

Bluebelle's harsh bray sounded from the nearest paddock, where Laurel kept sheep recuperating from illness or injury separated from the rest of the flock. For the past few days, an old ewe waited within the fencing to die.

After approaching the pen, Laurel opened the gate and spied the purebred Merino sprawled on her side in the far corner. Lifeless. The donkey sniffed the body and turned away. Grief welled in Laurel's throat. She hadn't been able to bring herself to slaughter the gentle mother once she stopped producing lambs. Would it have been more humane to have slit her throat and been done with it? For some, life went on too long. For others . . . not long enough. No one knew where they fit into the pattern or why, least of all Laurel.

She jumped at a shrill whistle that pierced the quiet. Keeping her gaze on the barn, her nerves on alert, Laurel crept toward the large double doors and grabbed the scythe still propped against the side of the building. Becky had used it last. Although Laurel told the child not to leave tools out in the weather, this time, she was thankful for her daughter's carelessness. Hopefully, whoever was in the barn couldn't hear her rustling approach as she limped through the half-cut grass and weeds.

She eased open the door and peered around it to see faint lamplight coming from the rear of the barn. Laurel raised the scythe, prepared to take on the intruder.

A human figure sat in the dirt next to a covered feed barrel holding the source of the light, his lower body shadowed. One hand cradled a small object. The other held what appeared to be a knife. It moved from back to front, creating a scraping sound.

"You can put that down, ma'am. I'm no threat."

He could not fathom the threat she considered him, nor of the elation his impending departure produced in her. Tomorrow meant the end of walking on cheval glass that reflected her shortcomings. It meant the end of waiting for her reserve to crack under his charm. It meant returning to normal.

She let out a curbed breath and lowered the tool, setting it against an inner wall. "Why are you in my barn in the middle of the night, Mr. Spencer?"

"I hope you'll forgive me for not rising, ma'am." The tip of the jackknife in his right hand pointed to his horse's stall. "You've taken good care of Ruthie. I thank you."

She ambled down the aisle and stopped three feet away from him. The closer proximity allowed her to use the lamp to see into his bearded face. The light sprinkled the top of his dark head with copper streaks and added amber sparkles to his blue eyes. His crooked grin—

Laurel averted her gaze and counted to five to refocus her thoughts. "That is not an answer to my question, Mr. Spencer."

"I wanted to see how my horse was faring."

"With a knife? What else were you doing?"

"Whittling, Mrs. Tillman. It's what I do when I can't sleep." He set the knife amid the curled shavings on the ground and looked up at her. "And you? Ladies don't wander outside in the night without a good reason."

Laurel remembered the thin wrapper covering her nightclothes and the cool air seeping through the material. She crossed her arms in front of her and crushed the high neckline of her gown in her fist, refusing to run out the door like a scandalized maiden. "Are you saying I am not a lady?"

His lips pinched together in a tight line she imagined was to hold inside the retort he longed to speak. While she had trod upon his patience for weeks now, he had remained a gentleman. With her reply, she felt even less like a lady than normal.

Laurel tilted her head toward the stall and changed the subject to something safer. "Why Ruthie?"

"I beg your pardon?"

"Why choose that name for your horse?"

"Used to be Tulip." He chuckled. "A man gets in too many scuffles defending a horse named Tulip."

She swallowed her amusement. "And Ruthie stops those scuffles?"

"Not really. That mare has followed me from post to post like the Biblical Ruth. It seemed natural. Why doesn't your buckskin have a name?"

"He never told it to me."

The barn filled with Quinn's laughter and raised an answering bawl from the milk cow. When his merriment settled, a hush took over the space between them while Ruthie and Princess chewed hay in the cribs.

Quinn broke the silence. "Couldn't sleep?"

He might have confessed his own insomnia, but there was no way on God's green earth Laurel would confess hers. "I came out to see how the sick ewe in the paddock fared."

"How is she?"

The image of the animal came unbidden and, so too, her answer. "Dead."

"I'm sorry."

His softened features and whispered voice wrapped her in an embrace so sympathetic she failed to shake it off. "Th-the ewe was the last survivor of the original flock my husband purchased. I should have made mutton stew with her years ago, but—"

"But she provided a link to a better time?"

She lifted a shoulder and changed the subject. "I heard a whistle."

He placed the piece of wood he'd whittled against his lips and blew. At the ear-piercing noise, Ruthie stuck her head over the stall door, her ears perked forward. "A flute for Becky."

Laurel struggled not to smile. "I am not sure I should thank you, Mr. Spencer."

"Mrs. Tillman, the day you are sure might be my last day on this earthly sod." Once again, his deep laughter echoed throughout the barn. It had been years since she'd enjoyed the masculine sound. "As I've told the others, I would prefer to be called Quinn."

Her smile died, but her resolution remained strong. "Good night, Mr. Spencer." She spun around and started for the barn door.

"Good night . . . Mrs. Tillman."

Laurel walked away without looking back. The war ended years ago. Why did she persist in fighting him?

CHAPTER SIX

Laurel sat in the porch chair next to the butter churn and turned the crank on the cylinder slowly, counting each rotation. While Momma and Camille relied on prayer to ease their concerns, this and climbing the hill out back suited Laurel.

She couldn't say why she felt a need to churn today but suspected it had to do with Quinn's departure. Somehow, she had allowed herself to be talked into letting him stay longer than she'd initially planned.

"I would prefer to be called Quinn." As if he could gain her amity through the simple exchange of Christian names! The crank spun.

Her thoughts swirled over their conversation and his surprise gift for her daughter, so much so, she had gone to bed having forgotten about the dead ewe. This morning, she found the spot of bare earth in which he had buried the animal. How had he done such a deed in his condition? Surely, it took him most of the night to dig the grave and move the heavy carcass. Why would he?

"Isn't it a little warm to churn butter?" Issy settled on a step and wiped her brow with a dirty kerchief. Her sly grin told Laurel she knew exactly what was going on.

"I'd be right happy to do that chore for you, Miz Tillman."

Ernie put one foot on the step, and Issy grabbed her shirt sleeve. "Oh, no you don't. No one dares take that chore from Laurel. She'll stick you inside that cedar barrel and slap you around with the dasher until you cry uncle."

Laurel smiled at Ernie's owl eyes. "Stop frightening the poor child, Issy. I appreciate the offer, but I like to churn. It eases my mind." She stopped short of confessing she did so with an empty barrel again today. The others caught on to her method of beating away her concerns one day long ago when she claimed to churn, then the butter ran out the next morning.

"Eases your mind, but not our stomachs." Issy pointed toward the carriage near the barn. "I see Mr. Bruner is here. Looks like Quinn's leaving us today like he said. Where are they, anyhow?"

"He's attending to his mare. I'm sure he's looking her over thoroughly, not trusting our care." Guilt stabbed Laurel in the chest for telling such a boldfaced lie.

"Oh, Laurel, you know—" Issy stared down the lane leading to the house. Dust swirled in the distance as a chestnut horse trotted toward them, its rider sitting tall in the saddle. She huffed and mumbled, "Here comes Mr. *MacNot-a-man*."

Laurel stopped churning and stepped off the porch to await her neighbor's arrival. Too bad she didn't have her carbine handy. Then again, seeing Issy's black look made her glad it was nowhere nearby.

Murphy MacMahon stopped his horse two feet from them and crossed his arms over the saddle horn. Leaning forward, his brazen gaze raked Issy from head to toe. "Well, if it isn't the little shepherdess with the big mouth."

Issy stared back with an expression cold enough to freeze a flame. "Why, lookee here Laurel, it's the little cowboy with the big ranch."

Laurel pressed her fingers to her temples. The animosity between those two started long before Issy came to work for her. Neither would admit to why they went at each other like wild dogs over the same kill. "What do you want, Murphy?"

He turned his bronzy brown eyes to her. "First, I want the hired help dismissed from taking part in our discussion."

Issy rose from the step. She made a show of dusting off the seat of her britches as though dusting away the presence of the rancher. "Why would I want to sit here and listen to some chuckleheaded cattleman who wouldn't know the meaning of the word no if it up and bit him in the—"

"Issy, I believe my gelding has a loose shoe. You and Ernie see to it he's reshod."

"Yeah, shepherdess, don't keep the fella waiting." Murphy's deep laughter vibrated through Laurel. "Be a shame for you to pass up the rare chance for a male's attention, whatever the species."

Ernie reached out and grabbed the back of Issy's shirt as she lunged for Murphy. "Come on, he ain't worth bloodyin' your hands over."

While being dragged away, Issy spouted a string of coarse insults aimed at the rancher.

Once they were gone, Laurel let loose her own opinion. "You two are worse than children. I've a mind to set you both on a stool in a corner until you learn to talk nice to one another. Now, what do you want?"

Seemingly unfazed by her anger, Murphy dismounted and leaned against his horse as though he hadn't a care in the world. Similar in the breadth of their shoulders and muscular frame, the youngest MacMahon brother stood a few inches taller than Quinn Spencer, but he didn't intimidate her half as much.

"You know what, Laurel."

"Royce sent you?" The muscle jumping along his jaw answered her question. "When are you going to step away from your brother's shadow and become your own man, Murphy?"

"I am my own man. The Triple M belongs to both of us. I came to ask you once more—politely, ma'am—to sell out to us."

"And I am saying once more—politely, sir—that you and your brother will never get my property."

He straightened and stared at the house, then waved an arm through the air. "For Pete's sake, look around you, Laurel. The place is falling apart. Would John have wanted to see it this way? Would he have wanted you to work so hard only to fall further behind?"

For a moment, Laurel thought she saw compassion in his expression. "Don't worry about La Casa del Fuego, Murphy. We do just fine without men."

He took in several deep breaths. "You and your misfit friends have become a laughingstock around here."

"My 'misfit friends' work hard and—"

"What kind of future will Becky have when she grows up? No man in his right mind will offer her marriage. Gentlemen don't want just females, Laurel. They want ladies who wear yards of frill." He gestured toward the corral where Issy and Ernie worked in trousers and overly large shirts. "Not flannel and leather."

Laurel swallowed hard, faced with the truth of his words. Had she done her child a disservice and ruined her chance of a good match? "My daughter will find a man worthy of her, someone who won't let what a woman wears or thinks scare him away." Or would her stubbornness force Becky to settle for anyone willing to take her?

Several times after John's death, Laurel had considered selling the ranch—even to the MacMahons. Every time, her husband's plans and the memory of what he had done for her prevented her from selling out. But perhaps his dreams were better fulfilled by someone else, someone more capable of earning the respect of his neighbors.

Sometimes, she grew tired—tired of the hostility, tired of the responsibility she felt for the others, and tired of never knowing an hour of tranquil rest.

Quinn hobbled from the barn, leading Ruthie. He tied the mare to the rear of Arthur's carriage and rolled his shoulders. Tickling beads of sweat dripped down his back. Mid-September days still swirled with hot air. When wearing his frock coat, the shirt underneath stuck to his skin.

He turned toward the house where the hottest air blew around two people near the porch. Laurel faced his direction with hard eyes that matched the voice raised in a heated exchange with a young stranger. The man squared his shoulders, clenching and unclenching the hands near his thighs.

Arthur moved next to him. "Sounds as if Mrs. Tillman has an unwelcome caller. It's best that we don't interfere."

Quinn would have agreed if it weren't for the stranger's fists. "I'd better save that man from himself."

"Pardon?"

"If I don't intervene, we could end up representing him in court for striking a woman." He adjusted the crutches and limped forward with Arthur in his shadow. "Is everything all right, Mrs. Tillman?"

The visitor stared at Quinn. For the briefest moment, something akin to concern flashed across the man's face. It disappeared, replaced by condescension. "We're having a private chat, mister."

"It isn't private when you're heard all the way to the barn."

"It's all right, Mr. Spencer. Mr. MacMahon was about to leave." She glared at her neighbor. "Disappointed again."

Ah, one of the rancher brothers mentioned by Camille. Royce or Murphy? Quinn judged him to be in his mid twenties, so probably Murphy.

"Royce is eager to finish this, Laurel."

"We have finished. From now on, you and your brother keep yourselves and all that belong to you off my land, or I'll be tempted to shoot first and ask 'How do you do?' second."

Quinn hoped she didn't mean that, but he couldn't be sure. "Mrs. Tillman—"

MacMahon's glare flashed a "Mind your business" warning. The cattleman mounted and swung his horse around. Digging in spurs, he sent his ride galloping down the drive. Quinn closed his eyes to keep out the grit kicked up by the animal's hoofs.

"I'll put the rest of your things in the carriage, Quinn." Arthur walked away, shaking his head.

Laurel's fair-skinned cheeks glowed red. She hugged the porch post as if it provided an anchor to keep her from being swept away by her own wrath. "Royce and Murphy think they can bully me. After all these years, they still . . ."

"Have the MacMahons given you a fair offer?"

"Fair? What do you think is fair, Mr. Spencer?" Her soft, southern drawl and feline smile prickled the hairs on Quinn's neck.

"I'm not familiar with property values in the area, ma'am, but I'd be pleased to look into it for you once I'm situated in Bold Creek."

She splayed her long, thin fingers on her hips. Piano fingers. Fingers his musically inclined mother had possessed. "You'd waste your time. I have no intention of selling."

Her cavalier attitude grated. "Then perhaps remarrying will ease your burden."

Laurel batted her eyes and leaned closer. "Are you offering, Mr. Spencer?"

He took a step backward and heat flamed his skin. He hated the reaction her outlandish behavior provoked. No wonder men refused to work for her.

"No, Mrs. Tillman, I am not, nor will I ever." Quinn's tone matched her soft, yet firm, voice. "However, I agree with the cattleman. It may be in your best interest and the best interests of the other La Casa del Fuego women to turn to more traditional roles. I assure you, I am only concerned for your welfare."

"And who on this ranch concerns you most, Mr. Spencer? Camille?"

He sighed and touched a finger to the brim of his hat, weary of the verbal game she played. "I appreciate your hospitality these weeks, Mrs. Tillman."

As he walked toward the carriage, she called out, "I didn't ask for your advice, Mr. Spencer. Nor will I ever."

Quinn stopped at the mocking reference to his own comment. "And I can assure you, madam, that I won't make the mistake of providing you with any in the future."

CHAPTER SEVEN

Quinn tapped his good foot on the dusty floor of the carriage, reliving his exchange with Laurel. He regarded himself as a gentleman, one who treated the fairer sex with dignity and respect. Never had he met anyone who belittled him with such blatant delight. "Why? Why is she holding tight to a place that will probably work her into an early grave?"

Arthur eased back on the reins, slowing the trotting bay as they turned from the lengthy drive of La Casa del Fuego onto the road that paralleled the river. "Laurel Tillman is an independent sort. Too bad she won't listen to your common sense and sell her place to the MacMahons."

Quinn turned his face to the passing scenery—hills, pastureland, and protruding rock. "*I didn't ask for your advice, Mr. Spencer. Nor will I ever.*" Without question, she was as thorny as that prickly pear cactus alongside the road. God had provided the plant with a way to protect its tender insides by giving the flat, paddle-like branches spiny barbs. Anyone who brushed against it immediately regretted the move. He gripped the carriage frame as it jostled along the rutted road. He wished never to have brushed against Laurel.

Still, he could not shake her melancholy expression and strained voice as she spoke of the dead ewe. He had spent much of the night and his flagging strength burying the animal—without receiving a word of thanks.

Like the cactus, did her barbs guard a vulnerability, protecting her from whatever might hurt her? An inner response reminded him that Jesus had the power to change anyone's heart, even one surrounded by thorns, like Laurel's.

He slumped in the seat, closed his eyes, and tilted his aching head back to rest against the top of the thinly padded leather. The carriage continued its bounce along the road, adding to his growing discomfort.

Arthur guided the carriage along River Road, reins in one hand, while the other pointed straight ahead. "Isabel Krueger grew up on a farm about five miles in that direction. Believe me, people know the quirks of that young lady. As I am sure you've learned, she's one of those who enjoys defying her role in society."

More than once in the past three weeks, Quinn had heard Issy Krueger spout her case over the inequality between the genders. His lips crimped in a frown. Females should accept who God created them to be and not attempt to infringe upon the duties and decisions of males. God made men and women different for a reason. He hoped Issy would learn that before she drove away every eligible male in Texas.

Oddly, Camille possessed the soft-spoken and ladylike gentility and movement of a female raised in circumstances far from the one in which she now lived. He sensed she didn't care for her work, so why stay?

"What do you know about Miss Arneau?"

Arthur laughed. "Other than she's an enigma? Nothing really. Mrs. Tillman returned from a trip four years ago in her company. Miss Arneau has remained on the ranch ever since. Some people believe she's harboring a terrible secret."

What secret would cause a pretty young woman to bury herself on a sheep ranch doing work she didn't like? Camille claimed to follow Christ and had stated that everyone hid sins they wished to protect from prying eyes. Did she conceal a past life that brought her shame and sent her into hiding?

"I would recommend that you stay away from the ladies."

He glanced at Arthur. "Why?"

"For your well-being, son. Some in Bold Creek consider Mrs. Tillman unfriendly and, frankly, unreasonable. Their influence may affect your business and political future. Of course, people will understand the predicament you found yourself in. They won't hold your time of recovery on the ranch against you. But it won't do to alienate our clients by calling on Mrs. Tillman or her friends in the future."

"I see." Quinn's head pounded as the warning reverberated through his skull—a warning he'd heard that first day from Mrs. Tillman's own lips.

They crested a hill that overlooked the town of Bold Creek. It sprawled across a relatively flat landscape with three or four dozen homes that dotted side streets and spread out into the countryside. A white steeple at the far end of town rose above a line of businesses along each side of Center Street. Some buildings were brick, others limestone. Most were whitewashed or plain board siding. People scurried up and down the boardwalks like colorful insects. They went in and out of stores, the largest of which had its type of trade painted on the stone side in large, black letters—Schuler's General Merchandise.

Upon entering town, they drove past a combination livery and blacksmith on the left. Smoke rose from the chimney of a smaller structure attached to one side of the barn. A handful of farm wagons lined up near a feed store across the road.

Arthur turned the carriage between the marshal's office and the First Commercial Bank. He stopped the buggy in front of a large house on Quinn's side of the conveyance. A small sign dangled from the porch overhang that read, "Cedar Ridge Boarding House—Hedda Dillard, Proprietress."

Arthur focused forward. His fingers twisted the reins. "Please keep in mind, Quinn, that a businessman's success can depend as much upon social relationships as expertise in his chosen endeavors."

Quinn acknowledged the validity of his words. He had not achieved his military rank by opposing those with influence over his career. However, he had served at a fort manned by Buffalo Soldiers and saw bigotry first-hand. It had sickened him, as did the idea of conveying the same narrow-mindedness toward the ladies of La Casa del Fuego. Still, he abhorred the idea of the women flaunting convention.

Arthur pointed to the house. "Mrs. Dillard should have your room ready. She was sorry she couldn't offer you accommodation earlier. Her daughter's illness called her to Houston."

"I meant to ask. How was your trip?"

Arthur frowned, his fingers tightening on the harness reins. "You knew about that?"

"You mentioned it when you visited a couple of weeks ago."

"Ah, yes. I remember." Arthur's hands relaxed on the reins, and he shrugged. "It went as well as expected."

With no details volunteered, Quinn dropped the inquiry.

He eyed the simple two-story clapboard house with its peeling white paint. The neglected condition reminded him of the buildings around the sheep ranch.

Why couldn't Laurel admit she needed a man's hand before the place fell down around her? Missing shingles, loose porch boards and railings, gates fastened with faded ropes of old calico.

He blew out a breath, unsure whether he was more frustrated with her attitude or his own. Well, it wasn't his problem. Laurel — no, Mrs. Tillman — made that crystal clear before he left. And Arthur made it clear that he expected Quinn to keep a proper distance from *all* the women of La Casa del Fuego.

"The boarding house isn't much to look at on the outside, but Mrs. Dillard is a pleasant woman and an excellent cook. There's a small stable in the back for stalling your mare."

Quinn eased onto the ground and rested his weight on the crutches. He had grown tired of the single-mindedness of his thoughts. "I only care that my room is clean." And the tick stuffed with goose down.

Ned Bonner tilted his bowler to the back of his graying head and wiped his brow with a bright yellow bandana. Then he retied the cloth around his neck. "You drive a hard bargain, ma'am."

"I'm certain no harder than any other sheep ranchers you've dealt with this fall, Mr. Bonner." Laurel stared at the payment he handed her. Satisfied at the amount, she wrapped her fingers around the bank draft and smiled up at the businessman.

"No. Few have bested you in their negotiations with me this year." He winked. "But don't let it get around."

"But there have been a few? It sounds as though I'll need to do better next time."

Bonner's laughter echoed across the yard. "And cost me my job, Mrs. Tillman?"

She glanced to the pens holding the large flock of rams, lambs, and older ewes awaiting the drive to Austin and the train that would carry them to market. About half her flock remained, including the wethers, or castrated males, that would provide much of the wool production.

Laurel, Camille, and Issy had spent the week since Quinn's departure completing the culling of the market sheep, while Becky and Ernie kept watch on the remaining animals. Laurel had consulted the record book with her notes, seeking sheep with a triangle stamped on them after the spring shearing—a testimony to the shortened life of the animal.

The shearing had yielded over twice as much wool as last year. Even with the declining wool prices, between its sale in June and Mr. Bonner's purchase this day, she would mark the year 1877 as her best yet. If November's breeding went well enough to exceed last year's births and their newborn losses were minimal, La Casa del Fuego would remain financially sound.

So far, she'd seen no sign of the mountain lion that had attacked her sheep and Mr. Spencer. She hoped to keep it that way.

"As usual—"

"As usual, I will see that they're treated well on the journey to the railroad in Austin. You have a sturdy flock of Merinos, Mrs. Tillman. Even the ones you've culled are superior to some I've seen, so don't worry. It's been a pleasure to do business with you again, ma'am."

Ned Bonner called to the shepherds near the pen to move his newly purchased flock down the drive. Then he readjusted the hat on his head, untied his horse, and lifted his foot to the stirrup.

He hesitated. Lowering his boot back to the ground, he turned to Laurel. "Ma'am, I know you've faced a good bit of opposition since the passing of your husband. Few women would take on your task. No matter what anyone else says, I admire your persistence and hope to deal with you again next year."

Stunned to the point of managing only an "*Adios*," she stood by the porch while he followed the flock and disappeared around a bend in the drive. When had a man expressed confidence in her abilities and approved her choice to continue what John had started? Never.

"Well?"

Laurel swallowed the emotion Mr. Bonner's encouragement had produced and turned to face the approaching Issy, Camille at her side. She raised the bank draft in her hand. "Top dollar."

Issy hooted. Together, the three of them celebrated with cookies and tea on the porch. Finally, Laurel stood and brushed crumbs from her shirt. "There's still plenty of daylight left, ladies. Let's clip those animals that need extra shearing around their eyes. Even with their exceptional eyesight and hearing, I don't want to lose a sheep to a predator because it needs a haircut."

"Oh, but they look adorable that way." Camille smiled and set her glass on top of the porch rail, then followed Laurel to the tool shed.

Issy got there first. She opened the door and disappeared inside, reappearing with two pairs of shears. "One's missing."

"Missing?" Laurel limped around her and entered the shed. She let her eyes adjust to the dim light before seeking the wall with nails for three pairs of sheep shears to be hung. All three spaces were empty. "They must be around here somewhere. We haven't used them since spring, and I know we stored all three in their proper places. When did you see them last?"

Issy stepped beside her. "Not since sharpening them after shearing."

Camille dipped her chin, but Laurel glimpsed her stricken expression. "Well?"

"I suppose I should have reminded her to put them away."

"Who? Who would have had—" Laurel's jaw hardened with the realization. "Becky?"

Camille nodded. "About a month ago, she wanted to trim Charlie's beard."

"What beard? With sheep shears?"

Issy chuckled. At Laurel's scowl, the girl sucked in her lips, but her eyes shone with silent laughter.

Laurel marched toward the house with Camille following on her heels. "I'm tired of having to tell her over and over to put the tools where they belong. Where is that child's head?"

"I told her to leave them be, and I never saw her use them. You know she is an obedient girl. Do not accuse her until you ask."

Laurel halted and whipped around. "Don't tell me how to raise my child, Camille."

Issy opened her mouth to speak, then clamped her lips together. Camille eyed the ground.

Going off half-cocked and doing or saying things she regretted had always been Laurel's downfall. She had allowed her temper free rein with Quinn, pricking her conscience with the need to apologize. Now, she risked alienating her two closest friends, not to mention her daughter.

She pressed a hand to her forehead and held her breath as though that would restrain any unpleasant words. She released it only when feeling under control. "I can't afford to buy new tools at every turn. That girl must learn to put things away." She sighed. "All right. I'll wait to hear what Becky has to say."

It had better be that she never touched the shears.

CHAPTER EIGHT

Quinn handed the bank draft to the teller. "This is the amount I would like deposited into my account, Mr. Hornsby."

Though he found it prudent to distribute his funds among more than one bank, he'd transferred a significant sum into this one. It wouldn't hurt him to be seen as a man of some worth.

The door opened, and the teller dipped his head in greeting. "Morning, Mrs. Weaver. Miss Weaver."

"Good morning, Mr. Hornsby."

While Quinn waited for the teller to complete the receipt, the older of the women approached him. Her stout body, dark clothing, and inquisitive expression reminded him of a curious black bear. He nodded once to her and the lady at her side before turning his attention back to the teller cage.

The elder woman cleared her throat, a not-so-subtle command for his attention. Facing her once more, he stretched his lips into the warmest smile he could muster. "Ma'am?"

"You are Mr. Spencer."

She'd pronounced his name with such certainty that even if she were wrong, convincing her of the error would prove a waste of time.

"Yes, ma'am."

She reached out a hand as though expecting him to raise it to his lips. He transferred the walking stick that had taken the place of the crutches to his left hand. With his right, he clasped her fingers in a gentle grip before releasing them.

"I am Mrs. Alfred Weaver." She pointed to the closed door to her right. "That is my husband's office. He's the president of this bank."

"It's a pleasure to meet you, ma'am."

Mr. Hornsby slid the deposit receipt under the bars of the teller cage. Her eyes strayed to the paper and widened, confirming she had seen the monetary figure. Mrs. Weaver reached for the younger woman's arm and tugged her close to her side. "This is my daughter, Mary. *Miss* Mary Weaver."

Quinn eyed the plain, twig-like woman well into her twenties and received a bold inspection tinted with defiance. He trapped a grin that longed to escape. This girl had more spark than he first thought. He tipped his head. "Miss Weaver."

Her brown eyes brightened. For a moment, he thought she would smile. "It's—"

"I understand you are an attorney, Mr. Spencer." Mrs. Weaver cut off her daughter's reply with her own curt statement.

Quinn sensed the plans rolling through the mother's mind, plans he had no desire to satisfy. "I am."

"Excellent." She frowned at the walking stick. "You're healing well? I hope you sent for Dr. Cameron as soon as you escaped the clutches of those sheep women. Personally, I wouldn't trust their care."

"Mama . . ."

Mrs. Weaver sighed. "Though I suppose in life and death situations one has no choice in Good Samaritans. At least you survived that awful experience, Mr. Spencer. For that, we are most delighted."

"I appreciate your concern, however, I—"

"I'm sure you were nothing but a gentleman while you remained under that Tillman woman's roof. She and her . . . employees . . . are odd creatures. I am confident you were vigilant day and night to fend off their attentions, if you understand my meaning."

He understood all too well and battled the urge to shock her by saying he'd not made one tiny effort to fend off anyone's attentions. That would only do Laurel and the others more harm.

"She would be better off had she the sense to—"

The front door rattled. As if summoned by the conversation, Laurel came into the room. Despite the limp, her footsteps sounded quiet on the polished floorboards. Attired in her "go-to-town" faded blue dress, she had arranged her honey-colored hair under a straw bonnet trimmed with blue ribbon ties and a bouquet of dried daisies. Didn't she realize she could turn any man's head?

Laurel came to an abrupt stop upon seeing him standing on the other side of Mrs. Weaver. The astonishment quickly vanished, replaced by a stiffness that infected him, too.

The banker's wife took a few small steps toward her. "Good morning, Mrs. Tillman."

Wariness crept across Laurel's features as if she spotted a rattler in the middle of her path. "Good morning, Mrs. Weaver. Good morning, Mary." She acknowledged Quinn with a brusque, "Mr. Spencer."

He mumbled a greeting that barely made it past his own ears.

"How is your mother?"

Returning her attention to the inquisitive Mrs. Weaver, Laurel said, "Well, thank you."

"You must tell her that Mary and I are grateful for her care of Mr. Spencer."

Laurel's brows rose. She glanced from Mary to Quinn and back again. "I will tell her."

The heat of anger rose in Quinn, yet he chose not to embarrass Mary by denying the mother's implication. Instead, he tipped his head slightly. "Ladies, if you will excuse me, I must get back to work. Good day." He started for the door.

"Mr. Spencer?"

Quinn slowly turned. "Yes, Mrs. Tillman?"

"May we speak a moment?"

He looked from the suspicious eyes of the bank president's wife to Laurel's firm gaze. Whatever she wanted, a private conversation would provoke the opportunity for gossip and speculation.

Shifting his focus to the wall clock, he decided the best thing for him—for them both—was to leave. "I'm sorry. I haven't the time to spare." From the corner of his eye, he caught the satisfied smirk marring Mrs. Weaver's face.

Quinn left the bank as an inner urge prodded him to step back inside and apologize to Laurel in front of the Weavers. Instead, he stuffed his hands in his trouser pockets and marched straight to his office above the bakery.

Laurel moved from one window to the next. She drew every curtain in the house with unsteady hands as thunder rumbled through the walls and jagged bolts of lightning slit the dusky sky. Raindrops pelted the roof like small clods of dirt after an explosion of cannon fire.

The dream would come again like it did on nights when nature reminded her of the unnatural sounds caused by human hate. If God truly cared, her sleeping daughter would never experience the same agony.

Momma sat in the rocker near the fireplace, rocking back and forth while darning one of Becky's stockings. With each move backward, the chair joints creaked. "I hope Mr. Spencer's injury has healed. If I did right by him, he should have no lasting effects. Oh, it would be horrible to know I did something wrong."

"You did nothing wrong, Momma. Don't worry so."

Laurel had not seen Quinn since they met at the bank three weeks earlier—such an uncomfortable and disappointing encounter. She had wanted to apologize for her behavior the day he left—to explain why a visit by either of the MacMahon brothers flared her temper. He didn't give her the chance but hurried out of the bank as though she carried some dreaded disease.

She could almost feel sorry for him. No doubt, Mrs. Weaver bushwhacked him with her daughter. Or had he truly taken an interest in Mary? It hardly mattered to Laurel. She'd had her bed back for four weeks now and aimed to keep its comfort, even if she had worked so hard lately she could fall asleep on cobblestone paving.

Next time she saved a stranger, she would drive him straight to town and let someone else worry over him.

"You provided him with excellent care, Momma. I am sure he's doing fine."

Her mother's needle moved in and out of the balled wool as easily as it had Quinn's leg. "I hope he'll pay us a visit soon. I dare to say, he's a genial man. Don't you agree?"

Lately, Laurel had tried to keep her opinion of Quinn Spencer to herself, mainly because it ticked back and forth like the pendulum of a metronome. Swinging to the far left meant she despised the man who had sided with those responsible for the invasion of the South. Swinging to the far right meant acknowledging his easygoing and kind manner when in the presence of others. Usually, she hoped to ignore the memory of him, leaving it stuck in the center.

The door blew open, banging against the inside wall. Ernie rushed inside looking as though she swam from the bunkhouse with her nightclothes on. Rain trickled down her face, dripping off each side of her jaw. Her auburn hair hung limp over her shoulders. She shivered in the cool evening air while water puddled around her bare and muddy feet.

"Pardon, Miz Tillman, but Camille sent me. She said to get whatever can hold water."

Laurel hurried to the door and looked out. She covered her eyes at the latest flash of lightning. "What's wrong?"

"That bunkhouse is floodin' somethin' fierce, ma'am."

"Oh, fiddle-faddle. I should have patched that roof after the last storm. We haven't had a good rain in so long, I forgot."

Actually, Laurel had not forgotten so much as she had put the task off. It required climbing a ladder and balancing on a sloped roof. Though she had no fear of heights, her stiff leg begged her to avoid the needed repairs.

Thunder rumbled in the distance. At least the storm wasted no time in moving on toward the east. Soon, they could clean up the mess inside the building.

Her mother fetched four pots and bowls from the kitchen and shoved them at Ernie. "These should help. Would you like me to get towels and rags?"

"Yes, thank you, Momma."

Wet as cats, they mopped up the water from the bunkhouse floor. They had partitioned the structure, previously one large room, into a sitting room and bedroom. Thankfully, most of the water dripped into the sitting room with a lesser amount in the bedroom. At least the bunks remained dry.

"Poor Issy." Camille stood at the door, squeezing the water out of a towel and onto the ground. "I hope she found shelter before getting drenched."

The women took turns staying with the flock. This was Issy's time, meaning she was caught out in the storm.

"She's probably holed up in that old cave near the river." Laurel wiped her hands on her damp skirt. "I'm more concerned about the thunder having scattered the flock. Once we're done here, I'll check."

"Charlie is with her. I would not worry."

Laurel looked up. A drop of water landed on the bridge of her nose and slid down to drop off the end. She wiped a hand across her face. "I'll go to town tomorrow and order new shingles."

"We should all go." Camille wrung water from a rag into a pail. "We have not been to town together in months."

As summer moved into fall, the women had worked back-breaking hours. They culled the sheep, repaired the breeding pens, and separated first-year lambs from those old enough to be bred. They chose the rams capable of improving the ranch's stock. Soon, they would slaughter several of the older ewes and two of the hogs, preserving the mutton and ham for the coming seasons. The end of each day brought barely enough time for a quick meal and a wash-up before they collapsed into their beds.

"I suppose we're due a few hours of distraction," Laurel said.

"Also, I need more thread for my frivolité."

"Glory be, Camille. When have you found spare moments to use what you purchased last time? Do you tat in your sleep?"

Laurel already knew Camille often worked the shuttle during her time to watch the sheep. Lately, they had all been too busy for simply watching. How long would her cultured friend put up with raising smelly sheep? It would be so easy to ask why she remained on the ranch. What had she run away from? The last thing Laurel wanted was to swap stories of the past . . . or lose her best friend through nosiness.

Camille laughed and wagged a finger. "If you are good girls, I will buy our meal at the café."

"This has been our best year thus far. In time, I might pay you a decent wage. How can you afford to treat us, Camille?"

She turned away and spread the damp cloth over the porcelain washbasin. "If I could not afford it, I would not offer."

Aware her question went unanswered, Laurel turned to Ernie. "If she wants to throw her hard-earned money away, I don't see how we can turn down such an offer, do you?"

Ernie's hazel eyes resembled those of a captured mustang—pupils wide, round and terrified. "If y'all don't mind, ma'am, I'd rather stay here."

Laurel studied the young girl. Ernie hung her head and bore a hole in the damp floor. She hadn't stepped a foot over the ranch's boundary line since her arrival. One more person seeking a hideout. "You can take Issy's place with the sheep."

"You sure you want to leave Ernie alone, Laurel?"

"I'm sure, Issy. She'll be more comfortable."

Following Momma, Laurel climbed onto the wagon bench and took up the reins while Camille, Issy, and Becky found spots in the buckboard's bed.

"I wasn't worried about her comfort."

Remembering the stolen butterküchen, Laurel wondered if Issy had a point. No. Ernie had been hungry that day. In the past month and a half, she had proven to be an honest, hard worker. Laurel would bet next spring's lambs there was nothing to be anxious about. Half of next spring's lambs, anyway.

For all the good it would do, Camille snapped open her lace parasol and tilted it to provide a bit of spotted shade for Becky and herself. Issy depended on her small straw bonnet, not really caring one way or another about her already freckled skin.

"Issy, you worry too much and trust too little." The smile in Camille's voice diluted the reproof.

All morning, Laurel's friend had been much too cheerful over a mere trip to town. A suspicion wiggled into her mind that tatting thread might not be all Camille wanted from her visit to Bold Creek. Was she keen to see a certain lawyer again?

They rattled down the drive in the cool of the mid-October morning. The freshness of an overnight rainfall scented the air.

"We don't know much about Ernie," said Issy.

Laurel looked over her shoulder. "I didn't know much about you when I hired you, now did I? We've all gotten along these years by minding our own business. I think we should continue that way."

Issy shook her head. "Yes, ma'am."

The women kept up a constant chatter until Laurel guided the mules onto Center Street in Bold Creek. Being Saturday, many people came to town to do their errands. They crowded the business section with buckboards, buggies, and saddle horses. The air smelled of woodsmoke and manure.

"I don't see any open spaces, do you?" Laurel turned down the alley behind the mercantile. "We'll park the team here and go in the back door."

Three of them departed the conveyance with as much dignity as the act allowed. However, Issy, dressed in her bloomers, and Becky, in her Sunday best, jumped off the bed, splashing mud onto their boots. Laurel glanced around, thankful no one else occupied the alley to see the unladylike display by her daughter. It would spawn more fodder for gossip.

With four pairs of shoes tapping the wooden planks and Laurel's tip-tapping, they sounded like an army marching down the narrow aisle that ran through the back of the store to the main room. Laurel doubted anyone heard their arrival over the conversations and laughter going on around them.

She took a small sheet of notepaper from the bag hanging off her wrist and pressed it into her mother's hand. "I must see Mr. Hawkins and order the shingles before he closes his shop at noon, then I'll go to the cemetery. Will you collect what we need?"

Momma read the list and frowned. "You haven't written the size of the nails you want. What should I tell Mr. Schuler?"

"I'm not sure of the size myself. Tell him they're for cedar shingles and let him decide."

"Oh, well, yes. I suppose I can do that." Momma's shoulders relaxed. "If you don't mind, I'll visit the bakery when we're through here. I'd like to see how Frieda Oberlin is feeling today."

"That's a fine idea, Momma. Give the Oberlins my best."

"I believe I will visit May Simpson." Camille fingered the dusty shelf at her side and inspected her glove. "She asked me to call the next time I was in town."

Laurel would have asked Camille what she was up to had she not declared earlier that they should each mind their own business. Instead, she addressed Becky. "Why don't you come with me to visit Daddy and Johnny?"

"But, Momma, I want to go with Granmomma to the bakery."

It hurt to see her daughter's memory fade to the point she no longer wanted to go to the graves of her father and brother. Yet she was too young to be burdened with maudlin observances that meant nothing to her.

"Why do you want to go with Granmomma?"

Becky dipped her head. "Mr. Oberlin always gives me a treat."

At least the girl was honest—in this case. Becky still denied using the missing sheep shears on Charlie's "beard." Laurel had given her the benefit of the doubt, since Charlie showed no sign of having had his whiskers trimmed. But the shears remained missing.

"You shouldn't presume upon the man for treats, Peanut."

"That's not the only reason, Momma. I—"

Laurel held up her hand, fighting to keep her voice stern when she really wished to laugh. "The Oberlins enjoy having you call on them, so I am approving the visit." The smile Becky gave her made it worth standing by the gravesites alone.

"Thank you, Momma."

Before going their separate ways, they all agreed to meet at the café at noon.

On her walk to the carpenter's, Laurel approached the bakery and breathed in the luscious scents. Her gaze strayed to the office on the second floor where a dark-haired man in rolled shirtsleeves and vest stood with his back to a street-side window. He stretched his arms out as though he'd sat for hours and fought cramps in his muscles. He'd had his hair trimmed recently, removing most of the little waves in the back.

Laurel hitched her skirts to cross the muddy street before Quinn saw her.

Quinn turned to the window and planted his knuckles on the sill, staring at the mud-spattered boardwalks and traffic-furrowed streets.

A freight wagon clattered past, and its right front wheel sank into a hole filled with last night's rain. The muddy water splashed up and onto the dark skirt of a woman awkwardly crossing the street. She paused long enough to be splattered again by the rear wheel. Standing with her back to Quinn, her foot tapped the mud to the rhythm of a Virginia Reel. He needn't see her face to recognize Laurel Tillman's pique.

To his shame, Quinn recalled the day they met inside the bank. Not only had he allowed Mrs. Weaver to disparage her and insinuate a false relationship between him and Mary, he had all but run out of the building to avoid being linked with Laurel.

He was a military man. He never retreated from an enemy.

I am sorry, Father. I know I must seek You rather than the approval of others, but I'm finding it difficult. Give me strength.

Laurel continued down Center Street without looking up at the window above the bakery, and he breathed a sigh of relief.

CHAPTER NINE

Laurel stood at little Johnny's resting place, reliving memories for the thousandth time. His first toothless smile. His first steps. The time he stuffed the fly in his mouth and swallowed it before she could stop him. The way he dragged his worn blanket around the house.

With heartrending clarity, she witnessed again his feverish body, the aches and vomiting, the smallpox rash, his cries of pain. She felt her five-year-old's last breath on her cheek.

Tears trailed down Laurel's face. Why do this to herself?

Her husband had suffered in the same manner, dying a week later and leaving Laurel and her mother alone with a three-year-old, a struggling ranch, and a flock of two hundred sheep.

Removing the lace-edged handkerchief from her reticule, she wiped away the irritating wetness. Each visit to the cemetery led to this appalling display of weakness. No wonder Becky stayed away.

"It's turned into a pleasant morning, Mrs. Tillman."

Engrossed in her memories, Laurel flinched at the unexpected voice. She drew in a ragged breath and turned away from the cold headstone.

Reverend Perry removed his black hat and ambled closer. "I'm sorry if I startled you."

She pulled her wool shawl closer around her shoulders. "It's all right, Reverend." If he noticed her blotchy cheeks and watery eyes, he didn't bring attention to them.

The baby-faced man wore a black frock coat and black trousers— fitting for his place of business next to a cemetery. However, his smile and bright blue eyes could light up the darkest corner of a room, quite unlike the fire and brimstone preachers she had heard back home in North Carolina.

"I see you here more often than anyone other than Mr. Bruner."

Not even his customary kindness could put her at ease in such surroundings. "I visit whenever I come to town."

Reverend Perry nodded and gestured toward the church. "I have prayed you would come to God's house as often as you come to the cemetery. Perhaps we'll be fortunate enough to see you tomorrow?"

If anyone could persuade her to enter a church building, it was this gentleman. "I don't believe so, but thank you, Reverend."

His smile never faltered. "Please let me know if I can do anything to assist you or your family."

Before she could provide a polite reply, his attention shifted to something behind her. "Ah, speaking of Mr. Bruner. Good morning, sir."

"Reverend Perry." The lawyer dipped his head. "Mrs. Tillman."

The three exchanged greetings and light conversation before the pastor said his goodbyes.

Arthur Bruner stepped to Laurel's side. "This is an attractive spot for a resting place with its rolling land and shade trees."

"Yes, it is."

He pointed to a far corner. "My Harriet rests over there."

Laurel followed the direction in which he pointed. An oversized headstone marked the site. "Is that a Hawthorn shading her grave?"

"Yes. I planted it when she died. Harriet loved the Hawthorn's white blossoms in spring and those red berries in fall." He pointed upward. "Mistletoe has invaded that mesquite tree. My wife, a true romantic, always hung it in our home at Christmas."

She stared into his face and saw the same sadness that filled her. "You miss her terribly."

"As you miss your husband and son."

"Yes."

They stood in silence until Arthur cleared his throat. "I never knew Mr. Tillman, but I saw your wedding photograph when I first visited Quinn. He served in the war?"

His mention of that time covered her in an even thicker shroud of self-pity. She absently tucked the handkerchief in the reticule and straightened her spine, determined to show the man strength rather than weakness. "My husband was a captain in the Army of the Confederate States—a brave and worthy soldier." Why add that last part?

He stared at John's headstone. "Those on both sides of the conflict were all too capable." He emphasized the statement with a grim smile. "I'll pay my respects to my wife now. Excuse me."

"Good day, Mr. Bruner."

Laurel left the cemetery and returned to town fighting a heavy heart. She refused to let her time in this place of sadness ruin the time with her friends and family.

A little after noon, Quinn left his office and walked to the café. He stepped inside the busy restaurant, removed his hat, and stopped to let his eyes adjust to the change in the light. Someone at the back of the dining room called his name and a small figure skipped forward, her crooked-toothed grin warming him. It surprised him to realize he had missed her.

"How are you, Mr. Spencer?"

He glanced toward the rear wall where the rest of the women, minus Ernie, had gathered around a table. They looked his way. With their attention focused on him, it was too late to back out the door.

"Fine, Becky. And you?"

"Good as grapes." She tugged on his hand. "We're back here. Come sit with us. We sure have missed you."

Did he imagine the chatter in the room dwindled from a roar to a soft buzz? He glanced around to find himself the focus of several pairs of eyes. "Actually, Becky, I'm in a bit of a hurry—"

"A man's gotta eat."

Quinn pinched his lips together and choked back laughter. "True. A man's gotta eat."

Trapped by his recent prayer, he presented her with an exaggerated bow. "Lead on, Miss Tillman."

He followed her to the back corner where two square tables were pushed together. Becky slid into a chair and slapped the seat of the one next to her. "Sit down, Mr. Spencer."

Quinn hesitated, unsure of his welcome by the others, particularly after the way he had treated Laurel the last time they met. Also, he hadn't visited the ranch since his leg healed. If for no other reason, proper etiquette dictated he make a social call. "Good afternoon, ladies."

Four of the five occupants smiled at him. The fifth stared into her teacup and fussed with her napkin.

Camille gestured to the lone vacant chair. "Please sit, Quinn. It will be a delight to have you dine with us."

Laurel's frown grew deeper with each plea from the others for his company. He pulled out the chair across from her and sat with his back to the door.

"Momma ordered shingles for the bunkhouse roof 'cause it leaked last night like a . . . like a . . ." Her brow crinkled.

"Sieve?"

"Becky."

"Mr. Hawkins said they wouldn't be ready until next week. Maybe you can come out to the ranch and help us fix the roof."

The warning in Laurel's voice had failed to deter her daughter. "Rebecca!"

"Why, Momma, I am only being hospitalable. Ain't that what you want me to be?"

Quinn fidgeted in his seat and noticed Laurel did the same.

"Have your legs healed fully, Mr. Spencer?" Thankfully, Laurel's mother saved him from committing to Becky's invitation.

"Completely, Mrs. Chamberlain. Dr. Cameron examined them my first week in town." At her downcast expression, he quickly sought to reassure her. "He had nothing but compliments for your ability, ma'am, and asked me to pass along his praises."

"That was several weeks ago." Laurel raised her chin. The accusation in those green orbs pierced Quinn with an intensity to rival her fork as it pierced the chicken on her plate.

Before he could assemble an excuse for his neglect, the waitress, Lillian, appeared and asked for his meal order. He concentrated on the chalkboard menu, though he knew every dish the Green Meadow Café offered. There were only three. "I'll have coffee and the pot roast, Lillian."

Rather than answer Laurel, he turned back to her mother. "I never asked where you learned your nursing skills."

"My late husband was a physician. I assisted him until he joined the Confederate cause. Orin worked in field hospitals until his death."

He nodded. "I'm sorry for your loss."

With a shrug of her shoulders, Ellen Chamberlain hid behind the act of eating.

"Momma went to the cemetery to talk to Daddy and Johnny today."

"Rebecca." Laurel's scowling face squelched any further comment from her daughter.

The matter-of-fact tone in Becky's statement took Quinn aback until he recalled being told that John Tillman and his son had died six years ago. She was probably too young to retain an emotional attachment. To the child, carved headstones in the local cemetery were the embodiment of her father and brother.

"How is your work coming, Quinn?"

He answered Camille's smile with one of his own. "Very well, thank you."

Quinn told them about his trip to Austin and watching the state legislators as they discussed various bills. "The trip was informative, but after three days of Arthur's introductions to the lawmakers, I was more than ready to return to Bold Creek and rest my recently healed legs. The experience left me questioning whether I still want to join the ranks of pompous politicians."

He didn't discuss the long hours reading law journals, running errands, writing letters for Arthur—mindless drivel satisfied only because he could not expect to become a general without first learning the basics as a private.

Light conversation continued until Lillian brought Quinn's meal. She squeezed between Mrs. Chamberlain's chair and the one at the next table. As she picked up an empty plate, her elbow bumped the arm of a man seated behind her. His coffee sloshed over his hand and onto the plate of food before him. He growled and turned in his seat. "Watch it, you clumsy cow."

Lillian used her apron to mop up the spill dripping off the edge of the table. "I'm sorry, sir."

The disgruntled diner stared at the waitress with eyes of narrow slits that crinkled the wine-colored blotch running across his temple and down his left cheek. His hooked nose wrinkled as though he'd caught a whiff of something foul. "If you ain't able to do your job proper-like, missy, you'd best find one you're good at, like sloppin' hogs."

Quinn wiped his mouth and slowly set his napkin on the table, using the time and the deed to pray over his next words and actions. He slid around sideways in his chair. "It was an accident, sir. The young lady apologized for the mishap. I suggest you apologize for your coarse remarks."

The man rose from his chair. "I ain't got no bone to pick with you, mister, so keep your snout out of this."

Quinn's chair scraped against the floor as he stood and glanced from table-to-table. People had paused in the middle of their meals to watch the show. He prayed the performance would disappoint them.

Lillian stepped between them and put her hand out. "Please, Mr. Spencer, don't let it bother you. I've dealt with worse than the likes of him."

"What's goin' on here?" Ira Jessup, cook and owner of the café, worked his way between the tables of the crowded restaurant. Topping out at only around five and a half feet, his weight not much more than a young woman's, he hardly appeared intimidating. Then Quinn noticed the rock-hard set of his bony face and the hand resting on the revolver poking from the waist of his trousers. Jessup eyed both men.

"Your ham-fisted gal here spilled hot coffee all over me." The man patted his wet hand and sleeve with a napkin.

Quinn stared him down. "She apologized."

"That truc, Lillian?"

"Yes, Mr. Jessup. I didn't mean it—to bump him, I mean."

The café owner bobbed his head. "Your meal's on Lil, mister."

The ill-mannered lout had the nerve to grin with pleasure. Quinn wanted to protest the verdict, but Jessup was the law in his establishment.

Before he walked away, the wiry little cook eyed the troublemaker. "I don't cotton to people bein' ugly to my hired help, mister. Find another place to eat from here on out."

The customer threw the napkin on the table and picked up his hat from the chair beside him. "Don't know nothin' 'bout fixin' pork chops, nohow."

Satisfied, Quinn returned to his seat. To turn the attention away from the incident and back to benign discussion, he brought up the young girl's absence. "Miss Goodman isn't here. I hope she's well."

"Oh, Ernie's fit." Issy offered him the plate of bread. "Laurel left her at the ranch."

With a slight shake of the head, Quinn declined another piece of cornbread and shifted sideways in his seat as the stranger abruptly stopped and turned toward them.

"It was her decision, Issy. I couldn't make her come to town."

At her statement, the man stared at Laurel, his fingers crimping the brim of his worn hat. A half-smile crooked his mouth. When he realized he was being watched, he left the café.

Quinn spent the rest of the meal looking over his shoulder. Why had the man taken an obvious interest in Laurel?

CHAPTER TEN

"Did y'all have fun in town?" Ernie reached out a hand to help Laurel's mother to the ground.

Camille closed her lace parasol and clutched the brown paper-wrapped package containing her silk tatting thread. "Delightful."

"We saw Mr. Spencer again." Becky placed the small flute to her lips and blew. One of the mules brayed a protest at the ear-piercing noise.

Laurel winced at both sounds. Or perhaps it was her daughter's mention of the man. "Please, Peanut. You'll frighten the animals."

Quinn's appearance at the café had removed much of Laurel's appetite. His constant glances around the room left the impression he would rather have been anywhere else but in their company. He didn't fool her for a minute. If Becky hadn't dragged him to their table, he would have stolen back out the door without acknowledging them.

In truth, their only common desire was to avoid one another. She eyed the condition of the buildings around the homestead. Anyone could see that Quinn objected to her way of life. He believed it was beyond a woman's ability to make the ranch a success.

She was determined to work harder to keep the place up. Reshingling the bunkhouse roof was a good place to start. She snorted at the memory of the way Quinn slid out of accepting Becky's invitation to help by ignoring the subject. For that, at least, she was grateful.

"The noon meal could have been better." As if remembering Camille's generous treat, Issy added, "The food and company were ideal, though. The company at our table, anyway."

Camille straightened her skirt and brushed imaginary dust from her bodice with fierceness, as though afraid it might eat through the layers of material to her skin. "Sí, *mon ami*. That man was horrid, was he not?"

"What man?" Ernie released the mules from the shafts while Becky filled a bucket with oats from a barrel in the barn and added them to the corral trough.

Issy removed the mules' harnesses. "A foul-mouthed stranger seated at the next table took exception to Lillian bumping him . . . typical male insults."

"Yes, but Quinn, who is a gentleman, stood up to the man."

His defense of the waitress had been commendable, though something Laurel would expect from any honorable man.

Having set down a twenty-five-cent piece before leaving the café, Laurel tried to cover most of the stranger's meal. A slight error shouldn't cost Lillian, a young widow with two children, to lose what little she earned. A last glance at the table showed Quinn had done the same.

"I believe Ira Jessup had a greater hand in quashing the incident."

Issy laughed. "Laurel's right. Everyone knows better than to mess with Ira."

"That mark on the stranger's face gave me goose skin." Becky rubbed her arms and sneezed.

"It was only a birthmark, Peanut. Nothing to be afraid of." Laurel pressed a palm to her daughter's forehead. "Are you feeling sickly?"

"No, ma'am. I got oat dust up my nose."

Laurel reached into her reticule for her handkerchief and came away empty-handed. She glanced into the wagon. Nothing. Her chest ached when realizing she had lost Camille's Christmas gift.

Ernie stopped while leading the mules through the gate of the corral. "What'd the mark look like?"

"It was purple and right here." Becky pointed to her left temple. "Looked like the Devil himself put a finger on him."

"Rebecca Tillman, where do you get such ideas? The man can't change the way he was born any more than you can change the color of your eyes."

Becky hung her head. "Sorry, Granmomma."

The mules tugged at the lead lines in Ernie's hand, pressuring the motionless girl to let them reach the feed in the corral. Instead, Ernie stared off into the distance, her face the shade of a sun-bleached bed sheet. Was she the one taking sick?

Laurel's mother motioned to Becky. "Come along and let's get you out of that dress before it's stained beyond help. My word, look at the mud on your shoes. Honestly, Rebecca, what are we to do with you?"

The girl brightened. "I lug me?"

"Just the answer I would have expected from your momma at your age. Come here, you rascal." Ellen Chamberlain wrapped an arm around her granddaughter's shoulders and led her to the house.

Once again, the change in her mother struck Laurel. More and more often, she showed signs of becoming the self-confident woman Laurel remembered from her childhood. The change had begun during Quinn's stay. Everything in her rebelled at the idea that he caused the difference.

As she sat in the saddle, the chill of the autumn morning washed over Laurel, bringing an end to the oppressive heat of summer.

She guided the buckskin up a slight hill, the mottled tan of the animal's coat blending with the grassy fall landscape. Stopping the horse at the top, she twisted in the saddle to peer at the sheep grazing behind her. In the distance, portions of buildings peeked from between clumps of trees surrounding the homestead—trees that more resembled bushes compared to the lofty oaks, hickories and ramrod pines of her North Carolina birthplace.

How she missed her younger years—the parties and dances, friends and suitors, those days spent prowling the woods disguised as a boy so she could join her brother on his hunting adventures. Sometimes, when she stood on the hill behind her house and looked off to the east, she imagined herself sixteen again, safe from the tragedies to come.

Who would she be now had the war not broken out sixteen years ago?

With a drawn-out sigh, she turned her back on the house. One made choices in life. The prudent learned to live with them.

Laurel urged the buckskin down the other side of the hill. They crossed the pastures, then meandered along a rocky path through brush and trees that led to a creek bed. After dismounting, she allowed the horse to drink from the cool, clear stream.

He raised his head and pricked his ears, water dripping from each side of his mouth and running down the steel of the bit. She followed the horse's gaze down the creek. A small doe approached the edge of the water and stopped to listen before drinking, timid in her vulnerability.

Years ago, Laurel and her brother Lance would have competed to see which one of them would provide the venison for the family's smokehouse. Oft times, it was Laurel, but even then, her mother insisted Lance take credit. She could hear Momma's disappointment as though it were yesterday.

"What proper girl prowls the woods with a gun?"

"But I like to hunt, Momma. What does it matter?"

"It matters. What if someone should see? Do you want to ruin your reputation?"

"I don't care what others think."

"Well, you should, young lady. It's important for your future. Society is unforgiving of those who do not follow its standards."

That was in the days before Daddy and Lance . . .

Laurel picked up a twig from the ground and snapped it in two.

"Momma, you were so right. One day I will rid myself of these trousers and wear only fine dresses again. I will be a lady." She just didn't know how to make that happen and still keep her promise to John.

Gathering the reins in one hand, she placed her left boot in the stirrup and prepared to swing her right leg over the saddle.

A gunshot echoed in the distance, stilling her movement. Then another. And another. Grass and brush rustled farther down the creek bank as the deer sprinted to safety.

The buckskin danced to the tune of more shots. With her left foot propped in the stirrup and her right remaining on the ground, Laurel's weak knee gave way. She lost her footing and fell. Clutching one rein, she struggled to her feet as more shots popped.

"Whoa." Soothing words and gentle strokes to the neck settled the gelding, yet did nothing to lessen the thumping of her heart.

She shook off the memories threatening to paralyze her. Almost as one motion, she mounted and whisked the carbine from the scabbard. She dug her heels into the horse's sides, and they tore across the landscape.

Laurel reined in the gelding near the fence the MacMahons strung to separate the southwest boundary of La Casa del Fuego from the northeast tip of the Triple M Ranch. She brought him from a run to a trot, then to a complete stop. The wide brim of her felt hat shaded her eyes as she leaned forward. Was that a horse among the trees ahead or a shadow?

Feeling too exposed in the open pastureland, Laurel slowly raised the weapon in her right hand while keeping her gaze fixed on the unknown. She'd counted close to a dozen shots fired. Now . . . silence.

The shadow moved. She levered a shell into the chamber as a rangy bay broke from the tree line. Every nerve on alert, she squinted, straining to identify the rider as he stopped to stare at her. Something about him rang familiar. The blotch that stained his face drew her attention. She knew that mark. In a flash, the man jerked his horse around and bolted.

"Stop!"

Laurel braced the carbine against her shoulder and cocked the hammer, judging the distance between herself and the target—a hundred yards and growing. Still within range. She could drop the bay with ease but aimed down and a few feet to the right. With a squeeze of the trigger, dust and bits of grass flew up near the animal's side. The horse reared, almost unseating its rider. Almost. The man regained control of the bay and disappeared from the rifle's range.

She heard a prolonged, agonized bawl. It came from the other side of the trees. She spun the gelding and galloped toward the sound. When she reached the source, her stomach lurched, and she squeezed her eyes shut. Blocking the sight did nothing to dull the gruesome images of the cattle carcasses sprawled on her land and the memories they raised.

Upon hearing another pathetic cry, she forced her eyes open. One of the Triple M-branded Longhorns raised its head from the ground, its curved horns stretching close to six feet from tip to tip. It stared at her with dark, pleading eyes. She choked down the nausea and dismounted. The wound in the beast's belly told her the steer would die a slow, tortured death if she didn't act.

Laurel straightened her shoulders and cleansed her mind of the past and any qualms over what she must do next. She raised the gun and aimed for the skull.

The blast echoed in her ears and left them ringing.

She stood for several moments until the sound of hoofbeats pounded toward her from the rear. Laurel whipped around, pointing the gun toward the newcomers. A wagon approached from the right. She lowered the weapon. "Oh, it's you."

Royce MacMahon sat in the farm wagon as though he owned the world. "I saw you shoot that steer, Laurel." He glanced from one dead animal to another, then back to her. "Are you ready to pay the price for what you've done?"

Quinn flipped through the papers on his desk and mumbled, "No wonder Arthur travels so much."

Going through the files the past couple of weeks had answered his curiosity about the office's sparse furnishings. How had Arthur thought to drum up enough business to support the two of them?

Turning his chair to the window, Quinn leaned back with his hands interlocked behind his head. He stared outside at the buildings across the street. Tantalizing aromas from the Oberlin's bakery wafted through the open window aided by the currents of a slight fall breeze. They tempted him to go downstairs and purchase bread or a pastry rather than eat lunch across the street at the café.

He liked the Oberlins. He liked the food at the boardinghouse and café. He liked this town and many of its people. That made the decision to leave Bold Creek in the future a hard one.

Arthur's aim for Quinn to take on Henry's role of working alongside him could put them both in the poorhouse. And if he made his home in Bold Creek, he might end up attempting to fulfill someone else's vision of his life rather than his own.

At a gentle rap on the door, he straightened in the chair. "Enter."

Creaking on the hinges, the door slowly swung open, pushed by the toe of a woman's shoe. The waitress from the Green Meadow Café peeked into the room. "Am I bothering you, Mr. Spencer?"

He stood and donned his suit coat. "No, ma'am. Please come in."

Lillian stepped into his office and stopped. She held a tray with two small plates, a large bowl, a cup, and a small coffee pot. Even through the napkins covering the dishes, the mixed aromas of chicken soup, bread and some sweet dessert made his mouth water.

He walked across the room and took the heavy tray from her, then set it atop the papers spread across his desk. Why the food? "I didn't order anything."

Lillian pointed to the tray. "I wanted to show my appreciation for what you did Saturday. It isn't much, mostly left over from our supper last night." Red in the face, she backed toward the door.

"It smells delicious. This wasn't necessary. I'm afraid I wasn't much help. Mr. Jessup made a better impression on the man."

"It wasn't just you standing up for me. You left enough to cover that nasty man's meal. Your kindness meant my own children being able to eat. I-I can't thank you enough."

Quinn lifted a corner of the napkin covering the soup and recalled the two bits Laurel slid under the rim of the bread plate when she thought no one saw. "Mine wasn't the only coin left on that table for you, Lillian."

Her eyes widened. "No?"

"No. Mrs. Tillman—"

Shouts traveled upward to his second-story office. He turned toward the street and stuck his head out the open window. Others stepped from shops to stare at the band of noisy cowmen down the street. They gathered in front of the jail. The leader sat in a wagon, the back filled with fence posts. He demanded the marshal appear in terms that left no argument as to the importance of his business.

Lillian hurried over and poked her head out the window next to Quinn. "Royce." The name spilled from her lips in hushed awe.

Quinn switched his attention from the rancher to the smaller figure sitting beside him, red-faced and ready to boil over. Murphy MacMahon remained on his chestnut and held the reins of Laurel's buckskin. Quinn's stomach clenched.

A cowhand dismounted and jerked Laurel by the arm. She toppled from the wagon seat and stumbled while being jerked up the jailhouse steps.

Before he could convince himself the affair was none of his business, Quinn ducked back into the room and rushed out of the office.

90

CHAPTER ELEVEN

"So help me, Royce MacMahon, when we're through here . . ."
Laurel fixed her neighbor with a glare intended to melt him into a
mass of quivering jelly. Her intention failed.

"What's going on?" Marshal Wade Ruiz stood near the door of
the jailhouse, his hand on the grip of his revolver.

"These idiots think—"

"She shot our—"

"One at a time!" He stepped to one side. Royce and Murphy
looked down on him as they neared the doorway. The marshal might
lack Royce's impressive height and youth, but he made up for it with
confidence and authority. "Get in here before we have the whole
town gathering for this spectacle."

Someone shoved Laurel's back, and she lost her balance again.
Murphy reached out and caught her right arm. He steadied her with
a surprisingly gentle hold, then let go.

Once inside the office, the marshal's gaze shifted from Laurel to
Royce, then back to Laurel. He pointed to her. "You, Mrs. Tillman.
What's this about?"

She wrenched her arm free from the pinching, leather-gloved fingers of the lackey at her left side. "They claim I shot their Longhorns."

Royce stood with his feet about a foot apart and crossed his arms over his chest. "Marshal, we heard the shots. By the time we got there, five of my steers were dead. We saw this woman shoot the sixth one in the head. We're witnesses." He turned to his hired hands. "Aren't we?"

Laurel gritted her teeth at the two concurring grunts and nods. Although she couldn't deny what happened, the men would say anything their boss wanted them to say.

The office door opened behind her. Firm footsteps sounded on the floorboards as the newcomer entered the room. The latch clicked. Laurel refused to take her gaze from Royce to identify the new witness to her humiliation. She had a more important concern. If she couldn't convince the owners of the Triple M of her innocence, their influence would see her locked behind those iron bars in the back.

"How many times must I say it? You saw me put down an already mortally-injured steer."

Royce leaned forward until he was but an inch from her. His hot breath blew across her face and ruffled loose tendrils of her hair as he said, "An injury caused by this carbine you carry." He held up the Winchester.

"As usual, Royce, you don't know what you're talking about. It wasn't me."

"Where were these animals?"

Laurel moaned, recognizing the voice at her back. Had Quinn gotten word of her predicament and come to provide a character reference? In that case, she may as well lock herself in a cell right now.

Royce glanced up and over her shoulder. "Who are you?"

"Quinn Spencer."

Laurel turned as he stepped closer and put a hand out. Murphy hesitated a moment before shaking it. Then Quinn offered the same to Royce, who ignored the attempt at civility.

"This is private business, Spencer."

"I took your manhandling of Mrs. Tillman as my invitation to this meeting."

"He's a lawyer." Murphy aimed a smirk at Quinn. "He likes to butt into things that aren't his concern."

"Mr. Spencer, are you this woman's attorney?"

"Not exactly, sir."

"Then I don't believe we need you right now." Marshal Ruiz moved to the chair behind his desk. "Of course, if you and Mrs. Tillman have a personal understanding . . ."

"No!" Together, they snapped out a denial.

A corner of the lawman's mouth lifted, tilting the black mustache sprinkled with silver. "Let me hear these people out before you do any lawyering, Spencer."

Laurel waited for him to leave, but Quinn remained in his spot next to Murphy. "My question seems a logical one, Marshal. I see no reason why Mr. MacMahon can't answer it."

When Royce refused to speak up, Laurel did it for him. "The cattle were on my property."

"How did they get there?"

"Someone cut the fence I raised to keep her dirty sheep off my land." Royce moved to the desk and leaned against it with his fingers curled around the top edge, his blue eyes fixed on Laurel. "And we know who."

"Why would I want to cut a fence that keeps *your* animals off *my* land?"

Quinn touched her arm, his somber expression a warning. He might have been a dangerous adversary once, but she was no fool and took his warning to heart. Losing her temper further would do nothing to support her case.

"I suppose you found wire cutters in Mrs. Tillman's possession."

"Not exactly, Spencer."

She breathed easier. No one could prove she cut the fence because she possessed on her person nothing with which to cut it. If she were lucky, that would be enough to prove her innocence.

Royce nodded to one of his men. The hired hand pulled an implement from the saddle bag thrown over his shoulder and handed it to his boss.

Laurel's leg muscles quivered. She covered her mouth with one hand while bracing herself against Murphy with the other.

"Linc found these in the brush near to where her horse stood. Obviously, she was so busy dropping the cattle she missed the fact that she dropped these." He held up his evidence.

The missing pair of shears?

Laurel looked down, unable to bear the verdict flashing from Quinn's eyes.

Quinn studied the tool in Royce MacMahon's hand, the long, triangular-shaped blades. If he didn't say something soon, the rancher would insist the marshal lock Laurel behind the bars in the back room, even if she's not guilty. But what could he say? The sheep shears were incriminating evidence.

"I'll take those." The marshal grabbed the shears from the cattleman's hands and held them out to Laurel. "Are these yours, Mrs. Tillman?"

Quinn subtly shook his head. Fortunately, she understood his desire for silence and, for once, didn't allow her ill will toward him to overrule her common sense. He intervened. "That isn't the point, Marshal Ruiz."

Royce MacMahon sneered. "And what is the point, Spencer? We caught her dead to rights. The cattle had the Triple M brand. She knew full well they were mine and lured them onto her land so she could kill them."

Quinn hoped the man's arrogance would work for Laurel's benefit. "Why would she do that, Mr. MacMahon?"

"Because she's a pigheaded woman."

Quinn pounced on the last word. "And no woman should run a ranch?"

"Of course not. They ought to stick to raising the next generation of cattlemen."

"And leave the land ownership to men like you?"

Royce patronized Quinn with another smirk. "Now you understand."

"I understand you want Mrs. Tillman's land."

The rancher took a step forward. Quinn disregarded the intimidation tactic, concerned more with whether he should broach the subject burning in his mind. He smoothed the soft whiskers covering the sides of his face and running across his upper lip.

Over the years, he'd learned to recognize little nuances in language, both through the spoken word and physical expressions. Right now, he read quite a bit about the younger MacMahon's refusal to look anyone in the eye. Did Murphy hold a hint of doubt as to Laurel's guilt? Perhaps he knew more than he was telling. Quinn wanted to further explore the discomfort in the younger man's attitude. "Were you all together at the time of the cattle killing?"

Murphy hesitated before pointing to the ranch hands. "I was with them. We heard the shots and rode hard toward the sound. We reached the spot about the same time as Royce."

"I see. Do you know where your brother was before then?"

Royce stepped away from the desk. "Marshal, are you going to let him continue this circus?"

The man nodded. "Murphy, pretend the question came from me."

The young man darted a quick glance at his brother, then turned his attention to the lawman. "No, sir. I hadn't seen him since breakfast when he asked me to meet him in the north pasture about eleven o'clock."

Quinn eyed the older MacMahon. "That's convenient."

"Why don't you be of some real help, Murph." Royce glared at his brother. "Tell them what Laurel said she'd do the next time something belonging to the Triple M stepped foot on her property."

"I told you, Royce, I didn't think she meant it."

"He's right. I wouldn't shoot—"

Quinn held up his hand to quiet Laurel in order to continue his questioning. "Why didn't you think she meant it, Murphy?"

Royce glared at Ruiz. "You're letting this man take over your investigation? We should have gone straight to the sheriff."

"Ordinarily, I'd tell you to do that, but Sheriff Reading's heart attack left the office vacant. Now, Mr. Spencer is asking the questions I'd ask, so let your brother speak."

Murphy and Laurel stared at one another as though in some silent communication. When he looked back at Quinn, his spine appeared straighter and his jaw had hardened. "Because as tough as she is, I don't believe she'd shoot anyone or anything without proper cause."

Quinn relaxed and faced Royce. "Mr. MacMahon, it sounds as though you're attempting to remove a 'pigheaded woman' from her land. You only needed to make it appear as though she shot your cattle, so you could blame her."

"Now hold up, Spencer. I am not letting you and your fancy lawyer ways twist this to be my doing. I saw her shoot that steer."

"And she's explained the reason for it."

"Quinn—"

"What about the shears?" Royce ignored Laurel and pointed to the evidence he had produced.

"We don't know your man found them in the grass. You could have dropped them yourself. Do you have proof that they're Mrs. Tillman's and she used that tool to cut the fence? Did you see her do so?"

"You calling me a liar, Spencer?"

"What you didn't see, Royce, was me trying to stop the person who really killed your precious cattle." Laurel leaned in closer to Quinn and lowered her voice. "I've been trying to tell you. It was that nasty man from the café."

His heart raced at the revelation. "Are you sure?"

As he had done with Murphy, Quinn studied her face, looking for any telltale sign of a falsehood. Her gaze never wavered from his, those green eyes challenging his skepticism. He wished she had spoken up sooner. Then again, he hadn't given her the chance. He had been too eager to protect her.

"Of course I'm sure."

Royce walked around the desk and opened a drawer. He withdrew a set of keys and held them up. "Marshal, me and my boys have a whole mess of chores to finish today and you're wasting my time listening to a man who owes this woman a debt. Who knows what else he wants from her."

Ruiz placed a hand on Quinn's shoulder in restraint. "No call to insult the lady like that, MacMahon."

"Lady? She hasn't seen fit to live like a lady since her husband died."

Loathing for the man boiled inside Quinn, but he didn't rise to the bait.

Royce tossed the keys to the marshal. "You have her admission that she shot one of my steers. You have the shears belonging to her. And you have my word that I caught her destroying my property. What more do you need? Lock her up and be done with it."

"Under the circumstances, Marshal, I believe you know that would be a miscarriage of justice."

The lawman glanced from the rancher to Quinn. "I'd be obliged if you two would quit telling me how to do my job. I want everyone but Mrs. Tillman to step outside."

"Marshal—"

"Take your men down to the Golden Ace and get yourselves something wet, MacMahon. I got work to do."

If a malevolent stare could stop a person's heart, the lawman would be as dead as those cattle on Laurel's land. It failed to intimidate Ruiz, which raised Quinn's respect for the man, along with his hope for a fair investigation in a town where too many citizens held Laurel in low esteem.

Royce stood his ground, then with a grunt, signaled to the other three. "We'll be back."

The marshal waved him away. "I look forward to it."

The stomp of their boots echoed on the porch of the jailhouse. Quinn tipped his head and sent Laurel a silent request. He wanted to hear whatever she told Ruiz.

She faced the lawman. "I'd like Mr. Spencer to stay. He was at the café on Saturday and may provide more information about the man."

"As soon as he interferes in my questioning, he'll go to the saloon to keep the others company." Ruiz sighed and sat at his desk. He pulled out a sheet of paper and a pencil, then motioned for her to sit in the seat near the wall. Quinn stood to her right. "Now, Mrs. Tillman, who's this man you say shot the Triple M livestock?"

"I don't know his name. I'd never seen him until that day at the café."

The marshal picked up a pencil and began writing on a sheet of paper. "What about you, Spencer?"

"No, sir. Saturday was the first time for me, too."

"Go on, Mrs. Tillman."

Laurel related the incident involving the waitress, describing the physical appearance of the man and emphasizing the mark on his face. Marshal Ruiz scribbled as she spoke.

"Anything you want to add to that, Mr. Spencer?"

Quinn relived his unease when catching the man staring at Laurel. He wished now he had confronted him. Did he have a grudge against Laurel? She said she'd never seen him around here before, but what about in her past? Had she lied? He didn't think so.

"Spencer?"

"I'm sorry. I was recalling the situation. I spent the rest of the meal watching over my shoulder. Before he left, the man stared at Mrs. Tillman. It made me uneasy." Laurel gasped, but he avoided looking at her.

"How so?"

"He started to leave, but as soon as Issy mentioned Laurel by name, he stopped and turned. At first, he seemed surprised. Then he smiled as though he'd just won a fortune in a poker game. When he caught me watching, he left."

Laurel sprang to her feet. "And you didn't mention such a thing? Why didn't you warn us if he made you uneasy? What if, instead of shooting cattle, he hurt my family?"

Had he made a mistake by not warning her? Could he have stopped what happened today? "It was only a look, not a cause to arrest the man. What would you have had me do?"

Before she could answer, Ruiz rapped the end of the pencil on the desktop. "Did he threaten her, Spencer?"

"No."

"Did you feel a need to escort the ladies home?"

"At that time, no." He glanced at Laurel. "But I will accompany Mrs. Tillman back to the ranch this afternoon."

She threw her shoulders back. "You will not."

"Ma'am, as soon as you tell me your side of what happened, I suggest you let this gentleman see you safely back to the ranch." Marshal Ruiz held up his hand to stay further argument. "After we see if your story makes sense to me."

Laurel sat back down in the chair. "Let's get this over so I can go home. Like Royce, I have work to do."

She went into great detail, starting with leaving the ranch house that morning and ending with being dragged up the jailhouse steps. Both Quinn and the lawman frowned off and on. Those frowns grew deeper when she mentioned shooting at the stranger on her property. Though she claimed to aim in front of him, the woman owned no end of gumption.

The marshal picked up the shears from his desk and held them toward her. "Are these yours?"

Not bothering to seek Quinn's guidance this time, Laurel looked them over and said, "The handle has my flame brand."

"When did you see them last?"

"A few months ago, after we sheared the sheep. I own three pairs. We wanted to use them again a couple of weeks ago. You can ask Issy and Camille. They were with me when we discovered one pair gone."

"Marshal, I question whether those shears can cut a strand of fencing thick enough to hold cattle."

Ruiz glared at Quinn. "I am doing the questioning, Mr. Lawyer." He leaned forward and rested his arms on the desk with an attitude of gravity. "Where do you keep your tools, Mrs. Tillman?"

"In the shed next to the barn."

"Is there a lock on the door?"

Laurel sat straighter. A glint of hope lit her countenance. "No."

"Who's allowed to go in there?"

"Everyone on the ranch. I hired three itinerant shepherds to help us with the shearing last spring, but they used their own tools. I don't loan mine. After they left, we sharpened the shears and put them away—all three pairs." She gave a little snort. "Those wandering shepherds are the only men courageous enough to cross Royce."

"Why did you threaten the Triple M men?"

Laurel sighed. "Murphy threw his weight around on behalf of his brother. I'm tired of telling those two I won't sell, so I said I didn't want to see anything belonging to the Triple M on my property again." She lifted a shoulder. "Haven't you ever let anger cause you to say something you didn't mean? Besides, I just told him I'd shoot first. I didn't say I'd aim at anything."

Quinn curbed his amusement. Royce MacMahon should thank God she turned his marriage proposal down. What an explosive pair of wills.

When she finished her story, the marshal studied his notes for several minutes while Quinn mulled over Laurel's options if the lawman didn't believe her. Would she allow him to assist her if it came to needing legal advice? Since she'd bucked at the idea of him accompanying her back to the ranch, the answer was likely no.

They awaited the decision to arrest Laurel or let her go. Quinn fidgeted with the watch chain attached to his vest, the metal links jingling against each other. *Come on, man. You know you have no convicting proof.*

Ruiz relaxed and leaned back in the chair. He tossed the pencil on the desk. Turning to Quinn, he said, "I want to question those MacMahon fellas and their hands. I'll keep them here as long as possible. That'll allow you and Mrs. Tillman to get a good bit down the road without their interference."

Quinn released the breath he'd held. "It won't please them to discover you didn't lock her up."

Laurel rose from her seat. "Whose side are you on, Mr. Spencer?"

"I'm on the side of truth, Laurel."

"I don't worry over whether I make people happy." Ruiz tugged on the piece of metal pinned to his vest. "That isn't why I wear this badge."

"I meant no offense, sir, but Royce MacMahon doesn't strike me as someone who's easily thwarted."

The marshal laughed. "It does my day good when I can pinch that man's temper." Too soon, he sobered, aiming a glare at Laurel. "I'll be heading out to your place later. If I find any reason to think you've lied to me, young woman, you'll be back here quicker than a rattlesnake can strike. You might hire this man . . . just in case."

Laurel stared at the lawman. The muscles of her jaw worked back and forth. "That won't be necessary."

Quinn turned to the marshal. "If you'll stop by the ranch house, I'd like to be with you when you investigate the site."

"As a lawyer or a friend?"

Quinn eyed Laurel's set profile. Once again, guilt rippled through him for having repaid the hospitality of the La Casa del Fuego women by protecting his own interest. "I'm going as a friend. For now."

"Let me get Ruthie from the barn at the boarding house and I'll see you home."

Laurel untied the reins of the buckskin and reached for the saddle horn, prepared to mount. "Don't bother. The marshal gave me back my carbine. I need no nursemaid."

"Your willingness to use that gun got you into this trouble to begin with." Quinn gripped her arm, preventing her feet from leaving the ground, and she let out a surprised gasp. "You're getting an escort if I have to treat you like the MacMahons and tie you to that saddle. Now follow me." He let go and rounded the corner onto Cedar Street, mumbling incoherent words.

The depressed skin on Laurel's arm bounced back, and so did her ire. He expected her to tag along like some adoring puppy. "I am no moon-eyed mutt, Mr. Spencer."

Quinn was right, though. Royce was not happy. She rubbed her forehead. "Oh, fiddle-faddle." She tugged on the reins and trailed after the Yankee lawyer, voicing her share of incoherent mumblings.

While he saddled his mare, she stood outside the barn. The hens in the yard of the boarding house clucked and fluffed their wings. She inhaled the smell of a chicken frying. Laurel's head spun, probably because she hadn't eaten since sunup, but the past few hours had destroyed the appetite Mrs. Dillard's cooking should stimulate.

Why would she interest the man with the wine-colored blotch? Or was it her? Perhaps he had a score to settle with Royce and wanted to throw suspicion off himself by placing it on someone known to be at odds with him. Or perhaps Quinn had been right. Was Royce ornery enough to have arranged this situation in order to ruin her and have a chance at purchasing her land?

She struggled for a reason for the mess she'd landed in. She settled on one.

How long do You intend to punish me, God?

She blew a frustrated breath between her lips. What a silly question to ask. She knew the answer. Forever. He would punish her forever.

CHAPTER TWELVE

Laurel had never appreciated her surroundings more. She used every sense to soak up the countryside—the river to the left, the hills in the distance, and relatively flat pastureland to the right. The trees in bright fall colors and the air crisp.

If Royce MacMahon had gotten his way, she wouldn't be breathing in the freshness of this country air, seeing the dust kicked up by the horses, and smelling the sweaty scent of their bodies. She wouldn't be staring at the hawk circling above, waiting for the right moment to swoop down on whatever unsuspecting prey scurried through the thin grass. She wouldn't hear the breeze whistling through the trees or the water flowing over rock. She wouldn't feel the sun on her face or taste the sourness of the crabapple she'd pulled from a roadside tree.

She'd remain trapped inside an iron cage.

Shifting in the saddle, Laurel groaned as loud as the leather. Her back and head ached as her horse trotted down the road.

"Did those men hurt you?" Quinn slowed his mare to a walk, concern etched in the vertical lines between his eyes.

"No. I'm fine."

She kept up the pace. The sooner they reached the ranch, the sooner she could lock herself in her room for the good cry that threatened to break free. Today's ultimate humiliation would be to burst into frustrated tears in front of Quinn.

He caught up with her. "Why do you think the stranger from the café wanted to kill Triple M cattle on your land?"

"I don't know."

"You've never met him?"

"I don't know."

Quinn frowned, her answer clearly unsatisfactory. "Does that mean you might have crossed paths before?"

"It means I don't know."

"Do you think his argument might be with Royce? Could you be a convenient scapegoat?"

Laurel grew tired of the inquisition. "I. Don't. Know."

He halted Ruthie in the center of the road. "For Pete's sake, Laurel, stop pouting and give me an answer I can use."

She pulled back on the reins and turned her gelding to face him. "I have answered you, Quinn. Those are all questions I have asked myself. Why don't you ask Royce? He thinks he knows it all."

"I might do that." He ran a hand down his bearded face and sighed. "I'm only trying to help you."

Without Quinn raising questions about Royce's evidence, her neighbor might have convinced the marshal of her guilt, and right now, she would sit on a jail cell cot. She owed him more than terse answers to his questions. The proper expression of gratitude raked Laurel like a dried thistle tumbling around her insides, so she spit it out as quickly as possible. "I am obliged to you for your assistance in town."

Turning onto the lane leading to the ranch house, she squeezed the sides of her gelding, prodding him into a lope. Had their roles been reversed, that measly attempt at a thank you would not have satisfied her, but it was the best she could do.

Their arrival at the house created a fuss that was one squeal short of chaos. Quinn sat atop Ruthie while each woman on the ranch surrounded Laurel. Their mouths ran nonstop. Issy demanded to know why Triple M cattle lay dead on the ranch, and Camille mixed three languages into each sentence. Everyone chattered and scolded Laurel for being away for so long without a word.

A grin broke free of the frown Quinn had worn most of the trip from town. He shook his head. Not even in his three weeks recuperating here had he seen them so effusive. A swarm of stirred up honeybees buzzed around their queen.

God had created two distinct traits in the sexes—one protective, the other nurturing. The reminder sobered him. These women would never admit it, but they may need a man's protection in the coming days. Would he want to be that man? Laurel could decide for him. The reluctant appreciation he had received earlier didn't mean she would accept his help again if offered.

"I regret causing you to worry." Her lilting drawl rose over Camille's concerns, Issy's complaints, and Becky's questions. "Everything's fine, except for my starvation. Let's go inside and I'll explain what happened."

The mere mention of eating revived the hunger pangs Quinn had tamped down, and he pictured in his mind the food Lillian had brought him. It sat cold and unappealing in his office.

The ladies started for the house, forgetting about his presence, so he whistled the tune to "When Johnny Comes Marching Home." He stopped when Laurel froze on the porch steps with her back to him.

"Mr. Spencer was kind enough to see me home. Perhaps we should fill his mouth with something more worthwhile than the notes of that dreadful song." She continued into the house, humming the Rebel favorite, "Dixie."

Quinn's shoulders shook with laughter. Surely, if she had been on the battle lines, the South would have won the war.

"You're welcome to join us, Mr. Spencer. Of course, if you would rather not . . ."

"Thank you, Mrs. Chamberlain. I'll take care of the horses and be inside after I wash."

After stalling Ruthie and turning out Laurel's nameless buckskin into the small pasture behind the barn, Quinn removed his suit coat and rolled up the sleeves of his shirt. He raised a full bucket from the well and dipped his hands in the cold water.

While scrubbing his face, he contemplated removing the beard tomorrow morning. He wasn't sure why he had left the task so long, except that the beard hid the scar on the underside of his jaw. His fingers ran through the softened facial hair. He'd give it some thought.

Feeling somewhat clean again, he entered through the side door to the small kitchen. Three women bounced off each other as they prepared a meal for the prodigal.

Camille took his coat and hung it on a hook near the front door. "I hope you like lamb stew."

"Sounds good."

Issy pointed to the long table that took up a good portion of the space in the room. "The meat is fresh."

Camille glared at her. "Thank you. I am sure that did wonders for our appetites."

Quinn chuckled and sat down. Issy sloshed stew into his bowl as Laurel eased into the chair opposite him. She had taken the time to freshen up and re-braid that marvelous length of hair and must have pinched her cheeks to encourage the healthy color.

While they ate, Laurel told the story of the cattle kill and her trip to Bold Creek. At one point, she kicked Quinn under the table when he opened his mouth to expound upon certain details she had left out of her version. She glossed over her treatment by the MacMahons and stressed her role as a witness rather than a suspect.

He concentrated on the stew, his newly healed leg throbbing with a fresh bruise. Who was he to deny her effort to keep the others from worrying? For now, he would bow to her wishes.

"Mr. Spencer, you were a gentleman to escort my daughter home."

"It was my pleasure, ma'am."

"Marshal Ruiz will be here soon. Quinn wants to ride with him to see where the cattle were shot. They hope to find something that will lead to the man responsible." Laurel dabbed at the edges of her mouth with a napkin and then fussed with smoothing it across her lap.

"You said you saw this man." Camille approached the table, gripping the towel-covered handle of the coffee pot, and refilled Laurel's cup. "Did you recognize him?"

"Yes."

"Well, who was it, Momma?"

She swished her fork through the stew. "It was the unpleasant man from the café on Saturday, Peanut."

Camille gasped and Issy pronounced him "a low-down skunk." Ellen Chamberlain wrung her hands while Becky started for the door.

"Rebecca, where are you going?"

"To the barn to check on Pru and the pups, Granmomma. I don't want that low-down skunk hurting them like he did those steers."

Laurel frowned at Issy, who looked not the least repentant for her part in Becky's name calling. "I want you to stay around the yard until the marshal arrests that man, you hear me?"

"Yes, ma'am." The little girl stopped and turned with her fingers wrapped around the doorknob, her expression as serious as her mother's. "Remember, Mr. Spencer, we're fixin' the roof on Saturday. Granmomma's gonna make a sweet potato pie and we're havin' a picnic. You'll be here like you promised, won't you?"

Like he promised? When did he do that?

The smiles on three additional faces awaited his answer. He prepared for a protest from Laurel, but she merely sipped her coffee. For once, he would have welcomed her objection, allowing him to turn the girl down without guilt. "Becky, I—"

A loud rap on the front door was a blessed interruption. "Mrs. Tillman, it's Marshal Ruiz."

As Camille rose to let the lawman inside, Laurel captured Quinn's gaze. "I want to go with you."

"Why?"

"Because it's my fu—" She glanced at her mother and lowered her voice until he had to lean closer to discern the words. "Because I'm interested in what you find."

Quinn matched her whisper. "You don't need to be accused of interfering with the evidence. I'll keep you informed of anything important."

She appeared on the verge of arguing when her mother grasped her hand. "Is there something wrong, dear?"

Laurel's glance flicked to Quinn and darted away, but not before he noticed her eyes narrow with concern. "No, Momma."

Quinn rose with the rest of the women and left the table. He questioned Laurel's desire to return to what he was sure would be a gruesome scene. Was she afraid he and the marshal would discover something to prove her guilty of destroying the Triple M's Longhorns?

Ruthie's neck muscles quivered, failing to shake loose a fly soaking up the sun and heat from the horse's body. Quinn brushed the stubborn insect away, only to have it land on the left ear of the marshal's horse. More insects gathered around the wounds on the dead cattle.

"I told Royce to give me a few hours to investigate before he got rid of these carcasses." Marshal Ruiz swatted a fly presumptuous enough to light on his hand.

"Did you speak with Ira Jessup and Lillian before you left town?"

"I did. They haven't seen the stranger since Ira told him not to come back. His name's Reg Ferrell. At least, that's how he signed the register at the hotel."

A surge of optimism rose in Quinn. "He's staying at the Sherwood?"

"Checked out Sunday morning."

"Yesterday?" Quinn's hope of a moment before died. "Do you

know for sure he's left town?"

"Nope. He waited for Schuler to open this morning and bought enough supplies to last for several weeks on the road."

"That doesn't mean he left the area. If he checked out of the hotel yesterday, where was he last night?"

"You know what I do, Spencer. It won't bode well for your lady friend if I can't locate this Ferrell character."

Quinn pointed to the dead cattle and dismounted. "Then let's find something that proves he did this."

Searching the ground, he and the lawman searched for anything that might confirm Laurel's claim that Reg Ferrell had caused the butchery surrounding them. As they approached carcass after carcass, a bothersome notion hid in the nether regions of Quinn's mind, refusing to reveal itself. What was it about these animals that troubled him?

They searched for another hour, finding little besides a couple of partial boot prints in the barest areas of grass. They spotted Laurel's—smaller, and with the left imprint deeper than the right. However, it was hard to know who made the rest.

The marshal kicked a tuft of grass several yards from a Longhorn. He reached down and picked up something from the ground. Holding it between two fingers, he examined the piece made of brass and steel. "It's a casing from a .44—same caliber used by Mrs. Tillman's '66 Winchester." He searched around for more. "I don't see any others. Do you?"

"No. And you can't rely on that casing as evidence when Laurel admitted to shooting a steer from close range." Quinn turned a full circle to scan the area. "The man shot the other cattle from a different spot. It could have been anywhere."

"True." Ruiz pointed to four different carcasses, including the one nearest him. "Each required a second or third bullet to make the kill. Whoever's responsible doesn't appear to be much of a shot." The man flipped the rounded metal casing into the air and caught it. It glinted when held up to the sunlight. "I think I'll dig out those bullets and see if they're all the same as your lady friend uses."

Quinn wanted to demand he stop referring to Laurel as his lady friend, but a revelation stopped him. He grinned and slapped the marshal on the back, earning a growl from the lawman. "Mrs. Tillman is innocent."

"What makes you so sure?"

"I've seen her expertise with a rifle. She would never need to shoot twice."

He related the story of having watched Laurel practice her shots. On the second occasion, she'd nailed the end of a board to the tool shed and marked a three-inch circle in the center. At over thirty yards, the first bullet hit inside the circle. She stepped back five paces and shot again. Over and over. Every bullet had hit inside the circle. When he'd asked why she felt the need to practice her shots, she said, "One never knows when another war will break out."

He'd thought it an odd answer from an odd woman.

"You'll have to do better than that, Mr. Lawyer. She could have made this deed look like someone who couldn't hit a wall if she stood next to it."

Quinn removed his hat and brushed the back of his hand across his damp forehead. "You don't believe Laurel's story?"

Ruiz shook his head. "It doesn't matter what I believe, does it? I gotta go by the evidence."

And, right now, that evidence pointed in only one woman's direction.

After kissing Becky goodnight and seeing her snuggled under the covers, Laurel stepped outside. She rubbed her shoulders and the back of her neck, not realizing until then how tight the muscles had become over the past hours.

Quinn had ridden back without the marshal. He reported nothing more than the guilty man's name. After asking if it meant anything to her, one raised eyebrow testified to his skepticism when she told him no.

The peaceful morning had turned into a challenging afternoon. So many questions circled inside her brain. Who was Reg Ferrell? Did she know him from the past? If not, why would he take an interest in her?

She stared at the half-moon, its light casting mysterious shadows around the yard. Why shoot Triple M cattle? Another matter confused her. What made Quinn Spencer rush to her aid today when he clearly disapproved of her?

Laurel paused at the last question, her thoughts befuddled by the emotions the Yankee wrought in her. In the past twelve years, she had met plenty of northerners and former federal soldiers. Even her mother grew up in Pennsylvania. She'd learned to ignore most, neither reviling nor liking them. But something about this northerner both drew and repelled her. Occasionally, he seemed familiar, yet any recollection of him sidestepped her memory.

She moved toward the butter churn and halted, surprised by a dark figure hunched over in the porch chair and turning the crank. "Ernie? You should be with the flock."

The girl let go of the handle and jumped to her feet. "Yes'm. Issy said she'd trade me a night."

"I see. What are you doing here, child?"

Ernie shoved her hands into her back pockets as if hiding her imitation of Laurel's habit. "Nothin'."

"It's getting late. Don't you think you ought to be in bed?"

"I reckon so." She made no move toward the bunkhouse.

Laurel took her place in the chair and leaned back. She waited to see if Ernie would confide in her. Something bothered the girl to the point she had been skittish as a rabbit for hours.

Shutting her eyes, Laurel breathed in the cool night air, thankful this day would end soon. "Nice evening. We won't need to bail out the bunkhouse tonight."

The girl remained silent.

Laurel opened her eyes. "Is there a problem? Something you'd like to discuss with me?"

"No, ma'am." She shook her head and toed a warped plank. "Yes, ma'am. I think I'd best be moving on in the mornin'."

Gripping the churn handle, Laurel cranked while planning her response. Why the sudden decision to leave?

In less than two months, this sweet girl had wriggled her way into Laurel's heart. She didn't want to see her go. Although almost full grown, Ernie displayed a child-like innocence, much like Becky's. Laurel hated to see that innocence lost to some lout who took advantage of her along the road or in some filthy cow town.

"I suppose you have distant family to find, people who miss you."

"No, ma'am. Since Ma passed on, I ain't got nobody."

"That's a shame." Laurel rotated the crank again. "Where do you plan to go?"

"Don't know. Maybe California. They say that ocean is mighty purty and you can't see its end."

"Before the war, my father took us to Wilmington. That's in my home state of North Carolina. My brother and I dipped our bare toes in the Atlantic Ocean." She smiled at the memory of building a wall in the sand, only to have Lance kick it down and laugh when a wave flowed through the breach. Laurel had gone a full two hours without speaking to him. "How will you get to California? Trains and coaches are costly."

Ernie shrugged. "Walk, I guess."

"That's a long way. Winter's coming on."

"Which is why I best get started."

Desperate to understand what the girl was thinking, Laurel said, "I thought you enjoyed working here. Momma says you're coming along fine with your lessons. I can hear it in your speech."

Ernie jerked around. "Oh, yes, ma'am. I ain't . . . haven't . . . never been in such a fine place. I just . . ."

"Has Issy been teasing you again?"

"Issy don't bother me none. If I was to have a sister, I'd want one just like her."

A thought occurred to Laurel. "Ernie, does this have to do with what happened today? It was not my doing. I hope you believe that. I didn't kill those cattle." Well, one.

She hung her head. "I know that, ma'am."

"Good." Perhaps approaching things from a different direction might prove more successful. "You're welcome to stay as long as you like, Ernie. Although we aren't all related through blood, we're like kin here. You are part of our family now."

Her hazel eyes grew wide. "I am?"

Laurel stood and stretched. She stepped next to Ernie and placed a hand on her shoulder. "Whatever you're running from will catch up with you one day. Those ghosts will find you. Here, you're not alone. You have us to help fend them off."

"I ain't runnin' from ghosts." She stared off into the darkness. Laurel thought the sun would shine before Ernie said another word. "Guess California ain't . . . isn't . . . gonna disappear into that water anytime soon, so maybe I could stay a mite longer."

"Good."

"Here you're not alone."

Laurel shivered. She learned years ago it did no good to run. The ghosts always found her. Even with others to help fend them off.

CHAPTER THIRTEEN

"More roast, Mr. Spencer?"

Quinn's landlady interrupted his worrisome thoughts. Two days had passed, and Laurel remained free. But how long would that last?

"Please, Mrs. Dillard."

She passed him a platter loaded with enough sliced meat to feed half a company of men. Beef, potatoes, onions and carrots dispersed an appetizing aroma throughout the rooms of the boarding house.

"Thank you." He helped himself to more meat and potatoes, then passed the platter to Harry Kepley, who sat across the table from him. "I must compliment you again on your excellent meals."

"I'll add my own compliments to you, ma'am. Memory fails when recalling a more delightful repast." A solid man with wiry orange hair, thick sideburns, and a drooping, rust-colored mustache, Harry represented a jewelry manufacturer in New York City. He traveled the southwest selling the trinkets he kept locked inside a small trunk in his room. When in the area, Harry stayed at the boarding house, saying he preferred Mrs. Dillard's hospitality over a hotel staff's indifference.

Hedda Dillard's wide smile would have cracked the face of a less robust woman. She waved a hand through the air. "Oh, go on with you, both of you. A woman enjoys nothing more than a hungry man who appreciates the fruits of her labor."

"Anyone who cannot appreciate the fruits of your culinary labor, dear madam, has lost his ability to taste."

Quinn concentrated on the number of his chews. Counting them prevented him from laughing out loud at Harry's blarney and Mrs. Dillard's cackling. In her fifties, the plump widow fed on flattery with an appetite rivaling her boarders' enjoyment of the delicious meals.

A knock on the front door halted all conversation. Quinn's landlady set her napkin beside her plate and rose from her seat. They might be in a small nowhere town in Texas, but propriety demanded the gentlemen do likewise.

"I wonder who is calling at this hour."

As she strode toward the door, Quinn and Harry seated themselves once more. From the hallway came indistinct voices. Quinn disregarded them to finish the last of his beef.

"Mr. Spencer, Mr. Bruner has asked to speak with you in private. I've shown him to the parlor. I told him he was welcome to stay for dessert, but he declined a piece of my peach pie." Mrs. Dillard stood in the doorway of the dining room, her eyes wide and her head cocked, as though finding it unfathomable that someone would turn down the offer of her peach pie.

For a widower to decline a woman's charming company and mouth-watering dessert meant this wasn't a social call. Arthur had been out of town since Monday morning. What brought him to the boarding house? Surely, he was tired after his travel. Quinn excused himself and walked to the parlor.

Arthur stood with his forearm propped on the edge of the fireplace mantel, his fingernails drumming Mrs. Dillard's polished oak while clenched teeth worked his jaw muscles.

"Arthur?"

The man turned with an expression black as a thunderhead with no rain. "Quinn."

"Unpleasant trip?"

"Not at all. But the news I received upon my return has me concerned."

"News?"

His employer pointed to the sofa, so Quinn took a seat and waited. Arthur glanced toward the dining room across the foyer, where laughter rose above the sound of silver clinking against china. As if satisfied the others were occupied and unable to overhear, his features softened and his mouth formed an awkward smile.

"I understand a situation involving the Triple M Ranch occurred on Monday."

Ah. "The MacMahons lost a half dozen steers."

"Yes. I heard the circumstance regarding their loss. The incident seems to be this week's gossip."

The muscles along Quinn's abdomen rippled with apprehension. While Mrs. Oberlin and a few others applauded him for opposing the MacMahons in favor of protecting Laurel, others expressed their disapproval. Arrogant as Royce MacMahon might be, many of the townspeople treated him with more respect than they did Laurel.

Pressing against the padded back of the sofa, Quinn crossed his legs, hoping to show a relaxed attitude contrary to the discomfort building inside him. "Marshal Ruiz is looking into it. We think the man responsible was a stranger named Reg Ferrell—"

"We? Does the marshal share your belief?"

"He has an open mind."

"So you speak of Mrs. Tillman and yourself?"

"Yes, sir." Quinn hurried on with his explanation. "Wade Ruiz is still investigating but hasn't located Ferrell. We think the man left town."

Arthur linked his hands behind his back, as Quinn had seen him do in a courtroom when questioning a witness. He paced in front of the fireplace. "You felt it necessary to jump to the aid of Laurel Tillman, even though I warned you against associating with her?"

"I did." He chafed at Arthur's words and tone, reminded of the time when, at ten years old, he'd caught Henry and Quinn sharing a cigar behind the carriage house. While they coughed and choked on the smoke, Arthur lectured them about the ills of tobacco use, even though Henry had snatched the cigar from a wooden box in his father's study. "If Royce MacMahon had gotten his way, Mrs. Tillman would face an undeserving charge."

"I understand Royce saw her kill one of their steers. Isn't that true? To say the charge would be undeserved seems incorrect."

"It is when she's innocent. Sir, she put one animal out of its misery after someone else shot all six."

"What makes you sure she's telling the truth?"

Even though each deformed bullet the marshal dug from the dead steers was a .44, it was a common caliber. Still, a persistent voice reminded Quinn of her threat to shoot anything on her land belonging to the brothers. And the cattleman found her sheep shears at the scene. What convinced him of her innocence?

"I speak from experience when I say she has no trouble being forthright. But I've also seen her compassion." Quinn recalled comparing Laurel's thorns to those of the cactus. Yet, her love for her daughter, her treatment of Ruthie, her grief over the dead ewe—every one of those actions told him she was incapable of a malicious animal killing. "I believe her, Arthur."

"Don't allow a personal attraction to interfere with your opinion. She is lovely on those occasions when she allows herself to be a woman."

Hearing Harry Kepley in the hallway, Quinn delayed his answer until after the jeweler climbed the stairs and the door to his room closed. "I have no personal interest in Mrs. Tillman. My involvement in what happened Monday was professional."

"Did she hire you to give her legal advice? Have you billed her for your time?"

Quinn had talked himself into a hole, and Arthur threw the first shovelful of dirt over him. "No, sir. When I saw Royce MacMahon and his men pushing her toward the jail, almost knocking her to the ground, I felt it only right that I see to her safety. I would have done the same for any woman treated that way."

"Yes, I heard of your support for that waitress at the café."

Quinn flexed his fingers. Did nothing get past the gossips in this town?

"Few women would have found themselves in the same circumstance as Mrs. Tillman, Quinn. Besides, the marshal was there. I am sure he could have handled the situation without you."

For years, Quinn had stood before various disgruntled senior officers as they censured a soldier—sometimes, even him. And he had been one of those disgruntled officers enough times to know excuses and self-justification made things worse.

"First, you dine with the ladies at the café, then you rush to Mrs. Tillman's aid like a medieval knight defending the scullery maid. It has people talking."

His temper held in check by a resolve as fragile as a spider's silken thread, Quinn rose from the sofa. "I beg your pardon, sir, if my actions have reflected poorly upon you."

"You have integrity. I admire that. But I have been the lawyer for the Triple M Ranch for several years. I cannot afford to lose Royce's business because my associate supports his foe."

Quinn's anger dissolved. How could he have forgotten? No wonder Arthur came here upset. If Royce discontinued using Arthur's services, others in the area might follow, and Arthur's finances would suffer.

The older man sighed and slapped Quinn on the shoulder. "Let's consider this situation water under the bridge. I doubt anything will come of it, even though she could have driven the branded cattle back onto Triple M land."

He ambled to the front door and stopped. "Between you and me, Royce MacMahon is as hotheaded as his late father, but he's also a reasonable man. I am sure he has no wish to prosecute a woman. Given a few days to cool down, he will see reason."

"I hope you're right, sir."

But Quinn wasn't convinced. Royce wanted Laurel's land. To get it, would he go as far as seeing her imprisoned?

"He said he'd help, Momma. Jehoshaphat! Where is that man?"

"Rebecca."

With no intention of waiting for Quinn to appear—a first visit since the trouble on Monday—Laurel moved the old ladder to the front of the bunkhouse. Propping it against the edge of the roof, she wiggled it until the legs rested firm in the soil. She examined the rungs to be sure the dry wood still had the strength to hold a person's weight.

Becky slapped her hands against her thighs. "Well, Momma, half the morning's gone. If he don't get here soon, we'll be done." She shook her head in disgust. "Men. Can't never depend on 'em."

Laurel clamped her lips together to keep from smiling at her daughter's indignation. She would have to ask Issy to restrain her vocal opinions about the opposite gender when around Becky. The girl was too impressionable. As it was, Momma complained that Ernie's grammar had rubbed off on her granddaughter, even while Ernie's had improved.

"It's only nine o'clock, Becky. Mr. Hawkins hasn't delivered the shingles yet. We can't start until then."

Laurel's mother tugged on one of the girl's braids. "It could be Mr. Spencer has something else of importance to do. People's lives do not revolve around your desires, Miss Tillman."

"I know, Granmomma, but he promised."

Laurel had reached her limit with the conversation. She was already beholden to Quinn for his help on Monday and wasn't eager to add to her debt. "No, you assumed. Besides, we can fix this roof ourselves. Now that's an end to it."

Just as she could handle the MacMahons without Quinn? Thank goodness, her explanation of events had appeased her family. She hadn't wanted to worry them.

Turning at the rattle of a wagon approaching the house, Laurel dusted off her dirty hands. "Becky, fetch Issy from the barn. Tell her Mr. Hawkins is here."

"Yes, ma'am." The youngster took off at a run.

"Walk, please."

Becky skidded to a stop, kicking up a cloud of dirt. With her arms out to the side as though balancing on a fence rail, she dipped and exaggerated a refined walk.

Exasperated by her daughter's impertinence, Laurel shook her head. She'd reaped the oats she'd sown.

Mr. Hawkins turned the freight wagon so the back end faced the bunkhouse. He stopped the mules and set the brake before jumping to the ground. The man had the face of an owl and the stinginess of a squirrel. "Howdy, Miz Tillman."

Laurel peered into the loaded wagon bed filled with cedar shingles and fancy fence pickets cut from the evergreen shrubs growing wild throughout the area—pickets she hadn't ordered. "I see I'm not your only delivery this morning, Mr. Hawkins."

"I ain't a man to waste my time makin' more'n one trip in a day." He opened the gate on the wagon and removed a bundle of shingles. "Where do you want 'em?"

"Over there." Laurel pointed to the bunkhouse and dragged another bundle closer to the edge, preparing to lift it from the bed.

Hiram Hawkins scowled at her under his dusty and worn hat. "You let me get them things, Miz. I ain't never let a woman do my work, and I ain't gonna start today."

Laurel raised her hands and backed off. Even when men had nothing, they kept their pride.

"Morning, Mr. Hawkins." Issy reached for the bundle and lifted it from the bed, grunting as she did so.

"Now, Miz Issy—"

"Oh, don't swallow your chew. I can carry it." She staggered and dropped the shingles. They landed on the ground with a thud. "They're heavier than I expected them to be."

Ernie laughed and reached down for one end of the bundle. "You get the other side, Issy. I reckon we'd best wrestle it together."

Paying no heed to Mr. Hawkins' protestations, the two of them carried the bundle to the front of the bunkhouse. No doubt the incident would become fodder for more talk.

Finished unloading her order, he climbed up and onto the wagon bench. He glanced back at the bunkhouse. "You sure you don't need help fixin' that roof, Missus?"

"How hard can it be to replace a few shingles?"

"Humph." He released the brake, ready to move on to his next delivery. He reached into his pocket, withdrew an envelope, and handed it to Laurel. "Nearly forgot."

She turned the plain cream-colored envelope in her hand, suspicious of its contents. "Mr. Hawkins, if this is your bill, we agreed I would pay you next time I came to town."

"Yes, ma'am. That ain't mine. I found it tacked to the shop door this mornin' with a note to give it to you."

"Oh, I see. Thank you."

"But, now that you mention it, I wouldn't mind gettin' my money sooner'n later, especially since them MacMahons're het up to see you troubled."

Laurel saw no reason to defend herself yet again over Monday's incident. "You will get your money as we agreed. Thank you for the delivery, sir." She turned and headed toward the bunkhouse, leaving him no choice but to drive off without receiving a penny from her.

She tore open one end of the envelope, removed a folded sheet of paper, and read the contents. Her mouth dropped open. "Of all the sorry scoundrels . . ."

"Are you all right, dear? What is it?"

Refolding the paper and sliding it back into the envelope with shaky fingers, Laurel tried in vain to dampen the anger and disillusionment. "It's nothing important, Momma."

She jammed the envelope into the pocket of her trousers and pushed the matter from her mind. She would deal with Mr. Spencer's outrageous demand later.

CHAPTER FOURTEEN

When Becky put her foot on the ladder, Laurel grabbed her arm. "You have other chores to do."

"Aw, Momma."

"Scoot. Your first job is to check on Charlie and Pru."

"Pru sure misses her babies when she has to work."

Laurel hoped she had prepared Becky well enough for the upcoming sale of the five puppies scrambling around the temporarily caged area in the barn. "She'll get used to being away from them. Like the rest of us, Pru has to earn her keep."

Sheep dotted the acreage surrounding the yard, their bleats singing in the background. So they could take this day to make repairs around the yard, Laurel had ordered the animals brought closer. For the next few hours, she trusted Becky and the dogs to guard the flock and warn them of danger.

Laurel stacked shingles across her forearm while Issy climbed the ladder. Ernie followed, stopping halfway. "Here." Laurel reached up and handed the girl several shingles. Ernie handed them off to Issy.

Once the shingles from the first bundle rested on the roof, Ernie scaled the rest of the rungs. With her feet planted on the old wood, she twisted, her hands fisted on her hips. "It's sure purty up here."

"Please be careful, Ernie." Momma wiped her hands on her apron. "I'm afraid you'll fall."

"Don't worry." Laurel raised her voice to a near shout. "They both have heads harder than a hickory and twice as dense."

"I heard that." Issy peered over the eave and attempted an offended expression, but her lips broke into a grin. When Laurel stepped on the bottom rung of the ladder, Issy said, "You stay where you are. That stiff knee of yours can't climb ladders and hobble across a roof. We'll handle this job."

"She is right, Laurel." Camille walked down the steps leading from the kitchen door. "This is our dwelling. We can make the repairs."

She nodded. It was for the best. Walking a roofline required concentration, and Laurel battled to keep her mind off Quinn's disturbing correspondence.

"Fix only the section where the shingles are cracked and causing the leak. That'll do until I get the extra money to replace the rest of the roof. There are other repairs to be made."

"Here he comes!" Becky had climbed the wooden rails of the hog pen and perched at the top. She pointed to the drive.

Ernie looked toward the rutted lane, one hand shielding her eyes. "It's Mr. Spencer all right."

He rode the mare up to the porch of the house and greeted the rooftop chorus of hellos with his own, "Good morning, ladies."

Laurel's fist crushed the paper in her pocket. The man had the gall to show up this morning. Well, she would see that the others learned what kind of scalawag they had befriended.

She waited for him to dismount before she pounced. "You have more nerve than a carpetbagger, Mr. Spencer."

He wrapped the reins around the porch rail, keeping his back to her. "What is it now, Laurel?"

His calm and innocent demeanor sent her temper soaring higher. "You know the problem full well." She jerked the envelope free of her pocket and shoved it at his chest. "I don't remember hiring you.

But I do remember you telling Marshal Ruiz you were assisting me as a friend."

Quinn took the envelope and removed the paper inside. His eyes narrowed and his lips formed a tight line as he read the notice. "This is a mistake."

"To me, it looks like a bill for the services of a Mr. Quinn Spencer, Attorney. You are that man, are you not?"

"I didn't prepare this bill."

"Gracious me. How could I have been wrong?" The sarcasm oozed through her parted lips. It wasn't the money. Well, yes, it was the money. Cash didn't grow on the cypress branches along the creeks. He claimed to help her as a friend. Friends didn't expect repayment. "It seems your acquaintance comes at a price."

She moved to snatch the bill from his hand, but he jerked the paper from her reach. "Where did you get this?"

The others circled around them, invested in the conversation. That was what Laurel had wanted, wasn't it? But Quinn's tight expression gave her pause. Had he told the truth about the bill? "Mr. Hawkins found it tacked to his door this morning and brought it with the delivery of the shingles. Why not bring it yourself?"

He glanced at each of the women and girls gathered around, their eyes circles of concern. Becky stood on the porch and peered over his shoulder. Off and on, her lips moved as she read the words on the bill. Quinn refolded the paper, and Becky frowned.

"Mrs. Chamberlain, will you bring me a pen and ink, please?"

Her mother sought Laurel's approval. Unwilling to ask why he needed the writing instrument, she said, "Go ahead, Momma."

Laurel wanted to look away but refused to break eye contact with Quinn. They waited in silence. When her mother returned, he took the pen and dipped the nib into the ink bottle. He unfolded the paper, wrote something on it, and gave the pen and bottle back to Momma. Quinn blew the ink dry before handing the bill to Laurel. "This settles the matter."

Her eyes widened at reading the three added words, "Paid in full."

She searched his face, her mouth incapable of asking the question that raced through her mind. Why? Why would he send her a bill, then mark it paid without receiving a nickel?

"I told you, Laurel. This didn't come from me. I still owe you more than it's possible to repay. You saved my life." He patted the neck of his horse. "And you saved Ruthie's."

The world around Laurel went still as she sought to read this man whose candid stare jumbled her senses. "You owe me nothing."

For the first time in years, Laurel could say those words to a Yankee—and mean them.

Quinn slid a shingle into place after removing the old wood from a four-by-six-foot section. While hammering the slat to the lath, he mimicked Laurel's description of the roof's problems, exaggerating her southern drawl. "'Two *tiny* places leak. They're the only ones in need of fixing. Then the entire roof will be fit as a fiddle.'"

Delusional woman. She would resolve the worst of the leaks, but the bunkhouse would drip until she replaced all the shingles.

After examining the areas to be repaired, he had chased the other helpers from the roof. "The more walking done on these shingles, the more chance for damage. Climb down and let me take care of this."

Camille descended the ladder without a word. Issy insisted she could do the task every bit as good as a man. Fortunately, Ernie tugged on her shirt sleeve, encouraging her to the edge and down the ladder. Quinn was in no mood to argue with one more person.

Arthur's visit to the boarding house nailed down—as tight as these new slats—the fact that it was not in Quinn's best interest to take on Laurel's case, if there was one. Quinn had tiptoed around the office the rest of the week, avoiding the topic of what Arthur considered an unethical and professional mistake.

Quinn set a nail in place and raised the hammer, careful to control his frustration. He used enough force to drive the nail into the wood, but not enough to crack it.

The lawyer in him insisted on speaking with Marshal Ruiz about his progress in finding Reg Ferrell. The practical person inside advised him to mind his own business, which he had done. After all, as Laurel proclaimed, she had not hired him. The bill Arthur sent by Hiram Hawkins tempted him to change his mind about representing her. The action, taken behind his back, left a bad taste in Quinn's mouth that the lemonade served to him before starting work hadn't washed away.

After installing a row of fresh shingles, he turned in time to see Becky peep over the edge of the roof. Would her mother approve of her being so high off the ground? He couldn't pinpoint what had caused Laurel to turn from a wasp into a warbler, but the gentle breeze had carried her singing to his ears several times while he had been on the roof. He wouldn't rush to get on her bad side again so soon.

"Climb down, Becky."

"What's it like to be on top of the world?"

Chuckling, he pounded another nail that joined the shingle to the lath underneath. "This isn't the top of the world."

In fact, the pitch of the low gabled roof was a gentle slope. She would see more of the world from the crest of the hill behind the house. Still, he had no time to worry about the girl's safety. "Go on now." He turned away from the downward slant of her mouth and protruding lower lip. Was it a Tillman family trait to whip up guilt in those they met?

"But I want to help you."

Stubborn as her mother. "No."

He should have been honest when faced with Becky's invitation. Knowing the girl had expected him to put in an appearance at La Casa del Fuego this morning, Quinn had risen undecided, surly, and without an appetite for Mrs. Dillard's johnnycakes. The incident with Lillian last Saturday sidetracked him from saying no to Becky, but he should have told her on Monday.

Once upon a time, he had charged Confederate bullets and the weapons of the Comanche with lauded courage. Nowadays, he worried more about his reputation. What did dreading the disillusionment of a nine-year-old mean?

"Verily I say unto you, Inasmuch as ye have done it unto one the least of these my brethren, ye have done it unto me."

Christ's words from the book of Matthew had repeated in Quinn's mind all the while he wrote letters and filed paperwork early that morning. Before he'd finished, he slammed the desk drawer shut and walked out of the office.

"Granmomma sent me to tell you to come eat." She started down the ladder, her small feet stomping the rungs in a fit of Tillman temper.

She had no father, and for some inexplicable reason, she looked up to him. With one curt word, he may have changed that.

In the years since Amy's death, he hadn't given thought to children—anyone's children. But this towheaded girl with freckles across her nose and a few crooked teeth had attached herself to his core like a snail to a leaf.

"Becky."

Braided hair, parted in the center, rose above the edge of the roof. Then he saw a sun-browned forehead and a pair of eyes the shade of a watermelon skin. "Yes, sir?"

"Once I'm finished, I'll bring you up for a few minutes to see the world . . . if your mother approves."

Those green eyes sparkled, and her cheeks rose until she resembled a chipmunk with both sides of its mouth packed full of seeds. She nodded. "Thanks, Mr. Spencer. I'll tell Granmomma you're coming as soon as you wash."

"You do that."

Quinn laughed as she raced across the yard to the kitchen door. She almost ran into her mother when Laurel limped down the steps carrying a bowl and wearing her blue dress. "Careful, Peanut."

"Sorry, Momma."

Had Laurel ever faced life with the same enthusiasm as her daughter?

"Oh Momma, Mr. Spencer says he'll take me up on the roof later, if it's all right with you. Please, Momma? Pleeease."

Laurel glanced over her shoulder, catching Quinn's gaze. He expected to hear the same "no" he had given Becky, but she just shrugged. "As long as you obey Mr. Spencer and don't do something foolish, I have no objection."

"I will. I mean I won't. I mean . . ."

Laughing, Laurel patted the top of Becky's head and walked away. Quinn sat still, soaking up the prolonged mirth, devoid of its usual trace of mockery. The pleasant sound washed over him, leaving him wishing to hear more of it in the future.

Quilts and blankets spread on the grass under a tree behind the house became their table and chairs. The center contained a platter mounded with fried chicken, as well as bowls of pinto beans and turnips, and plates of pickles and sliced bread.

After washing at the well, Quinn settled on a corner of a bright, multi-colored quilt. Camille sat on one side and Mrs. Chamberlain on the other.

"It's been years since I've enjoyed a picnic," he said.

Camille passed him the bowl holding Ellen Chamberlain's pickles. "We are happy to have you join us, Quinn."

Catching Laurel's soft gaze on him, he felt the first warm welcome he'd received from her, and he thanked God for prodding him to come here today.

The women's conversations rattled on, and he marveled at the bond they had formed—a bond of trust and respect. He envied them that connection. His last close friend had been Henry Bruner. And that hadn't ended well.

Quinn swallowed the last bite of sweet potato pie as the women around him rose like a flock of blackbirds to clear away the food and dishes.

"No, Momma. You cooked." With a hand on her mother's shoulder,

Laurel eased her back down on the blanket. "We'll clean up."

"You remain seated also, Quinn." Camille smiled down at him. "Have more tea and keep Ellen company. There is plenty of time to finish the roof."

Left alone with Mrs. Chamberlain, they sat in awkward silence for several moments until it occurred to Quinn that women enjoyed talking about their families. "Becky is a lively little girl."

"Yes. She is very much like her mother."

The physical resemblance between the younger woman and her daughter was evident, as was the occasional defiant trait, but he couldn't keep his mouth from asking, "How so?"

Ellen Chamberlain's broad smile removed the strain from her appearance. Quinn glimpsed strength and familial pride in the lifting of her chin and the glow in her eyes.

"Like Becky, Laurel had an undeniable curiosity about everything around her. When she was young, she followed her brother everywhere and drove me mad with her need to do all the things Lance did. They played together, read books to one another, defended each other against all threats. They were inseparable."

Quinn caught the note of sadness in the last statement. "Where is your son now?"

She glanced toward the house before leaning closer. "He died . . . the war." She didn't wait to hear Quinn's expression of regret. "They were twins, you know. Twins are closer than most siblings and mine were no exception. Lance was more serious, but, oh, how my girl could make him laugh. Hardly an hour went by that we didn't hear their laughter throughout the house, just as we do Becky's.

"And dance. As a girl, she danced until she wore blisters on her feet. Young men stood in line, waiting for their turns to escort her across the floor. All her friends were envious because she had the choice of any eligible lad in town." She lowered her eyes. "You must think me nothing but a doting mother. But she was a true delight. Many said so."

"I'm sure she entranced everyone." Before hearing Laurel's laughter and seeing the more carefree side to her personality this day, Quinn would have considered his comment a polite lie.

The woman grew somber. "Lance's death changed everything—for both of us. And then John and my grandson died. Now she rarely laughs, and it breaks my heart. As for dancing . . ."

Quinn didn't need to hear the rest. He could finish the sentence himself. Laurel's dancing days ended with whatever injury she had suffered. Her husband, her son, her beloved brother and father, her ability to move in a normal manner—to dance . . .

How fortunate he felt to have enjoyed the rare sound of her laughter at various times that afternoon.

Quinn put forth a question that he feared bordered on excessive curiosity. "May I ask how Laurel injured her leg?"

Like a threatened turtle, Ellen Chamberlain shrank back into her shell of uncertainty. "I should go inside."

He rose and helped her to her feet. "I shouldn't have pried. It isn't my concern."

Squeezing his hand, she gave him a timid smile, her brown eyes glassy. "I have prayed for years that God would send someone who understands what my daughter has faced. Someone to help her see that He longs to forgive all those who seek that forgiveness, no matter what they have done. From the day we met, Quinn, I have believed in the pit of my soul that you were that person." She released his hand and walked to the house.

Quinn climbed the ladder, the perplexing conversation rolling around in his mind until he missed a rung and slipped. He caught himself before falling to the ground. Why would Mrs. Chamberlain think God had sent him as an answer to her prayers? He didn't know what Laurel had faced.

Balanced on the roof, he picked up the hammer and grabbed a new shingle. Was that his purpose for being here? To lead Laurel to God's forgiveness for whatever sin plagued her? Why him?

Laurel stood under the tree's canopy, shaking out then refolding a quilt. Carrying it up the hill behind the house, she disappeared over the crest—over the top of the world. Quinn set the next shingle in place.

Leading her to God's forgiveness seemed an impossible task. She retreated from him at every turn.

How can You expect me to help her, Lord, when I don't know her burden?

CHAPTER FIFTEEN

"Watch for scorpions. They like to hide in dark corners." Laurel reached up with the broom and handed it off to Ernie, who stood on the loft floor and sneezed. "Those rafters have collected cobwebs for years. Open the loft doors for fresh air."

"Yes'm." Broom in hand, Ernie edged along the haystack to reach the small double doors.

Hooves pounded the dry earth. Laurel stepped outside and crossed her arms as both MacMahon brothers stopped their horses within ten feet of her. "What are you doing here?"

"I see you're unarmed today."

Royce's leer sent a shiver of apprehension skittering through Laurel. Too aware that she and Ernie were alone at the ranch house, she cursed herself for leaving the carbine in its rack above the fireplace.

"You have no worries from me, Laurel. Not when you look so . . . earthy."

His ridicule left her wanting to hide in a dark corner of the barn with the scorpions. They would be safer company.

A desire gnawed at Laurel—a desire to be seen as she once was, genteel and dressed in frills, rather than as she had become, hard and

132

unadorned.

She gritted her teeth with the reminder that dealing with people like the MacMahons didn't allow her to soften.

Not much irritated Royce more than being ignored, so Laurel turned her attention to his brother. "What do you want here, Murphy?"

"We came—"

Royce moved his horse closer. "I want reimbursement for the cattle you killed."

I, not *we*. How long would Murphy allow his brother to run roughshod over him? Royce treated him no better than a hired hand.

"Marshal Ruiz may not think he has enough evidence to see you jailed yet, but I know you destroyed my property." Royce leaned forward in the saddle. "I want twenty dollars a head for those cattle you shot. In case you can't multiply, at six head, that's one hundred and twenty dollars that I'm losing in Dodge City."

"Don't bluff me. Dodge was overrun with cattle this summer and nobody's getting twenty dollars a head. You'd be fortunate to get half that amount." She forced laughter from deep in her throat. "I won't pay you a cent."

His answer began with a malicious grin. "You took your hatred for the MacMahons out on my property."

"I don't hate you. Momma always said I shouldn't hate." When had that stopped her? "But I see nothing wrong with comparing you to a long-tailed rodent."

Laurel glanced at Murphy, who sat in the saddle staring at the horn as though he'd seen it jump. His lips twitched. She turned her attention back to Royce.

His eyes narrowed. "My lawyer assures me I can hold you liable."

Lawyer? He had consulted Arthur Bruner? Or had Quinn advised him to go for the money? Not after Saturday, surely. Not after what he'd said about how much he owed her. But perhaps . . . No. He would not turn on her that way. At least, she hoped not.

"I didn't shoot your cattle. A stranger named Reg Ferrell did. Go get your money from him."

"Ferrell left town on Monday morning. He makes a convenient scapegoat, though, doesn't he? You have until the end of the year to pay for those cattle, Laurel. I'm being generous by giving you almost eight weeks."

"Or what?"

"Or I'll sue you." He twisted in the saddle, glancing in all directions. Sizing up future holdings? He turned back to her. "Are you willing to risk this place becoming mine?"

Sick to her stomach and sick of him, she waved her hand through the air as if brushing away an annoying pest. "Get off my land, Royce."

A shrill cry and a loud thump echoed from the barn. Laurel whipped around. "Ernie?"

She moved as fast as her rigid leg would allow and ran into the barn. Sprawled on the dirt floor, the girl groaned and attempted to sit.

Laurel bent. Using her hands for balance, she went down on her left knee. The stiffer right leg angled out to the side. Sliding an arm behind Ernie's back, she eased her upright. "What happened?"

"I-I fell off the loft." She cradled her left hand with her right and drew in a sob. "I reckon it broke."

"Let me see." Murphy knelt in the dirt on the other side of Ernie. With care, he grasped the injured arm.

"Let's go, Murph. I don't have time for you to play doctor." Royce's dark and massive form blocked much of the barn's doorway.

With a gentle touch, Murphy probed Ernie's wrist. His caring expression softened the usual hard lines—an expression she remembered her father using while attending the sick. So familiar.

"Can you wiggle your fingers for me?" He nodded when they moved like the girl played a slow tune on a piano. "That's good."

"Murphy, I won't tell you again. She's fine. Now get a move on. We've got work to do."

Sighing, the young man looked up. "You go on, Royce. I'll be along in a minute."

"Make your choice, brother."

Murphy rose with his back to Laurel, his unyielding stance opposing Royce's ominous order. She held her breath as the two of them squared off. This would be the moment Murphy would stand up and become the man she suspected longed to be freed from his brother's rule. The two men stared at one another. Even Ernie, in her pain, remained still and silent.

Then Murphy's shoulders slumped. He looked down at Laurel, a whipped mongrel satisfied with the scraps left him by a bigger beast. If he had a tail, he would have tucked it between his legs. "It's only a sprain. Try to reduce the swelling and wrap it. She'll be fine in a few days."

Laurel turned away, unwilling to add to his shame by letting him see her disappointment. "I'm obliged to you, Murphy. Go on and get out of here."

She had hoped his honesty and defense of her that day at the jailhouse meant he had grown a backbone. Even though he hadn't shown it today, Laurel suspected that one day Murphy would turn on his brother for good. She hoped to be there when he did.

"Is he really gone?"

Laurel removed her hand from the crank of the butter churn and glanced at Ernie's shadowy outline. Those were the first words the girl had spoken all evening. Sitting on the porch steps, Ernie stared off into the darkness with her injured arm supported by a white sling made of old sheet linen that glowed in the moonlight.

Upon returning from taking Becky fishing in the creek, Momma had agreed with Murphy's diagnosis that it was only a sprain. She had applied a hot, wet bandage to reduce the swelling and wrapped the girl's wrist. Other than being spoiled for the next week, Ernie would be none the worse for wear.

"Is who gone?"

"The man that shot them cattle. Reg Ferrell."

Laurel noted the slight tremor in Ernie's voice when she said the man's name. "So I've been told. Why do you ask?"

Ernie played with the skirt folds of the green calico dress Camille had made for her. "No reason, but I hope so."

Marshal Ruiz had assured Quinn he still sought the man. So far, though, Ferrell had left no trace as to his whereabouts. Laurel remained vulnerable to arrest, or at the least, Royce's lawsuit. She could lose everything, including her freedom. The MacMahon brothers' visit had sent her to the porch after dinner to churn away the worry.

"If he isn't found, I have no way to prove I didn't shoot the Triple M cattle."

A gasp rose over the chirping of crickets. "It's all my fault. I can't let that happen to you, Miz Tillman."

"Why would you think this situation is your fault, Ernie? You didn't shoot those cattle, so I'm afraid there's nothing you can do to change things."

Ernie hung her head. "I'm not so sure, ma'am."

Silence streamed between them as Laurel waited for Ernie to open up. Something had bothered the girl for over a week. She was jumpy as a toad, afraid to be alone or leave the ranch. If she didn't speak soon—

"I know Ferrell."

A rush of foreboding flowed through Laurel and sped the thumping of her heart until it pained her. "What do you mean?"

Silence.

Laurel moved from her chair to the steps. She cupped Ernie's damp cheeks in both hands and turned the girl's face toward hers, then let go. "Ernaline?"

"You recollect me talkin' about Virgil Hicks? How he wanted me to marry him?"

How could she ever forget the man who forced Ernie to run away from her home? "Yes."

"Virgil musta sent Reg Ferrell to find me. If he caught wind I'm h-here..." Her voice broke on a sob.

Laurel tented her hands against her lips and thought about the incident in the café. The man sat next to them the whole time they were eating. Had they mentioned Ernie by name? She didn't think so. She shut her eyes and tried to recall the scene.

At Lillian's gaffe, his eyes had blazed and his words scraped across a tongue sharp as a razor. What else happened? They continued their conversation and . . . Laurel groaned.

"Miz Tillman, you all right?"

She wrapped her fingers around Ernie's cold, uninjured hand. "I know how he discovered you were here. We mentioned your name at the café, Ernie. I'm sorry."

The girl pulled her hand free and wiped away the tears dripping from her chin. "It isn't your fault, ma'am. I should've told you before about him."

"That's why you wanted to leave, wasn't it? You feared he would find you."

She nodded. "That and I didn't want no one hurt. I knew him as soon as Becky spoke of that mark on his face."

"And today in the loft, after I mentioned his name to the MacMahons, you fell soon after."

Ernie frowned at the bandaged wrist. "Just hearin' the name again sent the shivers trottin' through me. I ran for the ladder, but I reckon I missed the top step. H-he's meaner'n a mad dog, Miz Tillman. Please don't let him get me."

"He can't take you anywhere you don't want to go, Ernie. I'll tell the others about this. From now on, someone will always be near to see to your safety. And Virgil Hicks has no hold on you, either."

"I reckon he does, ma'am. My ma owed him money when she passed. He made me work in his store to pay the debt. He fed me and gave me a bed in the back room. At first, I was obliged for his help, thinking he was being kind." Ernie tucked a strand of hair behind her ear. "Then I found out he kept one o' them account books and wrote down what he said I owed for my food and the room. It was almost as much as he paid me."

Laurel struggled to control her outrage against a man who took advantage of a helpless and grieving girl.

"Then he started comin' downstairs at night. He scared me, Miz Tillman. Virgil Hicks don't take to hearin' the word no from nobody, leastwise, someone like me. But he started puttin' his hands on me and sayin' the only way to pay what I owed was to marry him. I hightailed it out of town."

"Marry him? Why pick you, Ernie? There must be women closer to his age in that town you're from." And why marry the child when he could overpower her and take what he wanted?

"Weren't many without a man and he wanted . . . he . . ." She paused, finding something interesting about a strand of hair on her sleeve. She raised her head. "He wanted young'uns … red-headed ones, Miz Tillman. Said his ma had red hair. Don't—Doesn't that make him crazier than a loon?"

Laurel managed a weak nod. "Sounds like it."

"He can't make me marry up with him 'cause I owe him money, can he?"

"Of course not." Laurel attempted a smile that she knew fell short of reassuring either of them. At least now she understood Ferrell being on her property. But why shoot the Longhorns? How did that help him return Ernie to Arkansas?

"Everything will work out. Go on to the bunkhouse and get some sleep. Rest is the best thing to heal that wrist."

"Yes'm." She rose from the porch step. After reaching the ground, Ernie turned back to give Laurel a one-armed hug. "Even when Ma was sick abed, she prayed the Lord Almighty would lead me straight to a new home. Ain't it wonderful how He works? G'night, ma'am." Ernie trotted to the bunkhouse, looking from right to left in the darkness.

Alone, Laurel raised her gaze to the stars twinkling like laughing eyes. "If this is your doing, God, what made You pick someone like me to be responsible for that girl?"

CHAPTER SIXTEEN

"Why didn't you tell us about the trouble you had with those brothers, Laurel?" Momma flipped the eggs in the skillet. The spatula in her hand trembled, but not from fear. Momma was madder than a wet hen. Madder than Laurel had seen her since Lance stole an apple from a street vendor back home. "You led us to believe you were a witness to the shootings. You said nothing about being a suspect. I don't like this one bit. What if they threaten you again?"

The smell of bacon grease and fresh coffee made the world right no matter what bedlam whipped around Laurel. She set forks at the six places around the table. "I didn't want to worry anyone. I only tell you now for Ernie's sake. I doubt there's any danger from them or the law. And Royce will not risk his precious reputation by injuring a woman."

He might not touch her, personally, but he hadn't stopped his hired men from doing so the day of the shooting. She had hidden the bruises they inflicted on her arms, intending that her family never learn of the men's rough treatment. She only told them now because Ernie had witnessed the argument yesterday. The news of her predicament should come from no one's lips but hers.

"That no-account Murphy. He knows dang well you didn't shoot Royce's stupid cattle." Issy knocked over the saltshaker on the table. The crystals scattered and blended into the white of the tablecloth. She began brushing them away. "Given the situation, though, don't you think you should tell Marshal Ruiz about their visit and this Ferrell fella's connection to Ernie?"

Camille shoved the breakfast plates at Issy's middle. "You should also tell Quinn."

"We don't need to consult Quinn Spencer at every turn." Laurel wrapped the handle of the coffee pot with a towel and carried it to the table.

"Do not be stubborn. He is the one who made certain you could come home. His interest in your plight prodded him to accompany the marshal to the place of slaughter. Why would you resist seeking his advice now?"

Why, indeed? Because she wasn't ready to let him claim further influence on her life. He had inserted himself into her affairs and her thoughts too often in the last weeks. And she had succumbed to placing more trust in him than made her comfortable.

And why did Camille persist in bringing him into the discussion? While Laurel poured the coffee, a mirthless chuckle escaped at the answer—an answer that caused an unexpected twitch in the pit of her stomach. If Camille was interested in Quinn, of course she would want to drag him into this problem.

"Laurel, this isn't only about you." Issy jerked her head, gesturing toward Ernie, seated in a corner of the kitchen, her feet tapping on the floor planks.

"You can't tell the lawman." Worry etched Ernie's youthful face with the lines of an older woman, lines that matched the ones Laurel had seen in her own mirror that morning.

"Why not, Ernie?"

"Cause he'll arrest me. I run away without paying Virgil what I owed."

Camille set a dish with bacon on the table and wiped her hands on her apron. "How much did your mother owe Mr. Hicks, Ernie?"

"Near fifteen dollars."

"How long did you work for him?"

"Six months."

"Six months?" Issy fell into the chair next to the young girl. "I'd say you only owe that skunk a spit in the face."

"But the law'll arrest me or send me back."

"No one will send you back, Ernie." Laurel set the coffee pot on the stove and tossed the towel on the counter. "This has to stop. I'll ride into town and talk to Marshal Ruiz today."

"And Quinn."

No, Camille. Not Quinn.

"Why, Mr. Spencer, I almost didn't recognize you without your beard." Mrs. Weaver set her basket on the mercantile counter and swished her way to his side. She examined his right profile as if appraising a marble sculpture. "Why you men desire to hide your good looks from those who appreciate them, I will never comprehend. I can assure you, Mary would agree." She elbowed him in the side. "If you understand my meaning."

He could be an earthworm and understand her meaning. Over the years, that predatory look had lit the eyes of more than one mother hungry to feed him to her unattached hatchling. The trickiest ones to escape had been the wives and offspring of his commanding officers. Somehow, he had fended them off while still preserving, not only a congenial relationship among the mothers and daughters, but his rank. Many a colonel respected his general but feared his Mrs. Colonel. Quinn hoped to be as fortunate in evading the plans of the banker's wife.

For once, the local gossip mill worked in his favor and allowed him to change the subject. "How was your trip to San Antonio, Mrs. Weaver?"

"Lovely. Just lovely." She slapped her hands together. "Oh, you should have seen my Sylvia. There will never be a more beautiful bride." As though realizing her mistake, she elbowed him again, her laugh shrill. "Except for Mary. Only she can give her sister competition, of course."

"Of course." Though she might one day make a passable bride, he'd heard it was Mary Weaver's withdrawn personality that sent Bold Creek's few eligible males on a run in the opposite direction.

"Mr. Weaver and I are having a small supper party on Saturday evening at seven. Nothing fancy, mind you, just a gathering of like-minded people, if you understand my meaning. Alfred and I would be pleased to have you join us."

Quinn searched for an excuse to avoid the trap being laid for him. He found none. Though feeling no responsibility toward making either Mrs. Weaver or Mary happy, he didn't want to upset Arthur, who represented Alfred Weaver and his bank in legal matters. "The pleasure will be mine, Mrs. Weaver. Thank you for the invitation."

"You're most welcome, Mr. Spencer. I am sure a bachelor like you craves a delicious meal now and again. My Mary makes mouthwatering rhubarb pies. Her homemaking skills are excellent."

"Yes, ma'am." Mrs. Dillard's meals were top-notch, and he felt no need for his own homemaker.

"I will see you and Mr. Weaver on Saturday, ma'am." Putting an end to the discussion, Quinn turned and smiled.

She pressed a hand to her cheek. "Oh my. Where did you get that scar?"

Without thinking, he ran his fingers over the three-inch, pinkish line of skin along his left jaw—the reason he had grown the beard. It seems his reasoning had been justified. But he refused to let the rude comment goad him into growing it again. "In defense of the Union, madam."

Quinn stalked toward the door, his way blocked by three farmers gathered in the center of the mercantile.

"I tell you he set my teeth on edge, and it weren't that mark on his face, neither."

"Heard Jessup threw him out of the café a while back and he left town. What'd he want with you?"

Quinn stopped and picked up a can of milk from the nearest shelf, pretending to read the label while listening.

"Wanted to know who sold the best horses in these parts. I tell you, when that no-good looked at me mean-like, Rolf, I raised my shotgun a bit."

Quinn expected to hear the straps snap on the proud farmer's overalls. He set the can back on the shelf and addressed the man in the stiff and faded clothing. "Pete, is it?"

The farmer's eyes reflected his suspicion. "Yep."

"My name is Quinn Spencer. I couldn't help but overhear your discussion."

"For someone who couldn't help but overhear, you sure was takin' your time readin' that can, mister."

Heat spread up the back of Quinn's neck. He grinned to break the tension. "I apologize, but your conversation piqued my interest."

The second, unnamed farmer, pointed in his direction. "He's the one got in the tussle with the fella at the café."

"The man's name is Reg Ferrell. Are you aware that Marshal Ruiz is looking for him?"

Pete crossed his arms. The sun-browned creases around his eyes deepened. "Why arrest him for insultin' a woman?"

"He's a wanted man?" Rolf's eyes widened.

Quinn shook his head. "The marshal wants to talk to him regarding a different matter. When did you see him?"

"Yesterday afternoon."

Yesterday? Ferrell was still in the area when they had assumed he left three weeks ago? "Did he say where to find him or which way he intended to travel?"

"Can't remember." Pete scratched the back of his head, cocking his dirty hat forward. Then, he pointed a crooked index finger in the air. "No, wait. He said somethin' about needin' the horse for a trip he planned to take soon's he got paid."

"He works around Bold Creek?"

Pete shrugged. "Didn't ask."

"When he left your place, which way did he go?"

"Reckon he went to the Triple M."

The pulse in Quinn's neck throbbed. "Why do you say that?"

"Cause that's where I told him to go. Murphy raises good mounts. When I pointed out the direction, he said he already knew how to get to the place."

Quinn paused, stunned that his suspicions about the rancher stood on the verge of being verified. He shook the farmer's hand again, with more vigor this time. "Thank you, sir. I'll make the marshal aware of Mr. Ferrell's visit to you. He may have more questions."

He stepped outside, the autumn sun warmed his face and hands, and the good news directed his course. So Ferrell expected pay for a job and knew the way to the Triple M. He hummed all the way down the boardwalk.

Royce MacMahon must know Ferrell. And the question to be answered? Did Royce *owe* Ferrell?

He crossed the street and entered the marshal's office. The door clattered shut behind him. The lawman sat with his feet propped on top of the desk, muffins and coffee nearby. He crossed his arms over his lean abdomen and stared at Quinn with an expression of foreboding.

"Marshal Ruiz, I need to talk to you."

"Mornin' to you too, Spencer." He motioned to the chair opposite the desk.

"Good morning." Grinning, Quinn sat in the hard seat Laurel had occupied the day of the cattle shootings. "Reg Ferrell is still in the area."

Marshal Ruiz straightened in his chair, his sharp gaze never leaving Quinn's face. "Where'd you see him?"

"I didn't." When the marshal blew out a frustrated breath, Quinn told of meeting a farmer named Pete in the mercantile. "I think we should ride out and talk to Royce MacMahon."

"You mean *I* should ride out and talk to him." Ruiz stood and stretched, groaning as he did so. His grimace at the half-eaten muffin spoke of an unfulfilled longing. He grunted and grabbed his hat off a peg and belted a holstered Colt around his middle. "Tell me, Spencer, did Mrs. Tillman ever hire you to represent her?"

Quinn hesitated before replying, suspecting his answer would prohibit him from accompanying the marshal this time. "No."

"Then I'll consider you an interested citizen, and I don't take citizens on investigations."

Biting his tongue, Quinn considered it best not to remind the marshal that he had gone along to investigate the site of the cattle shootings.

"Marshal, why six head?"

"What?"

"I believe the MacMahons hired Ferrell to kill the cattle and lay the blame on Laurel."

"Losing six steers isn't like losing six sticks of penny candy. If what you're suggesting happened, Royce could have saved himself some money by only killing one."

"But it wouldn't raise the outrage against her."

The marshal opened the door. "Evidence, Mr. Spencer. Evidence."

Quinn trudged back to his office above the bakery, rolling the last thirty minutes through his mind. Ruiz hadn't been as impressed as he had hoped. Maybe his efforts were a waste of time and he shouldn't become further involved. So far, Laurel's problems had been trouble for him.

He should give his time to someone suitable for marriage, such as the mayor's daughter or the seamstress, May Simpson, or heaven forbid, Mary Weaver. Camille Arneau's lovely features should make him want to ignore everyone's warning and call on her, but they didn't.

Instead, he dwelled on Laurel's courage when facing down the MacMahons, that misplaced, stubborn determination to prove herself capable, and the strength of devotion to those under her care. He saw her trudge up the hill and disappear over the other side like a specter, heard her mother speak of a past spent laughing and dancing and attracting beaux.

He had allowed a precocious nine-year-old imp to steal her way into his affections, but it was her mother who stole every spare thought.

Quinn closed his office door behind him and drifted over to the window, knowing he would continue to search for the proof that Laurel did not shoot the Triple M cattle. Then what?

He looked down on the town. Then he would leave Bold Creek and get on with achieving his original goals.

CHAPTER SEVENTEEN

Laurel dismounted in front of the marshal's office and tied the buckskin's reins to the porch column. She patted the gelding's neck, his mottled coat growing thicker with the approach of colder weather. "I'll be back soon."

She climbed the same two steps MacMahon's men had shoved her up three weeks ago and opened the door to the marshal's office. The aroma inside enveloped her with the smell of home—coffee from the pot on the little stove and the sweetness of pastry. She touched the side of the tin cup sitting on the desk . . . a tick shy of being cold. A half-eaten apple muffin sat beside it and a whole one nearby.

"Marshal?" With no answer, she called out again. "Marshal Ruiz? I need to talk to you."

The only sound was the creaking of the floorboards when she limped toward the doorway leading to the jail cells. She poked her head inside that section of the building. "Anyone here?" Two vacant cells testified to the emptiness.

Laurel waited in the chair near the desk. She had not ridden seven miles to miss the marshal because he stepped out for a few moments to stroll through town, gossip with store owners, or visit the privy out back.

When he didn't return after ten minutes, she left to look for him, leading her horse down the dusty street. Laurel squinted at the businesses on each side of town, peering into the windows as best she could for a glimpse of the lawman. She walked the boardwalks, then stood in front of the café with her hands on her hips. "Well, boy, I can't find him. There's no sense wasting more time if he isn't even in town." The buckskin nudged her from behind with his head, pushing her forward. She turned and rubbed the spot between his eyes with her knuckles. "You ready to go home?"

Preparing to mount, her gaze strayed to the second floor above the bakery and to the window in Quinn's office. She barely saw the back of his dark head.

Like a sorcerer, the lawyer drew her across the street, her feet moving at their own will. She tied the horse to the post in front of the bakery and climbed the stairs, pausing at the top. She was about to give Quinn permission to get more involved in her life. That wasn't what she wanted. Was it?

Quinn dipped the pen in the inkwell and held it over the cream-colored paper. What had he planned to write? He stared at the blank sheet on the desk, willing the words to appear like magic. *Come, man, you're too young for such absentmindedness.*

But it wasn't age that made him forgetful. Ever since learning that Reg Ferrell remained in the area, the question of why burdened him. Why not ride on? Why did he need an extra horse? He tossed the pen onto the desk, asking himself who planned to pay Ferrell. The MacMahons? No one could answer his questions until they found the stranger.

The slight *tip-tap, tip-tap* from the other side of the door snatched his reverie. He recognized the echo of Laurel's limp on hardwood. As he opened the door to his office, she whirled around and started toward the stairs.

She wouldn't venture into town for a social visit dressed in trousers. For her to have come to see him, something must have happened. So why leave without speaking to him?

"Laurel?"

She stopped on the first step. Her shoulders rose and fell with the release of a sigh. "Hello, Quinn."

"Is everything all right?"

She turned as if weighed down with lead-filled pockets. She raised her chin and formed a smile. "If you have a moment, I . . ." The words faded while those green orbs grew large and her mouth went slack. She blinked. One. Two. Three times. "Your beard."

He rubbed his clean-shaven cheek. "It must be a shock to see me without the whiskers. I've meant to do this for a while."

Laurel stood at the top of the stairs. Her chest heaved to draw in a breath, and her stare never left his face. She craned her neck left, then right, searching with a keen intensity. An emotion akin to panic flashed in her eyes, and she backed away until her boots hit the wall with a thump.

For the second time that morning, Quinn covered the scar with his fingers. It might be unattractive, but seeing his face shouldn't cause her sheer terror. But terror was what he noted in Laurel's wide eyes as her mouth opened in a silent scream. He would never have expected her to respond with fear and abhorrence over something as trivial as a facial blemish.

"I am not so repulsive." The icy rumble surprised him. Why should he care how she saw him?

She pushed away from the wall, ready to bolt like a deer caught in the crosshairs of a rifle scope.

Arthur's office door opened, and he stepped into the vestibule. He glanced back and forth between them, a frown pinching his lips, then stepped over to Laurel. "I thought I heard voices out here. Good morning, Mrs. Tillman."

She focused on his extended hand and clamped it tight with her own, like a mooring line anchoring a boat to the dock. One that secured her courage? Arthur winced.

"G-Good morning, Mr. Bruner. I don't mean to intrude, but . . ." She turned her head in Quinn's direction, then back to Arthur. "May I have a moment of your time?"

"Of course." He wrenched his hand from her grasp and swept the offended arm to the side while flexing his fingers. "Please come in."

Laurel lowered her head, but Quinn caught her sidelong glance. She looked away and entered Arthur's office without speaking another word.

Once Arthur closed door, Quinn stepped back into his own office, sealing himself and his battered pride inside the bleak little room.

He sat behind his desk with his fists balled on the paperwork lying on top, gritting his teeth until the ache forced him to relax his facial muscles or crack a tooth. Did she purposely seek to cause offense at every turn?

Quinn rubbed his jawline with his forefinger, tracing the rough skin on the left side. The scar wasn't that bad. As the minutes wore on, the resentment faded, allowing him to think rationally.

Something was amiss. Why would Laurel Tillman—a woman with a more serious deformity—react with revulsion at the sight of his scar? It made no sense.

Granted, he couldn't claim to predict her reaction in every circumstance, but he felt certain she would never faint with terror at a mere scar.

When Quinn stood, he caught his reflection in the window glass. Using it as a mirror, he peered at the lines of his face, the straight nose and high cheekbones he hadn't fully seen in months. He breathed a wry chuckle.

Maybe she just doesn't like your looks, Major Spencer.

He sank into the chair, leaned his head against the back, and closed his eyes, asking God to tell him why he shouldn't leave Bold Creek today.

As soon as Laurel reached the outskirts of town, she set her horse at a steady lope. The shock ebbed somewhat with the gentle rocking motion of the animal's strides. Yet the pace didn't free her of the blows she had taken lately. Decisions must be made—decisions that could change her future and the futures of those under her care.

Arthur Bruner had expressed a belief that she had no chance if charged with the deaths of the Triple M cattle and urged her to reconsider compensating the MacMahons for their loss. "Under those circumstances," he had assured her, "Royce will file no charges, and you'll have the issue behind you."

Even if she wanted to pay the scoundrels—the very thought of doing so grated on her—where would she get the money?

This had been La Casa del Fuego's most prosperous year, but after paying the mortgage, the women's salaries, feed bills and other expenses, the rest would need to carry them through until early summer when they would sell the wool. Besides, she had done nothing wrong.

She surveyed the countryside surrounding her—its gentle slopes, wispy grasses, short trees and rocky base. Land. She was rich in land, and land was what Royce wanted most. He would gladly take a portion of her property to settle the issue. Only he would demand the best, acreage worth far more than a few bony Texas Longhorns.

If it came down to paying an outrageous sum that she considered extortion or going to prison, could she trade her pride for liberty? Issy was right. This wasn't only about her. Imprisonment would leave Momma to raise a child alone and Becky without her mother. The others would have no employment. What would happen to poor Ernie?

Laurel flexed her shoulders to relieve the tension that traveled from there to her neck and into the back of her head.

Intuition told her that if she had spoken to Quinn, he would have had different advice for her. After a moment of indecision in which she had turned to leave the office, she would have shored up her courage and, setting pride aside, begged his help. She would have consulted him—if he hadn't shaved that blasted beard!

How could she have not known? All those weeks in her house, the times they were together . . . how had she missed it? The scar was there the whole time, hidden by whiskers.

Take away a few age lines around the eyes and mouth and thin his face . . .

She swore she would never forget that face. How could *he* have missed not recognizing her, either? Or had he? Perhaps guilt, not gratitude or friendship, played a part in his intervention between her and the MacMahons.

Common sense took hold, and she understood. It was highly unlikely Quinn recognized her after all this time. Few people would.

"Right fine day, Mrs. Tillman."

Wrenched from her self-pity, Laurel jerked the reins. The buckskin slid to a stop with his back legs tucked under his belly. She reached for the carbine.

"Don't do it, ma'am. I ain't gonna hurt you."

He held no weapon, so Laurel withdrew her hand from the gun. Her horse heaved, and a stab of guilt raced through her. She had been so lost in her thoughts she had not taken care to rest the gelding properly. Now he stood in the middle of the road, his tawny coat darkened with sweat. He couldn't outrun the fresher bay.

"You're in my way, Mr. Ferrell."

"Yes, ma'am, I reckon I am." His sneer stoked a fire of apprehension in Laurel. Her fingers tightened around the reins, and the buckskin regained the energy to dance. Ferrell didn't miss the horse's reaction. "Relax. I said I ain't gonna hurt you."

"What do you want?"

He crossed his arms over the saddle horn and leaned forward. "Well, ma'am, I reckon you know what I come for."

She affected a smile. "And I reckon you know you can't have her."

He kicked the bay and moved closer, never taking his menacing eyes from hers. Ignoring the urge to flee, she called up past discipline and held her ground.

Ferrell puckered his lips and shook his head. "Now, ma'am, I heard you got yourself in a right good pickle, and frankly, I don't appreciate you dragging me into it, too."

"Dragged you? I don't recollect forcing you to shoot those steers."

He snorted. "I didn't shoot nothin'."

She didn't believe him but hoped he would say why he did what he did. "You were there. If you're as innocent as you say, then you saw who was responsible. You need to tell the marshal."

"Maybe I saw you."

"What?"

"The marshal's lookin' for me. Maybe I will mosey on into town and answer a few questions. Of course, that don't mean I have to tell the truth, does it?"

Even on a cool afternoon, rivulets of moisture ran down her back. "In other words, you'll trade the truth of what happened in exchange for Ernie."

Ferrell laughed, a high-pitched, highly amused guffaw that made his horse prance. He cuffed the poor animal's ear. "You beat all, Miz Tillman. No, ma'am. I get Ernie and, in exchange, I disappear without telling the marshal I saw you shoot every one of them steers dead."

"You'd be lying." Laurel stopped herself from rolling her eyes. As if this man cared about telling a lie.

"Well, I ain't above a little fib to get what I want." His facial muscles tightened. "I also ain't above replacing that female with another one if you get any idea to run to the marshal to set a trap against me. I'll be watching."

Laurel went cold. Did he refer to Becky? Issy? Another innocent girl from the area?

"This time tomorrow you bring the girl to the spot where it all happened and we'll swap. Her for your freedom. Or I'll visit the marshal myself and see he gets my version of what happened." Not waiting for an answer, he started past her, then pulled his horse up. "I changed my mind. You be prompt and I could throw in a note saying I saw who really shot those poor, unfortunate animals."

Ferrell kicked the sides of the bay and disappeared across the grassy terrain before Laurel gathered her wits.

Smoke coiled from within the branches of a tall hickory in the distance. The bullet twisted, turning in mid-air as it approached. The flattened point floated toward her, the metal gleaming in the sunlight. Laurel smelled the burnt powder, heard the whir.

No. Not right. She should not be able to see it, smell it, hear it. She should expect it to hit her square between the eyes with no realization the weapon had been fired until it was too late.

No one should know when they were about to die. No one should die without seeing the face of their murderer.

She tried to evade the bullet, tried ducking her head, but her body wouldn't obey. Closer. Closer until it filled her line of sight.

Sweat poured down her face. Her mouth opened—the only part of her capable of movement. From somewhere nearby, a scream filled her ears. Her body jolted with the impact when the bullet slowly pierced the skin of both upper arms. How could that be? It should bore through her skull. She fell backward to hit the soft ground.

"Laurel? Laurel!"

Her eyes flew open to stare through the darkness at the barely discernable wood slats of a coffin lid. She reached up to touch it, but it was too far away. She blinked and swallowed. No. Not a coffin.

"Wake up, dear. Are you all right?"

The ceiling of her room. The bedcovers in disarray. Her mother leaning over her, eyes wide and fearful hands clutching her upper arms.

"Momma?"

Letting go, her mother eased onto the edge of the bed. "You had another bad dream?"

Laurel covered her damp face with her hands and rubbed the sleep from her eyes. She breathed deeply, willing away the horror of the past moments. Propping her back against the headboard, she clasped her mother's hand. "Yes. I'm all right."

Momma's eyes reflected doubt as she brushed clumps of wet hair from Laurel's clammy forehead. She gently stroked her cheek. "What brought this one on?"

She let go of her mother's hand and her fingers played with the braid draped down the front of her body. "What brings any of them on?" But she knew.

"Was it the visit by the MacMahons yesterday?"

"No, Momma." She attempted a smile, though suspected her lips twisted into something more resembling a grimace. "Since when have you known me to be frightened by those two?"

Since she spoke with Arthur Bruner that afternoon. Since he assured her Royce had a right to bring a lawsuit against her and she would be smart to compensate them for their loss.

"Well, something happened. It's been quite a while since you've cried out in your sleep. I'd hoped you had gotten past the nightmares."

Laurel stiffened. Her mother had that "Jesus is waiting for you" look on her face.

"I hate to see you suffer like this. He's waiting, Laurel. All you have to do is walk toward Him. 'Come unto me, all ye that labor and are heavy laden, and I will give you rest.'"

"Momma, please."

Her mother sighed. "Then will you at least tell me what bothers you?"

Did she dare tell her mother or keep it to herself? Why should she weigh her down with news that would upset her? No. This was between her and Quinn . . . and her and Ferrell . . . and her and the MacMahons.

"I suppose I'm fatigued by life lately. That's all."

Momma rose and trudged to the chest of drawers. She picked up the photograph of Laurel and John and ran a finger over the images. "Sometimes, I feel more like your child than your mother. It's my fault. I don't know what happened to me. I was much stronger when your father and brother were alive. Then you left and . . ." She set the framed photo back on the dresser and bowed her gray-streaked head. "Forgive me, dear, for allowing myself to depend on you for too long, standing idly by while you take too much of the burden for all of us upon yourself."

"Oh, no, Momma. I should—"

"We are each responsible for our actions, Laurel. The Lord has told me that mine have been weak and cowardly, adding to your load. He's urged me to help you and not hinder you."

A help? Why would God tell her mother that? Oh, if only she could feel the rest that Jesus promised. The peace. But her sinful actions were too great.

As she walked back to the bed, Momma carried herself with the self-assurance and authority Laurel remembered from her childhood. She sat on the edge of the bed. "I have *always* been so proud of you, of your courage. Now allow me mine. Permit me to carry some of the load for you by confiding in me. I am stronger than I appear sometimes, and I promise to be stronger in the future."

Laurel straightened the covers and slipped farther down in the bed. She crimped her eyes shut. It was as though their roles had reversed and she had become the uncertain one. All at once, Momma's candid appeal overcame Laurel's reservations. "Quinn shaved his beard."

Her mother leaned back and studied her a moment before saying, "Shaved his beard? I don't understand, dear. How could that cause your nightmare?"

She gripped her mother's hand. "Momma, he's the man who gave me my limp."

CHAPTER EIGHTEEN

Laurel sat on the barn floor and rubbed her burning eyes, convinced someone had wrung every drop of moisture from them during the dark hours. This nightmare had frightened her more than any in some time.

Awed by the way Momma handled the news about Quinn, she swelled with child-like pride in her parent. No wringing of the hands, no fearfulness, and no wavering in her good opinion of him. Her mother merely reminded Laurel it had been a time of war.

"God extends His forgiveness to all those who ask for it no matter what they've done, Laurel. And with what I know of Quinn, I suspect he has asked."

If God forgave Quinn Spencer, perhaps He would forgive her. Except Quinn had fought with honor. She, however—

"Isn't she pretty, Momma?" Becky sat cross-legged in a corner of the pen. She held up a whimpering, multi-colored puppy.

"Lovely, Peanut. But you'll do well to remember we'll sell them as soon as they're weaned." Laurel entered the pen with the puppies and the half-dozen sheep that were their constant companions. The sooner the dogs became accustomed to the sheep, the more inclined they would be to protect them.

"But Momma, you said we could keep one."

"I said no such thing. I did say it would be nice, but a good sheep dog is valuable, Becky. You know I keep a list of people who want a pup from Charlie and Prudence. We need that money."

"But Prudence isn't getting any younger. What happens when she can't have no more—"

"Any more."

"—any more pups? Wouldn't it be best to keep one girl and get us another boy so we'd have more dogs to sell?"

Laurel picked up a puppy that popped in and out from beneath a ewe. She hid her grin behind its body. "Child, you either have a good head for business or a desire to see us begging. This is a sheep ranch, not a kennel."

Even without training, she could sell each pup for a tidy sum. Laurel had plans for the money, not the least of which would be more ranch repairs—unless it went straight into Royce's hands.

"Your idea may be sound, but I don't have the time or inclination to train sheep dogs."

"I can do it." Becky pointed to a female sporting a peculiar black spot on her back. "I like that one. I'm going to name her Diamond."

She studied her daughter's anxious face. The child asked for little. Would it burden them to let her keep one pup to work with? "We'll see."

Leaving the pen, Laurel strolled into the cool depths of the barn, her mind reverting once more to last night's conversation with her mother. Not willing to lay too much on Momma's strengthening shoulders, she'd kept the situation with Reg Ferrell to herself. Laurel hadn't asked Mr. Bruner's advice on the subject, but she'd seen to it no woman left the ranch yard alone and that they watched Ernie and Becky at all times. She had thought to offer Ferrell the balance of Ernie's account to give to Virgil Hicks, hoping it would ensure the old goat held no hold over the girl and Ferrell would return to Arkansas alone.

Probably a pipe dream.

"Mrs. Tillman?"

Laurel jumped at the unexpected male voice. She turned, squinting at the shadowy figure standing in the barn's doorway. "Marshal?"

"I was told I would find you here." He stepped closer until his features cleared.

Her hands broke out in a sweat and the tips of her fingers became like ice. Had he come to arrest her? Had he found Reg Ferrell and listened as that man accused her of the shootings to save his sorry hide?

If Ferrell remained free, he expected to deliver Ernie back to his employer. Even if Laurel went to jail, others would see to it he came nowhere near that young girl—or the females in Laurel's care.

She walked to the entrance. The marshal's face glowed in the beam of sunlight. "What can I do for you?"

He studied her for a moment. "You look played out, ma'am."

The mirror in her room had revealed as much. She'd even found a couple of gray hairs. "Ranching's hard work."

"So's worrying."

He only knew a portion of her worry.

"I understand you were looking for me yesterday."

"Let's go to the house." Passing the lawman, Laurel left the barn. "It's nippy this morning. I'm sure you could use something hot to drink after your ride."

"Sounds good."

"Becky, time for your lessons with Granmomma."

The girl ran to the house ahead of her.

Once inside the kitchen, Laurel took the marshal's hat and hung it from a peg, then motioned toward a chair at the table. She poured them each a cup of coffee and set a plate of her mother's biscuits in front of him. A friendly delay, but one that couldn't last forever. "I'm sorry you came so far to see what I might have wanted. I thought I'd ask if there had been any progress in seeing to my innocence."

"I have news about the man you said you thought shot the Triple M cattle."

She breathed in the coffee's aroma and blew on the steaming liquid before taking a cautious sip. Heat traveled downward and settled inside her nervous stomach, causing it to burn. The saucer rattled a tad when Laurel set her cup on it. She straightened against the chair back and gazed into the marshal's lined face. "You found him?"

"Not yet, but he contacted Pete Callahan two days ago about buying a horse. Pete sent him to the MacMahons."

His pause gave Laurel the impression he held back additional information. "And?"

Marshal Ruiz gulped a mouthful of the hot coffee in his cup, then winced and swallowed gingerly. "Evidently, this Ferrell fella didn't wait for directions to the Triple M but headed that way on his own. Took Pete by surprise, the man being a stranger and all."

She gripped her cup in a stranglehold while contemplating the significance of the marshal's words. "You think Ferrell knew the MacMahons already?"

If so, what relationship did Ernie's pursuer have with the ranchers? Ferrell hinted at knowing who actually did the shooting that day. She fought against letting her hopes rise.

"Royce and Murphy swear up and down he never showed up at the ranch."

Never showed? Her hope crashed. "You believe them?"

"I spoke with several hands. No one saw him."

"No one saw him, or no one admitted to seeing him?" Perhaps the marshal hadn't asked the right person. "What about Reuben Stockard? He's the only one on that ranch I'd trust to tell the truth."

He shook his head. "I talked to him first. He said no one rode into the yard on Tuesday who didn't belong."

"Ferrell may have changed his mind and gone somewhere else to buy a horse."

"Possibly. I'd like to know why he needed a second mount."

Laurel couldn't make her tongue spit it out. She lowered her chin and cut her eyes toward the front room where her mother and Becky worked, debating the wisdom of telling the truth. It seemed a simple matter to say Ferrell wanted the horse to return Ernie to Arkansas. The truth refused to leave her mouth. "Perhaps he plans to travel a distance and wants to rest one horse while riding another."

"Sounds like a reasonable account." He took a bite from a biscuit. "Mmm, your mama's a fine cook."

Just tell him about Ernie. He can help.

But what if he couldn't find Ferrell in time to keep him from harming one of her friends or Becky?

Laurel smoothed a wrinkle in the tablecloth. It was bad enough that Ferrell threatened to accuse her. It would be Laurel's word against his, and Royce witnessed her shooting one of the steers.

She picked a biscuit from the plate for herself and tore off a small piece, mashing it in her fingers until it was flat and doughy.

You planned to tell him yesterday.

That was before she met with Mr. Bruner and Ferrell ambushed her. If the marshal realized the man's connection to the ranch through Ernie, it would give him more reason to believe Laurel made up the story about seeing Ferrell when the cattle were shot. Besides, the girl shook like a leaf in a stiff gust every time anyone mentioned that the law should know her situation. Each time Laurel tried to reassure her that Ward Ruiz was a fair man, Ernie crumpled into tears.

"It seems to me, Marshal, you should be out looking for Reg Ferrell instead of sitting here drinking my coffee and eating Momma's biscuits." To her regret, the argument with herself had sharpened her tone.

"Where would you have me go, Mrs. Tillman?"

Where indeed? She could offer to take him to Ferrell herself if he'd wait a few hours. But she didn't.

Ruiz leaned back in the chair until the two front legs came off the floor and the back of his head pressed against the wall. His brown gaze bore into Laurel. Using the force of her will, she kept her own eyes steady.

"Someone is lying to me, Mrs. Tillman. I'm not sure who, but I'll find out."

Laurel wanted to shout, "It isn't me!" But she balked. Over the years, she had gotten good at lying by never saying a word.

The chair legs hit the floor with a thump. "You sure that was all you wanted to see me about yesterday?"

Laurel sipped at the coffee that had grown tepid. As long as Marshal Ruiz didn't find Reg Ferrell, her guilt remained a matter of her word against Royce's. If caught, she knew the Arkansas stranger would try to save himself by pointing a finger at her.

She set her cup down and pushed the saucer away. She also pushed aside the inner voice that warned her away from what she was about to do. "Royce and Murphy paid me a visit on Tuesday. Royce threatened to sue me over the loss of the cattle. He insisted on a ridiculous amount of money, which I refused to pay. His demand amounted to extortion."

"That's a serious charge."

"He wanted twenty dollars a head for cattle worth half that." She controlled the rise of her voice and kept fear from taking hold. "Another thing. While they were here, Ernie fell from the loft and sprained her wrist. Royce became irate when Murphy tried to help her. He showed no more concern for that girl than if she were a dying fly on the windowsill." Or a bullet-riddled cow lying on the ground.

The marshal's crinkled brow hinted that she'd struck a vein of doubt regarding the older MacMahon. She mined deeper, seeking to expose more nuggets of suspicion. "A man with so little compassion wouldn't care about a few dead Longhorns. He might even welcome their slaughter if it meant placing me and my land in a perilous position."

Ruiz's chair scraped across the floor as he stood and reached for his hat. Laurel held her breath, awaiting the announcement of his intention to ride to the Triple M and confront Royce.

"Was that Spencer's idea or yours, ma'am?"

She inhaled a quick breath. What had Quinn to do with this? They had not spoken of the matter. In fact, she wished not to speak to that former blue belly again.

"I don't understand your question. Mr. Spencer knows nothing of—"

"From the beginning, you two have pushed the theory that the MacMahons are involved. You've pushed it hard. Don't think you can dupe me into accepting any story you and your lawyer friend conjure up. I'm not so easily deceived, Mrs. Tillman." He set his hat on his head and gave her a curt nod. "*Adios.*"

She stared at his back as he left by the front door. Only when his boots echoed on the porch steps did Laurel move to the window to peer through the glass. The marshal straddled the saddle and reined his bay around, sending it down the drive at a quick, jarring . . . angry trot.

Laurel turned and placed her palms on the tabletop, resting her weight on her arms. She had gone too far. Her insides stung with biting dread. Had she made an adversary of the lawman when she desperately needed him as an ally?

Issy fastened the throatlatch of the bridle and arranged the buckskin's black forelock over the brow band. "Where're you headed?"

Laurel slid her left boot through the stirrup and used it to pull her weight off the ground. How much should she tell Issy? Common sense suggested someone should know where to look in case she didn't return. With effort, she bent her bad knee as far as it would go and settled her right boot in the other stirrup.

"I'm headed for White Creek. I'll be back in a couple of hours." Laurel reined the horse around and stopped. "Make sure Ernie is never alone."

"We've watched over her ever since you told us about that Ferrell character still being around."

"I know, but don't let your guard down and,"—the next order would send an additional alarm through her friends—"be sure you and Camille are armed and ready."

Issy grasped the reins. "Now you're scaring me. What's going on? Why are you going out there again?"

"I'll tell you when I get back."

"Then I'll go with you."

"No." Laurel pressed the sides of the gelding, moving him forward until Issy let go of the reins. "There's no need."

Guiding her horse at a trot across the terrain, she hoped to arrive at the designated location before Reg Ferrell, so he would not see her ride up alone. She crossed the creek in a shallow spot that, except midsummer, usually held six to eight inches of water. Rain had been scarce this month, but not so scarce that there should be this little flow to the river. She would check it out another time.

Laurel dismounted near the tree line where the Arkansan had hidden the day of the shootings. Leading her horse through the brush, she tied the reins to a low limb and waited, breathing in the sharp smells of the evergreen junipers and rotting leaves. Occasionally, she crept from the clump of trees to scan the horizon. Each time, she returned to her horse, sulking and drumming her fingers on the saddle.

The sun continued its descent. Laurel estimated she'd waited two hours past the meeting time.

She untied the reins, led her horse from the tree line, and mounted. Turning the gelding toward home, a troubling sensation roosted in her gut, squirming until she thought she'd be sick.

Ferrell hadn't shown. Maybe he'd wanted to lure her away from the ranch so he could get Ernie without her around. Maybe harm would come to the girl or the others through her decision not to tell Marshal Ruiz of the meeting.

Laurel dug her heels into the buckskin's sides while pleading with God that He not take His anger with her out on her loved ones.

CHAPTER NINETEEN

"You did not tell Marshal Ruiz about Ernie and seeing Mr. Ferrell on the road?" The tatting shuttle in Camille's hands stilled, cocked at an angle. She set the instrument and partially finished piece of lace on her lap and leaned forward in the rocker. A plank in the bunkhouse floor creaked in protest of the chair's movement. "Why not?"

"Telling him didn't seem a good idea." With her hands clasped behind her, Laurel propped a shoulder against a wall, affecting a relaxed position. "Ferrell threatened to accuse me of shooting the cattle." Why hadn't Ferrell shown up after demanding she meet him?

Laurel arrived home that afternoon in a panic to find a state of calm and everyone accounted for. It didn't ease her mind.

Issy entered from the adjacent room. "Why would he believe that skunk?"

Why, indeed? So far, he had not rushed to judgment or bowed to Royce's demand. Perhaps she should have trusted him.

"You did not make up the story of seeing him near the cattle."

"No, but..."

"But what?" Camille's raised eyebrows appealed for candor.

"The marshal has the notion that Quinn and I have conspired

together."

"In what way?"

"To convince him that Royce hired Ferrell to kill his own cattle."

"That is *ridicule*."

"I agree with Camille." Issy walked toward Laurel in her nightclothes, a pink shawl wrapped around her upper body. In the lamplight, and with her pale hair draped over her shoulders, Issy's features softened into a femininity she hid during the day.

Had Laurel done the young woman a disservice by not being a proper influence? She may have damaged them all, allowing them to become social outcasts. Laurel had reached her fill of making the wrong choices.

"So, what did you tell him?"

"I told him about the visit Royce and Murphy paid me on Tuesday. I told him about their threat of a lawsuit against me." She straightened and stepped away from the wall. "I also told him I thought the amount they sought was as good as extortion."

"Hoorah for you."

Issy's cheer gave Laurel the boldness to continue. "And I told him about Royce's insistence that his brother not attend to Ernie's injury. I suggested that his callousness toward another human being might extend to the destruction of his own cattle to gain La Casa del Fuego." She waited for a vocal reaction from her astonished friends.

"Oh, Laurel, how shrewd." Issy clapped her hands and rubbed her palms together. "It serves that ornery cuss right."

Laurel smiled until the disapproval on Camille's face told her she could expect no applause from that quarter. "You don't agree with what I said?"

"Do you?"

"Then what would you have done?"

"We are not talking about me."

"That's right. We're not." Laurel strove to keep her voice steady. "You are not the one responsible for the safety of everyone on this ranch, Camille. You are not the one facing a possible jail sentence or, at the least, a large fine."

Camille's eyes shone with sympathy. "Do you believe Royce is guilty?"

Issy frowned and pulled her shawl tighter around her body. "What difference does it make? She's not testifying to it in court. She only made a suggestion, a reasonable one to me."

Both MacMahons were a thorn in Laurel's bustle. But did she really think Royce would go so far to get her property?

"Royce certainly had no trouble believing *me* guilty. As Issy says, it's reasonable. Why shouldn't I point it out?" She shrugged. "Who's to say he didn't hire Ferrell? According to the marshal, he knew the way to the Triple M without Pete Callahan telling him. It only makes sense to think he had visited the ranch before Tuesday."

Camille set her handiwork inside a small wooden box on a nearby table. "So you pointed a finger at an innocent to take suspicion from yourself?"

"Innocent? What makes you think he's innocent? The man is out to ruin me, Camille, to put me in jail. If he succeeds, where will you be? Where will you go?"

Camille walked over and reached her arms around Laurel, wrapping her in a hug. "I am not worried about me or Issy or anyone else on this ranch. What concerns me is the bitterness you harbor in your heart toward certain people—the MacMahons, Quinn Spencer, others around Bold Creek. I am worried that one day it will eat you alive, *mi amiga.*" She pulled back, still gripping Laurel's arms. "'Be not overcome with evil, but overcome evil with good.'"

Laurel wriggled out of her friend's grasp. "Camille, please stop quoting scripture at me."

"I am only quoting the way God wants each of us to live."

"And is this how He wants you to live?" She gestured to their surroundings. "Cooped up on this ranch? Gossiped about by people who think they are better than you? What bitterness do you harbor against—" Laurel slapped a hand over her wayward mouth. She had no right to take her worry out on others. A hurt she was sure went beyond the thoughtlessness of her words, momentarily wrinkled her friend's face. Seeing it, she reached for Camille's hand. "I beg your forgiveness."

In her regret, Laurel was tempted to break her own rule and ask more about Camille's history, ask why she had hidden out on the ranch for so long. She had met Camille in a time of distress and given her shelter in much the same way she had Ernie. As close as they had become, they had never confided to one another the more devastating details of their pasts.

"I am where God wants me for now. I pray I am, anyway, but sometimes I believe I am merely a coward." Camille stepped to the small table, picked up the Bible and placed it in Laurel's hands. "Here. I ask that you read the twelfth chapter of Romans, especially the last verses."

"But—"

Camille shook her finger. "Please. We can discuss your thoughts about it later."

"I can give them to you now."

The woman grinned. "I will wait."

Laurel scowled at the book, then at her friend. "Who is in charge around here, anyway?"

"I pray that is what you will discover."

She needn't discover anything, because Laurel already knew. And it wasn't her.

Laurel reached over to turn down the lamp and her hand brushed the Bible sitting on the bedside table. She breathed a sigh, knowing there would be no rest until she obeyed Camille's order.

She shuffled through the pages of Romans until reaching the twelfth chapter. While sliding her finger back and forth across the paper, she read the first sixteen verses. When she came to verse seventeen, she paused. Laurel's heart quickened and her lips moved in silence, her mind hearing each word.

"'Recompense no man evil for evil. Provide things honest in the sight of all men. If it be possible, as much as lieth in you, live peaceably with all men. Dearly beloved, avenge not yourselves, but rather give place unto wrath: for it is written, Vengeance is mine; I will repay, saith the Lord. Therefore if thine enemy hunger, feed him; if he thirst, give him drink: for in so doing thou shalt heap coals of fire on his head. Be not overcome of evil, but overcome evil with good.'"

Live peaceably with all men. Avenge not yourselves. Vengeance is mine. I will repay. Be not overcome with evil.

After carefully shutting the book, she set it on the table and extinguished the lamp's wick. The room sank into a blackness broken only by a slim shaft of moonlight beaming on her as it burned through the bedroom window. She closed her eyes and turned her back to the heavenly scrutiny. A steady flow of tears trailed across her nose and dripped onto the pillow.

"You're too late to take up your vengeance on my account, God. It is done."

Two male voices seeped through the wood of Quinn's office door. One belonged to Arthur. The other, deeper and with a native drawl, sounded familiar but too low to place.

A door shut, and the voices hushed. He returned his attention to the papers on his desk. Common, uninteresting paperwork—filing, writing letters. Without an office clerk, Quinn had assumed the role.

Most days, he shuffled through law journals and published briefs, enjoying the research and arguing various aspects of the recorded cases with Arthur. Where possible, he read the particulars of the litigation and before reaching the announced verdict, formed his own judgment, satisfied that his findings often matched that of the judge. Finally, he was becoming the lawyer he set out to be before the war and his years of hiding within the military.

Quinn's foot tapped the floor, keeping time with the pen he tapped on the edge of the desk. He should have resigned his commission years ago rather than using the military to avoid a return to Ohio. The memories raised by the troops of Buffalo Soldiers at his last post had become too much to bear and prompted him to leave. But the images followed him to this small town through his association with Laurel.

Folding a bill to be mailed to a farmer in a neighboring town—a man he wasn't sure could even read—he slipped it into an addressed envelope and laid it on the corner of his desk.

At a knock on his door, Quinn looked up from writing the next invoice. "Enter."

Arthur pushed open the door and peered around it. "Please come into my office, son. I am meeting with a client and would like your presence."

Quinn set the pen into the brass holder next to the inkwell. "Certainly, sir." He shrugged into his frock coat and followed Arthur to the office across the hall.

The occupant of the upholstered chair near the desk twisted to face him. Royce MacMahon sprawled in the seat with one elbow propped on the chair arm and his disdain aimed at Quinn. The rancher lowered his eyes and raised his hand to inspect the dirt under his fingernails, dismissing Quinn's extended hand for a second time.

"I believe introductions are unnecessary." Arthur motioned to a plain wooden chair near the wall. "Have a seat, Quinn."

He settled as comfortably as possible against the straight back, waiting to learn the reason they brought him into their discussion.

"I don't know why you insist on him being here, Arthur. My business is with you."

"Relax, Royce. Quinn is an intelligent man, fully able to assist you. As I am frequently out of town, I like to keep him abreast of the situations my clients face."

The rancher waved away the explanation. "Have it your way. Now, when can I expect Mrs. Tillman to pay what she owes me?"

"Have patience. I'm sure she hasn't that kind of cash on hand. It's why we gave her until the end of the year. However, in my conversation with her last week, I let her know it was in her best interest to recompense you for your cattle losses."

Quinn stiffened. He and Arthur hadn't discussed his meeting with Laurel the previous Wednesday. Annoyance over her reaction to his scar had discouraged him from asking about her visit. He hadn't offended Mary Weaver Saturday evening. In fact, the young woman had made it too clear she found him interesting.

"I'm sorry, sir, but why did you advise Mrs. Tillman to make restitution to the Triple M?" The words spilled from his mouth without permission.

Royce spit out a wry laugh that proclaimed Quinn a fool. "Because she stole my steers and killed them."

"I'm not aware of there being evidence she stole anything of yours, Mr. MacMahon. If you have proof, kindly inform me."

"You saw it the day I escorted her to the jail, Spencer."

"I saw circumstantial evidence. If Marshal Ruiz felt there was sufficient cause to arrest Mrs. Tillman, I'm sure he would have done so by now."

"The marshal is too incompetent to act on what's in front of his nose." Royce crossed his legs as though he hadn't a care. "I assure you, it means trouble for his future in this town."

"Are you threatening to see he loses his job?" Would Ruiz care about making an enemy of this man? If so, it might affect his investigation.

"I don't threaten, Spencer. I make things happen."

Quinn opened his mouth to ask if that included hiring Ferrell to shoot the cattle in an effort to drive Laurel off her land. He closed it again before uttering a word. After all, the MacMahons were clients. That brought up another matter. Arthur represented the Triple M. Why would he advise Laurel?

Arthur thrust a hand in the air. "Gentlemen, please. We're on the same side."

"Frankly, Bruner, I don't trust your clerk."

Ignoring Royce's insult, Quinn settled back in the chair again, letting the rancher continue his attack.

"I don't at all believe he's on my side. It's clear his loyalty lies with those sheep-loving harlots."

Quinn gripped the arms of the chair. "That was uncalled for, MacMa—"

"I told you earlier. I won't have him involved in my business, Bruner. You can see for yourself he favors Laurel and her girls. Why should I trust him?"

Arthur scowled at his client and rattled a stack of papers on his desk as if buying time while he considered how to handle the situation. He turned his attention to Quinn, who sat in silence while being studied by the older man. "I believe calling you into this meeting was a mistake. It would be best if you return to your office."

Quinn's chest heaved with suppressed anger. "As you wish. Good day, Mr. MacMahon."

His shoes pounded the planks as he crossed the hall. The chair behind his desk screeched when he fell into it. He stared out the window at nothing in particular and remained in that position, sulking over his dismissal like a scolded child dispatched to a stool in a corner of the schoolroom.

While in the military, Quinn had learned to control his opinions, bowing to the whims of his superiors, whether right or wrong. Sometimes it meant biting the side of his mouth to keep from letting an opposing viewpoint spew forth. He rubbed his tongue along the tender flesh. Why should an attack on the La Casa del Fuego women by a man who wore his spitefulness like a badge of honor cause Quinn to forget years of training?

"We should talk."

He flinched at the unexpected voice and swiveled in the chair as Arthur stepped into his office. Ready to face his discipline, Quinn drew his shoulders back and said, "I apologize if Mr. MacMahon misunderstood my concerns."

Arthur laughed, though the bark held no hint of actual humor.

"You feel a need to apologize for Royce?"

"I suppose my apology is for letting him rile me into being indiscreet. I didn't intend to stir up trouble between the two of you."

"Then what was your intention, son?"

Yes, why provoke MacMahon that way—other than Quinn found him to be loathsome?

"It seemed I walked into a conversation that had already taken place. Feeling at a disadvantage, I wanted to know why he was convinced Laurel Tillman owed him for his cattle."

"The law is clear, Quinn. Here, cattle theft is punishable by several years in the state penitentiary, as well as the possibility of a heavy fine."

"Yes, but no one has proven she cut the fence and drove those steers onto her property." Quinn held his breath while awaiting the argument he guessed was coming.

"However, the fact remains that my clients witnessed her killing their livestock."

"One that was already gravely wounded."

"And it is her responsibility to show any fact under which she could justify the shooting."

"She gave a reasonable explanation. To prevent the prolonged suffering of the animal. Half the cattle required at least two shots to kill them. Mrs. Tillman can demonstrate her exceptional ability with a weapon."

Arthur smiled in the way of an indulgent father. "Son, even you, who has yet to experience arguing a case in an actual courtroom, could convince a jury that she shot all six animals and tried to prevent suspicion from falling on her through the use of multiple shots. Is there a witness to say she did not?"

He placed a hand on Quinn's shoulder. "I agreed to speak to her, not as an attorney—I have not billed her for my services—but as a fellow member of this community." His comment proved a reminder of their previous disagreement over Arthur having billed Laurel. "I suggested that, rather than face the possibility of spending time in prison, she should consider Royce's charitable offer and be done with the whole affair. Mrs. Tillman has a child to raise. How can she do so from inside a prison?"

"You're so sure she's guilty?"

"Are you so sure she is not?"

No matter how hostile her attitude toward him, Quinn could not forget that horrid day and Laurel's shock and vulnerability while Royce and his men threw accusations at her. His belief in her innocence and the belief of twelve other men may prove different. And how would she find a fair hearing with the attitude of many around Bold Creek? If it ever came to a trial, he would do his best to seek unbiased jurors. That, of course, presumed she would trust him to represent her.

"I thought as much."

The statement yanked Quinn from his pondering. "I beg your pardon, sir?"

"I asked you to the meeting to discover where your loyalties lie, Quinn. I see they are written on your face."

Quinn could not deny the charge. "I believe there's more going on than we see on the surface."

Arthur released his doubt in a huff. "If she is tried and convicted, at the least, she faces a misdemeanor and would owe a fine that could be more than Royce has asked. But under the circumstances, I fear she'll receive no less than the maximum punishment of prison." He started for the office door. "I talked Royce out of pressing charges or filing a lawsuit, provided she admits to her guilt and agrees to restitution. I am sure, under those circumstances, the marshal will agree."

"She will appreciate your intervention on her behalf, sir." A lie. Knowing Laurel, she would dig in her heels and refuse to pay a cent.

"Mrs. Tillman is a . . . unique woman. I admire her courage but am left wondering about her obstinate ways—something attributable to her southern upbringing, I am sure." He turned. "I feel obligated to remind you, Quinn, that if she should contact you for legal help, you must refuse."

After Arthur walked out, Quinn sank into his chair. His research had confirmed the facts of their discussion. Depending on the charges, and if found guilty, Laurel could spend much of Becky's remaining childhood imprisoned for something he believed she had not done.

Short of acting as her lawyer, the only means to prove her innocence was for Reg Ferrell to admit the truth. But first, he must be found. So far, he had eluded those seeking him.

Quinn combed his fingers through his hair. What if the marshal found Ferrell and his testimony indicted Laurel?

CHAPTER TWENTY

From the crest of the knoll, Laurel sat atop the buckskin and scanned the landscape dotted with grazing sheep. So peaceful. The occasional bleats sang like a lullaby, weighting her eyelids and drooping her shoulders. Yawning, she stood in the stirrups and stretched before fatigue tumbled her out of the saddle and onto the grass.

Marshal Ruiz had not paid her a return visit—hopefully, a case of no news meaning good news. Still, when near the house, she caught herself watching the drive, anticipating his arrival.

She had pondered the verses in Romans until she could recite them from memory, seeing her name written in every sentence.

Recompense no man evil for evil, Laurel. Wasn't that what she tried to do when accusing Royce of hiring Ferrell?

Provide things honest in the sight of all men, Laurel. Regarding informing the marshal of Ferrell's connection to Ernie and her planned meeting with him, she had not been honest. Certainly, she had no desire to cause more trouble for Ernie, but she worried the lawman would use the meeting against her.

If it be possible, as much as lieth in you, Laurel, live peaceably with all men. When was the last time she cared to get along with her neighbors, be they the MacMahons or the residents of Bold Creek? Or even Quinn Spencer?

Since the latter months of 1863, little peace had lain within her. How could she live in peace with others when she found it so hard to live peacefully with herself? She blew out a sigh. The people around Bold Creek weren't the antagonists. That destructive trait rested inside her. She had done her best over the years to keep people at arm's length so they wouldn't discover her guilt.

And the most condemning: *Vengeance is mine; I will repay, Laurel.* Nothing else struck her with more terror. The tragedies in her life must be God's judgment coming to fruition.

She pressed her legs against the sides of the gelding and urged him down the gradual slope at a slow pace so as not to disturb the flock. Laurel reined in the buckskin once they reached Ernie. The girl sat on a large rock, watching from one side. Issy kept guard on the other. Charlie roamed the pasture, surveying the landscape for any danger, while he kept wandering sheep within sight.

"Hey there, Miz Tillman."

Laurel pointed to Ernie's wrist. "How's your sprain?"

The girl stretched out her arm and shook her hand. "Aw, like Becky says, it's good as grapes. Your ma's sure got a good hand for doctorin'."

"Yes, she does. It would be nice to have a doctor who lived closer, though. If something life-threatening happened, it might prove too confounding for her."

"Miz Chamberlain's right smart and got more common sense than most people see. Only she ain't learned to stop worryin' about what other people think." Ernie ducked her head. "I reckon I shouldn't oughta talk like that. I didn't mean no . . . any . . . disrespect."

Laurel thought about what she'd said and smiled. "It's all right. I think you're right smart too, Ernie."

The girl grinned. "Yes'm. Your ma's been learnin' me . . ." She gave the rock a frustrated kick with the heel of her boot. "She's been *teaching* me how to talk like a fancy lady."

"You'll be glad later. Now, I'm headed for White Creek."

Ernie squiggled to the ground, her eyes wide, agitated pools. "Ain't—isn't—that where the cattle were killed?"

Laurel dreaded the idea of returning to the area, but had no choice. "Last week I noticed water trickled downstream. This is my first opportunity to look into the problem." She withheld the real reason she hadn't gone to the creek. She worried about leaving the others unprotected to check it out. They didn't have the same ability to defend themselves as she did.

"I think something's damming the creek."

"You be careful. That Ferrell fella could still be around."

A chill snaked through Laurel, but she didn't want her fear to be catching. "With no sign of him for days, I'm sure he's long gone, Ernie."

True, Reg Ferrell never showed up at their meeting place, and she hadn't seen nor heard from him since last week. But the thought that he might still be out there put them on edge. The pastures nearest the yard hadn't been grazed in a while, so she had moved the flocks closer and kept everyone within a safe distance of the house.

"I'll see you at supper." Laurel turned her horse and headed west.

As she approached the area where she had crossed last week, the water still dribbled along the rocky bed. Laurel pushed through the brush but stopped at hearing a whinny. The buckskin looked to the right and his ears pricked forward.

She dismounted and dropped the reins. After slipping the carbine from the scabbard, she whispered near the horse's left ear, "You stay put." She winced at each crunch of soil and stone under her boot. Ahead, a black tail swished, long strands catching on a twig. "What are you doing here, Ruthie?"

"She brought me."

Laurel lurched backward at Quinn's sudden appearance on the other side of the saddle. She hadn't seen him since that day in his office. The scar on his jaw stood out like lantern light in a darkened room—then and now. She looked away.

"Your mother told me I'd find you somewhere along the creek."

To have reached this area ahead of her, he must have arrived at the house right after she left. Stopping to talk to Ernie had slowed her down. "What do you want?"

"I thought I'd help you find what dammed the water."

"That's not what I meant. What brought you to the ranch in the first place?"

His brows formed a vee. "I'm concerned for you. All of you."

"I appreciate your concern, but there's no need for it." She moved back to the buckskin and slid the firearm into its sheath on the saddle.

He followed. "Laurel, there is a need."

The skin on her arms prickled at his tone. "What do you mean?"

"I found something in the creek up ahead."

"Don't be so mysterious. What is it?" She started around him.

He grabbed her. "Don't."

"Let go of my arm, Quinn. If it's blocking the flow to the river, I need to remove it." She twisted free and tramped farther into the brush.

"Laurel."

Ignoring his call, she crashed through the foliage and limped down the low embankment. Breaking twigs and rustled leaves behind her said Quinn followed. At the creek bed, Laurel skidded to a stop.

Her mouth dropped open, and her ears roared. The din drowned out all other sounds as she stared at what remained of the water's obstruction. A man's body.

Other bodies floated in front of her. Faces long gone. Sounds and smells never forgotten. She pressed her hands against her eyes and turned away. Her chest ached with the effort to breathe, and her good knee buckled.

Muscular arms wrapped around her, holding her up as the side of her face slid down the wool of a coat that clothed a protective shoulder. She gripped the material in her fists and clenched tight until the horrific images faded and her breathing eased.

Quinn rested his chin on the top of her head and gently stroked her back. "You're so insistent. Why do you have to prove how strong and independent you are? Why do you have to take everything upon yourself?" His censure never rose above a whisper.

She gave in to the warmth and comfort she found while pressed against his chest. Her arms wrapped around him and Laurel breathed in the smell of wool and hair oil. A harmony vibrated through her chest as Quinn's heartbeat danced with hers. His strength absorbed her every fear, her every worry. Banishing their past to a far corner of her mind, she indulged in the embrace of this man—a man of peace and principle.

The tremors evaporated in the cool November air. She wanted nothing more than to rest in the arms of someone who cared for her.

Laurel pushed away and straightened her shoulders. The emotions were not real. Quinn held no special fondness for her. And how could she hold any for him when faced with the scar of their meeting years ago?

She resisted the urge to turn and look back at the creek. Today, her reality lay in that direction. Her reality was the rotting corpse of a man wearing the clothing she had last seen on Reg Ferrell.

Quinn clasped his palms together. The muscles in his forearms tightened. Upon finding Ferrell's ravaged, decomposed body, those same hands had shaken. He had seen hundreds of dead bodies during the war. They littered the battlefields like discarded trash. This body was different. This body condemned and shouted out the prime name on a list of murder suspects, for he was certain it was murder. That name was Laurel Tillman.

"Who do you think will be in Wade's mind to arrest?"

It was as though Laurel had read his thoughts. When his throat closed, trapping the answer, she turned away.

He walked up behind her. "Come. Let me show you something." Something he prayed wouldn't put a rope around her neck.

Quinn led her a few yards south, staying between Laurel and the creek to shield her from another glimpse of Ferrell. He pointed to a branch on a sapling. "Have you seen that before?"

She gasped and reached for the material caught in the small tree. He clasped her arm and stopped her before she could touch it. As much as he hated it, this was evidence he must show to the law.

"That's my handkerchief."

Hope dropped into his boots. "When did you see it last?"

Her brows drew together. She lowered her hand to her side and turned with her back to him. He waited, each moment of silence stretching his patience.

Laurel kneaded her temples with the tips of her fingers. "No, that can't be."

"Can't be what?"

"I lost it weeks ago."

Quinn moved to stand in front of her. "Tell me." If he asked her the hard questions first, she may be more prepared when the marshal demanded answers. "When was the last time you remember using it?"

Laurel gazed at the material, no longer white, but smeared with rust-colored stains. She rubbed her forehead as if the action would provide the answer she sought. "I lost it the day we all ate at the café. The day we first met . . . him."

"Did you leave it at the café?"

"If I knew I had, I would have returned for it." Laurel stared off into the distance. "I only know that when we arrived home, it was gone. I assumed it had fallen from my bag somewhere in town."

Quinn glanced toward the body. "You haven't seen Ferrell on your property since the day the cattle were killed?"

She averted her eyes. "No."

He might believe that answer had she not hesitated first. "Let's go. Someone needs to inform Marshal Ruiz."

Each time Quinn attempted to question her on the ride back to the house, he received one- or two- word answers that led him no closer to understanding why Ferrell's body would be lying across a creek on her land. Now they sat on the porch in silence, waiting until Issy returned with the marshal.

His patience dwindled further. Eager for her to confide in him before the lawman arrived, he opened his mouth, only to close it when Ellen stepped outside.

She handed them each a glass of water. "It's been quiet out here for quite some time. Have you told Quinn?"

Laurel encircled her glass with her long fingers and took a slow drink. She handed her mother the rest of the water. "Thank you, Momma. It quenched my thirst. Please let me handle this."

"But shouldn't you ..." Laurel's mother reached for Quinn's empty glass, his throat still dry. "I think you should."

Once she walked back inside, he asked, "What did she mean? What does she want you to tell me?"

"We'll discuss it when Issy returns."

She tempted him to shake the bullheadedness out of her. "If you tell me what you know now, maybe I can offer advice that will help when you speak with Wade."

She gave the crank of the butter churn a spin. "It sounds like you believe I'm guilty."

"That's not what I said." But was it his belief? Her shocked reaction at the creek appeared to have been real. "I want to help you."

"You are not my lawyer, Quinn."

His insides flinched as if she had slapped his face. Laurel was right, though. He was not her lawyer, yet he continued to insert himself into her troubles. What was he to her? Nothing.

Yet she had clung to him earlier when gallantry claimed his better judgment. If he could call it simple gallantry. Then she pulled away and took her warmth with her.

In the past few years, two or three worthy ladies had stirred his interest, women who returned his limited affection. But none twisted him in knots the way Laurel did. She ignited a fire of protectiveness and flames of passion, both good and bad, inside him—sensations that had lain dormant for years.

Quinn glanced sideways. Laurel's gaze melted the floorboards, and she gripped the handle of the butter churn in her fist until her knuckles turned white.

Before he could question her further, two riders galloped up the drive. Quinn walked down the porch steps, seeking the words that would keep Wade Ruiz from dragging Laurel off to Bold Creek's jail.

CHAPTER TWENTY-ONE

Laurel waited until the marshal reined in his mount, then wobbled as she stood on legs firm as wet paper. Strange. As the years passed, life's experiences made her more cowardly.

She asked Issy to walk and water the worn-out horses. Quinn and the marshal spent a few moments in a hushed conference, so she stayed on the porch and brushed dust from her trousers, trying not to worry.

Never had she felt so defenseless. Even growing up, she was always the strong one. Daddy and Momma both knew it. Though they used his young age as an excuse, they had denied her brother his request to take up arms against the Yankee invaders. When Daddy returned home for a few days of respite from the war, Laurel had overheard them talking. Momma feared that Lance would not last through the first fight, even if he were older. Daddy agreed, saying Laurel showed the greater ability to survive a conflict. Only Momma was privy to the accuracy of his words.

No, there had been one other. But John knew her weakness, and he had used it against her.

The thought strangled her memory of him. Throughout the years of their marriage and beyond, she had denied the truth of that statement, choosing to believe her husband protected her. But doubt flickered whenever he reminded her of her role in the conflict and his rescue of her virtue. Each time, she snuffed out the misgivings before letting them build into a conflagration that would engulf her in resentment and ingratitude.

Recompense no man evil for evil, Laurel. Vengeance is mine; I will repay, Laurel.

Camille had never once mentioned reclaiming her Bible, and Laurel could not force herself to give it back yet. Seeking a crumb of hope, she had returned to the beginning of the book of Romans. The writer spoke of faith and God's grace and finding joy in trials. She had never found joy in her trials.

Therefore being justified by faith, we have peace with God through our Lord Jesus Christ.

Peace? She had leaned on her husband for that elusive peace, but it never came. They shared contentment, but lately, she had formed a notion that John's love caused him to stoke her flames of guilt, keeping her indebted to him. What kind of love was that?

But God commendeth his love toward us, in that, while we were yet sinners, Christ died for us. He died for you, Laurel, a terrible sinner.

Why? Did she dare to think God loved her so much that He allowed the death of His own Son for someone like her? No. There must be an exception, a limit to His grace and mercy. A chuckle of disbelief escaped. The writer may as well have added, "The exception is you, Laurel Leigh Chamberlain Tillman."

How would Quinn have handled the skeletons in her cupboard? Would he have done like John and used the information to keep her close? Of course, that presumed he felt more than pity for her.

It wasn't as though Quinn would ever learn her secret anyway. She hadn't even told him about her connection to Ferrell. As the two men approached the porch, she expected the latter to change.

"Mrs. Tillman." The marshal removed his hat and ran his fingers through his hair to smooth it. "I understand Mr. Ferrell's been located."

She almost laughed. What an understatement!

"Marshal, I never said it was Ferrell." The lawyer intervened once more on her behalf. "I said it was someone who appeared to be wearing either his clothes or ones similar to his."

Ruiz faced Quinn. "Spencer, let's get one thing straight. I'm not looking to arrest your lady friend without just cause, so give me room to establish the facts for myself."

Laurel thought about coming to Quinn's defense, to tell Marshal Ruiz that he only wished to help. Quinn showed restraint in not replying, so she did, too.

The door opened, and Momma stepped onto the porch. "Good afternoon, Marshal. One of these days, we must invite you here for purely social reasons." She challenged him with a glare that said she would protect her daughter from him or anyone else. Laurel wanted to rush to her side and hide behind Momma's skirts like she did as a child.

Without so much as a "How do?" he asked, "Ma'am, what do you know about the relationship between your daughter and Reg Ferrell?"

Laurel stomped down the steps of the porch. "There was no relationship. Leave her alone, Marshal Ruiz. Please."

Her poor mother's eyes grew round and her face paled with discomfiture. She glanced from the marshal to Laurel to Quinn and back to Laurel, all the while worrying her hands.

"Momma, it's all right. I'll tell him the truth. I'll tell them both." Then she stared at Wade Ruiz and bloomed, her courage opening like a tulip in daylight. "I know he was a horrid man who threatened those I love."

"N-no you don't, ma'am." Everyone turned at the sound of Ernie's cracking voice. "I-I reckon it's my place to tell 'em."

Quinn's sympathy coiled around the young girl who had escaped

Arkansas and the perverted attentions of an older man. Camille and Issy stood beside Ernie, each with an arm around her. Becky watched from the opened door, having been ordered by her mother to stay in the house. Laurel hadn't instructed her not to listen.

"Miz Tillman told me not to worry about it none. She said she wouldn't let Ferrell have me. If it wasn't for her, I'da been walkin' alone to California by now. But she asked me to stay . . . said that, even though we ain't related by blood, I was family." Tears rolled down her ruddy face, and she sobbed. "H-Her and the others ain't never done nothing but make me feel like p-part of their f-family."

Quinn glanced at Laurel. She remained stoic next to the marshal, appearing unmoved by Ernie's expression of gratitude—except for the watery brightness of her eyes.

Wade Ruiz asked, "Did Mrs. Tillman say how she planned to keep Mr. Ferrell from taking you away?"

"No, sir." Ernie's eyes narrowed. "But she ain't done what you're thinking."

The marshal focused on Laurel, whose eyes shifted from one person to another. If Quinn could see her nervousness, so could the lawman.

"You have something you want to add, Mrs. Tillman?"

Once again, she glanced from Camille to Issy. They both nodded. Laurel drew in a deep breath, as though seeking to inhale any boldness they might have blown her way. "As I rode back from town on the day I stopped to see you, Mr. Ferrell intercepted me. He insisted I give him Ernie to take back to Arkansas."

Quinn stiffened. "Why didn't you tell me?"

The marshal glared before he turned back to Laurel. "And if you didn't?"

"If I didn't, he threatened to inform you he saw me shoot the Triple M cattle."

Marshal Ruiz pointed a finger at her. "Did he see you do it?"

His brusque question kindled a fire of indignation in Laurel's answer. "Of course not. I have already told you the truth of what happened that morning."

"Then why not tell me of meeting him when I rode out here the next day? You never mentioned seeing Ferrell, yet you knew I sought him."

Any hint of Laurel's anger seeped away, replaced by a surrender Quinn had never seen in her. "I kept quiet because I was afraid."

"Afraid of what?"

"Of what you're thinking now."

"And just what might that be?"

"That I'm guilty . . . of everything."

In a sign of frustration, the marshal clacked his teeth together twice. "Young woman, I wish you and everyone else would stop trying to read my mind. Haven't I proved you can trust me to be objective, to look at the evidence? *All* the evidence?"

Laurel searched his craggy face. "There's more you should know."

Quinn's breathing ran shallow. His outburst earlier had been a mistake, one Arthur would not have made. With all the restraint he could muster, he held his questions back.

Wade Ruiz nodded. "Go ahead."

"Mr. Ferrell insisted I bring Ernie to him the next afternoon. I kept the appointment without her. He never showed."

"Since you didn't have Miss Goodman with you as he asked, why did you bother going?"

"I hoped to bluff my way through the meeting by telling him that, even if I went to jail, the others would see to Ernie's safety."

"Where were you to meet him?"

She rubbed her hands together and looked away. "At the place where the steers were slaughtered. Close to where his body lies right now."

Quinn closed his eyes. He didn't know what to say. Obviously, no one else did, either, since the only sound he heard was the imagined voice of a jury foreman pronouncing a verdict: "Guilty of murder."

Laurel stood with an arm encircling the porch post while the marshal and Issy drove off in the buckboard. In the wagon bed, under an old blanket, rested Reg Ferrell's earthly body.

Quinn stepped off the porch. Despite what he'd said about being uncertain of the dead man's identity, there was no doubt in Laurel's mind. Although thankful Marshal Ruiz hadn't insisted she accompany him to town, she couldn't shake the feeling that would change soon. He had searched the area and found no undeniable evidence to arrest her, yet he'd warned her against leaving Bold Creek.

No evidence? "Did you give him the handkerchief?"

Quinn untied Ruthie's reins from the porch rail and turned toward the trail of dust that settled back onto the drive after being kicked up by the mules. "Yes."

A fleeting awareness of betrayal whipped through her, replaced by an unexpected sense of admiration for his integrity. Every crinkle around his eyes told her it pained him to have been the one to cause her more trouble. "Then why didn't he arrest me?"

"I'm not sure, but each time I'm in the man's presence, I hold a higher regard for him." Quinn settled into the saddle and paused, his gaze boring into Laurel. "Marshal Ruiz won't make an arrest until he's sure. But when he does, whoever he accuses will need a good lawyer."

As he rode away, her optimism dove deeper into hiding until she wasn't sure she would ever dredge it up again.

The door slammed behind her. "Momma?"

Laurel reached out and drew her daughter to her side, needing the warmth of Becky's small, innocent body. "Yes, Peanut?"

"Will the marshal take you away?"

She put all she had into a reassuring smile. "He has no reason, child. I did nothing wrong."

Becky bit her bottom lip before asking, "Will you teach me to shoot a gun?"

Laurel's heart constricted. "Why would you ask that of me?"

Tears formed in Becky's eyes. "Because I want to be like you,

Momma. I want to protect others from evil men like Mr. Ferrell. He would have hurt Ernie, but you wouldn't let him."

Laurel clutched Becky against her chest, soaking the girl's hair with the tears that ran down her cheeks. Did her daughter believe her capable of killing Ferrell?

Are you using my child against me, God? What more can I do to make things right with You?

"The answer is no, Becky. I will not teach you to shoot. And never ask me that question again."

CHAPTER TWENTY-TWO

Quinn played with the fried egg on his plate, swishing the firm white portion through the runny yolk and seldom putting the food in his mouth. He had been up since three o'clock, praying for wisdom and whittling away on a piece of wood he kept handy for such sleepless times.

For days, rumor and a warped version of truth had shot up and down the streets of Bold Creek like Comanche arrows. Most were aimed at the ladies of La Casa del Fuego, especially Laurel. Some chose Marshal Ruiz as their target for his refusal to arrest her. Quinn had fended off his own arrowheads of criticism for being at the ranch to discover the body. People asked why he involved himself in Laurel Tillman's affairs. Sometimes, he wondered the same thing.

The only arrows that pierced his chest were the ones let loose by Arthur. Being a gentleman, he softened his comments with a smattering of praise, as he had done yesterday.

Arthur had positioned himself on the corner of his desk while Quinn hoped to discuss a legal matter involving a property dispute between two farmers. His employer had another topic in mind.

"Son, you have the potential to be a benefit to me. You are

intelligent and charming. And unattached females find you intriguing enough to sway a few of their fathers toward seeking our legal advice."

True. Quinn had noticed a slight rise in the number of clients. He had hoped it came from a desire for his legal services.

"I fear, with your continued alignment with Mrs. Tillman, we will both pay the price."

Was this meeting a prelude to an ultimatum? Denounce Laurel or risk his relationship with Arthur? Even Mrs. Weaver had stopped pressing him to court Mary in her none-too-subtle manner.

"Sir, are you saying you would like me to leave your employ?" Quinn braced for Arthur's answer. Though he had planned to leave soon, the situation with Ferrell had kept him in Bold Creek—and if truth be told, other more personal reasons held him here.

"No. No, of course not. I only ask that you no longer interfere in the Ferrell investigation. If Mrs. Tillman is as innocent of the man's murder as you believe, the marshal will prove it."

"It isn't her innocence that he must prove, but her guilt."

"Don't split judicial hairs with me, Quinn. You know what I meant." Arthur walked around the desk and eased his lanky frame into his chair. "We've been over this before. Must I remind you we do not represent Mrs. Tillman? We represent the Triple M."

"What we are discussing is a different matter than responsibility in the deaths of six cattle. The current situation has nothing to do with the Triple M."

Not on the surface.

From there, the conversation slid downhill faster than a child using an old barn plank on packed snow. Any attempt at reasoning with Arthur met a deaf ear, which fueled a rigidity in Quinn he rarely showed.

"Would you like more coffee, Mr. Spencer?"

The question startled Quinn out of his reflections. He glanced up to find Mrs. Dillard hovering at his elbow, holding the coffeepot in one hand and reaching for his breakfast plate with the other.

He handed her the dish and shook his head. "No thank you. I'm running late as it is."

She looked at the picked-over food and clucked her tongue. "You ate next to nothing. You'll be hungry come mid-morning. I'll send you something."

"That isn't necessary, ma'am." At her frown, he grinned. "All right. I will receive it with pleasure and gratitude."

Quinn donned his hat and coat, preparing for the chilly, early morning walk to his office. His middle-of-the-night prayer and contemplation convinced him to offer Arthur an apology. He'd had no right raising his voice yesterday, but that was how their discussion ended—raised voices and an abrupt departure on Quinn's part.

"Have a good day, ma'am."

She followed him to the door. "Mr. Spencer?"

"Yes?"

"My dear husband told me that working with the hands kept worry from working on the mind." She pointed to a framed painting of a meadow overflowing with bluebonnets and the red and yellow blooms of Indian paintbrush and other wildflowers. Quinn had noticed its beauty the first time he entered the boarding house. "He painted this while our son suffered through smallpox. Mrs. Tillman, too, lost her husband and son to the same epidemic. Even in her grief, she visited me to express her condolences. I will never forget it."

Laurel's quiet deeds for others no longer surprised him. "Mr. Dillard was a talented painter."

She hooted. "Talented and messy. I cannot count how often I cleaned paint splotches from the floor and walls."

Quinn raised his attention to the ceiling. A renewed feeling of guilt engulfed him at leaving his room untidy. He should hurry back upstairs and brush the wood shavings into the fireplace.

"Mr. Spencer, a clean house takes little effort compared to gathering proper wisdom."

He kissed her cheek. "Thank you, Mrs. Dillard."

She responded with a middle-aged chortle. "Oh, begone with you. I have work to do." She waggled a pointed finger at him. "Never mind those biddies who have nothing better to do in a day than gossip. If they possessed an ounce of Christian charity, they would see Mrs. Tillman as a kind woman who doesn't need their approval. But she does need to accept God's grace before it's too late."

Ellen Chamberlain's words echoed in his mind. *I have prayed for years that God would send someone who understands what my daughter has faced. Someone to help her see that He longs to forgive all those who seek that forgiveness, no matter what they have done.*

Was he that person? How could he be? What did they have in common? What could he say to Laurel to lead her to what she needed? Quinn claimed to believe in the God of forgiveness, yet never once had he spoken to Laurel of that forgiveness.

None of the arrows he had felt thus far, including Arthur's, pierced deeper or truer than Mrs. Dillard's. Only hers were arrows tipped with a sincere burden for Laurel, neither gossip mongering nor warning.

He nodded to Mrs. Dillard and walked out onto the porch, pulling the door closed behind him. He had become a double-minded man, wavering in conviction while pleading for wisdom.

Breathing in the chilly morning air as though breathing in new life, he set off for his office to strengthen his faith and seek a way to help Laurel discover hers.

"Good afternoon, Mrs. Tillman."

The slight scent of the hair oil infiltrated Laurel's senses as she stood in the mercantile. More so after she caught herself purposely breathing deeply to inhale it. Quinn's voice came from her left, too near for her comfort.

Laurel willed reason to take over and turned her head to find his face within inches of hers, the scar running along his jawline level with her eyes. The disfigurement renewed an awareness of her own deformity and the reason for it. Her conscience contorted at the thinning of his lips and the wounded look in his eyes.

Casting aside regret over his disappointment, she turned back to the shelf and added a tin of tea to the empty basket hanging over her arm. "Good afternoon, Mr. Spencer."

"I came out of the barbershop a few minutes ago and caught sight of you entering the mercantile. I've been hoping to see you in town."

She slid sideways and pretended to look for something on the shelf, sweeping aside more tins and cans and rearranging them. "Why is that?"

"Will you join me for a midday meal at the café?"

His normal, deep and commanding voice engaged the interest of other customers in the store. Stares from all directions marched over her like ants. She had hoped to get in and out of the mercantile with little notice. Now he had brought attention to her presence.

Laurel stood dumbstruck. Should she accept his invitation or refuse?

Too much history came between them for her to be comfortable in his company. That's what she'd told herself over and over since the discovery of Ferrell's body.

Why had her emotions betrayed her that day? She had taken refuge in his arms and enjoyed every moment. The safety. The security. The ability to lean on someone else. She hadn't experienced such warmth and concern from a man in too long. But anyone could have prompted those feelings. It had nothing to do with the person standing next to her.

That didn't explain why her emotions betrayed her now. They urged her to accept his invitation when she should turn her back on this man who had been an enemy, who may still be one. He had never said he trusted in her innocence. And she couldn't say she trusted him. The past was an evil devil to fight.

The hum of whispers reached her ears. She leaned toward him and whispered, "I don't believe you want to associate with me, Mr. Spencer. It can't be good for you."

"Don't assume you know what's good for me, Laurel." He had lowered his voice, too, reminding her of two up-to-no-good conspirators. "I'm willing to risk being the subject of people's speculations. However, I must know if you're willing to be seen with me."

He fingered the scar, the hurt from her earlier gawking no longer mirrored in his eyes. In fact, they struck her as reflecting a baffling empathy. "What is it about this that continually draws your interest?"

Silence shouted between them as he awaited an explanation she had no intention of giving. Instead, for once, she allowed herself to act on impulse. Replacing the tea tin on the shelf, she slid her arm through Quinn's and had the satisfaction of seeing his eyebrows rise in astonishment, then draw together with wariness.

She took a step forward. "Shall we go?"

CHAPTER TWENTY-THREE

Quinn sipped his coffee while watching Laurel over the edge of the cup. She sat straight in the stiff restaurant chair and held her head high. An occasional twitch in a neck muscle was her only reaction to sporadic comments by those who didn't mind their verbal thrusts being overheard.

On the way to the café, he had been tempted to intercede on her behalf and must have telegraphed his intention through the strain of his arm muscles. In each instance, she'd tightened her fingers around his sleeve and tugged, prompting him to control his response.

Why had it taken so long to realize that Laurel Tillman had more grace in her thumbnail than some Bold Creek residents had in their entire bodies?

"I admire the way you've let the rudeness of others pass without comment."

"They believe I murdered someone, Quinn." She picked up her fork and pierced a piece of carrot with the tines, the intensity rending it in two pieces.

If she turned the other cheek at the rude behavior, why had she treated him like a case of typhoid upon his arrival? And she never answered his question about why his scar caused her to run from him the first time she saw it. Something about it had frightened her, and she was no coward.

Today, too, Laurel's sullen gaze had fallen on the mark, breaking open a wound he thought had healed the day he wrapped his arms around her and encountered a desire he hadn't known in years.

Then he realized his scar didn't repulse her, not in the way he had imagined. Laurel's grim face had displayed a dozen different emotions, among them, anxiety, shock, fear, sadness. But why? Soon, he would ask again and not settle for her skillful change of subject.

She set her fork on the table and shrugged. "Quinn, sometimes people have good instincts about a person."

His own fork clattered on the bowl in front of him and the food he had eaten weighed like a stone in his stomach. "Are you saying they're right? That you had something to do with—"

"No." She ripped a yeast roll in two and dropped the halves on her plate. "I am saying no such thing. But that doesn't mean my past is . . . as it should be."

"Laurel, no one's past is as it should be." He reached for the hand that rubbed her temple and pulled it down to the table, leaving his fingers enveloped around hers, hoping to warm the chill on her skin. "The only person in this world who never sinned was Jesus. His sacrifice gave imperfect human beings like you and me the way to become perfect in God's sight. And for that, I'm thankful."

"Religion is not a subject I want to discuss."

Laurel tried to pull away, but even knowing it was improper and people watched them, he held fast, unable to let her sweep the subject away like dirt on a floor.

"Why not?" Quinn became conscious that his thumb rubbed along the top of her bare hand. He stayed the unruly appendage and excused the motion as an effort to provide comfort. His grip loosened, and she pulled her hand free from his.

"Now isn't this a cozy little meal?" Sliding the closest empty chair up to their table, Royce straddled the seat and set his hat on the blue oilcloth table covering. Murphy stood nearby. The older MacMahon kept his attention riveted on Laurel and called out, "Lillian, honey, bring me what these folks are having!"

Laurel throttled her fork, but her lips stretched like molasses taffy and her words sounded every bit as sweet when she asked, "Quinn, did you invite this lout to dine with us?"

Murphy laughed and Royce shot him a scathing look, which failed to quiet the younger man. Quinn placed his elbows on the table and pressed his entwined fingers against the lower portion of his face. Even at that, his shoulders shook.

He lowered his hands and cleared his throat. "No, I didn't. Would you like me to remove him?"

She made a show of studying Royce's temper-reddened countenance. The cattleman choked the hat's broad brim in his curled fists and his knuckles blanched. Laurel set her fork inside her bowl and sat back in the chair. "He obviously has something dreadfully important he wants to tell us, so why don't we let him get it out before he faints dead away with apoplexy?"

Royce relaxed his hands and dipped his head. "That was amusing, Laurel. Let's hope you're as funny in front of a judge, because you'll soon need all the help you can get." Lillian set a steaming bowl of beef stew in front of him with a clatter. He glanced up, then discharged the young woman with a wave.

She didn't go far. Her scowl charred the hairs of MacMahon's auburn head. Many people in the restaurant abandoned their meals, and most listened with no concern over their ill-mannered eavesdropping.

Quinn had grown weary of being dismissed like a bothersome gnat by the rancher. If not for his curiosity over what Royce had to say, he would have insisted the man leave.

"Only another five weeks until the end of the year, Laurel. You know what happens then."

Ruddy spots colored her cheekbones and acid dripped from her tongue. "Yes, I do. Issy will be proved right, and we'll all smell the fragrance of the skunk you are, Royce."

From a couple of feet away, Murphy straightened and glared at his brother. "Royce, I didn't agree to meet you here to watch you browbeat a woman."

"If you have a weak stomach, Murph, why don't you go sit down? I'm only reminding Laurel that the days are passing. If she wants to avoid a lawsuit, she'll pay me for the cattle she killed."

"Pay you?" As calmly as possible, Quinn countered Royce's threat. "We've been over this before. She doesn't owe you reimbursement for an act she never committed."

"I suggest you talk to your employer. He has the papers ready . . . regardless of whether you agree." The eldest MacMahon brother rose from his seat and picked up his bowl. He weaved through the café, nodding and laughing with those he passed on his way to a vacant table at the front of the room.

Murphy bobbed his head. "Good day, ma'am. Spencer." He followed his brother.

Quinn speared a chunk of beef from the stew and stared at it, imagining it was meat from a Triple M Longhorn. He set the fork back in the bowl, his appetite gone. He laid the money for their meals on the table. "Shall we carry on our discussion outside?"

Laurel glanced around the room. People continued to watch them. Quinn might think her neighbors' comments didn't hurt, but in truth, since Ferrell's death, their hostility raked her flesh with fearsome claws. Should Marshal Ruiz ever decide to charge her, where would she find a fair jury?

She pushed back her chair with the screech of wood on wood and rose. "It seems prudent to leave them with a little mystery to my life."

They strolled down the boardwalk toward the edge of town. Laurel supposed Quinn slowed his steps so as not to overtax her hobbling movements. The gesture touched her more than she would have imagined. He was a gentleman, even if the thumb that caressed the back of her hand was anything but gentlemanly. A tremor quaked through her. From the November breeze cooling the back of her neck, or from the memory of that touch? Laurel shrugged deeper into her coat.

Silent and contemplative, Quinn walked on the street side with his hands clasped behind his back. Did he realize his mistake in the café and desire not to repeat it? After all, she was not Camille. Most likely, he wasn't particularly fond of her. She was only someone he sought to save from the trials of this life and the next.

Laurel eyed Quinn and the area once covered by a beard—lighter than the sun-browned skin surrounding it. She wished the scar and disparate flesh tones took away from his handsome features. But she feared they only added to the appealing quality of a man she tried to keep in the enemy camp.

After realizing she had been staring, she looked away. "I tried to convince the marshal that Royce hired Ferrell to kill his own livestock."

Quinn chuckled. "I admit to having made the same suggestion."

"Yes, I know. He thinks we conspired to dupe him." Her uneven footsteps provided an odd echo on the wooden planks. "He became angry with me and accused us of working together to put ideas into his head."

"Working together?" Quinn's dubious expression reflected her own thought.

Despite their connection, she smiled. "Amazing, isn't it?"

"A few months ago, it would have been impossible." He slipped behind her to allow another man to pass by, then stepped alongside her again. "Do you think Royce is responsible for all that's happened?"

"The killing of his cattle? Maybe. Murder? I wish I could say for certain. He's arrogant enough to think he could get away with it. I'm surprised the man's head fits through the front door of the Triple M—and it's a double door. He's like his father, both thinking themselves to be above the rest of us. When I turned down Royce's offer of marriage, he took it as a personal affront. It was the way he put the proposal that offended me most."

Quinn all but stopped walking. "You mean you might have married him had he put it differently?"

Laurel tried to picture herself as Mrs. Royce MacMahon, but all she saw was the jagged teeth of an animal trap biting into her ankle and holding her against her will. "Where has your common sense gone, Mr. Spencer?"

He laughed and took hold of her elbow to assist her down the steps and onto the dirt street. Then he tucked her arm in his and they continued their walk.

"What about Murphy? Would he be capable of shooting the cattle for some other reason? I see little familial devotion between the brothers."

She shook her head. "No, there is not. But I can't picture him doing such a thing."

Quinn's forehead crinkled. "That surprises me. Not because I believe Murphy played a role in what happened, but because you dislike both men. It's a revelation to hear you express even the slightest bit of faith in a MacMahon."

"Murphy annoys me because he won't stand up to his brother, but I hold no real animosity toward him. He only does what Royce tells him to do. One day, that will change."

"If the conversation in the café is any indication, I think he may prove your confidence in him. However, Issy certainly despises the man."

"Issy seems to have her own reasons for not approving of Murphy."

"Like you have your reasons for not approving of me?"

The comment stilled her, and she stared at the toes of the shoes peeking from under her skirt. Disapprove of Quinn? When had she gone from disapproving to . . .

How did she really feel about him? Certainly not the same as when they first met—after she rescued him from the mountain lion. Since the day he rescued her from Royce's accusations, he had whittled away Laurel's antagonism little by little, like he'd done to the piece of wood he'd carved into Becky's flute. Oh, she put up a good fight, especially after having seen the scar, but the shock had faded. She now understood that everything was her fault, not his. Had she not been where she didn't belong all those years ago, he would simply be another Yankee.

"Murphy is a hard man to fathom. Deep down, I think he's a good man. You two have more in common than you realize, Quinn."

She raised her face to find they had walked past the church and stood at the entrance to the cemetery. Had she led them there out of habit, like a wandering dog returning home? Most every time she came to town her feet carried her here.

Quinn stopped her when she turned to go back the way they came. "I owe you an apology, Laurel."

Heart thundering, her gaze automatically went to the area of her damaged knee. Did he recognize her after all? "An apology? Whatever for?"

Worry lines appeared between his eyes. "In the interest of my career, I've allowed people to influence my attitude toward you and the other ladies of La Casa del Fuego these past months. I readily came to Lillian's defense, yet stood by and let certain people say false things about all of you. I have wavered between helping you and ignoring your need for help. But God reached out and shook some much-needed sense into me recently."

"God shook sense into you? And here I thought you volunteered your acquaintance."

"You haven't exactly been a beacon of welcome and friendship." He grinned. "But I forgive you."

Her mouth tightened at his suggestion that she needed to be forgiven. She slammed her palm against the latch of the iron gate leading into the cemetery. The gate flew open and clanged against the stone wall. Laurel marched inside, her feet carrying her in a familiar direction. "You forgive me?"

"Yes." Quinn's composed answer sounded near her left ear. "And God waits to forgive you for whatever you think is unforgivable. He cares about you."

Was He waiting for her to come to Him?

Stopping in front of the two headstones marking the graves of her family members, she whirled so quickly her petticoats wrapped around her legs, threatening to trip her. "Don't be too sure." Her voice sputtered into a bitter mumble. He reached for her hand again, but she tucked it behind her back before he could touch it. "I think He seeks only to punish me."

"Punish you? Why?"

"Ask Him since the two of you are such close friends. He can explain why He's seen fit to chastise me at every turn. Not that I can blame Him."

She turned her back to Quinn and stepped closer to the smallest marker. Crouching before it, she traced the letters engraved on her son's tombstone. J—O—H.

Wearing gloves prevented her from feeling the cold, rough stone against her fingertips, prevented her from feeling close to her little boy. Her tantrum melted as she knelt by the grave. "He was only five."

"I truly am sorry for you."

Laurel turned at the sympathy in his voice. His eyes echoed the sentiment. "Have you ever lost a child, Quinn?"

"No. I never wed." He fidgeted with the bottom button on his coat, looking as though he expected it to pop off. "I nearly married. My fiancée died during the war."

"And you've never fallen in love again?" What was she doing by asking such a question? "I'm sorry. I had no right to be so forward."

In the ensuing silence, she rose from the ground and brushed from her black gloves the dirt that had gathered in the crevices of her baby's name.

He drew in a deep breath and released it. "Did your family own slaves?"

The abrupt change in topic stopped her with her hands together as though in mid-prayer. The reticule dangling from her wrist continued to sway back and forth. "No. No, Momma would never have allowed it. Neither would my daddy."

"Your mother wouldn't allow it?"

Laurel shook the brown grass from her wool skirt and smiled.

"Surprising, is it not? Once Momma was a strong, self-assured woman. Daddy counted on her opinion regarding decisions that affected the family. He believed the biblical idea of a helpmeet meant God also used his wife and her working mind to keep him on the right path. Thankfully, she's coming back to believing it of herself again."

Quinn removed his slouch hat and twirled it in his hands as the wind ruffled his hair. "My father believed the opposite. He considered the idea of a wifely helpmeet to be one who implemented the daily decisions he made. Don't get me wrong, he was a godly man who ran his household in an orderly fashion." He stared at the spinning hat. "Mother never seemed to mind."

"Did anyone ever ask her?"

Quinn stopped the hat's motion and gazed at her. "Not that I know."

The awed reply gave Laurel reason to think he had never considered doing so. "I suppose different methods work best in different families."

"I suppose." The twirling resumed. "It's good to hear that Mrs. Chamberlain is recovering her self-confidence."

"Yes." Laurel started toward the cemetery gate, hesitant to finish the sentence by saying she suspected him of having something to do with Momma's attitude. "What made you ask if our family had owned slaves?"

After walking out of the cemetery, Quinn closed the gate behind them with care. "We were discussing my fiancée."

"And I told you—"

"For the first time in years, I'd like to talk about it . . . with you."

Laurel wished she hadn't asked in the first place, because now she didn't want to hear about someone he once loved.

CHAPTER TWENTY-FOUR

"You aren't the only one who found the war costly, Laurel. There's a cemetery in Ohio with a similar stone. It's engraved with the name of Amy Grace Rendell."

Quinn paced in front of the ironwork fence. Forward for a few feet, turn and march back—all with the precision of years of morning and evening drills. Why this overwhelming urge to speak of Amy? And why, of all people, must it be with Laurel? If he discussed her with anyone, it should be Arthur, a man who had known her.

"Amy held a firm conviction against one human being owning another."

"Your fiancée was an abolitionist?"

"Yes. Her father had been a member of the Ohio Anti-Slavery Society for several years. I didn't know it then, but the Rendell's farm was a station on the Underground Railroad. Sometimes, her father and brothers acted as conductors, seeing people safely to the next stop."

"That was illegal. They risked a large fine and imprisonment for helping escaped slaves."

The censure implied in her comment stung. Quinn leaned with

the back of his head pressed against the knobby bark of a nearby oak tree. Above him, a squirrel perched on a partially bare limb, frozen with the fear of discovery. Did Amy freeze upon being discovered that night?

"They risked much more than that. Before the war, Ohio was a state divided on the slavery issue. While it wasn't legal to own slaves, many people feared escaped slaves would come north and take their jobs. The presence of abolitionists often sparked violence. The Rendells experienced it firsthand."

When asking Laurel to dine with him, he had planned to bring up the subject of her spiritual need. He had not intended to discuss the MacMahons, his family relationships, or his failure to protect the woman he had loved. Did God, in His omniscience, know that Amy's death somehow related to Laurel's situation?

She limped closer and placed her gloved fingers on his upper arm, the imagined warmth of the contact searing his skin through his coat. "I didn't mean to criticize. They sound like brave and caring people."

Nodding, Quinn pulled away, unable to concentrate on his story with her touching him. "Amy and I planned to marry in September of sixty-one, but by then the war had broken out and I enlisted in the cavalry. No one thought it would last so long. We thought the Rebs would—" Her raised eyebrow sent his explanation in a different direction. "Through Arthur's letters to Henry, I discovered her family's increasing involvement in the escape of slaves to Canada."

Quinn's worry had risen to resentment the first time he learned of their actions through a third party. Amy should have told him. Then the resentment grew into a concern that she felt unable to tell him something so significant, that she couldn't trust him to understand and approve. She should have felt free to tell him anything. They should have had no secrets from one another.

Then again, why should she trust him? He'd been vocal in the past when he didn't approve of decisions she made—just like his father.

"I trusted Amy's parents to keep her safe until I returned." He slapped the palm of his hand against the tree trunk. "We should have married before I left. Then she could have lived with my family, away from any threat."

"Sometimes, a man loves a woman so much, he fears losing her— or her affection—to the point of controlling her life."

Quinn glanced at John Tillman's tombstone. Had he tried to control Laurel while he lived? He couldn't imagine her allowing anyone to do that. "You're right, but I couldn't bear seeing her in danger."

"You wanted what was best for her. I cannot see how whatever happened to your Amy was your fault."

Quinn paused, grappling with the hurt that still pricked like an everlasting thorn. As usual, he wavered over who to direct his anger against. Her family? Or those in the South who opposed slavery but chose not to stop the abomination taking place in their backyards— people like the Chamberlains? He pictured Laurel doing what Amy had done. It wasn't hard. She was as strong and independent a woman as his fiancée—even more so.

"What we think is the right thing to do one day can prove to be the worst decision we ever made." Laurel's quiet words contained a melancholy wisdom and dissolved Quinn's ire with the ease of sugar dissolved in hot water.

He rubbed a hand down his face. Long ago, he had learned that anger brought nothing but regret. "Amy's father had arranged to conduct a family of five to Columbus. From there, they would have made their way to Canada. While working the farm that day, a cow kicked Elijah Rendell, breaking a couple of ribs and leaving him unable to travel. Amy's two older brothers were gone, or they would have taken his place. Bounty hunters prowled the area. Time was not on the side of the escaped slaves, so Amy—"

"She served as their conductor."

He nodded. "Later, I found out later it wasn't the first time. Though careful never to mention their activities by name for fear of my letter falling into the wrong hands, time and again I wrote her not to become involved in the disputes of her 'brothers.' It was a dangerous and foolhardy thing for a woman to do. Each time, I'd receive a return letter. She argued her case with the fire of a lawyer, while also using words that wouldn't give away her family's activities."

"Amy was an intelligent woman."

A chuckle escaped and caught him by surprise. "If she'd stood toe-to-toe with me in camp, she would have poked a finger at my chest. I'd hear the stamp of her foot as she insisted God didn't give a man the sole responsibility to do what was right. I have to admit that I read her letters over and over just to imagine that fit of temper from a woman whose manner normally reflected the gentlest of feminine spirits. No. Amy should have been no one other than herself."

What about Laurel? His gaze ran over the woman at his side, taking in the small, flowered straw hat cocked forward atop a mound of shining blonde hair. The simple black coat covered the upper half of the brown wool skirt. He breathed in the scent of lilacs from her soap, or maybe a dab of perfume. Today, every inch of her attire, her demeanor, proclaimed Laurel pretty and feminine.

To quell the growing pull toward her, Quinn forced his memory to conjure the other Laurel, the one he had first seen wearing the worn plaid shirt, denim trousers and chaps. Odd that, at first sight, he had thought she was a long-haired male. How could he have ever mistaken Laurel for a man?

Amy and this stubborn southern rebel were as different in temperament as Grant and Lee, yet, in their convictions, he saw them as sisters. Each took seriously a responsibility to protect others less able to protect themselves. Was it that quality that attracted him to both women? The notion that Laurel's appeal equaled the intensity of Amy's shook Quinn to his bones.

"What happened?"

He blinked away the internal upheaval. "What?"

"To your Amy. What happened to her?"

"After a while, I could only pray and leave her future up to God."

A frown passed over Laurel's face.

"Amy took it upon herself to save the slave family. She dressed in clothes belonging to her younger brother and crept out of the house that night. She didn't know the bounty hunters, two of them, suspected the Rendell's involvement in the Underground Railroad. They watched the road less than a mile away from the farm. As Amy drove the wagon, they stepped from among the trees, one in front and one behind. Because of the darkness and the attire, they mistook her for one of her brothers. They insisted on inspecting the cargo under the canvas in back. When she refused to let them, one man struck her. He may have meant to render her unconscious, but the blow broke her neck."

Quinn sighed, having finished the story dispassionately, almost as if he recited a stranger's tragedy. In fact, with the telling, it was as if a dark compartment in his mind opened, freeing him of the need to keep Amy's ill-fated exploit apart from his memory of the genteel woman he left for the war.

Silence stood between them until Laurel said, "You were ashamed of Amy."

Ashamed? How did she get such a ludicrous notion from his story? "Of course not." *Weren't you?* "I served alongside Buffalo Soldiers at Fort McKavett. I appreciated her dedication to saving slaves—human beings. I would never—"

"It's in your voice, Quinn. You may have loved her. A part of you may have respected her deeds. But a greater part was ashamed she wasn't the embodiment of femininity you admired."

A yearning to defend his principles engulfed him. "Yes, I disapproved of what she did. It was dangerous and imprudent and . . ." And not the actions of a lady.

In the mouth of the foolish is a rod of pride.

"I suppose once you heard about what happened, it strengthened your hatred."

He stepped away from the tree. "Hatred? Of whom?"

"Southerners. Confederates. Slave owners. God. Choose whichever fits."

"I hated no one, Laurel, least of all God."

"Why not?"

Was this the reason for her aversion to God? Had she been scorned for so long that she thought God had turned his back on her? "Laurel, I am not your enemy and neither is God. He loves you."

She laughed and swiped at the corner of her eye with her palm. "My goodness. If that's so, what more could happen if He hated me?"

"I don't think you've done anything that could make God hate you."

"Really? What if I told you—" Both lips drew inward until they disappeared, holding captive whatever she'd wanted to say.

Quinn ached at seeing torment in her face and breathed a quick prayer for the right words. "Laurel, if you sincerely ask God's forgiveness, He will grant it."

That narrow chin of hers rose in challenge. "What if I killed someone?"

Killed someone? He held his breath while scrutinizing her face.

"No, I did not kill Mr. Ferrell."

Then how to answer something like that? She had no idea how long it had taken him to forgive both himself and the Confederates. But he had done so and, with God's help, had even forgiven the bounty hunter who struck down Amy.

Quinn took a step forward. His gaze never wavered from hers. "He would still love you. God hates sin, but He stands ready with His grace to forgive the sinner."

"But He punishes that sin, does He not?"

"There are consequences to be paid." The trepidation in her voice brought out a gentleness in his. "God's own Son bore the penalty for our sins, Laurel. The death of Jesus on the cross was a willing sacrifice, so that, through his blood, we have peace with the Father. He might allow consequences to take place, but I don't believe He sits on His throne holding a hickory stick and beating us across the legs every time we make a mistake. If that were the case, walking would be very uncomfortable for me. Instead, His Spirit lovingly prods us back to the right path."

"Lovingly?"

"Some of us resist and need a little more pressure." He cocked his head. "Now, you didn't answer *my* question. What have you done that was grave enough to raise such anger in God?" He waited for her to say something, anything that would give him a clue about what tortured her.

After several moments of silence, her lips stretched into a lifeless smile as she walked away from him. "Nothing."

Quinn's shoulders sank with disappointment. "How can I help you if you—"

"President Hayes has declared a holiday of thanksgiving on the twenty-ninth." She stopped and turned toward him. "Momma has planned a feast, sure we owe God an immense amount of thanks for His care this year. Although, I can't think why with the way things have gone."

"Try harder."

Laurel ignored his goading. "As I was about to say, if you have no other invitation . . ." She made a face. "That wasn't how I meant to word it. If you would like to join us, we'll set a place for you at our table. Becky, Momma and Camille—all of us—will be happy to have you."

Quinn's jaw dropped with the ease of a broken handle on a well pump. Laurel was asking him to dinner? *The* Laurel Tillman who, only weeks ago, refused him a doctor and would have slammed the barn door on his backside in her eagerness to see him gone? True, he had dined with the women before, but never at her invitation.

Fighting to control his astonishment, he stammered a reply. "I-I accept."

"You invited Quinn for our Thanksgiving celebration?" Momma set the towel on the kitchen counter and faced Laurel with a round mouth and crimped eyebrows.

"Yes, I did."

"But what about ..." She peered around the otherwise empty kitchen and whispered, "You know."

"I am a grown woman. I can contend with the history that stands between us."

A sly smile tugged at her mother's lips. Laurel felt like a bug under her daddy's magnifying glass.

"What made you change your mind about him?"

"I have not changed my mind." Well, yes, she had—somewhat. All right, mostly. "I just ... I have not changed my mind."

"Laurel Leigh, do not lie to your dear mother."

Seeing the light of humor glowing in Momma's eyes, Laurel huffed with impatience. "You are enjoying this, aren't you?"

"And why shouldn't I enjoy the idea of my daughter's newfound ability to forgive?"

"Forgive? Are you forgetting what happened to Daddy and Lance?" And those who never saw the source of their impending death. They never saw her.

Ellen Chamberlain wrapped her arms around Laurel and whispered in her ear, "Daddy and Lance are ever on my mind, as is the price you have paid over the years. I pray this is the beginning of your ability to forgive yourself."

Laurel was ruing the day her mother rediscovered her self-assurance. Ever since, she'd felt set upon by Momma, Camille, and Quinn. They all expressed a desire to see her freed from the weight of her sin.

And whatever had she been thinking yesterday? Quinn told a sad story about a heroic dead fiancée and she invited him to dinner. Had there ever been such a sorry puppet?

"Oh, my. What will we serve?" Momma fussed with removing her apron and patted her hair as if the man would walk through the doorway at any moment. "I wonder what dishes he prefers. Did you ask him? Do you think he would rather have cornbread or yeast rolls? Or maybe my biscuits? He seemed to find those appetizing before.

Which do you think?"

Momma hadn't refreshed her entire store of confidence. Laurel laughed, the first such true amusement she had expressed in many a day. "Land's sakes, he is not royalty. He will eat what we eat."

"We want to make a good impression."

"Why? He spent three weeks under this roof. If he wasn't impressed by the time he left us, one meal won't make much difference."

"Yes, but he's your guest this time. He won't be here under the same circumstances. Wouldn't you prefer he enjoys himself?"

"My guest?" Laurel waggled her finger. "No, no, no. I invited him for the rest of you, since you have taken quite a shine to him. Camille, especially, should be grateful."

Had that whine actually come from her mouth? Laurel released a disgusted sigh and patted Momma's arm. "I have work to do. I'll leave the dinner in your expert hands."

Laurel had enough to worry about.

CHAPTER TWENTY-FIVE

Laurel lumbered up the porch steps while imagining the pleasure of her tired muscles soaking in a hot tub with steam rising toward the ceiling. She felt the soap cleansing the dirt from her face, neck, and hands. The image vanished with her mother's piercing laughter.

Taken aback by the responding masculine laughter, Laurel opened the door. Her mother stood next to the fireplace while Marshal Ruiz lit the kindling. What brought him here? Neither one noticed her. They had eyes only for each other.

"Ellen, that rascal picked cactus barbs from his feet for days."

"Oh, Wade, the poor man."

Wade? Ellen? Laurel rejected the idea there was anything personal between her widowed parent and the man who held her future in his hands. She stepped inside and gave the door a firm shove.

They both flinched at the noise. She forced a smile. "I wasn't expecting you, Marshal."

A hard stare replaced the humor in his face. "Mrs. Tillman."

This was it. He came to do his duty. She would have to forego the soothing bath that would wash away the smell of sheep. She might even have to forego her freedom.

215

"I came to talk to Miss Goodman. Has she returned yet?"

Laurel pressed a hand to her stomach. He didn't want her. Not today. "You came to speak with Ernie?"

Marshal Ruiz nodded. "That's what I said."

Laurel glanced from him to her mother and back to Ruiz again. "She's in the bunkhouse."

Momma moved away from the fireplace and "Wade." "I sent Becky out there a few minutes ago, Laurel, to await the girl's return."

Footsteps clomped across the porch planks. The front door opened, and Ernie stepped inside. Her skittish gaze moved between the adults, settling on Momma. "You wanted to see me, ma'am?"

"Yes, dear. Marshal Ruiz would like to speak with you."

Ernie took wobbling baby steps into the room. "Sir?"

The fierce professionalism the marshal had turned on Laurel melted into gentleness as he motioned Ernie to the sofa. Once the girl was seated, he pulled a slip of paper from his vest pocket. "I contacted the marshal of Lafayette County. That is where you're from?"

"Y-yes, sir."

With a soft grunt, he lowered himself to one knee in front of Ernie and held her gaze with his own. "I informed him of Mr. Ferrell's death and inquired about the man's connection with Mr. Hicks."

"You didn't . . . you didn't tell him about me?" Ernie's low voice cracked with alarm.

"I'm afraid I had to, Miss Goodman."

"Virgil Hicks sent Ferrell here to take Ernie back. What if he—"

"Mrs. Tillman." Her name spilled from his mouth with the tartness of vinegar. "For once, let me finish."

They glared at one another until Laurel waved a hand in resignation. She plopped into the rocking chair beside the fireplace and set the runners slapping against the floor planks. "Fine. Terrify the poor child."

Wade Ruiz scowled at her and turned back to Ernie. He unfolded the paper. "Are you aware, Miss Goodman, that your father is looking for you?"

"My pa? I ain't seen him in ages."

Laurel stopped the rocker. The no-good drunk who had abandoned his wife and child? But the awe in Ernie's voice spoke volumes about the girl's feelings for him.

"Seems he found the straight and narrow and returned to town for you and your mother. He wants to send money for your transportation home. That is, if you want to go back."

Laurel wanted to shout her objection. What if the father slipped into his old ways and ran out on his daughter again? She chewed her thumbnail and kept quiet. Only Ernie could make this decision.

"But what about that money I owe Mr. Hicks?"

"Seems your father has done well for himself in the time he's been gone. Hicks got wind of that news and thought he'd marry into money. Don't you worry about a bogus debt."

The teen's glance at each of them sought an answer to the dilemma. "I don't reckon I know what I want to do. I like it here, but . . ."

The marshal patted her hand. "You don't have to decide now. In fact, I prefer you wait a while. I'm not ready to let you leave Texas just yet."

"Why is that, Wade?"

"Ferrell's death investigation, Ellen. I can't rule out anyone involved in the matter."

His words weighed like a pile of boulders on Laurel's chest. Under her breath, she cursed the day Reg Ferrell stepped one foot over the state line.

"And I invited that man to partake in our celebration dinner on the twenty-ninth." Laurel's mother slammed the bowl of boiled potatoes down, apparently unconcerned with whether the force chipped the stoneware or left a mark on the table. "The nerve of him to suggest our precious Ernie would do something so vile. I should uninvite him." Her face contorted into an expression of indecision. "Shouldn't

I?"

"Momma, I think it's too late to take back your invitation."

Issy set forks at each place, the metal clanking against the plates. "He may not have come out and said it, but we all know what he meant."

"Issy, the marshal has his responsibility." Camille poured coffee into the cups. "We must allow him to do his job."

Laurel stirred the peas simmering in the pot on the stove while mulling over the quandary they found themselves in. Someone shot Reg Ferrell multiple times. It wasn't her, and she would never believe Ernie was capable of it, unless the man had tried to kidnap her. Laurel shook her head. The girl would never do it. Besides, that theory did not fit with the method of his demise. Ernie carried only a knife.

Who else besides the ladies on her ranch had a connection to the Arkansan? Quinn Spencer, but—

"Right, Laurel?"

At the mention of her name, she turned toward Issy. "Hmm?"

"Where have you been, dear? We've been discussing whether Ernie should return to her father in Arkansas or stay here. What do you think?"

Ernie stood in the doorway to the kitchen, her eyes wide in anticipation of Laurel's answer. What should she say? Did John Barleycorn Goodman deserve her? It was during times like these, when everyone looked to her for guidance, that Laurel wished for the wisdom God gave King Solomon.

"I think we should eat before our supper grows cold."

The ewe spawned a fretful bleat and tugged on the rope tied to a fence post by the barn. "Easy, girl. I'll be careful." Laurel removed the thick leather gloves covering her hands and separated the wool to better inspect the gash on the animal's shoulder. "It doesn't appear to be too bad, Camille. I wonder how she got it."

"If I make a guess, will you promise not to lose your temper?"

Straightening, Laurel tilted her head. "Is there a reason I should lose my temper?"

Camille spoke while trimming away nearly two inches of fine wool. "'Be swift to hear, slow to speak, slow to wrath'."

"And where is that scripture located?" Using a sponge, Laurel rinsed the cut with warm water to remove any dirt that might cause infection.

"James, first chapter, nineteenth verse."

"Fine. Then tell me quickly so I may hear quickly and get it over with."

Laughing, Camille applied an antiseptic salve to the wound. "That is not the point. You must be willing to listen and understand before you speak."

Laurel frowned at the hesitation of her friend to provide an answer for fear it might anger her. "Does everyone consider me a shrew?"

Camille bolted upright. "Not at all. Laurel, I spoke in jest. You have many worries at the moment, and your relationship with the MacMahons is so strained that I—"

"The MacMahons? What have they to do with my ewe's injury?"

"They have replaced the fencing along the border with your property and thrown a piece into our pasture. She became entangled in it."

Laurel glanced at the sheep's cut. "So help me, I—" At Camille's raised eyebrows, she lifted her hands, palms outward in surrender. "I feel no wrath. I am merely concerned for my animals." Laurel limped toward the gate of the pen. "This is nothing but a devil's rope with barbs. Let's tend to this lady and search for other stray pieces of wire. I won't send her out to be sliced like a Christmas ham again."

"Speaking of ham, Ellen would like a turkey for our meal of thanksgiving."

Laurel's stomach dropped to her knees. "And?"

"And you are to provide one from those that run wild in the area."

"Why can't she bake a chicken or two?" Something Laurel wasn't required to hunt and shoot.

"Because we are having guests. Your *mamá* is very excited. She wants the men to enjoy a special, home-cooked meal."

"Everyone knows Mrs. Dillard is a good cook. I can assure Momma that Quinn has not experienced deprivation. As for the marshal, he's an old bachelor. I would think, by now, he's learned to make a decent supper."

"Laurel," Camille's forehead crinkled, and she patted the ewe between the ears, "I have been told you invited Quinn for my sake. Why?"

"Why? Because you like him." And Laurel would never admit to any other reason for extending the invitation.

"I like him?" Camille spread her hands on both hips. "Yes, I like him as a friend. He cannot possibly be more."

Laurel looked away toward the hill. "Why not, Camille? He's an agreeable-looking man with prospects for the future. His manners are faultless and his character equally so." Her voice had softened without permission.

"Listen to yourself." Camille shook her head and muttered something in French—at least Laurel assumed it was French. "Quinn has no romantic feelings for me, nor do I for him."

He could be more to Camille, but Laurel would let it pass.

"You are wrong." Camille reached out and squeezed Laurel's arm. "Can you not see?"

"Evidently. What am I supposed to see?"

"Quinn Spencer is not enamored with me. You are the reason he cannot stay away from La Casa del Fuego." She laughed. "Anyone with an ounce of sense can read it in both of your faces."

Laurel's pulse quickened at the statement. "Don't be absurd." She walked away with Camille's words bouncing between her ears. There was nothing between her and Quinn.

And yet there was too much.

CHAPTER TWENTY-SIX

Quinn and Wade sat on the porch so the smoke from the cigars the marshal brought would not overpower the delectable aromas of the food inside. While the women peeled, chopped, rolled, and added finishing touches to the meal and table, the men socialized on their own. Ruiz's arrival dropped Quinn's eagerness for the day by a notch or two.

So far, their conversation had been amiable. He hoped it would continue to be pleasant. However, Ferrell's murder was bound to come up at some point. Hesitant to throw a shroud over the celebration in the ladies' presence, he broached the subject now. "I'm surprised to see you here, Marshal."

"Ellen wasn't happy with me when I requested Ernie stay in Bold Creek until my investigation ended. Good thing she'd already asked me to this fiesta. You can be sure I wasn't about to let her un-ask me." He laughed as a pile of ash fell from his cigar. With the toe of his boot, he kicked it off the porch edge and onto the dirt. "I really shouldn't be here, I suppose."

"It may cause talk."

"Yep." Wade drew his cheeks in, puffing on the rolled tobacco, and blew out a column of pungent smoke that curled upward in the air. "I'm sure it looks to some like I've ruled out this ranch as being a murderer's home."

Quinn jolted at the bluntness of the comment. "Then why did you come?"

"Why are you here?" The marshal winked, his grin a sly one.

Gripping his cigar a shade tighter, Quinn squeezed it between his thumb and forefinger. Why indeed? His visit would do nothing to mend his deteriorating relationship with Arthur. Nor would it make him popular with the more elite of Bold Creek's citizens. Strange, but he preferred the company of people like Wade Ruiz and Laurel— people who didn't run their lives based on the approval of others.

After a quick glance toward the house, Quinn answered his companion's grin with one of his own. "I came only because Mrs. Chamberlain is a fine woman and a wonderful cook."

Ruiz guffawed. "Never attempt perjury, Spencer. You're a terrible liar."

As he gazed across the ranch yard, Quinn sobered. "What have you discovered about Ferrell?"

"The man was a snake whose dealings with the law included charges of theft and blackmail. I don't think the marshal of Lafayette County was sorry to learn of his passing. I'm glad I've been spared the job of hunting him down for attempting to kidnap Miss Goodman. I guess that's why he wanted the extra horse. What I can't figure is why he didn't just steal one."

"How do you know he didn't?"

"I don't for a fact, but nobody's missing an animal, and Ferrell's horse showed up alone a couple of miles west of where you found him."

Quinn drew in the sharp taste of the cigar and released the smoke. Even though he rarely smoked, he had learned the proper method since that day he and Henry stole Arthur's store of tobacco.

The mere thought of the Bruner family turned Quinn's stomach into a mass of knotted nerves. His childhood friendship with Henry had grown into an adult friendship with the father, but since their confrontation, time spent with Arthur had been strained. These days, they barely spoke of anything other than business.

Weeks ago, he had reasoned that a necessary departure lay in his future. Only Laurel's troubles and the continued desire to remain under Arthur's professional guidance had kept him from taking such an action earlier. Now he may have waited too late. Besides the harm done to his relationship with Arthur, a growing fascination with Laurel had thwarted Quinn's will to leave. He wanted time to explore the appeal she held for him. Time suspicion might take away.

"So who do you think shot Ferrell?"

"I know it wasn't Ellen." Wade stood and leaned against the porch rail, crossing one boot over the other. "And I'd bet my Aunt Maria's prized heifer it wasn't her daughter."

The casual comment came while Quinn drew in a puff on the cigar. He choked on smoke and coughed. Removing the cigar from between his lips, he straightened. "Wh—" He coughed again. "Why do you say that?"

"Women aren't the only ones who can claim intuition, Spencer. I may be new to this area, but I possess good instincts about people."

"You're always touting the need for evidence, Marshal. Why the change?"

Taking the time to contemplate his answer, the lawman compressed his lips until his mustache hid his mouth. Finally, he asked, "While you were in the cavalry, did your enemy ever leave a trail showing he'd headed in one direction when, in fact, he'd gone the opposite way?"

Quinn nodded. "Sometimes."

"Did it work?"

"Sometimes. Other times I felt things weren't right, and I was being played for a fool."

"Well, that's how I feel when I follow the trail that leads to Laurel's guilt. For one thing, I tried cutting that fence wire with those shears. Got nothing for my trouble but a sore hand."

"What about the handkerchief?"

He shrugged. "That set of tracks also appear too obvious to be real."

"I see." The tension melted from Quinn like taffy in the sun. "Have you told her?"

"No, and don't you say anything either."

Quinn gritted his teeth. Laurel deserved a respite from the worry. "Why not?"

"It doesn't mean she's not the one putting down those misleading tracks."

He studied Wade. "You don't really believe that, do you?"

The marshal held the cigar up and inspected what remained of the tobacco. "Intuition isn't evidence, Spencer."

Laughter filled the kitchen and vibrated through Laurel. The people at the table formed a ring of believers in God's blessings while she remained outside looking in. Happiness saturated them soul deep. Laurel's dripped like a mist.

She longed to push into that circle and know God cared about her. She longed to give Him reason to bless her life rather than curse it. If she sought His forgiveness with her whole heart, would He really give it, as Quinn said? Would He remove the guilt and give her the same joy that filled those around her? It seemed impossible.

"Everything is delicious, ladies. Mrs. Chamberlain, you set a splendid table."

"Thank you, Quinn. I prefer to prepare the stuffing with oysters, but they're only worth buying when they're fresh."

Momma's face glowed with the compliments she received. It had been years since they had entertained in this manner, with her mother setting out china pieces and her best linens. She had stuffed a yellow pitcher with dried sunflowers and placed it on a square damask table covering. That morning, Becky gathered golden leaves from the oaks in the yard and scattered them around the pitcher.

And the smells. They cooked every day of the week, but today, the entire house came alive with the aromas of roasting turkey, apple pies, and greens.

"Momma doesn't cook much, but she shot the turkey, and Issy dressed it. You should have seen—"

"Rebecca, that's ... Oh." Momma's lips moved, but nothing more came out.

Laurel finished the rebuke. "That is not proper dinner conversation, Peanut. Now eat your food while the adults converse."

Becky sighed. "Yes, ma'am."

Across the table, Quinn caught Laurel's eye with a wink. Thunderstruck, she froze with her stuffing-filled fork raised in mid-air. Was he flirting with her in front of all these people? Her heart fluttered, but she dismissed as foolishness the idea that Camille may have been right about Quinn being attracted to her. His ... gesture ... meant nothing more than he found her daughter amusing.

"The girl takes pride in you, ma'am." The marshal chuckled. "That's something to cherish."

Becky's frown turned into a crooked grin.

Unsure whether his words were praise or chastisement, Laurel accepted them in a positive light. "And I take pride in my daughter, Marshal Ruiz."

"You do, Momma?"

"Of course I do."

"Granmomma said she was proud of you, too. She said you had courage."

Laurel smiled, pleased and intrigued by the statement. "Granmomma said that?"

"Sure, she did. She said it the night you had the nightmare, and she went into your room."

The smile on Laurel's face died. Surely the girl had not been awake that night and overheard her exchange with her mother. She glanced around the table to find six pairs of eyes staring at her. "Th-The nightmare?"

"Don't you remember? You were upset 'cause Mr. Spencer shaved his beard." Becky turned to Quinn, who sat to her left. "Why'd you make my momma limp, Mr. Spencer?"

CHAPTER TWENTY-SEVEN

Quinn's appetite disappeared as quickly as the room's lighthearted atmosphere. He longed to ask why Becky thought he caused her mother's limp. Apparently sensing the change in mood, the little girl spent the rest of the meal like her mother, eating in silence, her attention on her plate.

After dinner, he trailed Laurel to the top of the hill behind the house. It hurt him to hear she had suffered a nightmare over seeing his scarred appearance, but what had he to do with Laurel's limp?

"Go away, Quinn." She stood with her back to him, stiff and unapproachable.

He worked to keep his voice low and steady. "I can't go away until you tell me what Becky meant." He hadn't had a better day in many a year—the food, the laughter, the company. He'd allowed himself to believe this odd connection between them might grow into something deeper. Then everything came to an abrupt halt.

Quinn pressed harder for an answer. "Do you despise me so much that you would dream I caused you harm?"

She turned to face him. Tears illuminated her eyes and bunched her lashes. "I don't despise you. That's the problem. I should. I've tried, but I can't."

He reached out to touch her arm and withdrew his hand when she shrank away. "I have never hurt you. At least, I've never meant to. I have tried to be your friend."

"Enemies and friends. How does that go?" He strained to hear her mumbled words. She raised her gaze to the sky as though seeking the answer to her question in the clouds. "Oh, yes. 'Love your enemies.' Isn't that what the Bible says? Did you love your enemies during the war, Quinn?"

"Why are you bringing up something that ended twelve years ago? It has nothing to do with today or what we're discussing." She insisted on wallowing in her own bitterness. Why couldn't she forget and get on with living life in the present as he tried to do?

"Did you love your enemies, Quinn? Did you obey God and love those Johnny Rebs who shot at you? The ones with bayonets and cannons?" She stepped closer and, with the tip of her finger, traced the puckered flesh at his jawline. She whispered, "What about the one who gave you this?"

He jerked his head sideways to remove the touch that tingled his skin and sent his senses reeling. "What about the ones who presided over Libby Prison where I spent five months before escaping? Should I have loved them? What about the coward who shot my best friend from the limb of a tree seven hundred yards away? Should I love that man?"

Her eyes grew large, and her face paled. She swallowed. "Coward?" Her body trembled until he reached out for fear she might collapse. She avoided his grasp.

He lowered his arms. "You didn't wear your coat and you're shivering. Come. Let's go back inside and discuss this rationally over something warm."

Her voice rose as she said, "'If thine enemy hunger, feed him; if he thirst, give him drink: for in so doing thou shalt heap coals of fire on his head.'" She slapped a hand on top of the part in her hair. "My, my, it feels a slight bit warm up there."

"I told you, Laurel, I am not your enemy. I am heaping no coals on you."

"Then why does my scalp feel singed?" She laughed the high-pitched laugh of someone who is irrational. It ended as abruptly as it began. "You never answered my question. Did you love your enemies?"

Only those who had been in the bloody trenches and cannonball-pocked fields, heard the screams of the wounded, and gagged at seeing the faceless dead, or experienced the physical deprivation and suffocating odors that came with being locked in an over-crowded Confederate prison—only those men could understand his struggle to forget and forgive. This woman could only guess at the hardship.

"Not for a long time. I once hated every man, woman, and child with the slightest southern drawl. Does it make you happy to hear that, Laurel? Are you happy to hear it took years for God to get through to me that my unforgiving attitude only harmed myself?"

She peered into his eyes as though seeking a lifeline to save her from drowning in her own boiling sea of anguish. "But did He?"

"What?"

"Did God get through to you?"

The heart wrenching plea softened his exasperation with her. "Yes, He did. I have forgiven everyone involved, and I pray the ones I wronged during that time have forgiven me."

She paced back and forth in front of him. "Forgiven you? Is that the trick, Quinn? Do I have to forgive you? Do I have to forgive the others?" She didn't allow him time to answer. "Is that why I can't forget those blank faces?"

Blank faces?

She stopped pacing. "Why can't I forget your face like you've forgotten mine?"

"Forgotten yours? You're talking in circles. We only met a few months ago. Believe me, that was a meeting I'll never forget."

Another sudden bout of her laughter troubled Quinn. Her mind had become befuddled by more than Becky's question. She might truly be irrational. No, if anyone was crazy, it was him for casting aside his future for time spent with this tormented woman and her pixie-faced little girl.

Quinn searched his memory for where they might have met, convinced he had never seen her before that fateful day in August. "You've mistaken me for someone else. The first time I met you was the day you saved me from the mountain lion."

"No!" She shook her head violently. "You're wrong. It was the third of June in the year 1864." Her voice sputtered into a half-sob. "C-Cold Harbor."

Those two words sent a shiver of horrifying memories down his back. The sounds of the artillery pounding away. Shouted orders to overwhelmed soldiers. That shrill and unholy Rebel yell. The last moans of the mortally wounded—both man and animal. He gasped in remembrance of the suffocating heat and choking dust, of seeing his own exhaustion mirrored on the faces of battle-weary men forced to fight a determined foe for every mile marched in General Grant's effort to reach Richmond. The day was an utter failure in which thousands of federal soldiers became casualties.

"How did you know I fought at Cold Harbor?"

The irrational behavior vanished, and her eyes hardened with clarity. "We may have been on different sides, but we met there that day, Lieutenant Spencer."

The words took their time to seep in. Once they did, Quinn stepped back, his mind reeling. What she said—what she implied—was impossible.

Laurel lifted her skirt and petticoats, not caring if she did so in front of a male. She had done worse. After floundering in a barrel full of self-pity for the past hour, she dredged up a renewed anger at Quinn for his persistent ignorance.

His eyes widened, and he stood still as she bared her lower limb.

"What are you doing?"

"Providing you with proof. You are a representative of the court and like the marshal, you deal in evidence. Correct?"

He grasped her upper arm. "Have you no shame, Laurel?"

"I have shame enough for an entire regiment, Quinn." She wrenched free of his hand. Holding up her skirts, she raised the hem of her drawers above her right knee and rolled down her stocking.

He winced at the long, half-moon scar running up the right side of her calf, topped by a small crater in the flesh near her kneecap. "How?"

She captured his gaze with hers and refused to let go. "After all your time in the army, you don't recognize the result of a saber wound?" She raised the stocking, rolled down the leg of her drawers, and dropped her skirts, making sure they covered her ankles in a ladylike fashion.

"You don't know what you're saying."

She leaned toward him. "Don't give it another thought, Quinn. I suppose I can't fault you for not remembering one li'l ol' face out of the hundreds before you in your battles. I don't look the same. Gray, like black, is not a flattering color for me to wear. And this was shorter." She removed the pins and combs, letting her hair fall nearly to her waist, then ran her fingers through its thickness. She had missed its length during those wretched months and, ever since, had allowed it to be cut by only an inch.

"If it makes you feel better, I didn't recognize you, either, until you shaved your beard and I saw the scar. I could never forget your face." The poor man flinched as though she had slapped him. Maybe she should. It might release him from the shock.

"You are lying."

"Am I?" Laurel straightened her skirts and stalked off toward a group of mesquite trees, leaving him alone to ponder her words. Her deep sigh pierced the silence that enveloped her in its solemnity.

Over the years, she had hidden her actions from everyone but Momma and John. And, evidently, Becky. Why care if Quinn loathed her once she revealed what she had done all those years ago? His loathing could not equal God's . . . nor her own.

The dry foliage rustled behind her. Laurel stopped to let him catch up. They would settle everything, here and now.

"I want the truth. How did you know I fought at Cold Harbor? How could you know my rank that day?"

"Must I show you the proof again?" She raised her skirt.

"Don't. Don't do that." Quinn rubbed a hand down his face, but it didn't remove the deep worry lines between his eyes. "You must have seen me from the tavern nearby."

"I have never entered such a place. Surely, Quinn, you cannot be so slow to understand what I am saying."

He stepped backward. "There were women who followed soldiers from camp-to-camp. Some were wives who couldn't bear being separated from their husbands. There were others—less reputable females. Were you one of the former, Laurel? Did you follow John to war?" He asked, his voice pleading, as though hoping against hope she would answer in the affirmative.

"No."

"Then you were—" Quinn shut his mouth, and his jaw hardened.

This time, he did turn away, and Laurel's bravado shriveled at his disappointment in her. Having started this confession, she intended to see it through to the end. "No, Quinn. I was not one of the less reputable females, either. At least, not less reputable as you mean it."

He whipped around. Relief lightened his face. It was a short-lived relief as he apparently ran out of acceptable excuses for her to have been at Cold Harbor that day.

Laurel stared at the sun, partially covered by clouds. Thick, gray clouds of past mistakes darkened her whole life. How did she explain, to justify her action to him in a way he would understand? Most people would start with the beginning of their descent.

"My father was a country physician, Quinn, a man whose sole desire in life was to help those who needed him. During the first two years of a war he didn't support, he watched as men he'd befriended and doctored for ages—some he had welcomed into this world—

came home as cripples." She yanked a dying leaf from a branch above her and mindlessly shred it into small pieces. "Missing arms and legs. Head wounds that left them little more than idiots. Men undernourished and ill from their time in a federal prison. Of course, some never came back alive. He spent months torn between his hatred for war and his need to save lives.

"He volunteered, against Momma's wishes, saying he wanted to help where the help was needed—in the field hospitals. Four months later, we received word of his death. A Yankee prisoner had used Daddy's own scalpel to . . . He . . ." She took a deep breath when her voice threatened to crack. "Daddy only wanted to save the man's life."

Quinn stepped forward. She held out a hand to stop him, not wanting to be interrupted in her tale—not wanting to soften at his touch. This was the first time in twelve years she had discussed what happened with someone other than Momma, and she intended to finish her story. "Did you know I was a twin?"

"Becky mentioned it, as did your mother."

"It seems only the worst of my business has remained private until today." Laurel sniffed and waved a hand in the air. "Well, no matter, since I'm fixing to tattle on myself."

"Tell me. I want to understand what you went through, what causes you such grief."

You think that now, Mr. Spencer.

Laurel put a few more feet between them. "My brother Lance was smart, though a bit too serious." Laurel smiled. "After my uncle taught him to hunt, he became an excellent shot. In those days, I wanted to do everything Lance did and begged him to teach me. He could never deny me what I asked. We would go into the fields and set up targets, rarely missing when we fired. It wasn't long before I bested him at any distance. Momma feared talk from the neighbors and always made Lance take the credit for whatever bounty we brought home. He longed to join our men in their fight against the North. It became all he talked about, but our parents wouldn't give their consent.

"One day, we hunted deer on my uncle's farm near the mountains." Using the sleeve of her coat, Laurel swiped away a tear dripping from her jaw. "As I sat in the shade at the edge of the woods, I heard a shot. I stood, ready to shout my congratulations to Lance for his prize. That's when I saw a soldier running away—a blue belly. I searched the field, not seeing my brother. I called his name, but he didn't answer. When I finally found him . . ."

That vile image of years ago intruded, leaving her breathless. Her legs gave way, and she sank to the dirt on her knees, crushed by the memory of Lance's death. Quinn kneeled next to her and, like the day they found Reg Ferrell's body, he drew her close. Just as she had done then, she buried her face in the scratchy warmth of his coat, the smell of cigar smoke clinging to the wool. Her fingers dug in and clutched at the sleeves, seeking strength from more than the arms that encircled her.

Laurel needed every ounce of courage she could muster before burdening Quinn with the rest.

CHAPTER TWENTY-EIGHT

Quinn remained on the ground next to Laurel, his arms wrapped around her. Not like the day they found Ferrell. That day, he had drawn Laurel close, intending to protect a difficult woman from a gruesome sight. Today, he wanted to hold the wilted lady who stirred an urge to comfort, to do battle with her fears and help her overcome them. Gone was the headstrong, independent and spirited sheep rancher whose sarcasm could send Quinn's temper soaring.

Laurel touched a place inside of him left empty for far too long. Though he wanted to protect her, he wanted more—needed more—than to be simply a place of refuge for whatever plagued her.

His fingers wove into the blond hair, and he kissed her forehead before resting his chin on top of her head. "Laurel."

Her body stiffened, and she eased away from him. He loathed letting her go, but she struggled against his hold and left him no choice.

Laurel clambered to her feet. She backed away and ducked her chin, refusing to look at him. "You must understand, Quinn."

He stood, too. "Understand what? That we've breached the Mason-Dixon Line? That north and south no longer divide us?" He took a step forward, and she retreated two more feet.

"Please listen to me!"

Stopped by the incensed appeal, he did as she asked. "All right, I'm listening."

She clenched her hands together. "That day changed me. My heart turned cold on the very spot where a Yankee soldier killed my brother. From then on, all I could see was Lance's body. It didn't matter if I was awake or sleeping. I barely remembered him as he was when he lived—walking, talking, reading a book. My mind kept returning to that vision of him lying there, the ground around him turning dark with his blood."

Quinn swallowed the lump that blocked his throat and fought to keep his distance. However much fortitude was required of him, Laurel needed to finish her story before she would be ready to come back to his embrace.

"I suppose sanity abandoned me. I left home a few weeks before my seventeenth year to avenge Lance's death." She raised her chin and drew in a quivering breath. "For seven months, I fulfilled my brother's wish to be a soldier."

"A soldier?" Her meaning escaped him. "You mean a spy?"

"Not a spy. I joined my Confederate brethren as Private Lance Chamberlain."

"Priv—" He choked on the word and then laughed. Either she was jesting, or he hadn't heard her right.

"Do not laugh at me, Mr. Spencer. I am telling you the truth."

The laughter died. Yes, he could see by her scowl that she believed what she said. He had heard the rumors, but . . . "You fought in battle for the South? Pretending to be your brother?"

How could a woman dress like a man, live among men, fight alongside them, and no one see? Ludicrous. Seven months. His shameful gaze ran up and down her figure, seeking its shape under the layers of feminine clothing she wore, looking for anything to dispute her claim. She wasn't voluptuous, but her curves were not those of a man.

Would he have known had she taken up arms in his company? Maybe. In that moment when he first saw her, he'd believed a man rescued him. It had taken seeing her up close to realize his mistake.

Still, what she said was not possible. Was it?

"Someone would have known. Someone *should* have known." His voice rose with each word. "Were those Rebs blind?"

"Someone knew. John. He suspected, but like you, could not believe in his suspicion. However, he watched me. Then, one day, he followed as I went to the river." Her face flamed.

Quinn rejected the image her words generated. Instead, he concentrated on the fact that John Tillman had been aware of Laurel's deception. "Your husband knew you were a female. Did he report it?"

"He threatened it. By that time, though, the South needed all the able-bodied soldiers they could find." One eyebrow rose and her lips twisted into a smirk, revealing the impudent woman he first met. "I told you I was an excellent shot. You've seen it for yourself. And, though I felt sick to my stomach every time I fired my weapon, I stayed."

"Was your need for revenge so great that you continued to risk your life?"

"I would have welcomed the opportunity to return home in whatever way God saw fit. It only took pointing my weapon at one federal soldier to bring me to my senses and convince me of my wickedness. In time, I grew to despise myself. But walking away would have tarnished Lance's name. I couldn't allow others to think of him as a deserter."

Quinn tried to imagine what it would have been like for a young girl trapped in such circumstances—the filth from marching days or weeks on end without bathing or having a fresh change of clothing.

His face warmed. He had overheard disgusting things while the men in his company argued and teased one another. Had she heard the same vulgarities and jests? Most women would have fallen into a faint. Had she grown insensitive to the coarseness of the men around her? Not even the reckless action Amy had taken could compare with the deeds of Laurel Chamberlain. Both had abandoned convention to accomplish their aim.

But there was a difference. His fiancée's aim held a higher purpose than vengeance. Still, no woman should place herself in a position to experience the horror and danger of battle.

"John protected me as best he could."

A huff escaped Quinn's lips. "His best would have been to send you home as soon as he saw—"

She leveled her shoulders. "I had no intention of leaving and ruining my brother's reputation."

"So your husband kept your secret until when?"

"Until I received this injury and could no longer fight." She stared at him a moment before patting the side of her right leg. "John saved my life at Cold Harbor."

Quinn's heart plummeted. Laurel had been at the battle. She had taken part in it and expected him to remember her. Why?

Running a hand over his hair, his mind raced to sort through the jumble of memories. Then he stilled as a gut-wrenching fact penetrated all the confusion. If what Becky said . . .

He studied Laurel's eyes, searching for a reason to deny what he knew to be true. Instead, his face must have given away the awareness of guilt, for the green of her pupils radiated a moist emerald fire.

"Yes, Lieutenant Spencer. My blood stained the tip of your weapon that day."

Quinn's jaw slackened. His gaze darted from her ashen face to her knee and back to her face. Shame struck down his ability to think straight—to speak a word. He needed to get away, to wrap his mind around the idea that he once attempted to kill a woman.

He spun around and marched down the hill. A few minutes later, numb and hardly knowing what he was doing, he led a saddled Ruthie from the barn and rode away without looking back.

Laurel stood at the top of the hill, chastising herself for being heartless in telling him. Why hadn't she broken the news in a more merciful way? She had expected his scorn and unbelief, yet when he displayed it, she lost her temper and hurtful words flowed.

A cool breeze blew long strands of unfettered hair across her face. She brushed them away in order to watch as he galloped Ruthie down the drive.

She would never blame him for his reaction. Hers had been as dreadful upon first seeing him clean-shaven. The shock had been greater than each could handle. Quinn required time to come to terms with the fact that his saber left her with a permanent limp.

Once he'd ridden out of sight, she closed her eyes and let the wind cover her wretched tears.

Laurel had learned one thing from their time together today. Camille was right. Quinn had an affection for her.

At least he did before she drove him away.

Laurel returned to the house. The others stood on the front porch, chattering and questioning why Quinn rode off in such a hurry.

"He didn't even say goodbye. Why didn't he say goodbye?" Momma turned her way, eyebrows drawn together. "What happened to your hair?"

Confessing her past to Quinn opened a floodgate inside Laurel and forced the sordid story upon their ears. Once she finished, all but her mother stood frozen in their places on the porch, staring at her. Momma's glance darted back and forth to Wade.

They hate me for what I did. Momma hates me for ruining her budding relationship with the marshal.

Camille grasped her in a hug. "How horrid for you. I cannot imagine all you experienced. I am most happy you survived, *mi amiga.*"

"Now that's what I call an independent woman." Issy grinned and slapped Laurel on the back.

"Well, it seems you raised a girl with grit, Ellen." Wade grasped Momma's hand and squeezed it. "Guess she takes after her ma."

Laurel stood stock-still while trying to comprehend their reactions. "You don't condemn me?"

"Mrs. Tillman, I'm not one to throw stones. What I do in my life is between me and the Almighty." Wade's mustache twitched. "The same goes for you."

Later that night, Laurel stood in front of the mirror in her bedchamber and ran a brush from her scalp to the tips of the hair hanging at her waist.

"Between me and the Almighty?" She stared at her reflection, then raised her eyes to the ceiling. "They love me, anyway. Do you, God?"

Setting the brush on the dresser, she peered into the glass and fingered the fine lines that shot outward from the corners of her eyes. She examined the drooping mouth. In a few weeks, she would turn thirty-one, but right now, she felt more her mother's age.

Rumors had flown of women on both sides of the conflict joining the war as she had done. Conscription money baited poor girls who wanted to help their needy families. For some, fervor for the cause led them to enlist or become spies. As Quinn stated, others followed their husbands into the war.

Oh, if only her motivation had been so noble.

Laurel worked her fingers through her hair, braiding it for the night, while her mind relived those days of long ago.

Every minute for seven months, she had expected someone would discover her gender. Keeping her secret wore on her almost as much as the fighting itself. A part of her hoped her deception would be revealed and her departure forced.

Why had her fellow soldiers never known? Had she been that plain and unrefined? In all fairness to them, they had not expected a respectable woman to cut her hair above her collar, dress like a male, and invade their ranks. At first, some had questioned her smooth baby face until they learned her age. Then they teased her for being slow to achieve manhood.

For the first few months, she blushed at every spoken and unspoken vulgarity. The men noticed and purposely intensified the coarseness in order to "educate the boy." After a while, she learned to ignore their bawdy words and deeds, which ended the worst of the teasing.

Laurel walked to the dresser and picked up her wedding photograph. "For my sake, John, why didn't you insist I go home after you found out?" She sighed, knowing why. "Because you feared losing my ability when the Confederacy needed it so badly. Then you feared losing me to some boy back in North Carolina. How selfish we both were, Johnny."

On her way to the bed, she passed the trunk, refusing to yield to the temptation to purge its contents. They were, after all, a reminder of her need for penance. As if she needed the reminder!

She crawled under the covers, knowing sleep would either be a fanciful notion or a barrage of bad dreams. The bedside table still held Camille's Bible. She had kept it at her friend's insistence and begun reading passages of the New Testament off and on, usually when she couldn't fall asleep.

She'd completed the gospels and turned the pages to the next book, The Acts of the Apostles. The stories of Jesus being taken up to heaven and the day of Pentecost captivated her. Peter's eloquent preaching to the multitudes and his words held her in awe. She blinked away sorrow at the stoning of Stephen. The early Christians had endured so much suffering without retaliation.

She reached the story that seized her soul. Over and over, Laurel read about Saul, a hated man who caused and witnessed countless deaths of believers. Jesus turned him into a man named Paul, someone whose past atrocities were forgiven and forgotten, a powerful man of faith.

Laurel sifted through the pages into the wee hours, searching various books for more about the apostle and his relationship with Jesus. Raised in the church, she had heard the stories but ignored them for more worldly pleasure.

Her spirit stirred inside until she could no longer lie abed. She slipped into her coat and tiptoed outside to the porch, clutching the leather-bound Word of God to her chest. There, she sat barefoot in the night, her toes becoming chilled and her hand wildly turning the crank on the butter churn while she compared her life to that of a fellow sinner.

"Oh, my Lord! My God! Murder demands Your eternal hate, doesn't it? Oh, Holy F-Father, You forgave Paul's sins and gave him a second chance. You used him mightily. Can you ever forgive mine?" She sobbed, the plea catching in her throat. "Is it possible? Paul committed his sins in the ignorance of thinking he defended You. I committed mine as retribution for the deaths of Daddy and Lance."

She dropped to her knees and bent forward, the Bible slipping to the floor of the porch. Resting her head in her hands, she squeezed her eyes shut. "I can't live like this anymore. I don't want to live like this. I am so sorry. Please. Please, Jesus." She sniffled and released a weary sigh. "Please."

CHAPTER TWENTY-NINE

Leaning back in the chair across from Quinn's desk, Arthur rested one long leg over the other. He forked a slice of apple cake into his mouth. If Mrs. Dillard continued to send refreshments to Quinn's office, both he and Arthur would need a thick rope, a large pulley, and a draft horse to get from the street to the second floor.

"I haven't seen a man so down in the mouth as you this past week, Quinn. What happened?"

They were in the middle of discussing a recent decision by the Texas Supreme Court, so the abrupt question caught Quinn by surprise. He hesitated in answering. If he said he was fine, Arthur would see it as a lie. Nothing escaped the older man's awareness. If he told the truth, a hearty "I told you so" would be in order. And he was in no mood to hear it.

In fact, Quinn was anything but fine after struggling to come to terms with Laurel's past and the part he had played in it. Never had he whittled more useless pieces of wood.

"Nothing to do with business. I'll try to conduct myself in a more acceptable manner."

Arthur stared. When Quinn offered no further clarification, his eyes narrowed. "I believe you spent Thanksgiving at La Casa del Fuego, did you not?"

"How did you know?"

Arthur lifted a shoulder in a half-hearted shrug. "It won't be long before I receive instructions from Royce to file the lawsuit against Laurel with the court. She stands to lose a great deal if she doesn't heed his offer to drop the matter after reimbursement for the dead cattle."

"You mean twice the value of the dead cattle. Don't you find a lawsuit a little rash? The marshal hasn't concluded his investigation. With Ferrell dead, there's no way to prove who shot—or didn't shoot—the Triple M steers."

"Interesting, is it not?" Arthur shoved another forkful of cake into his mouth.

Quinn kept his mouth closed on the veiled accusation.

"We are here to serve and advise our clients, including Royce MacMahon. In return, his business helps us eat more than these desserts Mrs. Dillard bakes."

"*His* business?" Royce clearly held the upper hand, but Quinn had thought the two sons had equal ownership of the ranch. "What about Murphy? Perhaps he doesn't want a lawsuit. How much say does he have in everyday decisions?"

"Very little. They both have equal ownership of the ranch, but their father emphasized in his will that Royce was to control the business. Murphy is only a glorified foreman."

Quinn felt for the younger MacMahon's circumstances. "Why doesn't he leave?"

"You've met them both. Royce rules everything in his little kingdom, including his brother. At the time of his death, Gavin MacMahon was at odds with his youngest son and made clear his preference for Royce." Arthur placed the fork on the empty plate and set the china on the front edge of Quinn's desk. "It partially stemmed from Murphy's going east to school rather than staying to help grow the ranch's interests—an attempt at rebellion on Murphy's part. It didn't set well with his father or his brother."

Even in his dealings with Laurel, Quinn acknowledged that the younger cattleman carried about him a certain air of sophistication that Royce, in all his arrogance, didn't own. "So Murphy is an educated man. In what area?"

"No one knows. He returned to Bold Creek a year or so ago, after his father died and his mother moved to Delaware to stay with her sister. He's worked under his brother's thumb ever since. As Murphy chooses not to discuss it, I don't pry."

Quinn understood the last comment as a warning. Besides, the MacMahons held no concern for him other than in their treatment of Laurel.

"Arthur, I am urging you to advise Royce against going ahead with his suit, or . . ." Or what? What legal recourse did Laurel have? And who would assist her if she did not consent to his help? Even if Wade didn't believe her sheep shears cut the Triple M fence, the marshal couldn't truthfully testify that she had not killed all six steers.

Quinn had spent the past week disgusted by everything Laurel had told him. Oddly, he wanted to protect her again. Why? His lips crimped at the answer. Because, even after her story, his interest in the woman had deepened. Some might call it guilt. Others might term it sympathy. Quinn knew it for exactly what it was. Love.

A sad smile stretched across Arthur's face. "Quinn, for the life of me, I cannot understand how you allowed yourself to develop a fondness for someone who cannot hold a candle to Amy. Mrs. Tillman's people killed many of our men, including my son, who died in a furtive, underhanded manner." His voice rose steadily and hardened upon the mention of Henry.

Quinn had never witnessed this level of raw hostility from Arthur. Why move to a southern state if he felt so strongly about its people?

"Valiant men like my Henry never stood a chance against shots fired by cowards who dared not show their faces."

"Cowards?" All these years, Quinn had kept secret the sordid details of the death of Arthur's son, unwilling to burden his friend with the facts. He had explained that Henry died as the result of a marksman's bullet—the truth, but not all of it. "Both sides employed sharpshooters. We had Colonel Berdan's men."

Arthur's palms beat the arms of his chair. "Do not defend Confederate trash to me! No one deserved to die in such a manner, especially my Henry. He had the right to face his murderer, Quinn. Instead, men like that abhorrent John Tillman hid within the branches of trees and behind stone walls, picking off anyone wearing the blue uniform. Just looking at that witch of a wife of his boils my blood."

Quinn's own wrath brewed with the offense to Laurel. Yet, he wouldn't reveal her secret. "Whatever John Tillman did during the war does not reflect upon his wife."

"She married the man, didn't she?"

"And you sired Henry. Does that mean his cowardice falls on you?" Quinn cringed at letting that information slip.

Springing from his seat, Arthur slapped his hands on the desktop, rattling the fork on top of the china plate. "Cowardice? How dare you accuse my son of being a coward. You've proven through your willingness to associate with those strumpets that you come nowhere near being the man Henry was."

A bolt of lightning burned through Quinn and set his skin afire. He glared at Arthur. "Henry died while fleeing camp in the middle of the night."

Arthur jerked. "You are a liar."

Quinn's anger deflated as quickly as it had ballooned. He had sworn to himself never to reveal his boyhood friend's failing. Truly, James spoke with knowledge when he wrote that the tongue was "an unruly evil, full of deadly poison." Now it was too late for regret.

God, forgive me my temper and help me finish telling Arthur the truth with compassion.

"When I saw Henry creep away, I tried to convince him to stay. Like all of us, he was afraid, Arthur. He had seen too much death and destruction. He panicked at the thought of dying in a bloody field or

being maimed for life. Henry wouldn't listen to me and rode off."
Quinn heaved a weary sigh. "I followed, begging him to turn around.
He rode on. It was a momentary lapse. Given more time, I believe he
would have changed his mind."

Arthur sank back into the chair, his shoulders hunched in misery.
"You were above him in rank. You had the power to stop him."

"And I will live the rest of my life regretting I did not save my
friend." Arthur was right. He could have stopped Henry with an
order, but declined to use his authority. "A half-mile from camp, a
shot rang out. Henry pulled back on his horse and remained still for
what seemed an endless time. Then he crumpled to the ground and
disappeared in the tall grass at the side of the road. I jumped from my
horse and waited for the next shot or the charge of a company of
Rebels. Neither came. Henry died from one bullet fired from one
gun—by one expert shooter."

Laurel's story opposed Henry's. Rather than stain her brother's
memory, she resolved to remain in danger. It opposed his own, more
recent story, too. Instead of staying to do battle with his hurt and
pride, Quinn had panicked and run on Thanksgiving Day—just as
he had run from Amy's memory for years. He was a greater coward
than Henry.

Arthur pushed out of the chair and trudged to the door. When he
turned, his sagging face had aged ten years. "If you had been a loyal
friend, my son would sit in that chair instead of you."

Quinn winced at the slamming of his office door.

He may have no power to change the past, but the future was a
different matter.

Laurel loosened the reins and let the gelding walk at his own pace.
Issy followed suit with her mare.

"It's been over a week, Laurel. We haven't seen hide nor hair of
Quinn. Why don't you go to town and talk to him?"

"My talking to him drove him away, Issy. I don't think he's ready to hear from me again right now."

Besides, she needed more time. Their pasts horribly crossed, but it was the present that assured they could be no more than acquaintances. Though her friends had not turned away upon hearing her story, it didn't mean others would wrap her in arms of acceptance. A relationship with Quinn was sure to prove detrimental to his future. The knowledge pierced her heart with a blade sharper than the edge of his saber.

The buckskin stumbled over a rock and Laurel jounced forward. She yawned, patted the horse on the neck, and said to him, "We're both a little lazy this morning, aren't we?"

"If you don't get some good sleep, you're going to fall right out of that saddle." Issy drew her mare alongside Laurel's buckskin as they rode through the south pasture toward the river. "Since you told us about the war. Well, we're all worried sick about you."

"I'm fine." For the most part, more than fine.

At the graying light of dawn the morning of her emotional entreaty to God, she had awakened on the porch, her toes cold as a fish in winter waters. But that elusive spiritual peace she had sought for so long sank deep enough to warm her soul.

She waited, though, to tell the others. Not because she feared this reconciliation with God might be temporary. It was eternal. But she needed to apologize to Quinn. Laurel wanted him to be the first to know she had reached out and grasped the forgiveness God longed to give her—the forgiveness stubbornness and ignorance had kept her from receiving. She wanted peace with Quinn and wasn't confident he was ready to give it to her.

"Your ma says you didn't get much rest last night. Anyone can see the dark circles under your eyes."

"You should look in the mirror, Issy. Red competes with the blue-green of your eyes. What's bothering you?"

Issy hadn't been her usual defiant and cocky self, not since her sister's unexpected visit to the ranch yesterday. Afterward, she had stomped around the yard, talking to herself when she wasn't pouting.

"You have your own worries, Laurel. You don't need to fuss over mine."

Shrugging, Laurel said, "If you don't want to tell me, that's your decision. We've always agreed not to interfere in each other's lives. I won't even remind you I'm your boss."

Issy stopped her palomino and answered in a strangely quiet voice. "Sophie wanted to tell me she's getting married again."

"Again? I didn't realize she had been married before."

The return laughter held the contempt of the Issy Laurel knew well. "I should have said she told me again that she's marrying. It isn't something new. Sophie was engaged once before—for as long as it took to make me look like a fool."

A fool? The ill-will between the sisters was no secret. Still—

"Pardon me for saying so, boss lady, but I really don't want to talk about it."

"All right. I know when to mind my own business." Laurel pressed her legs against the sides of the gelding. "Let's head to the river. I could use a rest along the bank."

As they approached the water, Laurel stopped the buckskin. From the direction of the slope leading to the river, she discerned male voices. She pressed a finger to her lips in warning, then mouthed, "Who is it?"

Issy lifted both shoulders and shook her head. With quiet care, Laurel reached for the carbine. Her hand stopped short of touching it. So far in her life, the unknown meant seizing a gun. A fine example she set for her daughter.

She withdrew her hand and dismounted with quiet care. Issy followed her to within a few yards of the river, where they crept up behind a large rock and peered over the top. Murphy MacMahon and Reuben Stockard sat at the river's edge with their backs to the women. Each man held a wooden pole. An open creel sat on the bank between them. Neither man appeared to be too interested in catching his supper.

"All I'm saying's I think you know what you gotta do." The silver-haired Stockard had been with the Triple M for years, ever since the ranch's founding by Murphy's father. It was common knowledge that Gavin MacMahon never minded his cook enjoying a closer bond with his youngest son than he'd enjoyed, something Laurel believed to be in Murphy's best interest.

"Maybe."

"No maybe about it, boy. You gotta do the right thing. You gotta tell the man."

Murphy replied in a voice too low for Laurel to hear the words, but Laurel grasped the edginess. Reuben laughed off the ill humor. "Fine, then we'll talk about what's really stickin' in your craw. Don't condemn her, Murph. Pray for her."

"Who?"

Reuben shook his head. "I figured you for a smart man."

"You have your mind set on ruining my day?" Murphy slapped his knee and the pole resting on it jumped. "What good will it do to pray for a woman with the heart of a snake?"

The heart of a snake? Laurel turned to leave. Because of the way she tangled with the two brothers, who else could he be talking about but her? She had no intention of listening further. Eavesdroppers heard nothing but bad about themselves. And she knew all that already.

"T'was a time you didn't think like that."

Issy backed away and tripped. She gripped Laurel's forearm to stay upright. The woman's nails dug into Laurel's coat sleeve and her stare never left the men, who remained unaware of their presence.

Casting his line into the river, Murphy's worm-baited hook splashed into the water. "So? She used her charms on me. That was a long time ago, Reuben."

"You sure you still ain't hooked by those charms?"

Murphy eyed the old man for a moment and went back to fishing.

Laurel tugged on Issy's sleeve. When her friend refused to move, she stepped in front of her and looked into eyes that brimmed with tears. Issy blinked, and they spilled over her bottom lashes.

Arm in arm, they ambled back to the horses, leading the animals away from the river. While Issy swiped at the wetness on her face, Laurel ventured a question. "At first, I thought I was the snake Murphy mentioned. But you know who he really meant, don't you?"

"My sister is a vicious person." Issy glanced toward the river and sniffled. "Too bad the engagement didn't last. They deserved one another."

"Murphy was engaged to Sophie?"

As they walked away from the river with the horses following, Issy said, "At thirteen, I imagined myself in love with Murphy MacMahon." Her fingers fumbled with the reins in her hand. "Crazy, huh?"

"What happened?"

"He was almost twenty and smitten with Sophie, who was barely sixteen. She thought it would be entertaining to encourage him. The more I argued with her to leave him alone, the harder she pressed Murphy. Before I knew it, they were engaged. A few months later, my sister broke the engagement." Issy stopped walking. "I've never forgotten that day. Like a doggone fool, I told Murphy not to be sad because I would marry him." She turned to Laurel, a black look clouding her face. "Do you know what he said?"

"You don't have to tell me."

"First, he looked at me in disgust. Then he said, 'You don't have the charm or beauty of your sister. Even if you did, I'm done with any Kruegers.'"

"He was hurt, Issy. I am sure he didn't mean—"

"It didn't give him the right to be cruel."

"No."

No one had the right to be cruel. Not Murphy. And not Laurel.

CHAPTER THIRTY

Laurel stared at the boarding house. Her slow inhalation failed to calm her nerves. She slapped her hands down the folds of the brown wool of her skirt and patted the upswept hair at the back of her head, tucking loose strands under her bonnet. When satisfied with her appearance, she trod the path to the porch, all the while asking the Lord to boost her courage.

She had spent the past two weeks loving God and basking in the forgiveness He had waited years to give her. Moments still intruded when guilt, not a foe to die easily, rose to brandish its weapon of guilt and cause her to cower. During those times, a quick prayer sent the enemy into retreat.

Doubt rose again now. Perhaps she should have waited to make this visit. Did Quinn need more time to reconcile their war connection and accept a truce between them? A nervous tingle settled in her fingers and toes. She squared her shoulders and mentally dressed in the armor of God as Paul exhorted in his letter to those in Ephesus.

Upon reaching town, Laurel had stopped at the lawyer's office only to be told Quinn had taken ill. The news did nothing to ease her disquiet, especially when Mr. Bruner hinted her visit might do him more harm.

She readjusted her shield of faith and once again filled her lungs with cool December air. Limping up the brick walkway to Hedda Dillard's front porch, she struck the heavy door knocker against the wood.

When the door opened, Mrs. Dillard's worried face greeted her. "Please come in, Mrs. Tillman." The older woman stepped back to allow Laurel into the hall.

"How are you, Mrs. Dillard?"

The smell of chicken soup wafted from the direction of the woman's kitchen.

"I'm perfectly fine." She wiped her hands on her apron and brushed strands of hair from her eyes.

"I understand Mr. Spencer is ill."

Hedda Dillard frowned and shook her head. "He felt poorly yesterday and remains in his bed this morning."

"Does he have a fever?"

"No, just a slight belly upset and weakness. He appears to be better this morning. I'm making him broth."

"Is he well enough for visitors?"

Mrs. Dillard raised her gaze to the plank ceiling. "I think it will tickle him to have your company. Please have a seat in the parlor while I check to see if he would like to come downstairs."

The clock on the mantle ticked away the minutes. Mrs. Dillard remained gone. Laurel tapped a toe on the carpet in front of the sofa. What was taking her so long?

The older woman appeared in the parlor doorway. Without Hedda saying a word, the grimace on her reddened face announced Quinn's rejection of Laurel's visit.

"I am sorry. He said to tell you . . ." She appeared uncomfortable with the message. "He thinks it's best that you leave."

Disappointment overwhelmed her previous hope. Laurel stood and tried to take a step toward the door, but a tug inside kept her feet rooted to the floor. Should she allow him to reject her without an argument? That inner pull urged her not to leave the boarding house until she had spoken with Quinn. She folded a hand on each hip. "It is a pity the poor man is delirious in his suffering and saying things he doesn't mean. Would that soup be ready, Mrs. Dillard?"

The woman's countenance brightened. She guffawed. "I am much too busy to wait hand and foot on every boarder in this house. Will you take him a bowl?"

"Certainly." Laurel grinned and removed her coat. "Together, ma'am, we are more than that Yankee can handle."

"Mrs. Tillman, you do not need me to help you handle him."

"No." She hung her coat on a hook on the hall tree. "I need the One mightier than both of us."

At the knock on his door, Quinn straightened in the armchair with a grunt. What did his landlady want this time?

He required time to recover the strength needed for an exchange with Laurel and had instructed Mrs. Dillard to send her away. Though Hedda Dillard argued, she eventually gave in to his order.

The knock sounded again. "Enter." He gaped as the door opened and Laurel limped into his room carrying a laden tray. He should have known his landlady would be no match for a woman who bluffed her way through a war. "I told Mrs. Dillard I didn't want to see you today."

"I heard." She set the tray on the dresser, outwardly unperturbed by his statement.

"Then why are you here? Don't you give people enough to talk about?" This time the flash of hurt on Laurel's face stabbed his conscience.

"My heavens. Aren't we grumpy today?"

He fidgeted with a crease in his trousers. "*We* are no such thing."

"Yes, I know. It's only you." She removed the napkin from the tray, shook it out, and arranged it across his lap. "I'm here to feed you your midday meal, Quinn. If the busybodies choose to condemn me for doing my Christian duty, let them."

"Hmmph. Your Christian duty?" Since when had she worried about that?

He studied her face. Even with the stubborn set of her chin and the snap in her eyes, he sensed something different about her—something restful and intriguing.

She picked up the suit coat thrown carelessly across the end of the bed and hung it on a hook. Yesterday, he'd shrugged out of it and collapsed onto the goose-down mattress without changing clothes. This morning, he managed to wash his face, run fingers through his hair, and clean his teeth, but his shirt and trousers looked like a rumpled pile of laundry hanging on a tailor's dummy. Now Quinn was thankful for his efforts, scant as they were.

"You may as well be pleasant, for I have no intention of leaving."

His lips involuntarily spread into the first genuine smile he had known in too many days. "Never?"

Moving the smaller chair next to his, she smoothed her skirt before sitting. "Why, Mr. Spencer, your attempt at humor says you are on the mend."

She reached around and grabbed the steaming bowl of soup, protecting her hands from the heat with a second napkin. She swished the spoon through the hot broth and blew on it. "This is very good broth. Mrs. Dillard allowed me a taste before I brought it to you."

"You didn't answer me." What was wrong with him? Two minutes ago, he had wanted Mrs. Dillard to send her away. Now he teased her in a brazen attempt at flirtation. Perhaps the illness had affected his mind.

Laurel pressed the spoon against his lips. "Open." It was obey or let the soup drizzle down his chin. While he swallowed, she set the spoon back in the bowl.

"I can feed myself."

"Have you sent for Dr. Cameron?"

"Unnecessary. I feel better. In fact, I'll be returning to the office tomorrow."

"So soon? Is that wise? Perhaps Momma should—"

"Why are you here, Laurel?"

Her brows drew together, and she looked away, revealing an unusual lack of confidence. "I came for several reasons. First, I owe you an apology for the way I spoke to you the last time we met. I set out to tell my story with no intention of being spiteful."

During the times he spent mulling over their conversation on Thanksgiving, Quinn had remained undecided over which appalled him more, Laurel's confession or his reaction to it. He leaned his head against the back of the padded chair, admitting the real reason he hadn't wanted to see her today. He'd run off like a spineless cad two weeks ago, and he hadn't been sure how to make it up to her.

"You don't owe me anything. I am the one who's sorry. I'm sorry for having hurt you all those years ago. And I'm sorry for acting like a child on Thanksgiving."

"I never blamed you for that day in Virginia, Quinn. It's just that when—"

"When you recognized me, it all rushed back?"

"Yes. Sights, smells, sounds . . . the pain. The same happened when I first saw the saber hanging from your saddle."

Each time a soldier relived a battle, he risked his peace in the present. And regardless of her gender, Laurel had been a soldier.

"I walked out on you and your family without a word. It was unforgivable."

"Nothing is unforgivable, Quinn."

He raised his head and examined her face again, seeing something in her smile, in her eyes, seeing . . . tranquility? "That wasn't your belief the day we spoke in the cemetery. What changed your mind?"

"The second reason I came to see you." Laurel placed the bowl on the tray and covered his hand with hers. "God still loves me. He never turned His back on me. Even though I turned mine on Him, He waited for me to return."

Quinn's breath caught and his heart thumped faster than it had in the past twenty-four hours. "That's an answer to my prayers for you."

"My guilt these many years was due to my own rebellion, not some heavenly plan to punish me. I still struggle with knowing I took lives in the way I did." She hung her head and spoke in a bare whisper. "I never even saw their faces."

"It was war, Laurel. We did things we never thought ourselves capable of doing. Everyone had moments when their actions failed to reflect an honorable cause. Did you truly think you were the only one to enter the conflict seeking retribution for wrongs done to you?"

"But how I did it—"

"No." Quinn slid his hand from hers and cupped her face. "'It is well that war is so terrible; else we would grow too fond of it.' Your General Lee said that."

"He was a wise man."

"And a respected soldier who defended his people. You think you entered the war for the wrong reason, but I think you defended your family and friends against a threat. If anyone placed you or Becky or your mother in danger, I'd spend my last breath protecting each one of you."

She searched his face as though seeking to confirm the veracity of his words. "I believe you."

One could hear the whisper of a mouse in the hush that followed. His gaze slipped to Laurel's lips—a bit weathered from time in the cold, yet so inviting. An inner argument raged inside Quinn. The fanciful notion had entertained him for weeks. Did he risk her scorn? Or was she in agreement? His pulse thrummed in his ears.

Illness forgotten, hunger won out as he leaned forward a fraction of an inch at a time. She remained still, her eyes wide with what appeared to be indecision. Dare he complete the move? He proceeded slowly, allowing her time to pull away.

They came within a feather's breadth of their lips touching when a man's heavy footfalls tramped up the stairs. Remembering the open door of his room, Quinn removed his hands from her face. He settled against the chair back with a groan as a new boarder entered a room down the hall.

Her sigh echoed his frustration. "It was for the best."

Laurel rose from the seat and walked to the window. She drew the thin curtain aside and stared out the glass, lost in thought. Quinn wished to know what she pondered, but her bearing signaled a distance he chose not to cross. Yet.

She leaned forward, looking outside, and cocked her head until her cheek touched the window. "Murphy is headed to the marshal's office. Royce must have sent him to learn when Wade will arrest me."

"He'll have a long wait."

"So you say." She closed the curtain and faced him. "Mr. Bruner wishes you well. He's concerned about your health and plans to pay you a visit today."

"I suppose he'll do so before he leaves town. There's a court case pending." Quinn covered a yawn that slipped out. "He'll be gone for a few days. That's why I must return to the office tomorrow."

She left the window and limped back to his chair. "Then I'll leave."

"No, stay. Please, let's talk more. You said you had several reasons for coming."

"I believe I have given you enough." Her lips quirked. "I thought you were concerned for my reputation."

He grinned. "Both our reputations are already suspect. Besides, your visit has been a true curative for what ailed me."

Laurel glanced toward the opened door before sitting. She took the bowl of broth in hand again. "All right. I didn't finish feeding you, anyway."

Though capable of lifting a spoonful of broth himself, Quinn was content to take it from her if it meant she stayed. How quickly things had changed. Only a few short months ago, he was eager to keep her name from being linked with his. Now he ached to spend more time with her.

Ever since hearing her laughter while working on the bunkhouse roof, Quinn had yearned for the day she would burn the men's attire and become the lighthearted girl her mother described. Now he realized he had no desire to suggest how she should run her life. He only wanted to share it.

"I would like permission to court you, Laurel."

The spoon rattled against the bowl. She dropped it inside, splashing the broth onto the napkin. "Court me?"

"Do you find it so astonishing? We've been moving toward this for several weeks."

She reached out and felt his forehead. "Are you sure you are over your illness?"

He clasped her hand, removing it from his head, but keeping it enclosed in his own. "Something binds us together, Laurel. Something having nothing to do with the war."

Her pained features stopped him. Had he been mistaken? Did he merely fantasize that she had wanted that kiss? In his disappointment, he released her hand. "Am I the only one who feels it?"

She played with a string at the hem of the napkin. "No. No, it's been with me since I first saw you lying helpless on my land."

He exhaled his uncertainty. "You did your best to fool me, Mrs. Tillman."

"I fooled myself, Mr. Spencer." Laurel's rich chuckle drove away his doubt.

"Then what is the problem?"

She paused as though searching for the right words. He waited until she found them, noting the ghost of melancholia that passed over her face. "It may be hard for you to understand, Quinn, but John loved me."

Not words he had expected to hear. "That isn't hard to understand." Not at all. "Are you saying you still mourn your husband? That there's no room in your heart for—"

She leaned in and pressed a warm finger to his lips. The subtle smell of lilacs filled his senses before she took her finger away and straightened.

"I am saying that my husband and I were well-suited in an unhealthy manner." Laurel handed him the bowl and stood. She paced back and forth, her shoes tapping the boards in a broken rhythm. "After returning home from the war, I needed to feel feminine again. I let my hair grow exceptionally long and took an undue interest in fashion."

Quinn eyed the softness of short blonde curls at her temples. She had massed the rest atop her head. On Thanksgiving, Laurel had released it from the pins to cascade like a waterfall. One day, he would see her wear it that way again. He knew it in his gut.

"As beautiful as your hair is, it is not where your femininity lies, Laurel. Nor does it lie in the clothes you wear." Hearing the words springing from his mouth gave Quinn a start. Convinced of their truth, he added, "Anyone with any sense knows that."

"That's good to hear, because since I began running the ranch, I have had no time for the newest hair styles or fashion. Have you ever tried shearing sheep in a dress?"

He laughed. "Not lately."

"John grew up with little in the way of affection and hoarded whatever he received. He feared losing me to someone else and the only way he knew to keep that from happening was by never allowing me to forget he saved my life, my honor, and my brother's name. In youthful ignorance, I failed to recognize the calculating remarks meant to convince me of my good fortune." With a wry smile, she added, "I didn't realize how he had manipulated me, though I think Momma knew all along."

Quinn gripped the chair arm, imagining it to be John Tillman's neck.

"Please don't misunderstand. My husband loved me. I say that without a shred of doubt, and we had a satisfactory marriage. But ours was a selfish love. I have been no less selfish in my desire to save the ranch. Even though I've found satisfaction in its success, I should have sold out to Royce years ago. Instead, I never learned from my mistake. I should have insisted Issy and Camille live like proper women and stop pretending to be what they are not."

Icy fingers of apprehension ran up his spine. "What has this to do with us?"

"Right now, my problems are too public—my future uncertain. You are a promising lawyer, Quinn—maybe even a potential leader in the state. Too many important people in this town don't like our friendship. It's already caused talk. If we were to court, you would have little future here and no political career. We both know that hasn't changed. I won't be selfish again."

She strode to the doorway, where she stopped with a hand on the knob. "You were right, Mr. Yankee. We tore down that Mason-Dixon line . . . for a short time."

Before he could respond, plead with her to listen to reason, she closed the door and disappeared down the hallway. Her uneven footsteps faded, taking with her any expectations for their future.

CHAPTER THIRTY-ONE

Unprepared for Quinn's request to court her, temptation had urged Laurel to accept his suit. Even now, a strong desire to change her mind enticed her to run back up the stairs to the second floor.

She remained on the wagon bench and took the reins in hand, reliving the moment he nearly kissed her. Her heart ached with the trouble it would have created. The mistake. But, oh, she longed to have made that mistake.

Laurel refused to look up to the second story of the house. Regardless of the burning pull at the core of her emotions, for Quinn's sake, she had given him the only answer possible. One day he would see—

"And how did you find Quinn, Mrs. Tillman?"

Laurel jolted at the unexpected voice behind her. She pressed a hand to the throb in her chest. "Oh, Mr. Bruner, you gave me a start."

"Forgive me. I'm leaving town but wanted to see how he fared. Does he feel up to more callers?"

She waited until the man reached the front of her wagon. Earlier, in the dimness of the office staircase, she had missed the dark circles forming a half-moon shape under his bespectacled, lifeless eyes. Quinn had appeared healthier. "He's better and intends to leave for the office in the morning. However, I told him of your plan to call."

"Then I'll make mine a brief visit." He doffed his hat. "Good day to you, madam."

"Good day." Laurel turned the mules and passed the Bruner carriage on her way to Center Street.

Looking left at the corner, she remembered seeing Murphy stroll toward the marshal's office. On a whim, she pulled the mules to a stop in front of the limestone building and set the brake.

The door rattled as she closed it, drawing the attention of Wade Ruiz and Murphy. The latter stiffened in the chair in front of Wade's desk. "What are you doing here, Laurel?"

"The question of my day." She moved closer to the men. "Mr. Spencer is ill. During my visit to him, I saw you come in here. Does it have anything to do with me?"

Murphy blew frustrated air through his lips. He exchanged a questioning glance with the marshal, who nodded. Rising from his seat, he swept his arm through the air, offering the chair to Laurel. "I found something inside Royce's desk."

Quinn pushed against the chair's arms and rose, ready to shuffle over and settle into his bed. Laurel's visit had drained him. Not her visit. Her rejection.

A knock on the door stopped him a foot from his destination. He grinned, hoping she had changed her mind. "Who is it?"

"It's Arthur. May I come in?"

Quinn moaned, in no mood to spar with the man this morning. "Of course."

The door opened partway, and Arthur peered into the room. "You still look pale. Perhaps I should come back."

Peering at his face, Quinn arrived at the same conclusion about his guest's condition. "No. Please come in."

Arthur stepped inside the room and reached for the chair Laurel had occupied. He glanced toward the tray. "Chicken soup? Ah, but you haven't finished it. Don't you know that chicken soup cures all ills?"

"I'm feeling fine without it. Besides, it's cold now."

"Then let me fix that. We can't have you relapsing." Before Quinn could protest, Arthur left the room, carrying the tray with the soup bowl. He returned a short time later, steam curling above the broth.

"No bowl for you?"

Arthur patted his stomach. "I ate a late breakfast and couldn't possibly find room for more." He placed the tray on Quinn's lap. "Eat. I'd like you well enough to return to work as soon as possible."

"About that—"

Waving a hand through the air, Arthur said, "Let's put that nasty discussion behind us. You misunderstood Henry's intention that night, and I have no desire to speak of it again."

"Yes, sir." He had misunderstood nothing. However, the office atmosphere had been icy for the past week and Quinn welcomed this attempt at a thaw. "I'll be in the office first thing tomorrow morning."

He gulped a few more spoonfuls of broth. It went down warm and soothing. Still, he crinkled his nose at the odd taste—bitter and sweet—that hadn't been noticeable earlier. Then again, he'd noticed little beyond Laurel's presence.

Quinn asked about the results of a meeting with the owner of the local mill. They also spent several minutes discussing a trial beginning in two days at the county's courthouse, the reason for Arthur's trip.

When talk of business ended, Arthur shifted in his seat. "Have you and Mrs. Tillman resolved the differences between you?"

Quinn had said little of what happened at Thanksgiving, only that he and Laurel had a difference of opinion. He set aside the bowl of broth, tired of the taste. "Yes, sir . . . to a point."

"To a point?"

He shifted on the bed. "I've asked to court her."

Arthur stilled. Quinn waited while several emotions passed over the older man's face. Concern. Anger. Exasperation. Resignation. He read them all.

"And what was her answer?"

"She refused me." The discernible relief lasted only until Quinn added, "I intend to change her mind."

"I see. Well, I have made clear my reservations concerning her suitability for you."

As Arthur chose not to speak of his son, Quinn chose not to argue their differing opinions of Laurel.

Arthur stood and stretched. "If I hope to reach my destination before dark, I must leave now."

"I'll pray for safe travel."

"Thank you. Get well, Quinn. I'm sure Mrs. Tillman and her daughter—Becky, is it?—will need you." He pointed to the bowl. "And finish that soup."

Quinn would need more than chicken broth to defeat what ailed him. He would need to change people's minds about the ladies of La Casa del Fuego. Without it, he would never change Laurel's mind about allowing him to court her.

The morning's issues vexed Laurel until she had sought the quiet tranquility of the cemetery. While there, she prayed for the strength to overcome her feelings for Quinn—to put his prospects before her own.

Murphy's announcement had raised another worrisome problem. That one she locked in a back corner of her mind to be given free rein later.

Returning from the cemetery, Laurel walked past May Simpson's dress shop on her way to the buckboard. From the corner of her eye, she noted the creations draped over dress forms inside. Normally, she would pass by without giving them a second thought. Today, the gowns drew her back to the large window. She stood outside the shop, her attention fixed on a dress of bottle green wool and black velvet, the tip of its short train almost touching the floor.

"That color would look lovely on you, Laurel."

"I suppose so."

Without her realizing it, the petite dressmaker had stepped from the shop to stand on the boardwalk next to her. "Don't you adore the velvet trim?"

"Yes." Yes, she did. "The double rows of pleats running along the bottom of the underskirt are a nice touch, too."

"They are, aren't they?" May asked the question as though the thought had just occurred to her. Her voice softened into a dream-like quality perfect for ensnaring potential customers. "I especially like the black braid on the cuffs. Do you agree?"

"Yes."

"Would you like to try it on?"

"Ye—" What was she doing? She had no occasion to wear such a dress and doubted her appearance made much difference to her woolly flock. "Besides being an excellent seamstress, May, your sales skills outshine those of a drummer."

The small woman laughed. "Trying on the dress will prove worthwhile in the end."

Laurel closed her eyes and shook her head, willing away the temptation. "Not today."

May presented Laurel with a coy grin. "The Christmas social is next Saturday. Think of all the heads you would turn."

"Oh, they would turn." In the opposite direction. "I never attend such functions."

"What difference do the mistaken opinions of some pretentious women make?"

"Careful, May. You're speaking of some of your best customers."

She laughed again. "I have named no names." The laughter died as she touched Laurel's arm. "You have more friends around Bold Creek than you believe, and that's not sales talk. Please stop pushing us away, as you have done for years."

Laurel swallowed a lump of emotion, her gaze straying back to the dress in the window.

"Now, how about that dress?" May walked back to the entrance to her shop.

Bracing herself against the lure tugging her inside, Laurel shook her head. "No. I'd better get home."

She passed by the dressmaker on her way down the boardwalk. After a few feet, she turned. "May?"

"Yes?"

"Thank you."

"I meant what I said, Laurel. If you don't believe me, look around you." May Simpson walked back into the shop and shut the door.

Laurel peered up and down the main street of Bold Creek. Had she allowed her guilt to color her perception of how people saw her? Some looked down their noses at all the ranch women and would always do so. She could not be held responsible for their snobbery.

May, Reverend Perry, the Oberlins, Wade Ruiz . . . Quinn. All had broken through her shell by sheer persistence. How many others had she pushed away?

A short, gaunt woman approached. Should she test May's claim? Laurel drew her lips into a wide, sincere smile. "Good afternoon, Mrs. Fleming."

The farmer's wife halted. She studied Laurel's face for a moment, then returned the smile. "Why, it's a mighty good afternoon, Mrs. Tillman—a beautiful day."

"Yes. The sun has taken some of the chill from the air."

"Among other things it seems." Mrs. Fleming dipped her head. "All's well with your family?"

"It is. And yours?"

"Judd's got rheumatism awful today."

"I'm sorry."

"Aw, he'll be fit soon."

They talked a few more minutes before Mrs. Fleming said, "Goodness. I can't lollygag all day. Been a pleasure speaking with you, ma'am."

"Yes. It's been a pleasure for me, too."

Laurel walked on, her steps becoming lighter and more even. On her way to the buckboard, she passed The Golden Ace. In the alley alongside the saloon, familiar voices drifted to the street in animated discussion. Curiosity got the best of her. "Is there a problem?"

Murphy and Wade left the shadows and hiked into the sunshine. Murphy slipped his hands into his denim pockets. "You know what we spoke of earlier?"

"Of course."

"We just had a little talk with Royce inside the saloon." Murphy's eyes glowed with angst and anger. "He admitted to writing the bill of sale I found in the desk."

"But he said Ferrell never came to the ranch. How could he—"

Murphy's lip curled in derision. "Because he's a liar."

Laurel turned to Wade. "What excuse did Royce give for lying?"

The marshal laughed. "That man's a swollen-headed cuss. No offense Murphy."

"None taken."

"According to Royce, he didn't lie. I just didn't ask the right questions. He said Ferrell approached him on the road one day, away from the ranch, and told him he'd trade the name of the person who shot the cattle for a hundred dollars and a horse."

"One of *my* best horses." Murphy removed his hat and beat the felt on his thigh. Dust flew everywhere. "I've trained that gray since he was a foal. Royce knew I'd kept him for myself."

Laurel felt sorry for the younger brother. It couldn't be easy to break trust with a brother. Then again, Royce didn't share the same scruples.

Wade eyed Murphy. "When I refused to give him back the bill of sale, his face turned red, and he looked like a keg of gunpowder about to blow, didn't he?"

For the first time, Murphy grinned. "Yeah."

Laurel was in no mood to join in their humor. "I am well aware of Royce's temper, but why would he bargain with Ferrell when I'd already said I saw Ferrell shoot those steers?"

"Did you, Laurel?"

She paused at Wade's question. Did she see Reg Ferrell fire a shot? "No. No, I didn't. I saw him nearby and assumed . . ." She bit her bottom lip.

"As Royce assumed you had done the shooting?" Marshal Ruiz placed a hand on her arm. "Ferrell told him it wasn't you."

She let out a gasp and faced Murphy. "Then why didn't he say something instead of insisting I owe him the value of the animals? He still planned to sue me, didn't he?"

"A hundred dollars is a lot of money."

Her shoulders dropped in disbelief. "That scoundrel! He intended to get money from me to make up for what he would lose to Ferrell."

The younger MacMahon nodded. "On my honor, Laurel, I didn't know until today."

Wade took a few steps toward the boardwalk. "I need to talk to Bruner."

Laurel followed him. "Mr. Bruner? Why?"

Murphy kept pace at her right. "Royce was supposed to meet Ferrell on November eighth. My brother mentioned the man's proposition to Arthur, who told Royce it would be best if he met with Ferrell himself. That allowed Royce as little involvement as possible. Later, Arthur said the Arkansan didn't show."

Laurel balled her fists to control the trembling in her fingers. "Ferrell expected to take Ernie away on the eighth. What time were they to meet?"

"Noon."

"Two hours before I was to meet with Ferrell. If he didn't keep the appointment with Arthur Bruner, perhaps he was dead already."

Who else had Ferrell planned to see that day? Why hadn't the lawyer said something?

The two men exchanged a deliberate glance. Wade Ruiz stared down the street, toward the lawyer's office. "I'll know more once I speak with Bruner."

"You won't find him in his office. He was leaving town after visiting Quinn."

"Leaving town?" Wade's brown eyes sharpened.

"Quinn mentioned a court case. He plans to be gone several days." She told of running into the man outside the boarding house. Something about meeting Bruner bothered her, but she couldn't place what it might be.

"Why don't we mosey over and check out his place, Wade? Maybe we'll find something in *his* desk drawer, too."

"The man's a lawyer, Murphy. He knows I'd need a warrant."

"I don't." The younger man stepped off the boardwalk and started across the street.

Wade called after him, "I didn't hear that."

The conversation whirled in Laurel's head. When she'd suggested Ferrell might already have been dead when Arthur was to meet him, Wade and Murphy glanced at each other as though sharing a silent secret. Now, they carried on as though they suspected the lawyer of—

She pressed her fists to her temples. What was it she couldn't remember?

"Is something wrong, Laurel?"

"I don't know. Something about seeing Mr. Bruner this morning ..." Laurel walked the boards—back and forth. Each discussion she'd had with the man earlier passed through her mind. First in his office, then in front of the boarding house as she was leaving.

"He said, 'I am on my way out of town.' On his way ..." A grunt of bafflement escaped her lips when the answer came. She stopped pacing. "No bag."

"What?"

"As I passed the carriage, I looked inside and saw no bag for a stay of several days, yet I understood he planned to leave town straight from the boarding house. What could that mean?"

Wade paused a beat, then said, "It means I need to catch up to Murphy." The marshal broke into a jog as he crossed the street.

Laurel rubbed her coat-covered arms. She turned and walked to the buckboard still parked in front of the jail, fully aware of what it meant. The marshal had set his sights on a new suspect.

CHAPTER THIRTY-TWO

"Mrs. Tillman! Mrs. Tillman, wait." Hedda Dillard stopped and bent her plump frame, resting her hands on her hips as she gasped for air. "I am . . . I am not accustomed . . . to running."

Laurel sat atop the wagon's bench, her gloved hands eating into the leather reins. "What's wrong?"

"It's Mr. Spencer." The woman breathed deeply and straightened her body. "His illness is worse."

Fear wrapped Laurel in a bear hug. Momma. No matter Quinn's opinion, she must send for her mother. Then she remembered the horse still tied to the post in front of the limestone jail, and the day Ernie sprained her wrist.

"Murphy is in town, either at Mr. Bruner's office or the man's home. When you find him, send him to Quinn." Laurel hoped she wasn't wrong about her neighbor.

She urged the mules into a trot down Cedar Street. Once at the boarding house, she jumped to the ground, ignoring the stiffness in her knee. Gripping each side of her skirt, she ran to the porch.

Inside the house, she climbed the carpeted steps as fast as her leg would allow, calling Quinn's name and receiving no answer. Laurel's heart constricted as she opened the door. He stood against the wall, doubled over in pain.

She ducked under his arm and wrapped one of her own around his waist. "What are you doing out of bed?"

"I'll be all right."

Laurel eased him onto the mattress. "And I am Lincoln's ghost."

She tucked the covers around him and plumped a pillow behind his back, breathing a quick prayer for his recovery. His face, pale and haggard, reflected an agony not present earlier. When she left him sitting in the chair, his skin was healthy and his breathing strong. What caused the sudden relapse?

After stepping to the window, she peeled back the curtain and scanned the empty street. *Quickly, Murphy.*

Quinn moaned and held his abdomen. "Feels like fire searing my gut." Sweat formed on his brow and each breath became shallower.

Reaching out, Laurel clasped his hand. He tried to squeeze it but managed a mere twitch of a forefinger. She brushed the damp waves of hair from his forehead. "I wish I knew what to do for you, but I didn't inherit my daddy's gift of healing. Mrs. Dillard is bringing Murphy." At his quizzical expression, she added, "Something tells me that man can help you."

The stair treads resounded with a heavy pounding. Laurel rushed to the door. Mrs. Dillard followed Murphy and the marshal into the room. Reverend Perry brought up the rear.

In a matter of four long strides, Murphy reached the bed. He grasped Quinn's wrist with the tips of his fingers, then bent over to lift Quinn's eyelids and examine his pupils. His voice barely perceptible, he said, "I wish I had my bag."

"Bag?" Wade Ruiz peered over Murphy's shoulder. "What kind of bag?"

"The bag that holds my instruments and medicines."

Anger darkened the marshal's eyes. "We've had a doctor around here all this time and you said nothing?"

Laurel's only reaction was a whispered, "Thank you, God." She pushed aside the lawman. "Wade, at least wait until he treats Quinn before you upbraid him. Go ahead, Murphy. You'd better get it right."

Turning around, Murphy said, "Why don't you ladies wait outside?"

Laurel wasn't going anywhere. "I have seen worse."

Murphy placed the back of his hand against Quinn's forehead. "I understand you were ill yesterday but felt better this morning. When did it come on you again?"

"A few minutes ago. The . . . The pain is greater this time."

"Where?"

Quinn touched his stomach. "Here."

Murphy tested the area, bringing a groan from Quinn and a wince from Laurel. "You have no fever, and I don't feel anything unusual in your abdomen. Have you eaten anything today?"

"A little . . . chicken broth."

"What about before you fell ill yesterday?"

"Breakfast." He drew in a pained breath. "And the noon meal."

"What have you had to drink?"

Laurel's nerves twisted like strands of spun wool. Was Hedda's broth bad? She touched her middle. Although she had only tasted a teaspoon of the soup, Laurel felt fine. "Why are you asking these questions, Murphy?"

"He has no fever. The nausea, weakness, slow pulse . . ."

Wrinkles streaked across Quinn's brow. "I had tea at the office yesterday. It tasted strange, like today's broth."

"They tasted the same?"

"They had the same slight bitterness."

Mrs. Dillard drew her plump frame as straight as it would go. "My soup is never bitter. The pot I made this morning is no exception."

"She's right." Laurel's eyebrows narrowed in confusion. "I tasted the broth before I brought it to you earlier, Quinn. There was no bitterness."

Murphy walked over to the tray. He raised the bowl to his nose and sniffed. Then he dipped a finger in the broth and licked it, wrinkling his nose. "How much did you ingest, Quinn?"

"M-Most of it."

Laurel took the bowl from Murphy and sampled a large drop of the broth. "This isn't what I fed him at noon."

Quinn sucked in a breath and grabbed his stomach. The spasm passed quickly. "Arthur took it to Mrs. Dillard. She added more to make it hot."

"Straight from what was on the stove." Mrs. Dillard twisted a corner of her apron in her hands. "I had some myself after Mr. Bruner left."

Wade straightened from the slouched position he had taken against the bedroom wall. "Bruner handled the broth when not in your presence, Spencer?"

The marshal and Murphy exchanged another glance that sent Laurel's pulse racing. They moved to a corner of the room and began whispering. Quinn clasped her hand with a weak hold and motioned with his head toward the others.

"Gentlemen, if you have something to say, we would like to hear it, too." The two men stared at Laurel. "Well?"

Murphy ignored her and turned to Mrs. Dillard. "Please get me some charcoal from the fireplace or stove. Put it inside a handkerchief and pound it into a fine powder."

"Charcoal?"

"Hurry, ma'am. And if you have any whiskey, bring that and a spoon."

"Whiskey? Oh, I keep it strictly for medicinal purposes, I assure you." Mrs. Dillard's face glowed with a deep pink, and she lowered her chin. "I'll return shortly." Wade Ruiz jumped aside as she nearly bumped into him in her hurry to obey Murphy's instructions.

After Hedda left the room, Laurel glared at the men. "Which one of you will tell us what's wrong?"

Murphy walked back to the bed and looked down at Quinn. "It's possible you've been poisoned."

Laurel covered her mouth with an unsteady hand. Poisoned?

Quinn struggled to rise. "What kind of poison?"

"The juice of mistletoe berries."

He whispered, "You got that from a simple examination? I've been nowhere near the plant."

"You only think you haven't, Spencer." Murphy reached over and picked up the bowl. "This tells a different story."

Wade took the bowl and set it back on the tray. "Before we were summoned here, Murphy found an old sugar sack in Bruner's kitchen filled with leaves and a good many berries."

"No." Quinn's head sank back into the pillow. "He has no reason to do what you're suggesting. He's . . ." His voice died. He shut his eyes and nodded as though accepting Murphy's diagnosis.

"I was told Mr. Spencer was ill." Reverend Perry stepped into the room. "Given what I just overheard, you may be interested in what I have to say, Marshal."

"Go ahead, sir."

"A few mornings ago, I looked out the window of the church sanctuary and spotted Arthur Bruner in the cemetery. He had removed a clump of mistletoe from one of the mesquite trees."

"It's nearly Christmas, Reverend." Laurel cocked her head. "He told me once that his wife liked to decorate with the plant during the holiday."

"Mrs. Tillman, I noticed him pacing in front of your husband's grave. His lips moved as though he talked to the stone," Reverend Perry paused before adding, "then he kicked it."

Laurel grunted as though Bruner's boot connected with her stomach. "He kicked John's headstone?"

The pastor nodded. "I started outside to speak with him, but the rage in his stance gave me pause. Had I done so, I might have spared your suffering, Mr. Spencer. I'm very sorry."

"That doesn't explain why he would poison Quinn."

Murphy lowered his bulk into the chair next to the bed. "It takes a good bit to kill a person, and I doubt you consumed enough, Quinn, but you'll suffer until it leaves your body."

Quinn's eyes reflected more than the pain of his illness. They revealed the pain of a friend's betrayal.

"The nerve of that man! Adding poison to my soup." Hedda Dillard sat on the parlor sofa and dabbed at her eyes with a handkerchief.

"Don't blame yourself, Mrs. Dillard." Reverend Perry sat next to her. He leaned forward with his hands in an attitude of prayer. "I am more responsible than anyone."

"No one is to blame but Arthur Bruner." Laurel walked away from the warmth of the fire and sank into a green velvet-upholstered chair across from the pastor. "And wallowing in guilt is not a productive pastime."

"Thank you for that reminder, Mrs. Tillman."

"Well, I don't know about you, but I bake when I'm upset." Hedda rose from the sofa. "Right now, I am upset enough to rival the Oberlins for business. If you'll excuse me, I'll be in the kitchen."

Once she left the room, the pastor walked to the entry to the parlor. "Murphy assured us that Mr. Spencer will be fine, Mrs. Tillman, but be assured I'll continue to pray."

Laurel nodded and shut her eyes. She began her own silent prayer that soon drifted away.

Her eyes popped open at the gentle shaking of her shoulder. Laurel pressed into the chair back, caught off guard by Murphy's burly frame bent over her. She rubbed her eyes and glanced at the mantle clock. Nine? Pots rattled in the kitchen. "How's Quinn?"

"Resting. There's nothing to worry about. He'll sleep off and on through the night."

Relief flowed through her. Murphy helped her stand. The man was a mystery. One minute hard, the next compassionate. "Why not tell people you were a doctor? Why hide it? Wade was right. We could have used your services."

He hung his head. "Your ma's done a fine job handling minor

ailments and Dr. Cameron is a good doctor. No one needed me."

"Ernie did, and you were needed today, but that doesn't answer my question."

"I won't talk about it, Laurel, and I've asked the others not to mention it to anyone. I'm asking the same of you." He walked toward the parlor doorway, then paused and turned. "How did you know, anyway?"

"I am the daughter of a physician. There is an assessing look in a concerned doctor's eyes when he sees physical suffering. I've seen that look more than once on your face, Murphy."

He started toward the front door of the house. "Your family was worried about you and sent Issy. She's waiting in the kitchen to drive you home."

Laurel glanced to the ceiling, tempted to go upstairs before she left. Instead, she walked out of the parlor and toward the kitchen.

Because of God's mercy, she would see Quinn tomorrow.

Laurel tossed and turned on her bed, listening to the hoots of an owl in between the bleats of sheep. Sleep refused to override her reflections on the day.

Before leaving for the county seat in the late afternoon, Wade had stopped by the ranch to inform her mother of the reason for Laurel's absence. Momma had sent Issy to drive her back, not wanting her to travel alone at night.

Saying a prayer for Quinn's recovery—one of an endless string—Laurel also thanked God for showing her Murphy's medical prowess through little observations. Otherwise, sending for Dr. Cameron to attend Quinn would have meant more hours of his suffering.

Arthur Bruner. Laurel ran the name over and over through her mind. Until Wade caught up with him, they wouldn't know for sure if he killed Ferrell and, if so, why. The marshal had spent the hours before leaving town gathering evidence against the man. Without being specific, he said it was ample enough for even a lawyer to plead him guilty.

Oddly, this time, Laurel experienced no desire for vengeance. She only wanted to know why Bruner sickened the man she loved.

Her pulse rate surged, leaving her breathless. Seeing Quinn lying in that bed, the shadowy growth of whisker stubbles being the only thing to save his pale features from disappearing into the whiteness of the sheet . . . She'd felt no greater fear of loss since caring for her dying baby boy.

After an untold time in restlessness, the night sounds blended into one. Memory mixed with dreams and the jostle of her bed.

Her eyelids fluttered, not fully opening. Through sleep-filled cracks, she thought an illusory figure floated across the floor of her darkened bedroom.

"Momma?"

The one word sounded like thunder, freezing the phantom into stillness. She opened her mouth again, but before a sound emerged, the apparition rolled into the night's shadows, leaving cold air in its wake.

CHAPTER THIRTY-THREE

Quinn tucked his shirt into his trousers, grateful for the strength to move, something he'd not had until well over an hour after his customary time to rise. He turned to Wade, who stood just inside his room. "Have you found Arthur?"

"Nope. The man never showed up at the courthouse or anywhere else along the way." He pulled a sheet of paper from his coat pocket. "I found this list in Bruner's house, along with a couple of photographs of men in Confederate uniform."

Quinn snatched the paper from the marshal's hand and read the names, stopping at Reg Ferrell's. Running a finger over Ferrell's name, he traced a large, black "X" made by a pencil, the same mark drawn across the other four names. As he rubbed a fingernail over something splashed across the bottom of the paper, he clenched his teeth. "Is this Ferrell's blood?"

"Possibly. Or it could belong to one of the others." Wade reached for the list and carefully replaced it in his pocket.

The casual statement gnawed at Quinn. The spasms and vomiting of the night before were nothing compared to the attack of pain upon hearing of Arthur's deeds. Would he have prevented what happened by being honest years ago? "Do you think he killed the others, too?"

"I won't know for sure until I can do some checking. Until we find Bruner, I expect it'll take time to identify those men. It's a fact he didn't go to the county seat like he said."

"I wondered why he would make his home in Texas. My guess is they're all former soldiers—former Confederate soldiers."

Wade's back straightened. "Any idea where he might be?"

While pushing his feet into his boots, Quinn searched his mind for any clues hidden in the comments Arthur had made over the past few days. Recalling their last discussion froze his fingers as he pulled his pant leg over his left boot. Why hadn't he paid more attention to the words and Arthur's tone of voice?

He finished the job, his movements driven by desperation. "Where is Laurel?"

"At the ranch. Why?"

Still weakened from his bout with the poison, Quinn made his way to the bureau and pulled the holster containing the Army Colt from the top drawer. He wrapped the belt around his hips.

God, please don't let me be too late.

"Spencer?"

The fragile control he possessed threatened to explode when his fingers fumbled with the prong on the buckle. It slid back and forth, marring the leather rather than slipping easily into the hole in the belt. "He may go after Laurel and Becky."

"Why?"

"The last thing he told me was to get well because they would need me. I was so caught up in Laurel's rejection of my suit that I paid little attention to what he said."

"That doesn't mean he intends to hurt them."

"Are you willing to take that chance, Wade?" He grabbed his coat from a hook and pushed past the marshal. "I am not."

Laurel patted the buckskin's head, stepped back out of the corral beside the barn, and latched the gate.

A high-pitched bark sounded from the center of the sheep pen where Becky worked with the pup. "How is the training coming along, Peanut?"

"Good as grapes, Momma. Diamond is real smart. She's . . ."

Pounding hoof beats drown out her daughter's words. Quinn and Wade galloped their horses into the yard. They pulled the sweating animals up near the barn.

"Howdy, Mr. Spencer. Howdy, Marshal Ruiz." Both men returned Becky's greeting.

The stormy look on Quinn's face rattled Laurel. "You ought to be resting."

He held up his hand. "Laurel, this is not a social visit." His attention shifted back to her daughter. "Becky, go inside. If I know your grandmother, she has cookies ready for you."

Becky's eyes widened at his firm tone, but she shuffled to the porch, kicking up dust with the toes of her boots. She ordered Diamond to wait outside.

The girl entered the house, and Quinn asked, "Where are the rest of the women?"

"Momma is inside. The others are with the flock."

Wade's mouth drooped as he turned to Quinn. "I imagine the other women are safe for now."

"Safe?" Laurel's hand tightened around the handle of the pail she carried until she thought her fingers would meld into the metal. "Why wouldn't they be safe?"

Quinn's hooded eyes and taut jaw muscles revealed both weariness and worry. "I think Arthur may come here."

Was this another nightmare? If so, she hoped to awaken before it took hold. She blinked, but it did no good. The men still stood before her with concern etched in deep lines on their faces. "Why?"

Quinn told her of Bruner's statement. When Wade mentioned finding the list with crossed-off names and two photographs of

Confederate soldiers, Laurel fought to draw a breath. This visit did not begin a nightmare, but continued one begun in the wee hours of last night. "It couldn't have been real."

"What's wrong?"

"I meant to ask Becky if she had taken it."

"What?" Quinn gripped her upper arms. "Taken what, Laurel?"

"My wedding photograph. I thought I dreamed someone came into my room last night. When I dressed this morning, I noticed the photograph was missing from my bureau."

Wade glanced around the yard. "It's time we get you into the house, too."

"You take her, Wade. I'll have a look around."

Inside, Laurel paced the kitchen floor while Wade checked the rest of the house. Momma sat at the table with her hands clenched together. Becky crumbled a cookie on a small plate.

When Wade stepped into the kitchen, Laurel halted her pacing. "What do you plan to do?"

"I have Mort Zucker putting out the word to watch for Bruner. I'll leave Spencer here with you and try to pick up a trail." He glanced at Momma and Becky and lowered his voice. "There are footprints outside your bedroom window."

That was the trouble with nightmares. They stemmed from reality. "If he wanted to hurt us, why not do so last night?"

"Maybe he didn't have time."

"Becky called to me. She must have scared him off."

At Diamond's fierce bark, everyone's anxious gaze moved to the side door. The growls and yaps punctured the wood, then grew quieter the farther the animal ran from the house. A gunshot cracked the air, followed by the puppy's shrill yelp.

"Diamond!" Becky dropped a half-eaten cookie and ran out the door.

"Come back here, Rebecca!" Laurel bolted after her daughter. Wade jerked her back inside.

Quinn tightened his grasp on the revolver and eased toward the open door of the barn he had searched. The shot came from near the bunkhouse.

He peered around the barn's opening as Laurel called out for Becky. The girl continued her chase after the frightened puppy. He had to get her attention. "Becky, come here."

She stopped near the bunkhouse and turned. Though he couldn't hear them, the rise and fall of her shoulders testified to her sobs. He stepped away from the barn.

A long, thin shadow slithered across the dirt until it reached the back of Becky's feet. Quinn opened his mouth to shout a warning. Too late. Arthur snatched the girl around the waist and lifted her from the ground. She screamed and kicked before they disappeared around the corner of the bunkhouse.

Quinn pounded the side of the barn. "No!" The sound of departing hoof beats urged him to action.

He untied Ruthie, jammed his boot into the left stirrup, and shouted to the horse to move. The mare jumped forward as he swung his other leg over her back and settled into the saddle. The door of the house slammed open. Laurel ran toward the barn, her carbine gripped in her fist. Wade followed.

Quinn raced across the yard, terrified that Arthur might hurt the girl, which would lead Laurel to hurt Arthur. As the distance grew between Quinn and the house, Ellen's voice drifted through the air, urgently calling the marshal's name.

The chilly wind created by his mare's speed whipped Quinn's face and made his eyes water. In the open, tall blades of winter-dried grass slapped his legs. A few tore off and caught between his calves and the saddle leathers just above the stirrups. Within the areas of scrub and mesquite, he dodged low-hanging limbs while the brush battered his arms and legs.

Arthur's horse appeared and disappeared from view as it sprinted across the rolling landscape at a pace Ruthie could not match after the race to the ranch this morning. Quinn fell farther and farther behind.

On a hilltop, he reined in Ruthie, both of them needing a quick rest. The effects of the poisoning still weakened his endurance, and his mare heaved air in and out through extended nostrils. They each dragged in deep breaths before resuming the pursuit.

Arthur's horse curved toward the river and vanished amid the trees. Quinn urged his tired mare into a lope and followed with caution. Near the bank of the river, he found the riderless gelding and tied Ruthie to a buttonbush close by. He set out on foot, stepping over rock after rock that bordered a pool with water clear as fine crystal.

Ahead, Arthur paused on a dry rocky ridge. In a few months, rain would swell the river, pouring water over the rock. For now, it made a bridge. He shoved Becky forward, and she tripped, falling to her knees. The little girl's scream pierced the serenity of her surroundings.

Quinn stood in plain sight on a lower outcropping of rock. "Release Becky and let's talk, Arthur."

The old man stopped and stiffened his grip around the rifle. "I'd hoped you would still writhe in bed. That Rebel bullet should have caught you years ago. Better you than my boy. You poisoned Henry's good name . . . spread lies about him."

"So you poisoned me? I spread no lies, Arthur. I've told no one but you."

Sunlight glinted off Arthur's spectacles. "I didn't try to kill you, though I wanted to see you suffer. But those who had a part in killing my son must be brought to justice."

"Mrs. Tillman and her child had nothing to do with Henry's death."

Arthur stepped to the edge of the rocky shelf and away from Becky. "Remember the day I pulled a nightshirt from the woman's trunk?"

"Yes." What had that to do with anything?

"She has a Whitworth hidden under the clothing."

Quinn's brow furrowed. "A Whitworth?"

Enfield rifles had been more plentiful and easier to obtain during the war, but the Whitworths that made it through Federal blockades were nothing to sneer at. Certainly, Major General Sedgwick could attest to that fact . . . had he lived.

"John Tillman killed Henry."

CHAPTER THIRTY-FOUR

Terror filled her daughter's face when that monster snatched her up and carried her off. If anything happened to Becky . . .

She wouldn't lose another child!

Laurel had bridled her horse and galloped away from the house, expecting Wade to be on her heels. Then Momma called him back, leaving her to follow the trail alone. She passed Ernie carrying the yapping puppy toward the house. With a raised thumb, the girl indicated Diamond was fine.

She didn't know what she would do when she caught up with Bruner. She could have remained at the house and trusted Quinn to bring Becky back safely. She could have done so much differently in her life. If so, her daughter would not be in danger now.

Laurel battled the guilt that fought to take control of her mind. Prayer. She covered the distance in a state of prayer.

A horse rushed up behind her. Laurel's upper body twisted on the buckskin's bare back, her carbine pointed at the rider. She lowered the gun when Wade Ruiz caught up to her. They both reined in their horses.

Wade clutched an all-too-familiar object and panic squeezed

Laurel's insides. "Where did you get that?"

"Ellen thought you might need it." He held out the Whitworth.

She shook her head and gripped the carbine tighter. "I can't."

"Looks like they're headed toward the river." He shoved the rifle at her again. "Take this one. I'll carry yours."

She reached out a trembling hand and then withdrew it. "That's a weapon for killing men in stealth. The old Laurel could kill Bruner that way, but I have not been that person for years. I cannot succumb to vengeance again." Her gaze flashed from the Whitworth to the carbine. She backed the buckskin to put a few feet between herself and the marshal.

"This is not vengeance, ma'am. That man threatens your daughter. This firearm may be the difference between her living and dying. If it comes down to it, the law gives me the power to order you to use this weapon in defense of that little girl." He moved his horse closer. "Your ma sent it."

She fixed her eyes on the gun, taking in the long barrel and the scope on the left side. Why would Momma dig it out for her to use again? Other than removing the Whitworth from the trunk occasionally to clean it, Laurel had not fired it in years.

Thinking of the trunk triggered a memory and provoked her gasp. "Oh, no."

"Mrs. Tillman?"

"I caught Bruner going through my trunk the first day he visited Quinn. He must have seen that." She pointed to the firearm. "He took my photograph because . . . he knows."

Laurel fixed her gaze on the rifle in Wade's hand. The air thickened and strangled her. Could she fire it again to save her daughter from a madman's revenge?

"You don't know he was responsible, Arthur."

Even though he never saw the weapon that killed Henry, Quinn had suspected it was a Whitworth. In his nightmares, he still heard the bullet of the British-made rifle whistle through the air. Confederate sharpshooters found its deadly range to be as much as fifteen hundred yards and put it into the hands of the best marksmen among the Rebels. What were the odds that Tillman shot Henry? Laurel had never mentioned the roles she and her husband had played during the war.

"Even if it's true, why punish his family?"

"It's justice, son. I can't kill Tillman, but I can take away what was his."

Quinn kept his voice steady while probing further. "Then what justice is there in killing innocent people like Reg Ferrell?"

"Innocent?" Arthur's laughter echoed along the river. "The man blackmailed me, then planned to tell Royce he saw me shoot the cattle. Innocent. Bah! He was another murdering Rebel."

Hate consumed Arthur, turning him irrational. He'd waste his breath reminding the man that any Confederate sharpshooter could have killed Henry. His friend was mad.

"So you tried to place the murder on Laurel by hanging her handkerchief from that branch?"

"I was fortunate to see her drop it in the cemetery one day."

Becky used the men's conversation to tiptoe across the rock. Quinn's hand inched toward his holster. He resisted the urge to shout at her to run. Instead, he attempted to keep Arthur's attention. "What about the other men on your list? The photographs?"

Arthur laughed. "Gentlemen I've met in my travels. Texas is full of Rebs. I found the photographs in their homes and took them as souvenirs."

As Becky crept over the rock with her eyes on her captor, the toe of her boot caught in a small crevice, and she fell to her knees.

Arthur twisted and lunged for her, yanking her in front of him. "You are going nowhere, girl."

Quinn whipped out the revolver and raced over more rock, splashing through shallow puddles of water. "Let her go, Arthur."

"Stop, Quinn." The old lawyer wrapped a forearm around Becky's neck. With his other arm stretched outward, he pointed his rifle in Quinn's direction. "I could easily render her unconscious and throw her off this rock to drown."

The words stung like hornets, burning Quinn's stomach worse than the mistletoe's toxin. He stared at the two of them, never feeling more helpless.

Becky coughed, choking with Arthur's grip around her neck.

"What do you want with her? She wasn't born at the time of the war." Quinn chanced taking a few steps closer as he talked. "Take me and let her go. I'm the one who insulted Henry's memory."

Arthur stepped forward, inches from the end of the ridge, dragging Becky with him. "You think you are clever, Quinn, but come any closer and this little one goes in the water."

Tears streamed down Becky's face, and her fear tore at Quinn. "What is it you want?"

"Tillman's rifle. I want the weapon that killed my boy. I almost retrieved it last night. Unfortunately, Mrs. Tillman woke up."

Quinn itched to yank the man from the rock and thrash him. "If you want the Whitworth, we'll arrange it. Not if you hurt Becky. Let me send her back to the ranch with word of what you want. Until she returns, I'll take her place." He stepped forward. "We'll talk this out."

"Liar!" Arthur's face twisted. He tossed Becky aside like a spent apple core. She shrieked and hit the rock, remaining motionless. "You're nothing but a liar." He aimed the rifle at Quinn.

Quinn dove to the side and landed on his stomach as a bullet exploded into limestone. Pieces of rock bruised his arm and rained onto his back.

At the awful, familiar whistle of another bullet, Arthur screamed. He fell over the ridge and into the pool of water below. For an endless moment, Quinn couldn't move, expecting another shot from the weapon that wreaked havoc during the war. With all his effort, he forced his thoughts to return to the present.

"Becky!" Relief escaped in a whoosh of breath when he found her huddled against a large rock. "Stay there."

Quinn tossed off his boots and jacket, dropped the gun belt on the ground, then plunged into the cold river. He swam to the center of the pool, where Arthur struggled to stay afloat. Grasping the injured man around the neck with the same fierceness with which he had held Becky, Quinn pulled him onto the escarpment. Arthur rolled on the stone, hugging his knee and moaning.

Quinn shivered as his clothing dripped water. He ran a hand through his wet hair, shoving it away from his eyes, and then grimaced at the rivulets of blood running down the stone slope near Arthur's shattered left knee.

Wade appeared on the ridge next to Becky. He examined the back of her head and then hugged her to him.

"Is she all right?"

"Bruised and scared, but fine." The marshal pointed to Arthur. "That one'll be lucky not to lose a leg."

They both turned at the clang of a horse's steel shoes speeding along the bank. Laurel tossed something into the nearby grass and hopped off the unsaddled buckskin before it even stopped. She ran across the rock bridge. "Are you all right, Becky?"

Becky stood near the edge. "G-Good as g-grapes, Momma. How is Diamond?"

Laurel sobbed a laugh and pulled Becky into her arms, rocking the child back and forth. "Ernie found her. They headed into the yard as I rode out. Not a scratch on her."

Quinn never saw Wade leave the ridge. The two most important people in his life had consumed his attention. The marshal appeared beside him and set down the weapon he carried. He went through Arthur's clothing, pulling a wet photograph from the man's pocket. Wade held it up for Quinn to see. "Here's more proof he was in Laurel's room." He handcuffed the whimpering murderer and picked up the rifle he had set down. "We'll let the doctor fix him up, but I'm guessing he'll hang just the same."

"Arthur believes John Tillman was the sharpshooter who shot his son Henry." Quinn pointed to the Whitworth clutched in the marshal's hand. "I never expected one of those would save my life one day. I know his future is in doubt, but I'm indebted to you for not killing him."

"Me?" Wade grinned. "The shot came from a tree canopy down river. My eyes ain't good enough for seeing that far, even with one of these." Wade fingered the distinctive scope mounted on the left side of the rifle. "I picked this up from the grass."

"If not you, then . . ." Quinn studied the only other person who could have made that shot.

Laurel met his questioning gaze. The area under her right eye sported a half-circle of reddened skin that hours from now would be a midnight blue. "If I had wanted Bruner dead, he would not sit there moaning right now."

Quinn stirred next to Laurel, opening and closing his mouth without a word escaping. Laurel waited until he was ready to ask the question uppermost in his mind.

During the ride home, while she hugged her daughter and praised God for allowing her aim to save Bruner's life and Becky's, Quinn had lagged behind, lost in his own thoughts. Even now, he sat brooding on the porch step beside her, wrapped in a striped woolen blanket while the others talked inside the house.

"Arthur believed John shot Henry. He wanted to ruin everything important to your husband."

"Yes, I know." She also knew what Quinn wanted to hear from her.

"And?"

"And was it me?" Laurel prayed not. "When did he . . . when did it happen?"

"Knoxville. November of '63."

291

Her relief escaped in a puff of air between parted lips. "I enlisted in late November of that year. My regiment was nowhere near Knoxville."

Quinn merely nodded.

The discovery cleared the air between them. They sat in tired silence for several minutes until Laurel broke the quiet. "You should return to Hedda's and rest."

"Thanks to Murphy, I'm fine. He's a confounding man, but I'm beginning to like him."

She played with the edge of the blanket. "I'm sorry about your friend."

"Me, too. Arthur admitted to seeking former Confederate soldiers to kill them. That isn't the man I knew. All those times he left town, I thought he simply met with clients. No wonder business was mediocre. When I think what he might have done to Becky—"

"I would rather not think about it. Thank you for going after her."

"It was my fault. If I had been honest about Henry years ago when Arthur's wife was still alive to help him through it, I may have saved lives."

"You don't know that he wouldn't have killed, anyway." Checkers bumped against her side. She stroked the cat's mottled fur.

Quinn leaned close and fingered the bruise under Laurel's eye. "That Whitworth has quite a recoil."

She tilted her head away from the too-pleasant touch. "I spent three months of the war with a black eye."

"I bet you were a sight. I'm glad I can't remember our meeting that day in Virginia." He gazed off toward the pen by the barn. "What did you do with it?"

"The rifle? Wade has it. He can keep the cursed thing. I don't need it anymore."

"It must have been difficult climbing that tree with your stiff knee."

"It's easier when your loved ones are in danger."

"You're an amazing woman, Laurel."

How did he manage to say that with such awe? "Amazing? I am not proud of what I did, Quinn—today or all those years ago. Do you know what it's like to hunt men like prey? To shoot them while hidden hundreds of yards away and know they never had a chance against your aim?" She stared into his ashen face. Of course he did. "Do you ever have nightmares?"

"Sometimes."

"Even the smallest reminders bring them about. My whole body shakes whenever I think of those days. I get nauseous and . . ." She wrapped her arms around her middle and squeezed, cutting off the rising torment. God had forgiven her. She must focus on that. "If it weren't for Bruner's threat against you and my daughter, I never would have loaded that weapon again."

Quinn grasped her hand in his and rested them both on his knee. "When I said you were amazing, I wasn't talking about your ability to fire a weapon. I was talking about you—your courage, your sense of duty and justice tempered by mercy, your willingness to help others." He grinned. "Your temper. Your stubbornness. I'm amazed by everything about you, Laurel."

Her throat swelled, and she bobbed her head. She wanted to tell him how just sitting next to him, here and now, thrilled her to the point of giving way to her feelings. Instead, she said, "You have taken years off my life in the past two days, Quinn."

"I suppose that puts us closer in age now. We'll toddle into our dotage together." His declaration both delighted and disheartened her. "At least I know you care for me."

"I never said so."

"You climbed that tree to save 'loved ones.' Plural."

His expression dared her to correct him. As hard as she tried, the denial failed to make it past a thought. "All right, I do. Very much. But Quinn, we have gone over this before. Nothing has changed."

His gaze held hers, drilling his determination into her. "That's right. Nothing has changed. I still intend to court you. I've seen the transformation in you, Laurel. Others will see it, too, if you let them."

She pulled her hand from his and looked away before those compelling blue eyes forced her to surrender. Once her emotions were under control, she turned to him again. "Why are you doing this? We agreed it was better for you not to be seen with me."

Quinn's lips compressed in a sign of frustration. "Where is your signed contract?"

She frowned. "My what?"

He threw off the blanket, gripped her elbow, and propelled her to her feet. "Where is this pact you say I agreed to? I don't remember any such thing, nor do I remember an oral agreement."

Laurel eased her arm free. "Don't be ridiculous."

"You may have decided the scope of our relationship, Mrs. Tillman, but I did not agree. Therefore, it's not legally binding."

"Why are you—" She counted to five and lowered her voice to a harsh whisper. "Why are you being so mule-headed?"

"*I* am mule-headed?" His thunderous laughter caused Ruthie to dance at the end of her tether.

She crossed her arms. "You are acting like a foolish man, Quinn Spencer."

"And you are—" He shook his head and walked to his horse. He paused long enough to say, "You are the woman I plan to marry."

Quinn left her to stare at his back, but unlike their separation on Thanksgiving Day, he rode off whistling.

CHAPTER THIRTY-FIVE

"Momma, hurry and decide. We'll be late."

"Yes, but . . ." Ellen Chamberlain's fingers fidgeted with her hair as she peered into Laurel's mirror. "Don't you think I'm too old to have these little curls along my face? Whatever was Camille thinking?"

Laurel kissed her mother's slightly creased cheek. "You'll never be old, Momma. And I know a gentleman more than willing to back my claim." She laughed at the rosy hue on her mother's face.

Today, for the first time, the women of La Casa del Fuego would attend Bold Creek's annual Christmas social. Once Momma left the bedroom, Laurel swayed and turned in front of the mirror. Camille had swept the sides and back of her hair upward in a fancy twist and allowed a portion to fall in ringlets, none of the tresses false as worn by some ladies. The bruise around her eye had faded to a yellow-green.

She fingered the velvet on the dress. May Simpson had been right. The green matched her coloring perfectly. The dressmaker had been right about something else, too. No more holding people at arm's length. If they didn't like her, they didn't like her.

She limped onto the porch. Issy and Ernie had the mules harnessed and the buckboard waiting in front of the house. "Everyone load up."

"Tell me why we're doing this again?"

"Because, Issy, we will no longer hide on this ranch like we have something to be ashamed of."

"You know as well as I do those ol' biddies'll ride us out of that church on a broken pew."

"Then we will ride back in."

Issy placed a hand on her stomach and frowned. "I can't breathe in this doggone corset. Why does it need to be so tight?"

"Ah, to have your figure." Camille settled onto the quilt spread across the floor of the wagon to protect the women's dresses from dirt and splinters. "You should wear such finery more often, Issy. You look lovely in that pale shade of blue."

Issy responded with a rude snort. Laurel acknowledged the truth of Camille's statement. Perhaps, together, they might help the younger woman see that she could be a lady as appealing as her sister. This night was a good start.

They arrived in Bold Creek as the sun sat atop a western hill. Laurel stopped the mules behind a line of other conveyances and set the brake. They walked toward the limestone building and stopped as a group a few yards away.

Outside, a small gathering of men stood with lit cigars and pipes, the smoke carried away on a slight breeze. Children chased one another, screaming and laughing. A young girl stopped upon seeing Becky. She waved her arm through the air, motioning for Laurel's daughter to join them.

"May I, Momma?"

"Of course, Peanut." Laurel smiled as Becky skipped away and joined the children in their games.

Violin strains of *Silent Night* drifted through the open windows while the women stood in the cold and stared at the buildin

Laurel's heart hammered. The faces of the others reflected her anxiety. Maybe this wasn't a good idea. By now, the whole town must know of her misadventures during the war. They certainly knew she had wounded Bruner. Had that made her a greater pariah than before?

Others would see the change if she let them.

Following Quinn's advice, Laurel straightened her back and led the way. "We won't learn how we'll be treated until we go inside."

"Good evening, ladies." Reverend Perry stood at the door. "I'm glad you came."

Each woman mumbled a "Thank you." He enticed them into the building by adding, "The stove is fired and the room warm."

Wade Ruiz appeared next to him. "I'll be happy to escort them into the party." He offered Laurel's mother his arm. She didn't hesitate to take it. The three other women followed.

Most of the pews lined the wall to accommodate the adults who milled around, talking and eating cakes, cookies, and pies. The sweet aromas of the refreshments competed with the special fragrances worn by both women and men dressed in their finest—extravagant or plain, dependent upon their means. Holly sprigs tied with red ribbons decorated the food tables, while garlands of ivy draped the front of the tablecloths in swags.

Laurel searched the crowded room, nodding to those who stopped their conversation in order to stare. Most people, however, went about socializing and paying scant attention to the newcomers.

She craned her neck to see over and around the bodies in her way. No sign of Quinn. Her certainty of his attendance had caused her to think long and hard about her own presence, particularly after the ill-advised declaration of his intentions. Marriage. How she wished. But no.

"Here I am." His breath tickled her bare neck as he whispered over her left shoulder and into her ear. The smell of bay rum filled her senses.

Schooling her face to show an indifference belying her true emotions, she continued to scan the room. "Don't you believe it arrogant, Mr. Spencer, to suggest I might have been looking for you?"

"I believe it deceptive, Mrs. Tillman, to suggest you were not." He stepped alongside her as she turned her head to frown at him. "May we get you ladies something hot to drink?"

"No, thanks." Issy stepped away from them. "I see a pew along the wall with my name on it."

"Thank you, no, Quinn." Camille flipped her fan open and waved it in front of her face. "I should speak to May Simpson before she plays the piano once more."

After Camille walked off, Wade said, "Ellen?"

"Yes. I could use a cup of hot tea."

Wade ushered her mother over to the refreshment tables, leaving Laurel standing alone with Quinn—alone and silent for what seemed an eternity.

"Quite a gathering tonight."

"Yes." She stepped to the right to put more space between them and bumped into the rotund barber. "Oh, pardon me."

Quinn grasped her arm. "Let's go over to the corner where we'll be out of the way."

Laurel planted her feet. "And let everyone believe we are here together?"

Anger flashed in his eyes and disappeared so quickly, she thought she might have imagined it. Disappointment replaced the emotion, then it turned to determination. "I'd hoped you had changed your mind about us."

She edged closer to plead with him. "Look around you. No one has greeted me with open arms."

"Have you greeted others that way?"

"I-I . . . No." She had reverted to her old habit and waited for them to make the first move. "It isn't easy."

"I understand, Laurel. Truly. Now, if you'll excuse me, I have something to attend to. We'll talk again in a few minutes." He left her standing with her mouth open as he weaved through the crowd toward the musicians. Leaving her was becoming a habit of his.

This was not working out. After being in the building all of fifteen minutes, Laurel itched to return home. She looked around for the others. Momma stood next to Wade and another couple, all four deep in conversation. Camille spoke with Emma Warren and May in front of the piano. To Laurel's satisfaction, Issy sat next to Peter Belton. The two of them carried on an animated discussion.

Perhaps she would have something to refresh her after all. Laurel limped to the table holding a punch bowl and ladled a drink into a cup.

"Delicious punch." Wade held his cup out for her to refill. "I understand Ernie's pa is coming next Wednesday."

"I suggested he travel here and allow his daughter to get to know him better. She deserves the time to decide whether to stay at the ranch or return to Arkansas."

"Seems like a sensible plan." He reached out for one of Mr. Oberlin's lebkuchen and bit into the spicy Christmas cookie.

Laurel handed Wade a full cup of punch to wash away the crumbs caught in his mustache.

"Ladies and gentlemen, may I have your attention, please?"

At the sound of Quinn's voice, Laurel set the ladle in the bowl and turned. He called out two more times before his audience stilled to listen. Her insides twisted as his serious blue eyes bore through her. What was that man up to?

"I have something of import to say." He grinned. "At least it's important to me."

Chuckles rippled through the crowd. Oh, the man could charm a snake. He will make a fine courtroom orator.

"I came here four months ago hoping to start a new profession and gain practical legal knowledge and experience, along with the respect of each of you. Nothing was more vital to me than establishing my career. Doing so meant seeking the approval of the local population, approval that could one day send me to the state capital as your representative."

She leaned toward Wade. "What is he doing?"

The marshal winked. "If we close our mouths and listen, Mrs. Tillman, we might find out."

Laurel sniffed and faced forward. Without a doubt, the old coot knew more than he would say.

Quinn scanned his audience. "I stand here to admit to you my sin of pride. That sin led me to fear being seen with good people—sisters in Christ. You know of whom I speak. These are women whose circumstances have forced them to support themselves in the best way they know how."

A man in the back shouted, "They wear men's pants!"

Quinn smiled. "Someone asked me recently if I'd ever tried to shear sheep in a dress." Sporadic chuckles floated around the room.

"What about Mrs. Tillman's actions during the war, Spencer?"

Laurel's muscles stiffened. Her irritation with Quinn rose. Why hadn't he left well enough alone? Why bring this up to humiliate her? She turned to leave. Without looking at her, Wade gripped her shoulder, forcing her to face forward again.

"She regrets her actions during that time. As you said, it was war. Women are no less affected by its consequences than men. God has forgiven her just as He's forgiven me for my mistakes—and you for yours." Quinn's voice had hardened. "Anything else?"

Laurel wanted to call out to him to hush before he ruined any hope of a good life in Bold Creek. She pressed her lips together. Anything she said would only provoke trouble.

He stood tall and confident. "Let's settle this right now, because starting tonight, I will not tolerate gossip regarding any of the women of La Casa del Fuego, especially Laurel, since I one day hope to marry her."

Mrs. Weaver gasped and drew Mary closer, as if protecting her daughter from Quinn's influence.

Laurel's mouth dropped. When her wits returned, she clamped her jaw tighter than the lid on a canning jar and waited for the storm that would surely rise from his announcement. The room remained silent as the gaze of many pairs of eyes strayed in her direction. From the other side of the room, a man cleared his throat. Both of the Oberlins pushed through the throng to Quinn's side.

Anton twisted his bowler in his hands. "Me und da wife have listened too long to da gossip without speaking. Without Mrs.

Tillman's kindness, my Frieda would not be here today. She an-anom..."

"Anonymously?" Quinn gripped the man's shoulder in a show of camaraderie.

The German smiled, his face growing a deeper red. "Ja, that. In secret, she paid for a doctor to cure my wife. We are grateful."

Laurel returned the couple's smiles. How long had they known of her payment to Dr. Cameron for his visits?

May Simpson stood next to her bench at the piano and faced the crowd. "Some have said Mrs. Tillman shouldn't try to save her ranch. She should sell out. Why should she sell her home? What woman here doesn't work hard for her family? Some choose other less moral methods, you know." At the whispers, her chin rose, and she smiled, looking proud of her shocking statement. "These ladies have selected hard, honest work—no different from most of you. And while speaking of hard work, you should know that my friend Camille Arneau tatted the lace on many of your frocks."

Laurel's eyebrows rose with the news. That was why Camille spent so much of her spare time working the shuttle?

May returned to the piano and stared at the sheet music in front of her as if shocked to realize what she had done. Laurel prayed her business wouldn't suffer for her outburst.

Camille stepped forward. Her fingers twisted the handkerchief in her hands. "You know little about us and, for that, we must take the blame. Mrs. Tillman offered me shelter four years ago, and I will be forever thankful to God for her kind heart. Without question or judgment, she took in a stranger ashamed and terrified of her own husband." She faced Laurel and mouthed, "*Merci, mi amiga.*"

A husband? Laurel bit her bottom lip, her eyes pooling with the understanding of what that declaration had cost her good friend.

Reverend Perry faced the gathering. "I have watched Mrs. Tillman on her visits to the cemetery. Several of you have spoken of her generosity over the years. Lately, she shared with me her newfound faith. She's a woman of courage and compassion—one who could teach any of us a lesson in God's grace and mercy. In fact, she reminds me a little of Paul. He considered himself chief among all sinners, yet once Jesus saved him, Paul looked upon Christ as his example and praised Him for his mercy." The pastor's smile wiped away the gravity of his speech. "That was not tomorrow's sermon, so I expect everyone to be in your seats at the proper time on Sunday morning." The crowd responded with heartier laughter than the jest demanded. "In the meantime, I could do with hearing another rousing carol from our musicians."

The music played and most people went back to their merry time like nothing awkward had happened. After patting her on the back, Wade walked away with a smile.

Quinn cut through the assembly, stopping to shake some hands and greet friendly faces. Mrs. Weaver ushered her daughter away from his path, and a few others followed, proving his argument and witnesses had not convinced everyone. There were still those who would shun her and, possibly, Quinn.

He reached her side and, without a word, slipped her arm in the crook of his and led her to a private spot near the back door. "It's up to you, Laurel. There are no more excuses."

She lifted her chin to roll her eyes at the ceiling but stopped when seeing something hanging from the top of the door frame a foot behind Quinn. Did the pastor know someone had hung it inside his church?

Her lips twisted in an effort to contain her amusement at the irony. Ever so gently, Laurel urged Quinn backward until he stood with his back against the door. "You believe that little speech took care of the problem, don't you?"

"I do."

"Hmm. Perhaps you should take care of that one."

When she pointed above his head, he looked up and moaned. "Mistletoe."

Laurel laughed. "Why the face? You have a fondness for it."

A wicked gleam lit his eyes. "Now that you mention it, I do." He wrapped his arms around her waist and bent his head. "Shall we call a permanent truce, Private Chamberlain?"

It was clear she could no longer withstand the Yankee's dogged barrage.

Laurel twisted her fingers in the lapels of Quinn's coat, rose to her toes, and tilted forward. Her lips brushed his, and she whispered, "I know when to surrender, Major Spencer."

Coming in 2026!

A LADY UNVEILED

HOUSE OF FIRE, BOOK 2

Amid receiving anonymous letters that shift into cryptic threats, an
independent-minded woman yearns for the respect and love of a
rancher blackmailed into keeping a secret.

In appreciation . . .

I originally wrote this book over a decade ago, so several authors had a hand in the shaping of the story. I appreciate Nicole M. Miller and Edwina Cowgill for their time and suggestions way back when. And I'll never forget the boost I got from the judges who read my unpublished entry in contests eons ago. (*"What? The amazing author [Anonymous] liked my first fifteen pages? Woo-hoo!"*)

My special thanks go to Heidi Chiavaroli for her amazing insights and encouragement. She's an advisor, cheerleader, and long-distance friend.

I can't end this without thanking you, a reader of Christian fiction. Without you and everyone else who seek out books with a Godly thread, I'd simply share stories with myself. I hope you enjoyed Laurel and Quinn's story. If so, please consider telling others through word of mouth or a written review or rating.

Of course, I reserve the utmost thanks for the One who gave me this story. While I strive to entertain, I also attempt to include some nugget of God's truth for readers to apply to their own lives. I hope it was there for you.

As an author of heartwarming and award-winning historical and contemporary romance, Sandra Ardoin engages readers with page-turning stories of love and faith. Rarely out of reach of a book, she's also an armchair sports enthusiast, country music listener, and seldom says no to eating out.

Visit her at www.sandraardoin.com.
Connect with her on BookBub, Facebook, X, and Goodreads.

Get all the latest news and specials!

Sign up for Sandra's Love and Faith in Fiction newsletter at: www.sandraardoin/newsletter.